PRAISE FOR *The Voyage of the Narwhal*

"[Andrea] Barrett's marvelous achievement is to have reimagined so graphically that cusp of time when Victorian certainty began to question whether it could encompass the world with its outward-bound enthusiasm alone—when it started to glimpse the dark ballast beneath the iceberg's dazzling tip."

—Annette Koback, *New York Times*

"A luminous work of historical fiction that explores the far reaches of the Arctic and of men's souls. . . . The novel is an excellent demonstration of Barrett's exceedingly fine and thorough hand at blending historical and natural detail with life-shaping conflict."

—Robin Vidimos, *Denver Post*

"Breathes with a contemporary urgency, an exhilarating adventure novel."

—Philip Graham, *Chicago Tribune*

"Breathtaking . . . exquisitely written in every way . . . fully worthy of the massive, dangerous subject it undertakes."

—*Cleveland Plain Dealer*

"Both cunningly cerebral and hair-raisingly visceral. . . . This is an astonishingly good book by a writer we must declare as major."

—*Newsday*

"Stunning. . . . Barrett shows the arrogance and delusion that drove the age of exploration better than any nonfiction book could."

—*Ft. Lauderdale Sun-Sentinel*

"A meditation on the nature of adventure and the scientific mind. . . . [W]ritten in the spirit . . . of a 19th century novel— solid, unhurried, reflective and totally wedded to plot. . . . *Voyage of the Narwhal* is [Barrett's] own creation, marvelously imagined and beautifully told. A first-rate novel."

—Peter Kurth, *Salon*

"Barrett delivers a stunning novel in which a meticulous grasp of historical and natural detail, insight into character and pulse-pounding action are integrated into a dramatic adventure story with deep moral resonance. . . . The denouement, when it arrives, is a triumph: a confluence of justice, retribution, spiritual faith, metamorphosis and love."

—*Publishers Weekly*, starred review

"[An] impeccably researched and stunningly written tale. . . . The intellectual range exhibited by this magnificent novel places its author in the rarefied company of great contemporary encyclopedic writers like Pynchon, Gaddis, and Harry Mulisch."

—*Kirkus Reviews*

THE VOYAGE

OF THE

NARWHAL

THE VOYAGE
OF THE
NARWHAL

A NOVEL

ANDREA BARRETT

W. W. NORTON & COMPANY
Celebrating a Century of Independent Publishing

For information about permission to reproduce selections from this book,
write to Permissions, W. W. Norton & Company, Inc.,
500 Fifth Avenue, New York, NY 10110

For information about special discounts for bulk purchases, please contact
W. W. Norton Special Sales at specialsales@wwnorton.com or 800-233-4830

Manufacturing by Lakeside Book Company
Production manager: Erin Reilly

ISBN 978-1-324-06597-5 (pbk)

W. W. Norton & Company, Inc., 500 Fifth Avenue, New York, N.Y. 10110
www.wwnorton.com

W. W. Norton & Company Ltd., 15 Carlisle Street, London W1D 3BS

1 2 3 4 5 6 7 8 9 0

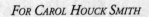
FOR CAROL HOUCK SMITH

CONTENTS

PART III

PART I

1

His Lists

(May 1855)

I try in vain to be persuaded that the pole is the seat of frost and desolation; it ever presents itself to my imagination as the region of beauty and delight. There . . . the sun is for ever visible; its broad disk just skirting the horizon, and diffusing a perpetual splendor. There . . . snow and frost are banished; and, sailing over a calm sea, we may be wafted to a land surpassing in wonders and in beauty every region hitherto discovered on the habitable globe . . . What may not be expected in a country of eternal light?

—MARY SHELLEY, *Frankenstein* (1818)

HE WAS STANDING ON THE WHARF, PEERING DOWN AT the Delaware River while the sun beat on his shoulders. A mild breeze, the smells of tar and copper. A few yards away the *Narwhal* loomed, but he was looking instead at the partial reflection trapped between hull and pilings. The way the planks wavered, the railing bent, the boom appeared then disappeared; the way the image filled the surface without concealing the complicated life below. He saw, beneath the transparent shadow, what his father had taught him to see: the schools of minnows, the eels and algae, the mussels burrowing into the silt; the diatoms and desmids and insect larvae sweeping past hydrazoans and infant snails. *The oyster,* his father once said, *is impregnated by the dew; the pregnant shells give birth to pearls conceived from the sky. If the dew is pure, the pearls are brilliant; if cloudy, the pearls are dull.* Far above him, but mirrored as well, long strands of cloud moved one way and gliding gulls another.

In the water the *Narwhal* sat solid and dark among the surrounding fleet. Everyone headed somewhere, Erasmus thought. England, Africa, California; stony islands alive with seals; the coast of Florida. Yet no one, among all those travelers, who might offer him advice. He turned back to his work. Where was this mound of supplies to go? An untidy package yielded, beneath its waterproof wrappings, a dozen plum puddings that brought him near to tears. Each time he arranged part of the hold more of these parcels appeared: a crate of damson plums in syrup from an old woman in Conshohocken who'd read about their voyage in the newspaper and wanted to contribute her bit. A case of brandy from a Wilmington banker, volumes of Thackeray from a schoolmaster in Doylestown, heaps of hand-knitted socks. His hands bristled with lists, each only partly checked-off: never mind those puddings, he thought. Where were the last two hundred pounds of pemmican? How had half the meat biscuit been stowed with the candles and the lamp oil?

And where were the last members of the crew? In his pocket he had another list, the final roster:

ZECHARIAH VOORHEES,
COMMANDER

AMOS TYLER,
SAILING MASTER

COLIN TAGLIABEAU,
FIRST OFFICER

GEORGE FRANCIS,
SECOND OFFICER

JAN BOERHAAVE,
SURGEON

ERASMUS D. WELLS,
NATURALIST

FREDERICK SCHUESSELE, *COOK*

THOMAS FORBES, *CARPENTER*

SEAMEN:

ISAAC BOND, NILS JENSEN, ROBERT CAREY,
BARTON DESOUZA, IVAN HRUSKA,
FLETCHER LAMB, SEAN HAMILTON

Fifteen of them, all hands counted. Captain Tyler, Mr. Tagliabeau, and Mr. Francis, who together would have charge of the ship's daily operations, were experienced whaling men. Dr. Boerhaave had a medical degree from Edinburgh; Schuessele had been cook for a New York packet line; Forbes was an Ohio farm boy who'd never been to sea, but who could fashion anything from a few odd scraps of wood. Of the seven unevenly trained seamen, Bond had reported for duty drunk, and Hruska and Hamilton were still missing.

Their companions, invisible in the hold, waited for directions—waited, Erasmus feared, for him to fail. He was forty years old and had a history of failure; he'd sailed, when hardly more than a boy, on a voyage so thwarted it became a national joke. Since then his life's work had come to almost nothing. No wife, no children, no truly close friends; a sister in a difficult situation. What he had now was this pile of goods, and a second chance.

Still pondering the puddings, he heard laughter and looked up to see Zeke hanging from the rigging like a flag. His long arms were stretched above a thatch of golden hair; as he laughed his teeth were gleaming in his mouth; he was twenty-six and made Erasmus feel like a fossil. Everything about this moment was tied to Zeke. The hermaphrodite brig about to become their home had once been part of Zeke's family's packet line; with his father's money, Zeke had ordered oak sheathing spiked to her sides as protection against the ice, iron plates wrapped around her bows, tarred felt layered between the double-planked decks. In charge of the expedition—and hence, Erasmus reminded himself, of him—Zeke had chosen Erasmus to gather the equipment and stores surrounding him now in such bewildering heaps.

Where was all this to go? Salt beef and pork and barrels of malt, knives and needles for barter with the Esquimaux, guns and ammunition, coal and wood, tents and cooking lamps and woolen clothing, buffalo skins, a library, enough wooden boards to house over the deck in an emergency. And what about the spirit thermometers, or the four chronometers, the microscope, and all the stores for his specimens: spirits of wine, loose gauze, prenumbered labels and glass jars, arsenical soap for preserving bird skins, camphor and pillboxes for preserving insects, dissecting scissors, watch glasses, pins, string, glass tubes and sealing wax, bungs and soaked bladders, brain hooks and blowpipes and egg drills, a sweeping net . . . too many things.

Erasmus stroked the wolf skins his youngest brother had sent from the Utah mountains. Just then he would have given anything for an hour's conversation with Copernicus, who understood what it meant to leave a life. But Copernicus was gone, still, again, and the wolf skins were handsome, but where would they fit? The sledges, specially constructed after Zeke's own design, had arrived two weeks late and wouldn't fit into the space Erasmus had planned for them; and he couldn't arrange the scientific equipment in any reasonable way. Every inch of the cabin was full, and they were not yet in it.

On the *Narwhal* Zeke slipped his feet from the stay, hung by one hand for a second, and then dropped lightly to the deck. Soon he joined Erasmus among the wharf's clutter, moving the theodolite and uncovering a crate of onions. "These look nice," he said. "Do we have enough?"

While they went over the provision lists yet again, Mr. Tagliabeau walked up with the news that their cook had deserted. He'd last been seen two days earlier, Mr. Tagliabeau reported. In the company of a red-headed woman who'd been haunting the docks.

Zeke, his hands deep in onions, only laughed. "I saw that hussy," he said. "What a flashing eye she had! But that it should be Schuessele who got her, with that monstrous beard of his . . ."

The wind tore one of Erasmus's lists away and sent it spinning through the masts. "We're leaving in three days!" he shouted. Later he'd remember this display with embarrassment. "*Three days.* Where are we going to find another cook?"

"There's no need to get excited," Zeke said. "The world is full of cooks. Mr. Tagliabeau, if you'd be so kind as to take a small recruiting tour among the taverns . . ."

"Wonderful," Erasmus said. "Do find us some criminal, some drunken sot."

They might have quarreled had not a group of young men dressed in Lincoln-green frock coats, white pantaloons, and straw hats trailing black ostrich feathers come dancing up the wharf. The United Toxophilites, Erasmus saw, making a surprise farewell to Zeke. The sight made him groan. Once he'd been part of this group of archers; once this had all seemed charming. Resurrecting the old sport of archery, flourishing the arrows retrieved from those first, magical trips to the Plains—as a boy, he'd participated in a meet that drew two thousand guests. But he'd lost his taste for such diversions after the Exploring Expedition, and he'd let his association with the Toxies lapse. Zeke, though, was part of the new young crowd that had taken over the club.

"Voorhees!" the Toxies cried. All around them, crews from other ships stared. "Voorhees! Voorhees!"

They gave Zeke three great cheers, hauled him down the length of the wharf, and formed a circle around him. Erasmus received courteous nods but no recognition. He listened to the mocking, high-spirited speeches, which likened Zeke to a great Indian chief setting off on a buffalo hunt. One youngster with a shock of red hair presented Zeke with a chalice; an elflike boy offered a patent-leather belt from which dangled a grease box and a tassel. Zeke accepted his gifts with a smile and a handshake, thanking each man by name and showing the poise that had made Erasmus's sister call him a natural leader.

Yet what had Zeke done? So very little, Erasmus thought as he eyed the grease box. A few years of sailing from Philadelphia to Dublin and Hull on the ships of his father's packet line, investigating currents and ocean creatures, although often, as he'd admitted to Erasmus, he'd been too seasick to work. Other than that all his learning came from books. As a boy he'd insinuated his way into Erasmus's family, through their fathers' friendship and an interest in natural history. Now they were further bound by Lavinia. But that Erasmus should be standing in Zeke's shadow, setting off for the arctic under the command of this untried youth—again he was amazed by his decision.

Zeke, as if he heard what Erasmus was thinking, broke through the circle of green-coated men, seized Erasmus's arm, and drew him into the center. "I couldn't do this without Erasmus

Darwin Wells," he cried. "Three cheers for our chief naturalist, my right hand!"

Erasmus blushed. Was this what he wanted? A kind of worship, mixed with disdain; as if Zeke wanted to emulate him, but without his flaws. But exactly this grudging caution had stranded him alone in midlife, and he pushed the thought aside. When the Toxies presented their green-and-gold pennant, he grasped the end marked with a merry archer and smiled at Zeke. Zeke made a speech of thanks; Erasmus made a shorter one, not mentioning that he'd known the club's founders or that he'd learned to shoot a bow when some of these men were still children. As he spoke he saw Captain Tyler hanging over the *Narwhal*'s rail, gazing curiously at them. His face, Erasmus thought, was the size and color of a ham.

The Toxies departed, Zeke climbed back on the *Narwhal*, and Erasmus was once more alone. He folded the pennant and tucked it into the wolf skins. Then he reconsidered the stowing of the sledges: back to front in a line down the center of the hold? or piled in a tight tower near the bow? He worked quietly for an hour, pushing down his worries by the repeated checking of items against his lists. Mr. Tagliabeau interrupted him, returning to the wharf in the company of a fresh-faced, dark-haired, blue-eyed boy.

"Ned Kynd," Mr. Tagliabeau said. "Twenty years of age." Zeke hopped down to investigate. After making introductions all around, Mr. Tagliabeau added, "Ned would like to join our expedition."

Zeke, hovering once more near the mound of supplies, looked Ned over. "You've had experience cooking?"

"In three places," the boy said shyly. As he listed them, all in the rough area by the wharves, Erasmus noted his heavy Irish accent.

"And have you been to sea?" Zeke asked.

Ned blushed. "Just once, sir. When I made my crossing."

"But the sea suits you?"

"My . . . circumstances then were not such that anyone could have enjoyed them. But I believe I would have, if I'd had work and meals and a place to sleep. I enjoyed being on deck very much. I like to watch the birds and fish."

"You'd be cooking for fifteen men," Erasmus said. "You're capable of that?"

"I wouldn't like to boast, but many a night I've cooked for three or four times that number. I was at a logging camp in the Adirondacks for some time, before I made my way to this city. Loggers are hungry men."

Zeke laid a hand on Erasmus's shoulder. "If he can feed loggers, he can surely feed us."

"You'd be bunking in the forecastle," Erasmus said. "With the seamen. They can be a bit rough."

"Not rougher than loggers, I wouldn't guess."

"Done, then," Zeke said. "And welcome. Gather your things and say your good-byes, we leave in three days." Off he went, bounding down the wharf like an antelope.

And so it was that Ned, hastily engaged to fill Schuessele's shoes, came to join the expedition. Later Erasmus would think many times how little might have steered Ned away. Mr. Tagliabeau might not have bumped into him beneath the chandler's awning; the Toxies' ostrich-feathered hats might have spooked him had he arrived but a few minutes earlier; Zeke might not have been there to interview him had he arrived but a little later. Any small coincidence might have done.

THAT NIGHT ERASMUS was sleepless again. In the Repository, his family's little natural history museum, he rose and paced the floors and tried to understand what he'd been doing. For twelve years he'd been camped out here, his world contracted to display

cabinets stuffed with dead animals, boxes of seeds and trays of fossils, the occasional stray beam of light shining through the windows
like a message from another planet. Framed engravings of eminent
naturalists leaned down from the bookshelves, watching benignly
as he bent to work that wasn't work, and went nowhere. Who could
understand that life? Or how he'd decided, finally, to leave it?

Across the garden loomed the house he hadn't slept in for more
than a decade. Everything showed his father's hand, from the carved
ferns on the moldings to his own name. He was Erasmus Darwin
for the British naturalist, grandfather to the young man who'd set
off on the *Beagle*; his brothers were named after Copernicus, Linnaeus, and Alexander von Humboldt. Four boys gaping up at their
father like nestlings waiting for worms. An engraver and printer by
trade, Frank Wells's passion had been natural history and his truest
friends the Peales and the Bartrams, Thomas Nuttall and Thomas
Say, Audubon of the beautiful birds and poor peculiar Rafinesque,
who'd died in a garret downtown.

On summer evenings, down by the creek, Mr. Wells had read
Pliny's *Natural History* to his sons. Pliny the Elder had died of his
scientific curiosity, he'd said; the fumes of Vesuvius had choked him
when he'd lingered to watch the smoke and lava. But before that he'd
compiled a remarkable collection of what he'd believed to be facts.
Some true, some false—but even the false still useful for the beauty
with which they were expressed, and for what they said about the
ways men conceived of each other, and of the world. Sometimes pacing, sometimes sitting on a tuft of grass, Erasmus's father had passed
down Pliny's descriptions of extraordinary peoples living beyond the
edge of the known. *A race of nomads with legs like snakes; a race of
forest dwellers running swiftly on feet pointed backward; a single-legged
race who move by hopping and then rest by lying on their backs and raising their singular feet above their heads, like small umbrellas.* Stories,

not science—but useful as a way of thinking about the great variety and mutability of human nature. How easily, he'd said, might we not exist at all. How easily might we be transformed into something wholly different.

In those old stories, he'd said, were lessons about gossip and the imagination and the perils of not observing the world directly. Yet although he was a great collector of explorers' tales he'd traveled very little himself; Erasmus had never known what his father would most like to have seen. As a counterpoint to Pliny he'd offered his sons the living, breathing science of his friends. They'd helped design the Repository and delighted Erasmus and his brothers with accounts of their travels. When Lavinia was born, they'd named her after her dying mother and tried to distract their friend from his grief with bones and feathers.

Now Erasmus followed the tracks of those men across the polished floor. He stopped at a wooden case holding trays of fossil teeth. Beneath the third tray was a false bottom, which only he knew about; in the secret space below the molars was a woman's black calf walking boot. His mother's; once he'd had a pair. Before the servants took her clothes away, to be given piece by piece to the poor, he'd stolen the boots she'd worn most often. For years he'd hidden them in his room, sometimes running his hands up the buttons as another boy might have fingered a rosary. Later, about to leave on his ill-fated first trip, he'd given Lavinia the left boot after swearing her to secrecy. This other he'd buried. Had it always been so small? The sole was hardly longer than his hand, the leather was cracking, the buttons loose. Where Lavinia's was he had no idea.

Four years ago, when his father died, he'd received the house, the Repository, a small income, and the care of Lavinia until she married. Which meant, he thought, that he'd inherited all the responsibility and none of the freedom or even the solid work. Was it his fault he hadn't known what to do? The family firm had gone to his middle brothers, who'd settled side by side downtown, within walking distance of their work: two moons, circling a planet that didn't interest him. Meanwhile Copernicus had headed west as soon as he received his share of the estate. Out there, among the Indians, he painted buffalo hunts and vast landscapes while Erasmus and Lavinia, left behind, leaned against each other in his absence.

Copernicus sent paintings back, some of which had already been shown at the Academy of Fine Arts. And sometimes—when he remembered, when he could be bothered—he sent packets of seeds, shaken from random plants that had caught his eye. His afterthoughts, which had become Erasmus's chief occupation. Erasmus had examined, classified, labeled, cataloged, added them to his lists. He filed them in tall wooden towers of tiny drawers, alongside the seeds his father's friends had brought back from China and the Yucatan and the Malay Archipelago, and those he'd salvaged— stolen, really—from the collections of the Exploring Expedition. When his eyes grew strained and his skin felt moldy, he retreated out back, between the house and the river and behind the Repository, planting samples in oblong plots and noting every characteristic of the seedlings.

But all that was over now. He put the boot away and returned to bed. *In Africa,* his father had said, *are a tribe of people who have no heads, but have mouths and eyes attached to their chests.* Sleep eluded him yet again and his lists bobbed behind his lids. In Germantown and along the Wissahickon, people sent him socks and marmalade and then dreamed of this expedition. Vicarious travelers, sleeping while he could not and conjuring up a generic exotic land. Lavinia had friends like this, for whom Darwin's Tierra del Fuego and Cook's Tahiti had merged with Parry's Igloolik and d'Urville's Antarctica until a place arose in which ice cliffs coexisted with acres of pampas, through which Tongan savages chased ostriches chasing camels. Those people sent six candles encased in brown paper but couldn't keep north and south straight in their minds, placing penguins and Esquimaux in the same confused ice and pleating a continent into a frozen sea.

None of them grasped the drudgery of such a voyage. Not just the planning and buying and stowing but the months sitting idly on the decks of a ship, the long stretches when nothing happened except that one's ties to home were imperceptibly dissolved and one became a stranger to one's life. No one knew how frightened he was, or the mental lists he made of all he dreaded. Ridiculous things, ignoble things. His bunk would be too short or too narrow or damp or drafty; his comrades would snore or twitch or moan; he'd be overcome by longing for women; he'd never sleep. Sleepless, he would grow short-tempered; short-tempered, he'd say something wrong to Zeke and make an enemy. The coarse food would upset his stomach and dyspepsia would upset his brain; what if he forgot how to think? His hands would be cold, they were always cold; he'd slice a specimen or stab himself. His joints would ache, his back would hurt, they'd run out of coffee, on which he relied; a storm would snap the masts in half, a whale would ram the ship. They'd get lost, they'd find nothing, they'd fail.

Giving up on sleep, he lit a candle and reached for his journal. On his earlier voyage this had been his constant, sometimes sole, companion, but tonight it let him down. Pen, inkpot, words on white paper; an inkstain on his thumb. He couldn't convey clearly the scene at the wharf. He gazed at his first messy attempt and then added:

Why is it so difficult simply to capture what was there? That old problem of trying to show things both sequentially, and simultaneously. If I drew that scene I'd show everything happening all at once, everyone present and every place visible, from the bottom of the river to the clouds. But when I describe it in words one thing follows another and everything's shaped by my single pair of eyes, my single voice. I wish I could show it as if through a fan of eyes. Widening out from my single perspective to several viewpoints, then many, so the whole picture might appear and not just my version of it. As if I weren't there. The river as the fish saw it, the ship as it looked to the men, Zeke as he looked to young Ned Kynd, the Toxies as they appeared to Captain Tyler: all those things, at once. So someone else might experience those hours for himself.

Irritated, he put down his pen. Even here, he thought, even in these pages meant only for his own eyes, he wasn't honest. He'd left out the first mate's self-important strut; the appalling sight of his own hands, which amid the onions had suddenly looked just like his father's; and the sense that they were all *posturing* in front of each other, perhaps for the benefit of the green-coated boys. He rubbed at the stain on his thumb. Nor was it true, or not wholly true, that he wanted to paint the scene as if he weren't in it. He *did* want his own point of view to count, even as he also wanted to be invisible. Such a liar, he thought. Although chiefly he lied to himself. He'd wrapped himself in a cloud. Beyond it the world pulsed and streamed but he was cut off; people loved and sorrowed without him. When had that cloud arrived?

STILL THEY WEREN'T ready to leave. Captain Tyler banished Zeke and Erasmus the next afternoon, while the men tore out and then rebuilt the bulkheads in the hold. The sledges hadn't fit after all, in any configuration; the wood took more space than planned and the measurements on Zeke's sketch had turned out to be wrong.

A clock ticked in Erasmus's chest: two days, two days, two days. They could leave no later, they were already late, the season for arctic navigation was short and the newspaper reporters and expedition's donors were ready to send them off on Thursday. Did he have enough socks? The right charts, enough pencils?

He was wild with anxiety and stuck here at home, with Zeke and Lavinia and her friend Alexandra Copeland. They were in the front parlor, all four of them working. Maps and charts and drawings spread everywhere. Without explanation he rose and ran to the Repository, which he ransacked in search of Scoresby's work on the polar ice.

He rolled the ladder along the shelves; the book was gone, yet he couldn't remember packing it. And couldn't bear the thought of explaining why it had suddenly seemed so crucial. The wry face Alexandra had made as he bolted embarrassed him. Yet her presence had been his idea—Lavinia couldn't stay alone, with only the servants for company, and she hadn't wanted to join Linnaeus or Humboldt. "A companion," he'd proposed. "Who'd like to share our home, in return for room and board and a modest payment."

Lavinia had chosen Alexandra, who'd accepted a pair of rooms on the second floor. When Linnaeus and Humboldt, unexpectedly generous, offered work hand-coloring the engravings they were printing for an entomology book, Alexandra had accepted that as well and made herself at home. Now there was no escaping her; sometimes she even followed him into the Repository. But she was good for Lavinia, he reminded himself. The way she pulled Lavinia into her work was wonderful. He took a breath and headed back.

At the parlor doorway he paused to watch his sister, who was frowning with concentration and shifting her gaze from the original painting pinned above her desk to the engraved copy she was coloring with Alexandra's help. Caught up, he thought, as she'd never been helping him with his seeds. The plates showed four tropical beetles. The sun lit the brushes, the water jars, and the ruffled pinafores so dabbed with gold and rust and blue that the beetles seemed to have leapt from the plates to the women's legs. "Has anyone seen my copy of Scoresby?" he asked.

"I've been reading it upstairs," Alexandra said. She touched her brush to the paper, leaving three tiny golden dots. "I didn't know you needed it."

Erasmus, admitting his foolishness, said, "It's not as if I have room for one more thing."

"I'll get it." As Alexandra put down her brush and moved away, Lavinia called for tea and leaned over the table on which Erasmus and Zeke had spread their papers: rather too close to Zeke's shoulder, Erasmus thought. As if she were pulled by the fragrance of Zeke's skin; as if she did not have the sense to resist the almost farcical beauty that made women stare at Zeke on the street and men hum with envy. It pained him to watch her betrayed by her body's yearnings. To him she was lovely, with her wide hazel eyes and rounded chin, now charmingly smudged with blue. Yet he suspected that to the gaze of others—perhaps even Zeke—she was merely pleasant-looking. She seemed to know that herself, as she knew that among her monthly meetings of earnest young women, gathered to discuss Goethe and Swedenborg and Fourier, she was valued more for her sensibility than for her brilliance. One by one those women had married and disappeared from the meetings, leaving behind only Alexandra and her. Once, when he'd been voicing his concerns about Zeke, she'd said, "I know I love him more than he loves me. It doesn't bother me." Then had flushed so darkly he'd wanted to pick her up and pace her around the floor, as he'd done when she was an infant and needed comforting.

As Lavinia traced their planned route with her index finger, past

Devon and Cornwallis and Beechey Island, where Franklin's winter camp had been found, then south along Boothia Peninsula and King William Land, Erasmus thought how maps showed only two things, land and water. To someone who hadn't traveled, their journey over that arctic map might seem a simple thing. Turn left, turn right, go north or south, steer by this headland or that bay. He and Zeke, who'd pored over their predecessors' accounts, knew otherwise. Ice, both fluid and solid, appeared and disappeared with consistent inconsistency; one year an inlet might be open, the next walled shut. Lavinia, unaware of this, traced the route backward and said with satisfaction, "It's not so very far. You'll be home before October."

"I hope," Zeke said. "But you mustn't worry if we're not—many expeditions have to winter over. We've provisioned for a full eighteen months, in case we're frozen in."

While Lavinia gazed at the deceitful map, Alexandra returned with Erasmus's book and then asked the question Lavinia might have been framing in her mind. "I haven't understood this all spring," she said. "If you take this route, which you say concentrates most efficiently on the areas in which you have some evidence of Franklin's presence, how can you also search for signs of an open polar sea? De Haven and Penny reported Jones Sound clogged with ice when they were there." She smoothed her paint-stained garment. "Ross found most of Barrow Strait frozen, and Peel Sound as well. Even if you manage to approach the region of Rae's discoveries, which lies south of all those areas, surely you can't also simultaneously head north?"

Erasmus lifted his head in surprise. The same question had worried him for months, but he'd pushed it aside; Zeke hadn't mentioned his desire to find an open polar sea since the evening that had launched them all on this path. Lavinia's twenty-sixth birthday party, back in November; Alexandra had been present that night as well, although Erasmus had hardly noticed her. He'd been full of hope that Lavinia was about to get what she most desired.

He'd spared no expense, dressing the Repository's windows with greenery and lining the sills with candles, scrubbing the dissecting table and shrouding it with crisp linen, on which he'd spread biscuits, a roasted ham, a turkey and a salmon in aspic. Lavinia had rejected her first three suitors—too dull, she'd said. Too weak, not smart enough. While her friends married and produced their first children she'd held out for Zeke and somehow won him. Erasmus had been terrified for her during her long campaign, then relieved, then worried again: his own fault. Zeke had asked for her hand but been vague about the details, and Erasmus had failed to press him. His father would have known better, he thought. His father wouldn't have permitted Lavinia to bind herself for an uncertain length of time. The damage was done, but secretly Erasmus had hoped Zeke might choose the party to announce a wedding date.

In the kind light of the candles Lavinia might have been a candle herself, radiant in white silk trimmed with blue ribbons. She stood perfectly still when Zeke, just as Erasmus had hoped, silenced the room and said, "I have an announcement!"

Erasmus had sighed with relief, not noticing that Lavinia looked confused. Zeke rested his elbow on a case that held a bird-of-paradise. "You've all heard the news announced by John Rae earlier this month," he said. He stood with his chin up, his chest out, one hand dancing in the air. "No doubt you share both my sorrow at what appears to have been the fate of Franklin's expedition, and my relief that some news—however fragmentary, and possibly incorrect—has been obtained."

He went on about the tragic disappearance of Franklin and his men, the many rescue attempts, the details of what Rae had discovered—old news to Erasmus, who'd followed every newspaper article. His guests listened, glasses in hands, among them women who would have listened with equal interest had Zeke been reciting the agricultural products of China; anything, Erasmus imagined them thinking, for this chance to gaze at Zeke blamelessly. Yet his own sister was the woman Zeke had chosen. "Perhaps you also feel, as I do," Zeke added, "that now that the area has been defined, someone has to search further for any possible survivors."

A guest stepped sideways then, so that Erasmus caught sight of Lavinia's face. She looked as puzzled as he felt.

"To that end," Zeke continued, "I've been able to obtain the backing of a number of our leading merchants for another expedition. Our valiant Dr. Kane has been searching for Franklin in the wrong area, and although we're all worried about him—and although I'd be the first to go in search of him if a relief expedition wasn't already being organized—something more is needed. I propose to set forth this spring, to search more thoroughly for Franklin in the areas below Lancaster Sound. While I'm there, I also propose to study the region, and to further investigate the possibility of an open polar sea."

Everyone had cheered. Erasmus had stretched his lips in something like a smile, hoping no one would notice his surprise. What merchants, when, how . . . did everyone know about this but him? Lavinia, even, who might have hidden her knowledge—but she wore a smile as forced as his own. Zeke must have made these arrangements in secret, taking pleasure in presenting his plan only when it was complete.

After the flurry of congratulations, after the first buzz of questions about where Zeke might go, and how he might get there, and what sort of ship and crew he envisioned, Zeke took Lavinia's hands. She beamed as if his announcement were the ideal birthday present, and when a guest sat down at the piano and began to play, she and Zeke led the crowd to the floor.

Erasmus went outside to have a cigar and calm the storm in his chest. He was watching the smoke rise through the still night air when Zeke appeared with two glasses and a bottle. He had to ask questions, Erasmus thought. Fatherly questions, although that role still felt odd: what this meant in terms of the engagement, whether Zeke wanted to marry Lavinia before he left—or release her, perhaps, until he returned.

Leaning against one of the fluted porch columns, Zeke filled the glasses and lit a cigar for himself. Erasmus opened his mouth to speak, and Zeke said, "Erasmus—you must come with me. When are you going to get another chance like this?"

Erasmus choked, coughing so hard he bent double. All the expeditions he'd already missed—was this what he'd been waiting for? Even Elisha Kent Kane had spurned him, sailing off with a crew of Philadelphians younger but no smarter than himself. Perhaps Zeke sensed his discouragement, and the extent of his wounded vanity.

"You're ideal for this," he said. "Where could I find anyone else as knowledgeable about the natural history of the polar regions? Or as familiar with the hardships of such a journey?"

The idea of serving under a man so much younger than himself was preposterous, but it seemed to him that Zeke was looking for a partner, not a subordinate. Surely Zeke wouldn't ask for his help if he didn't regard him as an equal, even—naturally—a superior? Erasmus said, "You're kind to think of me. But you might have asked me earlier—I have responsibilities here, and of course my own work . . ."

Zeke bounded from the porch to the grass below. "Of course!" he said, pacing before the columns. "It's a huge imposition—I wouldn't think of asking you if your work weren't so *invaluable* . . . but that's why you're the right person. I didn't want to bother you until I was sure I had backing for the expedition. Think of what we'll see!"

Somewhere in those icy waters, Franklin and his men might still be trapped in the *Erebus* and the *Terror*. Even if they couldn't be found, many new species, even new lands, were there to be discovered. Erasmus thought of being free, this time, to investigate everything without the noxious Navy discipline. He thought of northern sights to parallel, even exceed, his brief experience in the Antarctic; of discoveries in natural history that might prove extraordinarily important. Then he thought of his sister, who appeared on the porch with her white dress foaming like a spray of catalpa blossom.

"You should go in," she said to Zeke. "All the guests are longing to talk with you."

He leapt up the steps and she steered him inside. With a swirl of skirts she turned to Erasmus.

"Will you go?" she said.

Eavesdropping, he thought. Again. She'd done this since she was a little girl, as if this were the only way she could keep track of her brothers.

"Please? You have to go with him."

He had his *own* reasons, Erasmus thought. For going, or staying. "Did he keep this secret from you?"

"He *had* to, he said he needed . . ."

"Doesn't that worry you?"

"As if *you* ever tell me anything," she said. "And who are you to criticize him? Especially since Father died: all you do is mope around, sorting your seeds—do you think I haven't seen you at eleven in the morning still in bed? So Linnaeus and Humboldt can run the business without you. So you haven't found anyone to fall in love with since Sarah Louise."

Sarah Louise, he thought. Still the simple sound of her name made him feel like he'd swallowed a stone. A dull ache, which never quite left him. As Lavinia knew.

"Copernicus isn't married either," she continued, "but you don't see Copernicus moping around, you don't see *Copernicus* wasting his life . . . I *need* you."

A snarl of guilt and tenderness caught at him. As children, he and his brothers used to bolt for the woods and return hours later, to find Lavinia waiting by a window with an unread book in her lap. He'd been the one she looked up to, the one who tied her shoes and taught her to read. Sometimes, when the other boys weren't around and he'd remembered not just that her birth had cost him his mother, but that she'd never *had* a mother, they'd drawn very close. Then his brothers would tumble in and he'd abandon her again. Back and forth, oldest and youngest. He had failed her often enough.

She drew him inside, to a corner behind a case of stuffed finches. *"This is who I love,"* she said fiercely. "Do you understand? Do you remember what that feels like? What if something happens to him? You have to take care of him for me."

"Lavinia," he said. Her hands, squeezing his left arm, were very hot. Once, after Zeke had been describing the shipwreck that made him a local hero, Erasmus had found her weeping in the garden. Not with delayed fear over what might have happened to Zeke, not with hysteria—but with longing, she'd managed to make him understand. A boundless desire for Zeke. When he'd tried to remind her that Zeke had flaws as well as virtues, she'd said, "I know, I *know*. But it doesn't matter. What matters is the way I feel when he touches my hand, or when we dance and I smell the skin on his neck." The strength of her feelings had embarrassed him.

"You know this means waiting even longer," he said. "Has he mentioned a date?" His fault, he thought again. Why hadn't he asked Zeke himself?

"Not exactly. But when he gets home, I know he'll want to settle down."

Of course he wanted her to marry Zeke, not just to ease his own responsibilities but because he wanted her happy. Didn't he? She'd cared first for their father and then him. "You're sure . . ." he said. "You feel sure of his feelings for you?"

"He loves me," she said passionately. "In his own way—I know he does."

A blinding headache had seized him then, blurring the rest of the party. And through a process he still didn't understand, he'd been led to this table and Alexandra's pointed questions; to the fact that, in two days, he'd be sailing north in the company of a young man he'd known for ages yet couldn't imagine accepting orders from.

One of the maids came in with the tea tray: Agnes? Ellen? The servants were Lavinia's province; as long as meals appeared on time Erasmus didn't notice who did the work. He thought they didn't know this, although Lavinia sometimes reproached him. And although once he'd overheard the staff in the kitchen referring to "the seedy-man" and then laughing furiously. Now he avoided the eyes of the girl with the tray and drew a breath, waiting to hear what Zeke would say about the open polar sea.

"You read a lot," Zeke said to Alexandra. If he was startled that she'd remembered his comment at the party, it didn't show. "I've noticed that. So you must have learned about the stretches of open water persisting all winter and recurring in the same places every year. What the Russians call *polynyas*. Inglefield found open water in Smith Sound. Birds have been seen migrating northward from Canada. A warm current flows northward beneath the surface, several people have observed it—suppose it leads to a temperate ocean, free from ice, surrounding the North Pole beyond a frozen barrier?"

"Suppose," Alexandra said. Her right hand sketched an arc in the air, as if she were still holding her paintbrush.

"When Dr. Kane left," Zeke continued, "he said he was going to look for signs of this phenomenon if he could. So there's nothing so strange in my wanting to look as well."

Many times in the months since the party Erasmus had sat in the offices of wealthy men, while Zeke proposed their search for Franklin. A portrait of Franklin in full-dress uniform hung in the *Narwhal*'s cabin—Franklin, Franklin, Zeke had said, as he asked the men for money. It made sense that he concentrated on this aspect of the voyage—how proud the merchants were, contributing to such a good cause! In Zeke, Erasmus thought, they saw a young man who could succeed at anything. The man they'd dreamed of being, the man they hoped their sons might be. Other expeditions might have failed, but Zeke's would not.

"It's a theory," Zeke told Alexandra now. "An interesting theory. In the arctic one can never predict where the ice will allow one to go, nor one's speed, nor even always one's direction. My plan is to follow this route and search for Franklin. But were conditions to be unexpectedly good—were one of the northern channels to be open, say—it's possible we'd do some exploring."

"Possible," Alexandra said. "Hence you provision for eighteen months?"

"For safety's sake," Zeke said. He stroked his eyebrows, taming the springy golden tufts; perhaps aware that Lavinia followed the gesture intently. And perhaps, Erasmus thought, a bit annoyed that Alexandra didn't. A sensible woman, she seemed immune to Zeke's charms.

Lavinia, tearing her eyes from Zeke's hand, said, "I don't see here on the maps where you'd head north at all."

"Only if he were *driven* to it," Alexandra said. "Were he to raise this money to search for Franklin, and then purposefully head in another direction, that would be quite wrong."

Zeke gazed steadily at her, and she gazed as steadily back. "The maps never tell us what we need," he said, turning toward Lavinia. "That's part of the reason we go."

Later Erasmus would realize that for all his alertness to Zeke's gestures and the women's responses he hadn't been paying sufficient attention. The lamps were lit, the sun was setting, they were munching delicious chocolate cake; the maps beckoned and he was dreaming of glory. His own glory, his own desires. They might find survivors of Franklin's expedition; or if not, surely better evidence of what had happened than Rae's dispiriting tale. With any luck they'd find other things as well. All sorts of specimens, not just plants but seaweeds, fishes, birds—he would write a book. He'd sketch his specimens and write their descriptions; his talent was for drawing from nature, capturing the salient features as only a trained observer could. Copernicus, so skilled with color and light, would turn the sketches into paintings; Linnaeus and Humboldt would prepare the plates. Together they'd make something beautiful. For years, in the light of his disappointments, he'd pretended to himself that he wasn't ambitious—but he was, he was. And lucky beyond belief to be part of this voyage. A blaze of excitement blinded him.

"And you, Erasmus," Alexandra said. "What do you think of all this?"

"In the polar regions," he said, "it's true that one must be flexible, and take what opportunities are offered."

He looked down at the volume she'd relinquished. He would bring it, after all. Surely there was room for one small book. "Zeke and I will respond to what we find, and decide accordingly."

THAT NIGHT, IN her diary, Alexandra wrote:

> *It's not Lavinia's fault her brothers underestimate her. I know she'll*
> *be different once the men leave and we're on our own; her mind*
> *dissolves in Zeke's presence. I'll be glad when we can be ourselves.*
> *This house is so beautiful, so spacious—what would my parents*
> *think, I wonder, if they were alive to see me in these two gorgeous*
> *rooms I now call my own? The window over my bed looks down on*
> *a planting of dwarf trees. My bed-linen is changed weekly, by some-*
> *one other than me. And this painting is such a pleasure, so much*
> *more satisfying than needlework. So much better paid. Beneath the*
> *lining of my sewing box I've already tucked a surprising sum. Soon*
> *I'll be able to purchase some books of my own, an extravagance*
> *when I have the Repository shelves to browse through, once the men*
> *leave . . . I'm impatient for them to go, I am. And wish that, like*
> *Erasmus, I might have the luxury of sleeping out there.*
>
> *Does he know that he rocks the toe of his boot in the air when-*
> *ever Zeke speaks? I wonder what Erasmus was like as a boy. Before*
> *he grew so frozen, before he sat with his chin tucked into his col-*
> *lar like that, and his right hand wringing his left so strongly one*
> *wonders he doesn't break the bones. Lavinia says that when she was*
> *a girl he was fond of beetles and moths, and teased the succession*
> *of governesses who raised her. I can't imagine him teasing anyone.*

THE *NARWHAL* SET sail on May 28, in such a wild flurry that everything important seemed still undone and nothing Erasmus meant
to say got said. He and Zeke stood on the deck in their new gray
uniforms, waving their handkerchiefs. Above them the Toxophilites'

pennant streamed in the wind, snapping straight out then beginning to droop, snapping straight out again. Terns hung motionless in the high currents, and Erasmus felt as though he himself were hanging between two worlds.

The acquaintances of the *Narwhal's* crew gathered in little knots close to shore, followed by the cheering Toxies in their green outfits. Dotting the wharf in separate clusters were Zeke's and Erasmus's relatives and friends, their clothing splayed into wide colored planes by the wind whipping across the river. Alexandra had brought her entire family—her sisters, Emily and Jane; her brother, Browning; and Browning's wife and infant son—all of them huddled so tightly that it was as if even here, in the open air, they couldn't expand beyond the confines of the tiny house they'd shared since their parents' deaths. They were small, neat, and yet somehow fierce-looking; abolitionists, serious young people. They dressed in the colors of sparrows and doves but more closely resembled, Erasmus thought, a family of saw-whet owls. Browning had a Bible in his hands.

Later, Alexandra would write in her diary about the argument she and Browning had over the verses he read out loud. Later she'd sketch a portrait of Erasmus during these last minutes, which showed his hand clasped nervously around a stay, his graying hair curled beneath a cap that made him look oddly boyish, the tip of his long, thin nose sniffing at the wind. But for now she only stood silently, watching him watch everyone. In the oily water around the pilings wood shavings swirled and tossed.

To the left of Alexandra's family stood a group of employees from the engraving firm and some representatives from the Voorhees packet line; beyond them were Linnaeus and Humboldt, as plump and glossy as beavers, and Lavinia, leaning on both of them, overdressed in swirls of blue and green and flashing in the sun like a trout. At the tip of the wharf, befitting their support of the expedition, came Zeke's family. His father stood suave and proud, his still-thick thatch of ruddy hair moving in the wind and revealing his massive eyebrows and the lynxlike tufts on his ears. His mother, shrouded in black for the death of an aunt, was weeping. Not surprising, Erasmus thought; she was famous for the way she coddled her only son. Flanking her were Zeke's sisters, Violet and Laurel, beautifully dressed and seemingly contemptuous of their merchant husbands, who weren't sailing north.

They waved; the water opened between the wharf and the ship; the tune piped by the Toxies' piccolo player shattered in the breeze until the separate and unrelated notes merged with the calls of the gulls. *Behind the mountains and beyond the north wind,* Erasmus's father had once read to him, *past the cave where the cold arises, live a race of people called Hyperboreans. Here are the hinges on which the world turns and the limits of the circuits of the stars. Here there is no disharmony and sorrow is unknown.* The figures on the wharf began to shrink. Everyone, except the dead, whom Erasmus had ever loved; every person who might be proud of him or admire his courage or worry over his fate. The faces faded, and then disappeared.

2

Past the Cave Where the Cold Arises

(June–July 1855)

Of the inanimate productions of Greenland, none perhaps excites so much interest and astonishment in a stranger, as the ice in its great abundance and variety. The stupendous masses, known by the name of Ice-Islands, Floating-Mountains, or Icebergs, common to Davis' Straits and sometimes met with here, from their height, various forms, and the depth of water in which they ground, are calculated to strike the beholder with wonder; yet the fields of ice, more peculiar to Greenland, are not less astonishing. Their deficiency in elevation, is sufficiently compensated by their amazing extent of surface. Some of them have been observed near a hundred miles in length, and more than half that in breadth; each consisting of a single sheet of ice, having its surface raised in general four or six feet above the level of the water, and its base depressed to the depth of near twenty feet beneath.

The ice in general, is designated by a variety of appellations, distinguishing it according to the size or number of pieces, their form of aggregation, thickness, transparency, &c. I perhaps cannot better explain the terms in common acceptation amongst the whale-fishers, than by marking the disruption of a field. The thickest and strongest field cannot resist the power of a heavy swell; indeed, such are much less capable of bending without being dissevered, than the thinner ice which is more pliable. When a field, by the set of the current, drives to the southward, and being deserted by the loose ice, becomes exposed to the effects of a grown swell, it presently breaks into a great many pieces, few of which will exceed forty or fifty yards in diameter. Now, such a number of the pieces collected together in close contact, so that they cannot, from the top of the ship's mast, be seen over, are termed a pack.

When the collection of pieces can be seen across, if it assume a circular or polygonal form, the name of patch is applied, and it is called a stream when its shape is more of an oblong, how narrow soever it may be, provided the continuity of the pieces is preserved.

Pieces of very large dimensions, but smaller than fields, are called floes; thus, a field may be compared to a pack, and a floe to a patch, as regards their size and external form. Small pieces *which break off, and are separated from the larger masses by the effect of attrition, are called* brash-ice, *and may be collected into streams or patches. Ice is said to be* loose *or* open, *when the pieces are so far separated as to allow a ship to sail freely amongst them; this has likewise been called* drift ice. *A* hummock *is a protuberance raised upon any plane of ice above the common level. It is frequently produced by pressure, where one piece is squeezed upon another, often set up on its edge, and in that position cemented by the frost. Hummocks are likewise formed, by pieces of ice mutually crushing each other, the wreck being coacervated upon one or both of them. To hummocks, the ice is indebted for the variety of fanciful shapes, and its picturesque appearance. They occur in great numbers in heavy packs, on the edges and occasionally in the middle of fields and floes. They often attain the height of thirty feet or upwards . . .*

A bight *signifies a bay or sinuosity, on the border of any large mass or body of ice. It is supposed to be called* bight *from the low word* bite, *to take in, or entrap; because, in this situation, ships are sometimes so caught by a change of wind, that the ice cannot be cleared on either tack; and in some cases, a total loss has been the consequence.*

—WILLIAM SCORESBY, *The Polar Ice* (1815)

ZEKE STARTED HEAVING OVER THE *Narwhal's* RAIL before they cleared the bay. He had mentioned, Erasmus remembered, some seasickness on his father's ships—but this was no spasm, a few hours' illness and a night's recovery. This was endless retching and a white-faced speechless headache. As they passed New York and surged ahead of the ship heading off to search for Dr. Kane, the elation Erasmus might have felt was squelched by worry over Zeke's condition.

"Why didn't you warn me?" he asked. Around him the crew hovered, disdainfully watching Zeke respond to the slightest swells.

"I thought it would be different this time," Zeke whispered.

Erasmus, contemplating Zeke's falsehood, remembered an image he'd long forgotten. A pale, frail, yellow-haired boy reading mounds of natural history books and explorers' journals in a deep chair piled with pillows—that had been Zeke, aged thirteen or fourteen.

His own father, Erasmus remembered, had acted as a sort of uncle to Zeke during Mr. Voorhees's business trips: an antidote to a houseful of women. He'd brought armfuls of books during the year Zeke spent in bed after a bout of typhus, and had later welcomed Zeke's visits to the Repository. Erasmus, just back from the Exploring Expedition then, had been only vaguely aware that Zeke regarded him as some sort of hero. But after Zeke finished reading the journals of Franklin's first voyage, Erasmus had heard him say to his father, "This is how I want to live, Mr. Wells—like Franklin and his men, like Erasmus. I want to *explore.* How can anyone bear to live and die without accomplishing something remarkable?"

Erasmus had dismissed those words as boyish fantasies, watching unsurprised as Zeke was funneled into his family's business. He worked in the warehouse, he sat in the office, he traveled on the ships of the packet line; he complained he had no time for his own studies, yet acted like his father's right hand. Then a lightning bolt struck a ship he was on, burning it to the waterline and killing some of the crew. Flames shooting into the night, shattered spars, the cries of the lost; Zeke had saved twenty-six passengers, herding them toward the floating debris and caring for them until their rescue. His descriptions of the incident, Erasmus believed, had made Lavinia fall in love with him. Afterward Mr. Voorhees, as a kind of reward, had allowed Zeke a certain amount of time for his scientific investigations on each voyage.

Erasmus, thinking those investigations were just a hobby, had expected Zeke to mature into a merchant captain. Yet Zeke kept reading and planning and making notes—dreaming, while no one paid attention, of a quest that would make his name. Until finally, at Lavinia's birthday party, he'd surprised them all.

"In the water," Zeke had once told Erasmus, "while I was floating there, knowing I might easily die, I understood I would *not* die. I was *not* sickly, I was very strong; I could keep my head in an emergency. I was destined—I am destined—to do something remarkable. Men have made themselves famous solely by mastering a subject which others have not yet seen to be important. And I have mastered the literature of arctic exploration."

That mastery was of little use during the first ten days of the voyage, which Zeke spent flat on his back, flounder pale, his oddly large palms and short, blunt fingers dangling over the side of his berth. Erasmus cared for him as well as he could, remembering his promise to his sister and his own early misreadings of Zeke's character. Unpleasant work: yet for all his worry, there was still the great pleasure of being at sea again. The wind tearing the clouds to shreds, tearing his old dull life to shreds. In his journal he wrote:

How could I have forgotten what this was like? Thirteen years since I was last on a ship, waking to the sounds of halyards cracking

*against the masts, water rushing past the hull; and each day the
sense of time stretching out before me as rich and vast as the ocean. I
think about things I've forgotten for years. Outwardly this is much
like my last voyage: the watches changing, the ship's bell ringing, the
routine of meals and duties. Yet in other ways so different. No military men, no military discipline; just the small group of us, gathered for a common cause. And me with all the time in the world to
stand on the deck at night and watch the stars whirling overhead.*

RAIN, FOUR DAYS in a row. Erasmus stayed in the cabin for much
of that time, besotted with his new home. Between the bulkhead
separating the cabin from the forecastle, and the equipment shelves
surrounding the stepladder leading to the deck, everything else was
squeezed: hinged table and wooden stools; lockers, hanging lamp
and stove; and, stacked in tiers of three along the sides, six berths.
Mr. Tagliabeau, Captain Tyler, and Mr. Francis occupied the star-
board berths. On the port side, Dr. Boerhaave had the bottom, Zeke
the middle, and Erasmus the upper berth, which was lined and cur-
tained off with India rubber cloth. The rats creeping up from the
hold at night might have seen the officers arranged like cheeses along
their shelves and, on the opposite side of the bulkhead, the seamen
swaying in their netted hammocks.

Yet physical discomforts didn't seem to matter. With his curtain
drawn, Erasmus could almost pretend he was alone; almost forget
that Zeke lay just a few inches below him, Mr. Tagliabeau a few feet
across from him. Two wooden shelves held his books, his journal,
a reading lamp, his pens and drawing supplies. Compass, pocket-
sextant and watch hung from particular pegs; rifle, flask, and pouch
from others. Order, sweet order. Everything under his control, in a
space hardly bigger than a coffin yet warm and dry and lit. As the

rain tapered off on the fourth day he read and wrote in there, happy until he heard Zeke vomiting.

Delirious from lack of food, Zeke whimpered and called for his mother and sometimes for Lavinia. That boy in the invalid's chair was still apparent in his eyes, although he'd already managed to make it clear that he resented whoever helped him. Erasmus opened his curtain, fetched a clean basin, soothed Zeke's face with a damp cloth. Perhaps, he thought, Zeke wouldn't remember this day or hold these acts against him. When Dr. Boerhaave, still a stranger, said, "Let me see what I can do," and opened his medicine chest, Erasmus left Zeke in the doctor's hands and went to get some fresh air. Low swells, a crisp breeze, the rain-washed sails still dripping and the clouds parting like tufts of carded wool. Beneath that sky the deck was dotted with men picking oakum. Which was Isaac, which was Ivan? Erasmus had made a resolution, after watching Alexandra's ease with the same servants whose names he still forgot. On the *Narwhal,* he'd promised himself, he'd pay attention to everyone, not just the officers.

That was Robert, he thought. On that coil of rope. Sean, by the sturdy capstan. And in the galley, cooking as if he were dancing, Ned Kynd. A glance at the simmering carrots, a stir of the chicken fricassee, then a few quick kneads of the biscuit dough on a floured board.

Erasmus dipped a spoon in the stew pot and tasted the gravy. "Delicious," he said, thinking with pleasure of the live chickens still penned on the deck. Fresh food for another several weeks; he knew, as Zeke and perhaps even Ned did not, how much this was to be relished. "You're doing a fine job."

"It's a pleasure," Ned said. "A pleasure to have such a tidy place to cook in. And then the sea—isn't it lovely?"

"It is," Erasmus agreed. They spoke briefly about menus and the state of their provisions; then about Ned's quarters, which he claimed were fine. Never sick, always cheerful and prompt, Ned seemed to have made himself at home. Already he'd adopted the seamen's bright neckerchiefs and was growing a spotty beard. After a few minutes' chat about the weather and a spell of comfortable silence, Ned said, "May I ask you a question?"

"Of course," Erasmus said, praying it wouldn't be about Zeke.

"Could you tell me about this Franklin we're looking for? Who he is?"

Erasmus stared at him, a piece of carrot still in his mouth. "Didn't Commander Voorhees explain all this to you, when you signed on?"

Ned cut biscuits. "That Franklin was lost," he said. "That we were to go and search for him . . . but not much more than that."

Where had Ned been these last years? While Ned slipped the biscuits onto a tin, Erasmus leaned against the water barrel and tried to summarize the story that had riveted everyone else's attention.

"Sir John Franklin was, is, English," he said. "A famous explorer, who'd already been on three earlier arctic voyages."

The chicken simmered as Erasmus explained how Franklin had set off with over a hundred of the British Navy's finest men. For ships he had James Ross's old *Erebus* and *Terror,* refitted with hot-water heating systems and experimental screw propellers. Black-hulled, white-masted, the ships had left England in the spring of 1845, provisioned for three years. Each had taken along a library of some twelve hundred books and a hand organ, which played fifty tunes. The weather was remarkably fine that summer, and hopes for a swift journey high. Toward the end of that July they were seen by a whaler, moored to an iceberg at the mouth of Lancaster Sound; after that they disappeared.

"Disappeared?" Ned said. His hands cut lard into flour for a pie crust.

"Vanished," Erasmus replied. Everyone knew this part of the

story, he thought: not just himself and Zeke, but Lavinia and all her acquaintances, even his cook and his groom. "How did you miss this?"

"There was starvation in Ireland," Ned said sharply. "How did you miss *that*? I had other things on my mind."

The chronology of these two events fell into line. Ned, Erasmus realized, must have been part of the great wave of Irish emigrants fleeing the famine. He was still just a boy, he could almost have been Erasmus's son. "Forgive me," he said. He knew nothing of Ned's history, as he'd known nothing of his servants' lives at home. "That was stupid of me." Of course the events in Ireland had shaped Ned's life more than the stories of noble Franklin, unaccountably lost; or noble Jane, his wife, who by the time Zeke proposed their voyage had organized more than a dozen expeditions in search of her husband.

Ned sliced apples so swiftly they seemed to leap away from his knife, and Erasmus, after an awkward pause, explained how ships had converged from the east and west on the areas in which Franklin was presumed to be lost, while other expeditions traveled overland. All had made important geographical discoveries, but despite the rockets fired, the kites and balloons sent adrift in the air, the foxes tagged with messages and released, no one had found Franklin. Erasmus's fellow Philadelphian, Dr. Kane, had been with the fleet that reached Beechey Island during the summer of 1851, finding tantalizing traces of a winter camp.

Erasmus tried, without frightening Ned, to describe what that fleet had seen. Three of Franklin's seamen lying beneath three mounds; and also sailcloth, paper fragments and blankets, and six hundred preserved-meat tins, emptied of their contents and refilled with pebbles. But no note, nor any indication of which direction the party had headed on departing. Subsequent expeditions hadn't found a single clue as to Franklin's whereabouts. The Admiralty had given up the search a year ago, declaring Franklin and his men dead.

"Why would Commander Voorhees want to do this, then?" Ned asked. "If the men are dead?"

"There was news," Erasmus said. "Surprising news."

In the fall, just as Zeke had said at Lavinia's party, John Rae of the Hudson's Bay Company had startled everyone. Exploring the arctic coastline west of Repulse Bay, not in search of Franklin at all but purely for geographical interest, he'd come across some Esquimaux. A group of thirty or forty white men had starved to death some years before, they said, at the mouth of a large river. They wouldn't lead Rae to the bodies, and Rae had thought the season too far advanced to embark on a search himself. But the Esquimaux had relics: Rae purchased a gold watch, a surgeon's knife, a bit of an undervest; silver forks and spoons marked with Franklin's crest; a golden band from a cap.

"The part that set everyone talking, though," Erasmus said, "was the last story the Esquimaux told Dr. Rae."

Three pies were taking shape; he filched some apple slices. Was it wrong, he wondered, to bring up the subject of starvation with a boy who might have seen it directly? Was it wrong to talk so freely with a subordinate? But Ned, crimping the crusts together, said, "Well, *tell* me."

Erasmus, leaving out the worst parts, described the Esquimaux tale of mutilated corpses and human parts found in cooking kettles. There could be no doubt, Rae had said, that his countrymen had been driven to cannibalism as a last resort.

"What an uproar Rae caused!" Erasmus said. He registered Ned's pallor, but he was caught in his own momentum now. "You'd have thought he killed the men himself, from the public's response. The Admiralty dismissed his findings and said Englishmen don't eat Englishmen. But they declared the fate of Franklin's expedition resolved, despite the fact that Rae's story accounted for less than a third of the crew."

"You look for the rest, then?" Ned asked.

"*We* look."

He wound up with the facts that had set them off on their own quest. Although the Admiralty had given up, Lady Franklin persisted, bombarding the press with pleas for further, private expeditions.

"Until the ships are found," Erasmus said, "there's no proof that all the men are dead. Dr. Kane is still searching for them, but he headed for Smith Sound before Rae's return. Franklin might have reached that area if he'd headed north through Wellington Channel, but now we know he went southwest and that Kane's a thousand miles from the right place. We have all the facts Dr. Kane was missing, and our job is to search in the area Rae insufficiently explored."

Ned finished the pies and then looked up. "Commander Voorhees made it sound as if we were going to rescue *survivors*," he said. "Yet it seems we're only going after corpses."

"Not exactly," Erasmus said, flustered. "There may be some survivors, we hope there are. We go in search of them, and of news."

He left the galley feeling uneasy, a biscuit in his hand. He'd imagined that the ship's crew shared his and Zeke's thoughts: the story of Franklin clear in their minds, the goals of the voyage sharply defined and their own tasks understood. Now he wondered if they were like Ned, signed on for their own reasons, occupied with their own concerns, hardly aware of the facts. One was thinking, perhaps, about a belled cow walking high on a hill. Another about a pond and four locust trees, or about drinking whiskey or shoeing a horse, what he might buy when he was paid off, a young woman, an old quarrel, a sleigh's runners slicing the snow.

THE LAST TIME Ned had sailed on a ship, he'd been sick and stunned and hadn't known how to read or write. This time he'd do it differently; this time he'd keep a record. Before leaving Philadelphia he'd bought a lined copybook, of the sort boys used in school. That night he wrote:

The apple pies were very good. But Commander Voorhees still hasn't eaten a mouthful, nothing I make tempts him. Today I saw a large school of bluefish. Mr. Wells came to visit while I made dinner and told me about the explorer we're searching for. Except he is dead, also all his men I think. Not only frozen but starved. When he told me about the men eating each other I thought about home, and all this evening I've been remembering Denis and Nora and our voyage over, and all the others dead at home, and Mr. Wickersham who taught me to read and write, and everyone. I get along well enough with the seamen I bunk with, but don't yet have a special friend among them and wish I did. Although I've heard Mr. Wells asking the other seamen for details of their lives, he didn't ask me one thing about the famine years nor how or when I arrived in this country. Nor how it was that I happened to be free, with less than a dollar in my pocket, on the very afternoon Mr. Tagliabeau came looking for a replacement cook. Only he seemed surprised that I hadn't heard about the famous Englishman. If I hadn't tried to stop the fight between the two Spaniards that afternoon, and been fired for my pains and denied my last week's wages, I wouldn't have leapt at the chance for this position. When we return to Philadelphia in October I wonder if he'd help me find work away from the docks, perhaps in one of the inns out Germantown way.

OFF ST. JOHN'S, the scattered icebergs—pure white, impossibly huge, entirely covered with snow—cured Zeke like a drug. Captain Tyler, Mr. Tagliabeau, and Mr. Francis viewed them calmly, after their many whaling voyages. Erasmus, who'd seen similar bergs off Antarctica, restrained his excitement for the sake of appearances. But the men who hadn't been north before gaped openly, and Zeke was overcome.

"Look! Look!" he shouted, racing about the deck and then diving into the cabin for his journal. His first entry, dated June 15, 1855, was a series of hasty sketches captioned with rough measurements: *The largest iceberg is a quarter-mile across.* Nils Jensen, who couldn't read but had remarkable calculating skills, leaned over the drawing and murmured some numbers suggesting the berg's volume and area. Other excited men crowded around, but perhaps only Erasmus saw, behind the hamlike shoulders of huge Sean Hamilton, the officers exchanging glances and sarcastic smiles.

That night, with Zeke up on deck and not heaving into a basin, Erasmus slept soundly for the first time and so missed the actual collision. One great thump; by the time he woke and ran up on deck the *Narwhal* was moving backward, rebounding from a slope-sided iceberg and shorn of her dolphin striker and martingales. Past him ran Mr. Francis and Mr. Tagliabeau, Thomas Forbes on their heels with a sack of carpenter's tools. Shouts and calls and terse instructions; what was damaged, what intact; a dark figure draped over the bowsprit, investigating, anchored by hands on his ankles and a rope at his waist. Erasmus rubbed sleep from his eyes and tried to stay out of the way. Captain Tyler, standing next to Zeke as his crew worked, turned and said, "Had you taken the course I *suggested . . .*"

"This course is fine!" Zeke exclaimed. "The man in the crow's nest must have been sleeping. You there!" He tilted his head back and hollered at the figure on the masthead: Barton DeSouza, Erasmus saw. Was that Barton? "You look sharp there!"

The moon was full and the berg gleamed silvery off the *Narwhal*'s bow. Barton muttered something Erasmus couldn't hear. A hammer beat against a doubled wall of wood as Thomas and his helpers began repairing the damage. Nothing serious, Mr. Tagliabeau called back.

"It's late," Zeke pointed out. "They could do that tomorrow."

"Better to do it now," Captain Tyler said. "Suppose a squall were to strike in the next few hours?"

He turned his back, he called out orders, figures moved in response to his words. Zeke retreated—just when he should have asserted his authority, Erasmus thought. The men had instinctively looked to Captain Tyler during Zeke's illness, reverting to what they knew; on the fishing and whaling ships where they'd served before, the captain was the sole authority. Here, with an expedition commander who couldn't set a sail somehow in charge of the ship's captain, they were all uneasy. Erasmus overheard them now and again, a grumpy Greek chorus: *He's never been north of New York; he doesn't know how to roll a hammock; he changes his shirt twice a week*—Sean Hamilton, Ivan Hruska, Fletcher Lamb. Each time Zeke gave an order they turned to the captain and waited for his nod before obeying.

Erasmus saw all this, but couldn't fix it. For the next few days he focused instead on trying out the dredge and the tow nets. Already he could see that Zeke wouldn't share his scientific work; after all he was to be alone, as he'd been on his first voyage. He tied knots, adjusted shackles, replaced a poorly threaded pin, remembering how shyly his young self had hung back from his companions. While he was working up the courage to be friendly, everyone else had been pairing off, or clumping in groups of three or four from which he was excluded. Everyone had been courteous but he'd been left with no particular friend; and at times he'd thought he might die of loneliness.

He was older now, he was used to it. Yet still he felt grateful when Dr. Boerhaave, who'd been reading near the galley, edged up and broke his solitude. "Those little purple-tinted shrimps," he said, "are they *Crangon boreas*?"

Later, Erasmus would gain a clearer picture of Dr. Boerhaave's face. For now, what he first noticed was his mind: quick and shining, sharp but deep, moving through a sea of thought like a giant silver salmon. Dr. Boerhaave, Erasmus learned quickly, knew as much natural history as he did. Although he was the better botanist, Dr. Boerhaave was the better zoologist and was especially knowledgeable about marine invertebrates.

As they probed their captives, Dr. Boerhaave said he'd been raised in the port of Gothenberg, but educated in Paris and Edinburgh. His excellent English he attributed to his years at sea. Over a group of elegant little medusae captured in their tow net—"*Ptychogastria polaris*," Dr. Boerhaave said—he described his trips as ship's surgeon aboard Scottish whalers and Norwegian walrus-hunters.

"I was curious," he said. "I liked Edinburgh very much, but I didn't want to set up a practice there and see the same people for the next forty years. And the idea of returning permanently to Sweden . . ." He shrugged.

Erasmus, embalming a medusa, said, "Commander Voorhees told me you'd been twice to the high arctic. With whalers? Or were those more formal expeditions?"

"The latter," Dr. Boerhaave said. "On the Swedish exploring expedition I accompanied, we went up the west coast of Spitzbergen to Hakluyt's Headland—not as far as Parry got, but we saw some of the same places that Franklin and Beechey explored with the *Dorothea* and the *Trent*."

Franklin's first voyage, so long ago. For a minute Erasmus thought how that had led, by an unexpected web of events, to their own voyage.

"Later I went with a Russian expedition to Kamchatka Peninsula and the Pribilof and Aleutian Islands, then into the Bering Straits. We'd hoped to reach Wrangel Island but were stopped by icepack in the Beaufort Sea."

He drew an equatorial projection of the medusa before them, revealing the convoluted edges of the eight gastric folds. He had excellent pencils, Erasmus observed. The line they made was both darker and sharper than his own.

"What about you?" Dr. Boerhaave said. "Your own earlier journey—I read all five volumes of Wilkes's narrative of the Exploring Expedition, it was very popular when the first copies arrived in Europe. But I don't remember seeing your name mentioned. How is that so?"

Erasmus flushed and directed Dr. Boerhaave's attention to some questionable seals on the preserving jars. "It's a long story," he said. "I'll tell you another time. How did you decide to join us?"

"I thought it would round out my picture of the high arctic," Dr. Boerhaave said. "Different ice, different flora and fauna. Anyway I was already on this side of the ocean. I came to America several years ago, to visit some of your New England philosophers. Emerson, Brownson and the others—it interests me, what they've done with the ideas of Kant and Hegel. You know this young Henry Thoreau?"

"I don't," Erasmus said.

"I met him and some of his friends in Boston, which was delightful. But all along I also hoped to do some exploring, either out west or in the arctic. At a dinner party I ran into Professor Agassiz, whom

I'd once met in Scotland—we share an interest in fossil fishes. He put me in touch with some members of your Academy of Sciences, which is how I learned your expedition needed a surgeon. The position was just what I'd been hoping for."

"Was it?" Erasmus said thoughtfully. "You might just as easily have had mine—you're better trained. I expect you did both jobs at once on your other trips."

Dr. Boerhaave looked down at his drawing. "Differently trained, that's all. And in a way it's a relief simply to be responsible for the health of the crew and to have someone else in charge of the zoological and botanical reports. I've always thought both jobs were too much for one man to do well."

"But we must be partners, then," Erasmus said. "Real colleagues. May we do that?"

"Of course," Dr. Boerhaave said. With his pencil he drew a delicate tentacle.

DR. BOERHAAVE WROTE to William Greenstone, an Edinburgh classmate who was now a geologist of some repute:

Although we're not to Greenland yet, we've not been idle. I've examined all the men, so as to have an accurate point from which to assess their later health. On a journey this short, and with ample opportunities to acquire fresh food, there won't be signs of scurvy, but the alternation in day length and the sleep deprivation may cause changes.

It's an unusual situation for me, having an official naturalist on board. I worried that he—his name is Erasmus Wells—might be jealous of his position and equipment, and that I might have few opportunities for collecting and examining specimens. Yet in fact Mr. Wells is quite congenial and seems willing to let me share in his investigations. So far we've found nothing exciting but are in heavily traveled waters where everything we capture is well known. Yesterday we took a Cyclopterus spinosus *though: not quite two inches long, covered with the typical conical spines, and very like those I saw off Spitzbergen; I was surprised to see it this far south.*

I think I'll like my new companion. He's somewhat fussy and tends to be melancholy, but he's intelligent and well traveled. His formal education is spotty by our standards, but he's read widely and seems more—I don't know, more complicated than the usual run of Americans. Not quite so blindly optimistic, nor so convinced that one can make the world into what one wishes. Perhaps because he's older. Except for him and me and the ship's captain, the others are hardly more than children. I packed the bottom sampler you gave me carefully, and once we enter Baffin's Bay I'll do my best to obtain samples of the seafloor for you.

HERE WAS THE ARCTIC, Erasmus thought, as the *Narwhal* moved through Davis Strait and the night began to disappear. Or at least its true beginning: here, here, here.

His eyes burned from trying to take in everything at once. Whales with their baleen-laden mouths broke the water, sometimes as many as forty a day. Belugas slipped by white and radiant and the sky was alive with birds. The men cheered the first narwhals as guardian spirits and crowded around Erasmus as he sketched. With one of Dr. Boerhaave's excellent pencils he tried to capture the grooved spike jutting from the males' upper jaws and the smooth dark curves of their backs. Nils Jensen, out on the bowsprit, watched intently as each surfaced to breathe and called back measurements—ten feet long, twelve and half—which Erasmus noted on his drawings.

One day the coast of Greenland appeared, the peak of Suk-kertoppen rising above the fog and flickering past as they sailed to Disko Island. A flock of dovekies sailed through the rigging, and when Robert Carey knocked one to the deck Erasmus remembered how, as a little boy, he'd glimpsed three of these tiny birds in a creek near his home, bobbing exhausted where they'd been driven after a great northeaster. This one looked like a black-and-white quail in his hand. Bending over the rail to release it, he saw fronds of seaweed waving through ten fathoms of transparent water. As soon as they anchored at Godhavn he and Dr. Boerhaave sampled the shallows, finding nullipores, mussels, and small crustaceans. Then they saw people, floating on the water and looking back at them.

In tiny, skin-covered kayaks the strangers darted among the ice-bergs; their legs were hidden inside the boats, their arms extended by two-bladed paddles. Flash, flash: into the ocean and out again, water streaming silver from the blades. The paddles led to tight hooded jackets; the jackets merged into oval skirts connecting the men at their waists to the boats—like centaurs, Erasmus thought. Boat men, male boats. It was all a blur, he couldn't see their faces.

Sean Hamilton tossed them bits of biscuit and Erasmus revised his first opinion: *This* was where the journey began, with this first sight of the arctic men he'd read about for so long. That these Green-landers had traded with whalers for two centuries, been colonized by the Danes and converted by Moravian and Lutheran missionaries, made them less strange: but they were still new to him. On the first night in port, over a dinner of eider ducks at the huge-chimneyed home of the Danish inspector, he looked alternately at a bad engrav-ing of four Greenlanders captured near Godthaab and brought to Copenhagen and, out the window next to the portrait, at the jumble of wooden huts and sealskin tents into which the mysterious strang-ers disappeared.

———

ON THE *NARWHAL* the crew made their final preparations. Thomas Forbes, Erasmus saw, kept his carpenter's bench in perfect order. Ivan Hruska's hammock had a hole in it, which he repaired beautifully. Mr. Francis appeared to regard the boatswain's locker as a treasure chest, keeping close track of every marlinspike and bit of spun yarn he passed out. All this bustle pleased Erasmus. This was their last chance to ready the brig for her encounters with the pack, and finally, he thought, the men had been infected with the sense of urgency he'd had for months.

He and Zeke, equally busy, acquired sixteen ill-mannered Esquimaux dogs, a stock of dried codfish, bales of seal and caribou skins, full Esquimaux outfits for all the crew, and an interpreter, Johann Schwartzberg. After sharing a walk with him, Erasmus wrote:

> He's a Moravian missionary—an extremely interesting man. He's lived among the Esquimaux both here and in Labrador, and he knows their language as well as Danish, English, and German. He'll be invaluable if we meet Esquimaux around King William Land. When Zeke approached him, we learned that he'd followed the news of Franklin's expedition avidly and had already heard about Rae's discoveries. He seems genuinely thrilled to join us. The men call him Joe, and already I can see that he's sensible, mild-tempered, good-humored, and handy.

It was Joe who determined how many knives and needles and iron bars they should barter for the fish and the furs, and Joe who examined each Esquimaux outfit for proper fit. Zeke asked Mr. Tagliabeau and Mr. Francis to work with the dogs; when they tangled the traces and crashed the sledge and fumbled helplessly, it was Joe who demonstrated how to control them. Buff and brown and white and black, long-haired, demonic, and curly-tailed, the dogs were nothing like the well-mannered hounds Zeke kept at home. With a peculiar turn of the wrist, Joe directed the whip toward the head of the most recalcitrant creature and clipped off a piece of its ear.

Zeke, watching this with Erasmus, caught his breath and said, "Oh, how cruel!"

Mr. Francis shot a contemptuous glance back over his shoulder. "Perhaps you'd like to reason with them?" There was something weasel-like about him, Erasmus thought. That narrow chest; the thick hair growing low on his forehead and shading his deep-set eyes. "Maybe you can *persuade* them," Mr. Francis added.

"Would you take over?" Zeke asked Joe. He pulled Erasmus away. "A good commander recognizes those things that are abhorrent to him, or which he does badly, and gives others charge of them," he said. "Don't you think? Joe's a fine teacher, and Mr. Tagliabeau and Mr. Francis are coarse enough to be good drivers."

Joe also knew how to build a snow house and how to repair a sledge. And it was Joe who helped Erasmus overcome his initial discomfort around the short men with their glossy hair and unreadable eyes. *Hyperboreans,* Erasmus thought, recalling his father's tales. Was it Pliny who'd claimed they lived to a ripe old age and passed down marvelous stories? But his unease was grounded in experience, not myth. At Malolo in western Fiji, he'd seen savages murder two of the Exploring Expedition's men with no apparent provocation. In Naloa Bay he'd watched a native calmly gnaw the flesh of a cooked human head, which Wilkes had later purchased for their collection.

Yet the Esquimaux weren't violent, only a little sullen. Joe said, "You need to understand that they're doing us a favor—it hasn't been a good year for seals, and they don't have many spare skins. They're trading with us because the Danish inspector is sympathetic to Commander Voorhees's mission, and he ordered them to. You might give the men who bring you the best skins some extra token."

Erasmus offered small metal mirrors and was rewarded with smiles, which made him more comfortable. When he sketched the strangers, emerging from the skin tents scattered at the edge of the mission or rolling their delicate boats upside down and then righting them with a touch of their paddles, the orderly shapes he made on paper ordered his feelings as well.

After a last dinner at the home of the Danish inspector, the crew slept and then made sail early the following morning. Their wildly barking dogs were answered by the dogs on shore. Even that sound pleased Erasmus. They'd made good time so far and now, on this first day of July, they were finally ready. His lists had been worthwhile after all, and all the worry, all the fuss.

LATER, WHEN HE'D try to tell his story to the one person who might most want to hear it, he'd puzzle over how to recount the events of the next few weeks. The incidents had no shape, he would think. They were simply incidents, which piled one atop the other but always had to do with a set of men on a ship, moving fitfully from one patch of water to the next. At the rails he and Dr. Boerhaave gaped at the broken, drifting floes of sheet ice Captain Tyler called "the middle pack." A few inches thick, twelve feet thick; the size of a boat or of downtown Philadelphia; between these were the leads, the openings that sustained them. Without a sense of their passage through the pack, nothing that came later could be fully understood.

They saw the ice through a haze induced by the dogs, whose howling made sleep and even conversation impossible. No one knew what to do with them, nor how to manage their ravenous appetites; the loose ones broke into a barrel of seal flippers and gorged themselves until two died. Nothing was safe from them, and no one could control them but Joe. The constant noise and the lack of sleep made everyone nervous, and in the cramped officers' cabin Erasmus felt a split, which perhaps had been there all along, begin to widen. He and Dr. Boerhaave found themselves allied with Zeke, while Mr. Francis and Mr. Tagliabeau always lined up with Captain Tyler, as if the arrangement of their berths marked emotional as well as physical territory. Joe, who slept in the forecastle with the seamen, maintained a careful neutrality. When the dogs tried to eat a new litter of puppies, Joe rescued them, raising an eyebrow but saying nothing when Zeke took one for himself.

"Wissy," Zeke said, holding the squirming creature by the neck. "After the Wissahickon." He ran his hand over her fluffy, fawn-colored head, her white front feet, the black spot on her back, withdrawing it when she turned and nipped him.

"It's a river," Erasmus explained to Joe. "Back home." To Zeke he said, "Are you sure you want to keep her? They aren't bred to be pets."

"I don't think Captain Tyler appreciates having her in the cabin," Joe added.

But Zeke was adamant, working patiently to break her habit of chewing on everyone and everything, and she was by his side as they reached Upernavik. Nils Jensen counted the icebergs, cracked and grottoed or blue-green and crystalline, while Captain Tyler disagreed with Zeke about their route. A zigzag, west-trending lead had opened through the pack, and Zeke argued that they should try to force a passage directly west, as Parry had once done.

"The traditional route through Melville Bay to the North Water is longer in distance," Captain Tyler said, kicking Wissy away from his ankles. "But ultimately it's always quicker. Why don't you *discipline* this creature?"

Finally, as the lead narrowed and then disappeared, Zeke agreed to Captain Tyler's route and they slipped through the steadily thickening fog into the long and gentle curve of Melville Bay. Trying to describe this place to Copernicus later, Erasmus would seize a heavy mirror and drop it flat on its back from the height of his waist, so it shattered without scattering. Heavy floes grinding against each other on one side; against the land a hummocked barrier thick with grounded bergs and upended floes—and in between, their fragile ship.

In this mirror land they were all alone. "No surprise," Captain Tyler said irritably, after the lookout reported the absence of ships. "The whalers always take the pack in May or June, when there's less danger of being caught by an early winter."

"We left Philadelphia as soon as we could," Zeke told him. "You know that. It's not my fault."

Meanwhile the seamen told stories of ships destroyed when wind drove the drifting pack against the coast. There was a reason, they said, why Melville Bay was called the breaking-up yard. Ships crushed like hazelnuts, they said, or locked in the ice for months: as if saying it would keep it from happening. *We should have started sooner; we shouldn't be here at all; I knew four men. who died here*— Isaac Bond, Robert Carey, Barton DeSouza. Even as they grumbled, half-aware that Erasmus listened, the open water vanished.

Captain Tyler ordered the sails furled and sent a man to the masthead, where he could call down the positions of the ice. For two days, while the wind was dead but a slim lead was open, they tracked the ship. On the land-fast ice they passed canvas straps over their shoulders and chests, then fastened their harnesses to the towline. Plodding heavily, they towed the brig as a team of horses might pull heavy equipment across a field. Erasmus, who'd volunteered to help, could stop when he was exhausted, or when his hands froze or his feet blistered; here he felt for the first time how much older he was than everyone but Captain Tyler. Zeke, so much younger, would always pull longer but never finished a full watch. The men pulled until their watch was complete, and for all that, on a good day, they might make six miles.

On bad days, when the channel disappeared, they warped the brig like a wedge between the consolidated floes. Two men with an iron chisel cut a hole near the edge of a likely crack and drove in an anchor; a hawser was fastened to the anchor and the other end wound around the ship's winch. Everyone took his turn at the capstan bars. By the pressure of their bodies against the bars, the winch rotated, the hawser shivered, the ice began to groan. If the hawser didn't break, nor the anchor pull loose, the brig inched forward into the little crack. For hours they worked and got nowhere; an inch, a foot, the length of the ship.

THOSE DAYS BLURRED in Erasmus's mind. The great cliffs looming above him, the drifting bergs and shifting ice; brief bouts of sailing interspersed with long bouts of warping and tracking; the fog and wind and the brutal labor and the snatched, troubled bits of sleep; their wet clothes and hasty meals and Captain Tyler, red-faced, shouting at the men and occasionally whacking one with a fist or the end of a rope. Mr. Tagliabeau was somewhat less brutal with the men than the captain; Mr. Francis was worse.

"You have to do something about this," Erasmus said to Zeke one day. He was sweating horribly, itching from the wool next to his skin, and he thought he knew just how the men, working three times as hard as he was, felt. Fletcher Lamb had walked away from the towline after tearing the skin off his wrist, and Mr. Francis had hit him on the side of his head and chased him back.

Zeke shrugged. "What can I do? We have to make our way through this place, and there's no other way but to work the men as hard as they can stand. I promise things will be different when we reach the North Water."

It was like a single long nightmare, in which time passed too quickly and then, especially when they were bent to the capstan bars, refused to pass at all. The continuous light made things worse, not better: white, white, white tinged with blue, with gold, with green; white; more white. Their eyes burned, and as the sun looped around the sky, to the east in the morning, then south then west then finally in the north at night, with them still working, horribly sunburned, they began to yearn for the colors they never saw: sweet rich reds, the green of leaves. In their blurry sleepless state, with their bodies strained and aching, Erasmus wasn't surprised that they should lose sight of what had brought them there. It was all the crew could do to keep the brig moving and out of danger.

Zeke tried to keep the goals of the expedition alive by telling stories about Franklin; a way, he told Erasmus privately, of motivating the men. Off duty, they sprawled on the hatch covers or leaned against the boats while Zeke paced among them, describing Franklin's three earlier voyages. Franklin as a young lieutenant, seeking the North Pole by way of Spitzbergen, turned back by ice and returning to England with badly damaged ships. Franklin commanding an expedition through Rupert's Land, across the tundra to the mouth of the Coppermine River and exploring the coastline eastward in tiny canoes; Franklin in the arctic yet again, traveling down the MacKenzie River and exploring the coastline westward, nearly reaching Kotzebue Sound. In their winter camp on Great Bear Lake, Zeke said, Franklin had taught his men to read and Dr. Richardson, his naturalist companion, had lectured on the natural history of the region. After that last trip, Franklin had been knighted.

Zeke spoke as if he were transmitting the great tradition of arctic exploration, of which they were now a part. As if the stories would heal the crew's wounds and furies. But Erasmus noticed that Zeke never repeated these in the presence of Captain Tyler and the two mates. In a similar way, he was careful, himself, not to mention his disturbing dreams. Always he was sitting with his brothers at their father's knee, with Zeke, transformed into a boy their own age, hovering in the doorway and looking longingly at their family circle. Always his father was telling marvelous tales, as if he'd never taught them real science. *In ancient times,* his father said, *it was recorded that the sky rained milk and blood and flesh and iron; once the sky was said to rain wool and another time to rain bricks. It is always best to observe things for yourself.*

Erasmus tried not to think too much about what those dreams meant, or about the quarrels brewing. He shot burgomaster gulls and two species of loon, which the ravenous dogs tried to eat. Whenever they were stuck for a while, Joe tried to calm the dogs by unchaining them and letting them romp on the ice. They barked as if they'd gone insane and often proved difficult to retrieve; Zeke was forced to leave a pair behind when a berg suddenly sailed away from the brig. After that he no longer let Wissy run with the others but kept her tied to him by an improvised leash.

Ivan Hruska nearly drowned; a floe cracked as he was fixing an ice anchor, tossing him into the surging water. It wasn't true, as Erasmus had once believed, that immersion in this frigid fluid killed a man right away. Ivan was retrieved numb and blue and breathless, but alive. Fingers were caught between railings and lines, ribs were banged against capstan bars, skin was torn from palms and toes were broken by falling chisels. Dr. Boerhaave was kept busy attending to their injuries and preparing daily sick lists, which Zeke and Captain Tyler were forced to ignore:

Seaman Bond: abrasions to distal phalanges, left
Seaman Carey: two cracked ribs
Seaman DeSouza: asthma, aggravated by excessive labor
Seaman Hruska: bronchitis after immersion
Seaman Jensen: avulsed tip of right forefinger
Seaman Lamb: complaints of abdominal pain (earlier blow to liver?)
Seaman Hamilton: suppurating dermatitis, inner aspect of both thighs

Unromantic ailments, never mentioned in Zeke's tales. Meanwhile Joe tried to cheer the men. In Greenland, Erasmus learned, Joe had held services among his Esquimaux converts, during which he accompanied their singing with a zither. Now he plucked and strummed and taught the men songs, singing with them while they hauled.

A WEEK INTO Melville Bay, they were finishing their evening meal when the ice began to close in on them.

"If we cut a dock here," Captain Tyler said, indicating an indented portion of the large berg near them, "we should be safe, even if the drift ice closes full in to the shore."

"There's no time," Zeke said. "Suppose we make harbor inside this berg, and the floes seal off our exit? We could be here for weeks. And we've got the wind with us, for the moment."

They sailed on, with the men waiting tensely for orders. On deck, near the chained dogs, Erasmus and Zeke watched in silence. Soon the lead closed entirely and forced them to tie up to a floe. A second floe, which Nils Jensen estimated at some three-quarters of a mile in diameter and five feet deep, sailed past their sheltering chunk of ice, sheared half of it away without taking the brig, and proceeded serenely to shore. As it reached the land-fast ice, it rose in a stiff wave and shattered with a noise like thunder.

"Would you get out of the *way*!" Mr. Francis said, shoving Erasmus in his exasperation. Erasmus pulled back against the rail.

While Captain Tyler and Mr. Francis shouted and the men ran about with boathooks and pieces of lumber, a third floe pressed the *Narwhal* into the land-fast ice. Ned Kynd, his face as white as the ice, said, "We're going to be crushed."

He pressed into the rail beside Erasmus, who silently agreed with him. The ice on one side drove them into the ice on the other; the brig groaned, then screamed; her sides seemed to be giving way and the deck timbers began to arch. The seams between the deck planks opened. Zeke leaned toward Ned: two young men, one blond, one dark; one calm and one afraid.

"Don't worry so," Zeke said. He tapped Ned's shoulder and smiled at Erasmus. "I wouldn't let anything happen to us. Our bows are reinforced to withstand just this kind of pressure."

As if his words had been a spell the brig began to rise, tilting until the hawser snapped and they shot backward and across the floes like a seed pinched by a giant pair of fingers. For several hours they balanced on heaped-up ice cakes, until the wind changed and pulled the ice away and set them afloat once more with a dismal splash.

Zeke ordered rum for all the men and thanked them for their labor. To Captain Tyler he said, "You don't understand how well we've designed this ship to resist the ice. This is not your common whaler."

"If we had cut a dock," Captain Tyler said in a choked voice. His face was mottled, red on his fleshy nostrils and chin, white along his broad forehead and down the sharp bridge of his nose. His hands, Erasmus noticed, were hugely knotted at the joints. "If we had . . ." Abruptly he turned the watch over to Mr. Tagliabeau and retired below, where he wrapped his head in a blanket.

Later, perched on the hatch cover, Dr. Boerhaave whispered to

Erasmus that he'd feared their skipper might suffer an apoplexy. They looked out at the ice, too wound up to sleep and longing to talk: not about what had just happened, but anything else. They were still a little awkward with each other. Dr. Boerhaave said, "This is very different from the other expeditions I was on. Do you find it so? I'm curious about your earlier trip."

"I was twenty-three the last time I did anything like this," Erasmus said, watching the ice pieces spin in the tide. Twenty-three, barely older than Ned Kynd; often he'd been frightened half to death. When had his commander ever taken a minute to reassure him? The sky was lit like morning, although it was past ten o'clock; how delicious it was to be alive, under the shimmering clouds! Had the brig been shattered here, some of the crew would be dead by now and the rest drifting south on the fragments. He was alive, he was safe and warm. What was the point of keeping secret his time with the Exploring Expedition?

"When you asked why you never saw my name in Wilkes's book," he said, "there were nine civilians listed as 'Scientifics' among all those Navy men; I was the tenth. Wilkes never listed me because I joined the expedition at the last minute and didn't receive a salary."

He swallowed. Two floes touched and then parted, as if finishing a dance. "My father arranged it," he admitted. "The young woman to whom I was engaged"—*Sarah Louise Bettlesman*, he thought; still he could see her face, and remember her touch—"her lungs were weak, she died six months before we were to be married. I couldn't get back on my feet after that, and my father was worried. He pulled some strings, and after promising Wilkes he'd pay my keep for the voyage, he landed me a berth as Titian Peale's assistant."

"I am so sorry," Dr. Boerhaave said gently. "But I'm sure Wilkes felt lucky to have you."

While the ice waltzed around the bow and the clouds cavorted overhead, Erasmus told the rest of the story that had preoccupied him as he sorted and sifted his seeds.

The six ships of the Exploring Expedition had left Virginia in 1838. For the next four years they'd cruised the Pacific, from South America to the Fiji Islands, New Zealand and New Holland, the Sandwich Islands, the Oregon territory and more. Although Erasmus had been lonely, out of place, and often lost, he'd seen things he couldn't have imagined: cannibals, volcanic calderas, sixty-pound medusoids; the *meke wau,* or club dance, of the Fiji natives—natural wonders and also, always, Wilkes's brutality toward his men and his constant disregard of the needs of the Scientifics. The naval men had called the Scientifics bug catchers, clam diggers, and Wilkes had blocked their way at every turn.

They weren't allowed to work on deck, because of naval regulations and the bustle required to sail a ship. Below decks there was little light and less fresh air, and Wilkes forbade dissections there, as he found the odors distasteful and believed they spread disease. Their primary goal was surveying, Wilkes said, and he let nothing interfere with that. Day after day, Erasmus and his companions had watched the golden hours slip by while the naval men took topographical measurements of whatever island or coast was before them. Amazing plants and animals, always just out of reach. They'd set scoop nets when they could, consoling themselves with invertebrate treasures. When they thought they might expire from heat and anger, they threw themselves over the rail and into the swimming basin the men had made from a sail hung in the water. In early 1840, as they set off to explore the Antarctic waters and search for a landmass beneath the ice, Wilkes arranged to leave all the Scientifics behind at New Zealand and New Holland, so that whatever geographical discoveries he made need not be shared but might be wholly to the glory of the Navy.

He left all except Erasmus, too insignificant to worry about. On a shabby, poorly equipped ship, Erasmus and the sailors had nearly frozen to death. But they'd seen ice islands several hundred feet high and half a mile long, with gigantic arches leading into caverns crowned with bluffs and fissures. Ice rafts, some carrying boulders the size of a house. The sea had been luminous, lit like silver, and the tracks they left across it looked like lightning. Their boots leaked so badly they had to wrap their feet in blankets; their pea jackets might have been made of muslin; their gun ports failed to shut out the sea. Erasmus had been awed, and very cold, the night two midshipmen first caught sight of the Antarctic continent. Climbing up the rigging to join them, he'd seen the mountains for himself and then the wall of ice that almost shattered their ship. From that journey had come Wilkes's famous map, charting the Antarctic coast.

Everything after that was sordid; how could he tell Dr. Boerhaave? The quarrels among Wilkes and his junior officers, one ship wrecked and another sunk with all hands; crewmen massacred by the Fiji Islanders and then the retaliatory raids; floggings and a near mutiny and so many specimens lost. He fell silent for a minute. "The real point," he finally said, "isn't what we discovered but what happened when we returned. Everyone ignored us. Or mocked us."

"That's not in Wilkes's *Narrative*," Dr. Boerhaave said.

"It's not," Erasmus agreed. "Who ever writes about the failures?"

Yet this was the part he couldn't get past, the part that had twisted all the years since. Wilkes court-martialed on eleven charges and then, in a fury of wounded pride, impounding all the diaries and logbooks and journals and charts, and all the specimens.

"He took our *notes*," Erasmus said. "Our drawings, our paintings—he took them all."

Back in Washington, the specimens that hadn't been lost in transit disappeared like melting ice. Wilkes had compelled the Scientifics to work on what was left there in Washington, although all the good comparative collections and libraries were in Philadelphia. Then he'd ruined what work they completed. They'd come back to a country in the midst of a depression; what the men in Congress wanted wasn't science but maps and guides to new sealing and whaling grounds. Wilkes, with his endless charts, had satisfied the politicians. But meanwhile he delayed the expedition's scientific reports again and again.

"And then," Erasmus said, "after Titian Peale and I had spent years working on the mammals and birds and writing up our volume, Wilkes said it wasn't any good, and he blocked its publication."

He stopped; he couldn't imagine telling Dr. Boerhaave how he'd retreated from Washington to the safety of the Repository, turning finally to his seeds. Half living at home, half not; most of the privacy he'd required, without the fuss of having to set up an independent household. When he desired the kind of company he wouldn't want his family to meet, he visited certain establishments downtown or returned to Washington for a few days. Small comforts, but they were all he'd had as he wasted the prime of his young manhood. Although there were days when he'd deluded himself into thinking he might still salvage something resembling science from that voyage, in the end it was only Wilkes who'd triumphed. Despite his setbacks he'd had the great success of his *Narrative*. Even Dr. Boerhaave, across the ocean, had read it.

"It's such a *bad* book," Erasmus exclaimed. "Anyone knowing the people involved can see the pastiche of styles—the outright plagiarism of his subordinates' diaries and logbooks. Wilkes made those volumes with scissors and paste, and an utter lack of honor. He stole the book, then had copyright assigned to him and reprinted it privately. It made him rich."

"There's a certain unevenness of style," Dr. Boerhaave agreed. He picked at a frayed bit of whipping on a line. "I'm sorry. I didn't know—that's a terrible story." The string unraveled in his hand. "It's to your credit you've put that voyage behind you and joined up with Commander Voorhees."

"It's not a question of credit," Erasmus said. Although he felt a wonderful sense of pardon, hearing those words. "Only—I want the chance to have one voyage go *well*. I want to discover things Wilkes can't ruin. And—you know, don't you, that my sister is engaged to marry Zeke?"

"I didn't," Dr. Boerhaave said. "I had no idea. Commander Voorhees never mentioned . . . you'll be brothers-in-law?"

"I suppose," Erasmus said. "Of course." He picked up the scrap of string, unsure whether he should speak so personally. "My sister's very dear to me," he said. "Even though she's so much younger—our mother died when she was born, I helped raise her. I came on this voyage partly because she wanted me to watch over Zeke. He's so young, sometimes he's a bit . . . impulsive."

"So he is," Dr. Boerhaave said. "You're a kind brother."

Was that kindness? He'd lost the person he loved; he wanted to spare Lavinia that. Surely that was his simple duty. He asked, "Do you have brothers and sisters, yourself?"

Dr. Boerhaave smiled wryly. "One of each," he said. "Both in Sweden, both married—excellent but completely unremarkable people. They've never been able to understand why I wanted to travel, or why I should be so entranced by the arctic. We write letters, but almost never see each other. They're very good about looking after our parents."

He was cut off, Erasmus thought. Cut off from home; or free from ties to home. What did that feel like? "And in Edinburgh," he asked, ". . . does someone wait for you there? A woman friend?"

"Friends," Dr. Boerhaave said. Not boastingly, or in any indelicate way; just a simple statement. "Now and then, between trips, I've grown close to someone, and I stay in touch with them all. But every few years I go off like this, and it never seemed fair to get too entangled with any one woman, and then ask her to wait. I've been alone for so long it's come to seem normal."

He turned his head to follow a string of murres spangling, black and white, across the bow. "I love those birds," he said. "The sound their wings make. What about you? Are you . . . does someone wait for *you* at home?"

"No one but my family—not since my fiancée passed on."

"Such a pair of bachelors!" Dr. Boerhaave said.

There was a moment, then, as the murres continued pouring past them, in which anything might have been asked and answered. Erasmus might have asked what Dr. Boerhaave really meant by "alone"—with whom he shared that aloneness, and on what terms. Dr. Boerhaave might have asked Erasmus what he'd done since Sarah Louise's death for love and companionship: surely Erasmus hadn't dried up completely? But the moment passed and the two shy men asked nothing further of each other. Erasmus didn't have to say that he'd lived like a monk, except for brief entanglements that had left him feeling lonelier than before; that he'd not been able to move past the feeling that if he couldn't have Sarah Louise, he wanted no one. Or that, despite his love for his family, he'd often felt trapped living at home but hadn't been able to move. Where would he move to? Every place seemed equally possible, equally impossible. His father had tried to be patient with him but once, irritated by an attack of shingles, he'd spoken sharply. Erasmus, he'd said, was like a walking embodiment of Newton's Third Law of Motion. Set moving, he moved until someone stopped him; stopped, he was stuck until pushed again. Just like you, Erasmus had wanted to say. But hadn't.

———

THAT NIGHT HE lay in his bunk, mulling over what he'd revealed. Perhaps he shouldn't have mentioned that voyage at all—yet how could Dr. Boerhaave know him if he didn't share the biggest fact of his life? All those wasted days. While he'd been stalled a host of other, younger men had thrown themselves into the search for Franklin. Now that search was also his.

Back home he'd resisted the frenzy surrounding any mention of Franklin's name. That men sold cheap engravings of Franklin's portrait on the streets, or that because of Franklin he and Zeke had been interviewed in the newspapers and had gifts pressed in their hands, had nothing to do with him. The syrupy letters of a Mrs. Myers, saying she lived on a widow's mite but wanted to donate three goose-down pillows to aid in their search; the way, when he ordered socks in a shop, clerks came out from behind their counters to ask questions in breathless voices, as if not only Franklin and his men were heroes but so were he and Zeke—that puffery had made him uneasy. He'd focused on the practical, the everyday. Still there might be men alive, living off the land or among the Esquimaux; he and Zeke searched for them, not just for Franklin.

As he'd told Dr. Boerhaave the story of his earlier voyage, he'd seen how different it was from his present journey. This one was worthwhile. This one *meant* something. And when he finally slept, he dreamed he saw a column of men walking away from a ship. The ship was sinking, slowly and silently; the men turned their backs to it. Erasmus could see faces. A blond man with a broken nose, a short man with dark eyes and a mole on his chin. But not Franklin, nor any of the officers; no one whose portrait had been reproduced in the newspapers. Simply a group of strangers, waiting for help.

The dream both embarrassed and delighted him. Since the days of his first expedition, he'd not let himself admire anyone, nor been willing to bend his life to follow something greater. But he woke rejuvenated, feeling as if a great hand had reached down and brushed him from an eddy back into the current.

As they continued to struggle through Melville Bay, Zeke rolled off the names of the headlands they passed and said wistfully, "Wouldn't you like to have your name on something here?" Around his berth he'd built a rodent's nest of maps and papers. "Wouldn't it be wonderful to discover something altogether new?"

At night he pored over the accounts of Parry and Ross and Scoresby, sometimes reading passages aloud to the men while he paced the decks and they worked. He showed little interest in the amphipods Erasmus found clinging to the warping lines, or the snow geese and terns and ivory gulls that swooped and sailed above them. Nor was he interested in the miraculous refractions, which painted images in the sky near the sun. Sometimes whole bergs seemed to lift themselves above the horizon and float on nothingness, but Zeke no longer raptured over them. And Erasmus noticed that Zeke's journal—a handsome volume, bound in green silk, which Lavinia had given him—showed only a few scrappy entries.

"You've had no time?" Erasmus asked.

Zeke shook his head. "I keep meaning to," he said. "Lavinia made me promise I'd write in here, for her to read when we get back. But it's so large, and water spots the cover—and anyway I have this."

He showed Erasmus another notebook; he'd been keeping it for several years, he said, under his pillow at night and in his pocket during the day. Erasmus stared at the battered black volume, troubled that he hadn't known about it before.

"I started it when I began wishing I could do something to find

Franklin," Zeke said. "It's where I keep notes on things I've read, little reminders to myself, and so forth."

He held it out and Erasmus read the pages where it fell open. The titles of four books Zeke meant to read and seven he'd recently read, a letter to the Philadelphia paper praising Jane Franklin's continued quest for her husband, some thoughts about scurvy and its prevention (*FRESH MEAT,* underlined twice. *In the men, watch for bleeding gums, spots and swollenness of lower limbs, opening of old sores and wounds*), a recipe for pemmican, a drawing of a sledge runner, a Philadelphia merchant's quoted price for enough tobacco to supply the crew for eighteen months.

"Interesting," Erasmus said, although he was taken aback by this hodgepodge. Where was the urgency of their quest? "I can see this is where you kept track of what you learned while we were planning the trip. But what about now? Don't you—describe things? Write about what you've seen each day, and the progress we're making?"

"That's not important," Zeke said. On the cabin table a candle burned, casting improbable shadows. "Or not as important as planning ahead for what's to come. I like to use this for *thinking,* writing down what's really significant. Captain Tyler may run this brig on a daily basis. But I'm the one with the vision. I'm the one who has to keep us on track in the largest sense."

"I could do the mundane part," Erasmus offered. "Keep a record of our daily life, I mean. Then you'd be free to keep a more personal account."

"Why don't you take this?" Zeke said, indicating Lavinia's gift. "It's a good size, you'll have plenty of room." He lifted a stack of pages and let them slip along his thumb: a whirring noise, like wing beats. "When we get home, we can tell Lavinia we worked on it together."

THE WIND GREW fierce again. Not far from Cape York, Zeke gave in to Captain Tyler's wishes and ordered a dock cut in the landfast ice, where they might shelter until the gale passed. Above them a glacier poured between two cliffs crowded with nesting murres: black rock streaked with streams of droppings, the clean white river of ice; more soiled rock secreting waves of ammonia and an astonishing squawking noise. As birds left their eggs to seek fish in the cracks between the floes, a hunting party fired at them. Dr. Boerhaave, perched on a boulder, stayed behind to examine the parasites in the slaughtered birds' feathers. Zeke and Erasmus and Joe headed up the glacier's tongue.

They climbed joined by a long rope, which Joe looped around their waists as protection against the crevasses. Wissy, attached to Zeke by a separate rope, led; then Zeke and behind him Erasmus, who kept listing to the glacier's edge where it met the cliff, and where plants grew in the rocky, sheltered hollows. Chickweeds and sorrel and saxifrages, willows hardly bigger than his hand—but Zeke pulled on him like a farmer tugging a reluctant cow. In the rear Joe called out instructions when he detected a weakness in the ice. The lichens alone, Erasmus thought, would have repaid a week's visit; he didn't have a minute with them. The heaps of envelopes he'd brought for seeds were useless. The white bells of arctic heather like dwarfed lilies of the valley, the inch-high tangle of rhizomes, everything spreading vegetatively in a season too short for most plants to set seeds—he should be taking notes, copious notes, but they were moving too fast.

What was Zeke pulling him toward? A rough, craggy object half-embedded in the ice; he was missing his chance with the cliffside plants for the sake of a rock. By the time he caught up to Zeke, about to complain, Zeke was digging out one side of the boulder, assisted by Wissy's frantic paws. "What's so interesting?" Erasmus asked.

"I don't know," Zeke said. "It caught my eye, it looked so out of place—what is this doing here?"

Erasmus bent and saw that the side of the boulder opposite his hands was chipped and fractured in a way that suggested human interference. Elsewhere was a crust he recognized. "It's a meteorite," he told Zeke, annoyed that he hadn't discovered it himself.

Joe caught up to them, out of breath, and inspected the chipped side. "One of the iron stones!" he exclaimed.

"Why do you call it that?" Erasmus asked. He could feel where flakes the size of fingernails were missing.

"There are Esquimaux around here," Joe said. "The ones Ross called Arctic Highlanders. Even as far south as Godhavn we've heard stories of how they use the odd rocks stuck in the glaciers. They chip harpoon heads from them."

Erasmus inspected the rock more closely and probed it with his knife: a siderite, he decided, metallic iron alloyed with nickel.

A similar specimen had fallen in Gloucestershire in 1835—but how remarkable to find one here! And for Joe to know the story that made sense of it. "Ever since Ross explored this area, people have been wondering about the source of the northern tribe's iron," he said to Zeke. "They must have been getting it from this stone, or from others like it."

Joe nodded. "Somewhere near here are supposed to be three large ones, which the Esquimaux have named. And perhaps smaller ones like this as well."

Zeke tapped the lumpy, dull-colored rock. "We can't leave such an important discovery here."

"You can't *take* it," Joe exclaimed. "The natives need these. They call them *saviksue*, they believe they have a soul."

Erasmus looked at Joe, at Zeke, at the rock. He couldn't help himself, he coveted it.

"Them," Zeke said. "You acknowledge yourself that there are others. I'm only taking this small one."

Over Joe's protests Zeke and Erasmus chipped the ice away with their knives, until the rock was free. It was as heavy as a man. "Just help us roll it to the ship," Zeke begged; and Joe finally agreed.

In the eerie pink light they sweated and struggled and pushed, all the time hearing the distant gunshots and the indignant roar of the birds. Erasmus, as the angle of the glacier grew steeper, slipped near a patch of meltwater and fell. Joe and Zeke, roped on either side of him, tumbled seconds later. The meteorite, free of their hands, rolled clumsily as they untied the knots that tangled them. It gathered speed and lurched down slantwise, leaping over a last ridge of ice to plunge into the gap where the glacier had pulled away from the side of the cliff.

Erasmus heard it shatter and leapt to his feet. Running after it, too late to save it, stumbling and slipping and hoping, still, that he might retrieve a piece, he stayed upright most of the way down the glacier but skidded off the last, lowest ledge. He was flying; his eyes were open. He was arcing over the stony shore, heading for the ice, praying that he'd die quickly. He saw a patch of darkness the size of a dining-room table, an open pool in the ice; then he was underwater. Then under ice.

The water burned him like fire and scoured his mouth and eyes, but even as he thrashed and struggled and felt his limbs numb he saw the fish schooling around his legs, and the murres serenely swimming like fish, and the cool, green, glowing underside of the ice. He had a few minutes, he thought, remembering Ivan's near drowning. No more. Something shimmered white: belugas? He fainted, or froze, or drowned. When he came to himself again he was looking up at Dr. Boerhaave's anxious face.

"Am I alive?" he asked.

"Just barely," Dr. Boerhaave said. "Ned pulled you out."

"Did you see the meteorite?"

Dr. Boerhaave shook his head.

THEY COULDN'T RECOVER even a single piece of the stone before Captain Tyler hurried the *Narwhal* into a suddenly open lead. In his berth, recovering from his chilly bath, Erasmus rested for a day. When he felt better he thanked Ned.

"It was nothing," Ned said. "I was gutting a fish, looking right at the hole in the ice where you landed. All I did was run over with the boat hook."

With Dr. Boerhaave's help, Erasmus wrote up a description of the meteorite to send to Edinburgh. The weather grew fine—warm during the day; just below freezing during the gleaming north light that was as close as they came to night—and as Erasmus wrote to Dr. Boerhaave's friend he noted the odd combination of summer and winter features: cool air, hot sun; black cliffs, white ice. On the cloudless day when they reached the North Water, he felt as though he were home during harvest-time.

The air was warm, the water gleaming like steel and the icebergs elevated against the horizon. The men had stripped off most of their clothes. Mr. Tagliabeau was urging them on at the capstan bars when the lookout shouted, "We're here!" and the brig broke into open water. All hands stopped work and gave three cheers. Mr. Tagliabeau and Captain Tyler embraced one another and then, to Erasmus's astonishment, shook Zeke's hand. Joe broke out his zither and played several cheerful tunes; Captain Tyler ordered the sails set; and they were free of the pack.

3

A Riot of Objects

(July–August 1855)

It was homeward bound one night on the deep
Swinging in my hammock I fell asleep.
I dreamed a dream and thought it true
Concerning Franklin and his gallant crew.

With a hundred seamen he sailed away
To the frozen ocean in the month of May
To seek that passage around the pole
Where we poor sailors do sometimes go.

In Baffin's Bay where the whalefish blow
The fate of Franklin no man may know.
The fate of Franklin no tongue can tell
Franklin and his men do dwell.

Through cruel hardships they vainly strove.
Their ships on mountains of ice was drove

Where the eskimo in his skin canoe
Was the only man to ever come through.

And now my hardship it brings me pain.
For my long lost Franklin I'd plow the main.
Ten thousand pounds would I freely give
To know on earth if Franklin do live.
                    —"LADY FRANKLIN'S LAMENT"
                         (TRADITIONAL BALLAD)

IN HER DIARY, ALEXANDRA WROTE:

On the calendar Lavinia keeps by our desks, she not only crosses
off each passing day but counts the days remaining until October.
She's embarrassed when I catch her doing this, embarrassed to catch
herself doing it. When we visit Zeke's family, she wraps her arms
around Zeke's black dogs and buries her nose in their fur; the smell
reminds her of him, she claims, his clothes often carried a faint odor
of dog. But otherwise she puts up a brave front and tries not to talk
about her worries.

Still, I can see how distracted she is and how hard she finds it
to concentrate. Apart from her anxieties, she's not used to sustained
periods of work. I remind myself that at least I had my parents
throughout my childhood, while she had no mother at all: of course
this has shaped her, as has life with her brothers. On Tuesday,
while we were trying to mix a difficult shade of greenish blue, she
told me she was often invited to join in when their father read to

them—if she wasn't taking drawing lessons, or piano lessons, or being instructed in cookery or the management of the household—but she listened with only half an ear, sure she'd never use that knowledge. Erasmus and Copernicus would travel; Linnaeus and Humboldt would learn to engrave the plates and print the books that resulted from other men's travels. But always, she said, always I knew I'd be left at home. So why bother to learn those lessons well?

Because, I wanted to say. Because there is something in the learning; and because we can never tell what we may someday need. Instead I pointed to our paints. When you were taking drawing lessons, I said, did you ever think we'd be doing this? It is my hope to distract her with the pleasures of our task.

We completed the plates of the annelids today and then Lavinia worked on her trousseau, arranging piles of embroidered white lawn and ribbon-threaded muslin. Waists and knickers, nightgowns and petticoats—most made by two young sisters, half-French, from Chester. Her own stitching is clumsy, but she's good enough not to ask me for help even though she knows I've sometimes supported myself by sewing. I told her something she <u>didn't</u> know about me—in her back issues of the Lady's Book, *which she saves religiously, I pointed out the plates I colored by hand for Mr. Godey. A gown in green and yellow, not so different from a beetle's wing covers, made her smile. "You could do this," I told her. "If you don't like working with plants and animals, I could help you find work coloring fashion plates when we're done with the book." She told me her brothers would think that frivolous work, especially as she has no need to earn her living.*

We have two pair of cardinals nesting in the mock-orange near my window. A cecropia moth hatched from the cocoon Erasmus left on the windowseat. Last night my family came for dinner, and after we talked about the antislavery speeches Emily attended in Germantown, Harriet took me aside to whisper that she is with child again. Then Browning clumsily asked if we'd had any news. Of course this upset Lavinia. No mail, I answered quickly. Not yet. But it's too soon for the whalers with whom the brig might cross paths to have returned to port.

After they left we read out loud to each other, as we do most evenings. Lavinia reads from Mary Shelley's tale of Frankenstein and his monster; I read from Parry's journal. The journal of the first voyage, when Parry was hardly older than Zeke and when his men were all in their early twenties; the one during which everything went right. Fine weather, remarkable explorations, good hunting, starry skies. This is how Zeke and Erasmus are faring, I said.

But later, after we went to our separate rooms, I read secretly in the journal of Parry's second voyage. I never raise the subject of the Winter Island and Igloolik Esquimaux with Lavinia; if she knew what Parry hinted at about the women and their relationships with his men, she'd worry about this too. I lie in the dark and dream about that place and those people. I'd give anything to be with Zeke and Erasmus. Anything. I'm grateful for this position but sometimes I feel so <u>confined</u>—why can't my life be larger? I imagine those Esquimaux befriended by Parry and his crew: the feasts and games, the fur suits, the pairs of women tattooing each other, gravely passing a needle and a thread coated with lampblack and oil under the skin of their faces and breasts. I dream about them. I dream about the ice, the snow, the ice, the snow.

SURROUNDED BY THAT ice and snow, Erasmus dreamed of home—less and less often, though, as the brig passed down Lancaster Sound. Around him were breeding terns and gulls, snow geese and murres, eiders and dovekies; the water thick with whales and seals and scattered plates of floe ice; a sky from which birds dropped like arrows, piercing the water's skin. Sometimes narwhals tusked through the skin from the other side, as if sniffing at the solitary ship. They hadn't seen another ship since passing a few whalers at Pond's Bay, yet Erasmus was far from lonely. Dazzled, he looked at the cliffs, and knew Dr. Boerhaave shared his dazzlement.

"Anchor," he begged Zeke. "Let us have some time up there."

But Zeke said their schedule didn't leave a minute to spare. Finally, when they tied up to an iceberg to take on fresh water, Erasmus was granted four hours. Ned and Sean Hamilton rowed him and Dr. Boerhaave to the base of a kittiwake rookery.

"We'll climb," Erasmus told Dr. Boerhaave. He was trembling, longing to split himself into a hundred selves who might see a hundred sights. "Straight up, and gather what we can." To Ned and Sean, wandering along the bouldered shore, he handed a small cloth bag. "Put plants in here," he said. "If you see anything interesting, while you're walking . . ." Then he and Dr. Boerhaave began their ascent up the bird-plastered rock, guns and nets strapped to their backs.

Four hours, which passed like a sneeze. They brought back adult birds, eggs, dead chicks, and nests. On the *Narwhal,* Ned added the cloth bag to their treasures. "We walked east for a while," he said. "We found a little field." He reached into the specimen bag and spread handfuls of vegetation on the deck. "I brought you these," he said. "Are they what you wanted?"

Erasmus turned over the bits; Ned had picked leaves and branches and single flowers, rather than carefully gathering whole plants complete with the roots. Back home Erasmus had barked at the maid when she dared to move his drying plants; here he blamed the mess on himself. He hadn't realized anyone wouldn't know how to take a proper specimen. Still he and Dr. Boerhaave were able to identify the little gold-petaled poppies and four varieties of saxifrage. Ned, Erasmus saw with some chagrin, had found a regular arctic meadow, which he himself had missed.

"You did wonderfully," Erasmus said. "Thank you for these. Let me just show you the way scientists like to collect a plant."

Briefly he explained to Ned about root and stem and leaf and flower and fruiting body. Later, Ned wrote down Erasmus's words almost verbatim, along with a sketch of a proper specimen and some definitions:

> *Herbarium is the name for a collection of dried plant specimens, mounted and arranged systematically. The object with the flat boards and the straps is a press. Mr. Wells means to preserve samples of each interesting plant, to name those he can by comparing them against his books, and to keep a list: that is his job here. Dr. Boer-haave helps him. I may help too, they say, if I learn what they show me. It's like learning to read a different language—pistil, stamen, pinnate, palmate—not so hard but who would have thought a man could spend his life on this? I made salad from a red-leaved plant he calls Oxyria, which looks like the sheep sorrel at home. He was surprised that it tasted so good.*

WHERE BEFORE THEY'D been in waters familiar to Captain Tyler and the mates, and where Zeke was at a disadvantage, now they were in places none of them knew. Zeke had the charts of the explorers preceding him; Zeke had done his reading. It gave him a kind of power, Erasmus saw. For the first time, the other officers were dependent on Zeke's knowledge. It no longer mattered that Zeke had never been in the arctic before, nor that all his knowledge came from books. Ice was ice, islands were islands; channels showed up where he predicted. Book knowledge was all they had, and for a while Captain Tyler and the mates were rendered docile by their lack of it. No one argued with Zeke's orders.

Thousands of narwhals accompanied the brig up the ice-speckled strait, filling the air with their heavy, spooky exhalations—as if, Erasmus thought, the sea itself were breathing. Animal company was the only sort they had. In place of the great fleet filling the Sound four years ago, during Dr. Kane's first voyage, were those long-tusked little whales, and seals and walrus, and belugas everywhere. Extraordinarily beautiful, he thought. Smaller than he'd expected, a uniform creamy smoothness over bulging muscles, moving like swift white birds through the dark water.

Barrow Strait was empty as well. The stark and radiant landscape flashed by so fast that Erasmus found himself making strange, clutching movements with his hands, as if he might seize the sights that were denied him. Even when they reached the cairns on Cape Riley and then, on Beechey Island, the graves of three of Franklin's seamen and the relics of their first winter quarters, they lingered only briefly. These were, Erasmus and Zeke agreed, the very sites that Dr. Kane and the others had discovered in '51. From the water the gray gravel sloped gently upward, stopping at jagged cliffs. Against the background of those cliffs, the grave mounds and headstones were very small. Erasmus, Dr. Boerhaave, Zeke, and Ned examined the limestone slabs tessellated over two of the graves, and the little row of flat stones set like a fence around each mound.

"If we exhumed them," Dr. Boerhaave said, "even one, and could determine what he died from, we might gain some clues to the expedition's fate."

Zeke stepped back from the mounds. A tremor passed from his hands up his arms and shoulders and then rippled across his face. "We're not graverobbers," he said. "Nor resurrection men. Those are

Englishmen, men like our own crew. They're entitled to lie in peace. And what would we learn from violating them?"

"Suppose they were starving?" Dr. Boerhaave said. "Already, that first winter. In this cold, enough . . . remains would be left that we might determine that."

"If that was me in there," Zeke said, "if that was you—bad enough they've been left here all alone. Nothing you'd learn would tell us anything about where the expedition went."

He gazed down at the graves and then back at Dr. Boerhaave. "When you were in medical school," he said, "did you . . . ?"

"Well, of *course*," Dr. Boerhaave said. As Zeke shook his head and walked away, Dr. Boerhaave smiled at Erasmus, who smiled back at his friend.

After the three of them left, Ned lingered behind for a minute, placing a stone on each grave and saying a prayer. He told no one of the strange hallucination that seized him later. As he rinsed salt meat in water from the stream that trickled above the graves, he imagined that water seeping into the coffins, easing around the seamen's bodies, who had been young, like him. Beneath the first layers of gravel the ground was frozen, it never melted, and he saw the bodies frozen too, preserved forever; cherished, honored. The vision comforted him, yet also angered him. In Ireland he'd seen corpses stacked like firewood or tossed loosely into giant pits. Here, where no one might ever have seen them, three young Englishmen had each been given a careful and singular grave, a headstone chiseled with verses, a little fence.

TIME PRESSED ON them even more sharply after that first glimpse of the lost expedition. As the sails filled, bellied out in the brisk breeze, Zeke said, "Franklin must have turned the *Erebus* and the

Terror down Peel Sound after leaving Beechey Island. The ice is so heavy to the west, and when you think about Rae's report—where else could he have gone? It's the only place the earlier ships didn't look. They were all sure he'd gone north somehow, after finding the route blocked to the west. But how could any of his men have reached a place even close to King William Land, if not by way of Peel Sound?"

Simple logic, Erasmus thought. And so it must be true. Even Captain Tyler shrugged and agreed with Zeke. They turned south, sure they were following Franklin's trail. After thirty-five miles of hard sailing, fighting against the encroaching ice, the *Narwhal* was finally turned back by solid pack. No time for regrets, Zeke said. He retraced their route, rounding the walls and ravines of North Somerset and sailing down the east coast as far as Bellot Strait. Through here, Zeke hoped to pass back into Peel Sound.

Bellot Strait was completely choked with ice. The men stood mashed together on the bow, muttering with disappointment: "God damn this ice!" Captain Tyler said, before disappearing below. Their last chance to reach King William Land by water had just disappeared, Erasmus knew, and with it any chance of finding Franklin's ships. But they might still find traces of the expedition by land, as Rae had done. On Zeke's order they continued southward, along the massive hills and into the Gulf of Boothia.

Zeke grew cool and distant, hardly speaking except to give orders and treating Captain Tyler as if he were the skipper of a ferryboat. He allowed no stops, neither for the men to hunt nor for Erasmus to gather specimens. The winds and currents here seemed to concentrate the ice, which poured into the bay from the north and then swirled and massed, several times almost crushing the brig. The men grew nervous and muttered among themselves. Out here, far from the traditional whaling grounds, they seemed to wake as a group from a dream. Why had they come? Because they needed

work, Erasmus slowly understood; not because they were inspired
by the expedition's goals but because they'd needed jobs back in the
spring, when Zeke was recruiting men. They'd signed on because
the wages were good and because, despite all Zeke's stories, they had
not really been able to imagine their task. The men who'd never been
to sea before had had no useful information, no way to imagine what
lay before them; those with whaling experience must have imagined
that searching for Franklin would be like searching for whales.

The idea of moving just for the sake of moving, pressing deeper
and deeper into the ice with no assurance of reward, was as strange
to them, Erasmus thought, as flensing a bowhead would have been
to him. Every order Zeke gave brought a grumble: *we should have
anchored in Cresswell Bay; the men need fresh meat; the floes are scraping away the siding*—Mr. Francis, Ned Kynd, Mr. Tagliabeau.

Fletcher Lamb, who was stropping his razor when they crashed
into one of the monstrous bergs, jolted his hand and cut off the tip
of his left ring finger. Two of the dogs, knocked to their feet, turned
on each other and filled the air with chunks of fur and a spray of
blood; a kettle slipped overboard. When the *Narwhal* was finally
forced to stop, separated from King William Land by the full width
of Boothia, the men began clamoring to turn around the same day
they dropped anchor.

Discouraged, Erasmus stared at the charts. They'd not discovered even the smallest scrap of new coastline; the excellent map of
the Rosses detailed every cove they saw. Yet here, no matter what the
crew thought, they might begin their real search for any traces of
Franklin and his men. This was the place, Erasmus thought: the true
beginning after all. What began, instead, was the death of the dogs.

The dozen left after the earlier mishaps tore around the ship, raising and lowering their heads and tails and all the while barking furiously at some invisible threat. The lead dog, enormous and black, fell

first: a damp heap at the base of the mainmast. His white-footed consort followed, then two of the puppies Joe had earlier saved: red-eyed, fevered, frothing. They turned on Zeke and Erasmus and Dr. Boerhaave, who worked frantically to help them. Dr. Boerhaave wrote:

> *Why did I never make time for some veterinary training? In my autopsies I've found nothing more than livers that appear to be mildly enlarged, but I can't be sure of this: what does a healthy dog's liver look like? At Godhavn we heard rumors of a mysterious disease among the dogs of southern Greenland, but our own appeared to be in perfect health and continued so throughout Lancaster Sound. I should have been paying more attention. I'm not sure of the course of rabies in canines but was forced to consider this, and when four fell on their sides, pawing at their jaws, I ordered them shot to prevent the spread of disease. Commander Voorhees, who is sentimental about animals, was furious with me and we had an argument—he can't seem to grasp the idea that the sick dogs may endanger the men. In any event my efforts weren't successful: we lost the last adult today and only Wissy and one other puppy are left. I'm grateful none of us were bitten. On dissection I found no apparent brain inflammation, nor anything unusual in the spinal cord or nerves. Why didn't I think to bring along a book of veterinary medicine?*
>
> *The flesh on Fletcher Lamb's injured finger has begun to mortify beneath the bandage I applied. I've debrided and irrigated the wound, but remain worried.*

ZEKE HAD BEEN keeping Wissy in the cabin, where he hoped she might be safe, but the day after the other remaining puppy died she began running about, crashing off the bunks and the walls. Zeke held her in his arms, despite her mad strength; he tried to feed her tidbits and wouldn't let Dr. Boerhaave touch her. She squirmed and bit and then lay still, her head thrown back and her eyes blankly staring. Above her a tern cut through the rigging, back and forth and around the shrouds.

"You know what we have to do," Dr. Boerhaave said.

Zeke handed her to Robert Carey, who'd proved his skill with a gun by obtaining numerous birds on Beechey Island. Afterward Zeke wouldn't look at Dr. Boerhaave and nothing Erasmus said could console him. Dr. Boerhaave retreated to a corner on deck, turning a skull around in his long fingers and staring at his notes as if he might bring the dogs back to life. Caught between the two men, Erasmus wondered what the dogs' deaths meant.

Here they were, he thought, blocked from further sailing by ice, and blocked from overland travel by the lack of it. The snow on the land was mostly gone, except high on the hills and in hidden hollows; the land-fast ice was heaved and cracked and water-logged. Even if they could cross Boothia, the strait between its far side and King William Land could no longer be frozen solid, but must be a mass of loose and shifting floes. Sledging was impossible; sledge travel was meant for spring, when the sun had returned but the ice was smooth and solid everywhere. Why, then, had they brought dogs and sledges in the first place?

But he knew the answer. Ever since they'd acquired the dogs, he'd worried that Zeke meant to overwinter somewhere if the brig failed to reach its destination. Some of the crew must have guessed this as well, but they'd all wanted to believe the dogs wouldn't be needed. Then, after every stage of their desired route had been blocked, Ned had seized Erasmus's arm and said, "Some of the men say we won't go home this summer now. That we'll stay all winter, in the ice—is it true?"

Erasmus hadn't known what to say. He'd seen Zeke take out a

new set of maps and scribble in his little black book; but now the dogs were gone. Once, but only once, Zeke leaned his head against the mast and said, "I wonder if someone poisoned them."

"You know that's not true," Erasmus said gently. Everyone else pretended not to hear him.

Joe, perhaps wishing to deflect attention from the dead dogs and Zeke's foul mood, told stories that caused a different kind of uneasiness. The West Greenlanders among whom he'd lived, he said, had wonderfully designed harpoons and winter houses made of stone and turf with seal-intestine windows and seal-blubber lamps. How warm those houses could be in winter! So warm, he said, packed with bodies and lamps, that the women wore only fox-skin knickers unless they had visitors.

A hush fell over the men. For a moment, in that silence, they visualized warm, curved flesh decorated with those flirtatious frills. In Melville Bay they'd traded tales of the women who'd taken up with members of both Parry's and Franklin's earlier expeditions, and Ivan Hruska and Robert Carey had talked about Esquimaux men who'd brought their wives aboard the visiting ships and offered them in trade for knives and wood. Perhaps they'd all hoped for a similar chance.

"Of course we forbade this kind of display among our converts," Joe said. "No nakedness, we told them. And no exchanging wives." Afterward Erasmus, who'd overheard part of his story and seen the men's faces, spoke sharply to him.

EVERYONE WAS TIRED and hungry for fresh meat; with Zeke still sulking over the dogs, Erasmus took matters into his own hands and went ashore July 28 with Isaac Bond. The first caribou he'd ever seen bolted across the boggy ground, fleeing before the swarms of insects and then before Isaac, who shot four times and brought down two. They peeled the skins off carefully. In their hindquarters, Erasmus found freshly laid eggs of the warble fly and, in the hides, hundreds of holes where the larvae of a previous year's infestation had eaten their way out. Isaac, wielding a long knife, regarded the skinned purple carcasses and said they weren't so different from the deer he'd hunted as a boy. He cut off the heads, took out the tongues; peeled off the flesh, set the skulls aside.

Side by side they crowned a rock, antlers branching above white bone and lidless eyes. Erasmus, under their gaze, knelt and pointed out the joints most easily severed. Left went the knife, and right and left and down: intestines steaming, a large smooth liver, stomach pouring out masses of green paste. In another pile ribs and shoulders, haunches and loins and tongues. They wrapped the meat in the skins and Erasmus hefted his end of one bloody bundle and then froze at the sight of his own reflection in the eyes. The thread of their voyage had broken, he thought, the plot unraveled, the point disappeared; nothing was left but the texture of each moment and the feeling of his soul unfurling after years in a small dark box.

"Are you all right?" Isaac said. "Is this too heavy?"

The caribou were watching themselves being carried away. "Let's try to drag the bundles," Erasmus said. "Down to the boat."

The odd humming feeling persisted in his head. And when he and Isaac climbed aboard the *Narwhal* and found Zeke standing on the quarterdeck with Joe, talking to three Esquimaux while the crew gawked from the bow, at first Erasmus thought he'd hallucinated them.

"They're so *short*," Isaac whispered.

He stepped back toward the railing, and Erasmus involuntarily squeezed the meat in his arms. What if these strangers were dangerous? Or if the crew members did something to anger them? Zeke and Joe had no weapons; Erasmus, leaving Isaac to deal with the bloody mass, hurried to Zeke's side.

Joe and the Esquimaux spoke at some length. Then the Esquimaux stood quietly while Joe explained that these people, very different in dress and habits from those they'd met at Godhavn, wandered inland each summer in small family groups, searching for caribou. The camp of this particular group, Joe said, was several miles away, out of sight of the ship—they'd seen the hunting party, and had sent a delegation to investigate. "They invite our leaders to their camp," Joe said. "Three of us, to go with the three of them."

Zeke said, "You and me, of course." He was silent for a minute. "And Captain Tyler," he added.

Erasmus felt a little thrill at the idea that his figure, crouched near the skulls, had been the sight that drew the Esquimaux; then a fierce disappointment that he should not be included in the delegation. When he took Zeke's arm and begged to come, Zeke shook him off and said he couldn't ignore Captain Tyler's rank.

The crew watched in silence as the six men dropped down the side of the brig, rowed to shore, and disappeared over a low hill. Three and three, dressed entirely differently, Zeke's pale hair glowing behind the darker heads. The crew murmured behind them: *suppose they're murderers; suppose they're cannibals; suppose they're plotting to return with a great crowd and take over the ship*—Fletcher Lamb with his bandaged hand, Barton DeSouza, Robert Carey.

Out loud, over the muttered comments, Dr. Boerhaave said, "What if they don't come back?"

"There's no point in even thinking like that," Erasmus said. Although he was worried himself; if something happened to Zeke, how would he explain to Lavinia that he'd stayed safely on the brig?

"Shall we look at the bones from the mergansers?" Dr. Boerhaave said. "I finished the other set while you were hunting."

From the sea he pulled a dripping sack. The water was boiling with *Cancer nugax*; he and Erasmus had learned to take advantage of the little shrimps' hunger, hanging their roughly cleaned skeletons over the side in a fine-mesh net. Erasmus, still distracted, opened the sack to find that the voracious creatures had cleaned everything perfectly. The sight of the disarticulated bones calmed him a bit.

Dr. Boerhaave, making notes, said, "I'm ashamed to admit this, but—don't you sometimes experience the search for Franklin's remains as just . . . distraction? I wish our only task was simply to observe this amazing place and its creatures." In the breeze his soft brown hair with its streaks of gray lifted from his forehead and fell and lifted again, like partridge feathers.

"But it's not," Erasmus said, clutching a fistful of wing bones. He looked down at the beautiful planes and knobs in his hands. Zeke would be fine, he had Joe to help him; the Esquimaux had seemed quite friendly. "But I know what you mean. Would you pass me that wire?"

When he looked up again it was early evening, and Zeke and Joe and Captain Tyler were hopping back onto the deck unharmed. Erasmus followed Zeke down into the empty cabin, a jawbone still in his hand.

"Tell me," he said. "Tell me everything."

"It went well," Zeke said. "Joe didn't have much trouble interpreting—he says the dialect is similar to that of the West Greenlanders. They liked our gifts."

Up on deck, Captain Tyler began lashing down everything movable. "Esquimaux will steal anything," Erasmus heard him tell the men. "Everything. And you can be sure they'll be visiting now that they know we're here."

"But—what were they like?" Erasmus asked Zeke. "What were they wearing? What were they eating? What do their dwellings look like inside?"

"Interesting," Zeke said. "Different. I was concentrating on the conversation with our host. Don't you want to know if I heard any news of Franklin?" A huge smile split his face. "I've been waiting years for this," he said. "Don't you understand? Ever since I was a boy reading your father's books."

Suddenly he looked like that boy again, and Erasmus was reminded of something Lavinia had told him a few days after her birthday party. "How can I discourage him from this trip?" she'd said. "We fell in love talking about Franklin, you don't know how many hours I've spent listening to his stories and plans. He cherishes that in me, he says he loves the way I listen." Erasmus had asked her if she truly shared Zeke's enthusiasm, and she'd sworn she did. Or at least one part of it: "I admire Franklin's wife," she'd said. "Her steadfastness."

"I'm sorry," Erasmus said, abashed. "Of course I want to know."

"I asked the oldest man point-blank if he'd ever seen a ship frozen in the ice, or white men marching anywhere around here," Zeke said. "He said no but I thought I saw him exchange a look with the man sitting next to him. They've asked us to return tomorrow. Will you come?"

OF COURSE ERASMUS WENT, as did Ned, Mr. Tagliabeau, Thomas Forbes, several other men, and Joe—still their only interpreter, despite all the evenings Zeke had spent with him, transcribing into his black book Joe's version of the Esquimaux names for things. This time Captain Tyler, Mr. Francis, and a small detachment stayed behind to guard the ship. Dr. Boerhaave nearly stayed behind as well; Fletcher Lamb had returned to his hammock, complaining of shooting pains in his limbs and face, and Dr. Boerhaave was worried. But there was nothing he could do for Fletcher after giving him a few drops of laudanum, and so he joined the delegation.

They carried offerings of duff and dried apples, as well as knives and needles and files and beads to barter. Over the hills they went, into a rough and scrubby land bare of trees and veiled by a light drizzle. As they walked Erasmus listened to Joe, who was trying to teach Zeke some things about this group called the Netsilik. Now and then Erasmus bent to gather pebbles; he'd been lax, he felt, about examining the area's geological structure.

"You might want to be a bit more . . . cautious," Joe was saying to Zeke. "About asking directly for information; it's not these people's nature to respond to pointed questions, they dislike being cross-examined. And if I could let them know that we'll barter for everything they tell us, that they'll be rewarded?"

"Fine," Zeke said impatiently. "Fine, fine, fine."

Erasmus and the others could hardly keep up with him. In the treeless, featureless landscape, the six tents forming the camp stood out starkly. A bunch of dogs, tied away from the tents, howled like wolves.

"They'd eat the tents in an instant if they were free," Joe said as they approached. All around, on the rough stony ground, were dog carcasses, bits of rotted meat and blubber, and broken bones. Thomas Forbes tripped over something and Dr. Boerhaave, bending down, said, "I believe that's a human femur." The bone was still shrouded in bits of leathery skin.

Thomas leaped backward, stumbling on the shallow pit in which the bone had been interred. The flat pieces of limestone meant to cover the body were small and quite light, Erasmus saw, and had clearly been pushed aside by a hungry fox or a dog. Thomas cursed and then bent over, very pale.

Joe said, "It's not what you think. It's not that they disrespect their dead: but they believe that a heavy weight placed upon the deceased's body hinders the spirit from moving on. Of course the dogs uncover them, the dogs are always hungry."

"Savages," Thomas said. Later he would disappear for a day in the company of a young Netsilik woman, recently widowed, whatever discomfort he felt with the tribe's habits apparently overcome. But now Erasmus saw Thomas look with dislike on the man who emerged from a strong-smelling tent to greet them. The stranger had a sparse moustache and a tuft of hair between his chin and his lower lip; the bottom of his nose was bent to one side, as if it had been broken but not set. When he spoke, Erasmus heard the word *kabloona*.

"White man," Joe translated. In the light rain they stared at each other. The tent, Erasmus saw, was too small for them all to sit inside. They seated themselves on stones just in front of its opening.

Everything smelled of caribou. Behind him Erasmus could see how the rain saturated the hides, which hung heavily on the poles; how the rain dripped through the tiny holes drilled by warble flies when the animals had still been alive. Here too there were animal skulls, scores of skulls, jaws and eye sockets tilted among rocks and lichens. Zeke and the man who'd welcomed them—Oonali, he called himself—did all the talking, with Joe acting as interpreter. In return for the clasp knives and tobacco Zeke offered, and after Zeke had made it clear that he'd be honored to see Oonali's hunting outfit, Oonali brought out a bow and some arrows that Zeke admired.

"I'd love to bring these home to the Toxophilites," he said to Erasmus. "Wouldn't that be something?"

Erasmus was scratching steadily in Lavinia's journal—he couldn't write fast enough, he couldn't get down all the details. He sketched the bow: fir strengthened with bone and made more elastic by cunning springs of plaited sinew. He didn't sketch the curiously twisted bowstring or the slate-headed arrows, as Zeke had by then arranged to trade a pair of axe heads for the entire outfit. Next to him Dr. Boerhaave scribbled similarly, while Ned, who'd stuck his head beneath the door flap, turned his head slowly from one view to the next. Whalebone vessels and walrus-tusk knives, spoons made from what looked to be hollowed-out bones.

The camp was almost empty that afternoon: "The men are out hunting," Joe explained. But soon three women gathered around Oonali's tent and stood shyly gazing at Erasmus and the others. They were comely, Erasmus thought, despite the tattoos on their cheeks and hands. Less than five feet tall and plump, with tiny hands and glossy hair. He tried to sketch the black patterns twining up their arms while the women crowded around and laughed at his efforts. Zeke rose and offered each a steel needle.

The women made noises that seemed to indicate pleasure, promptly depositing the needles in little bags attached to their breeches. Each bag was made from the skin of a bird's foot with the claws still attached: charming, Erasmus thought. As he turned to ask Joe's help in bartering for one, the women reached toward Zeke and fingered his brass jacket buttons.

When Zeke pulled back, the women bent to Erasmus, still seated on his stone. He froze while the hands played over his chest. The slightest tugging, much more gentle than the crowding Fiji Islanders of his youth; it was the buttons they coveted, he realized, even more than the needles. Back in the brig, thanks to all his lists, he had a large tin of spares. With his knife he sliced off his three lower buttons and offered one to each woman.

Zeke frowned at him—but it was the buttons, Erasmus thought, that turned the tide of the afternoon. Four little boys pushed up to him, reaching for his journal and stroking the smooth white paper so insistently that he finally tore two blank pages from the back and handed them over. The boys grinned and ran away with their treasure; from the corner of his eye Erasmus saw them crowded on a stone cairn some way from the tents, tossing shreds that spun in the breeze like butterflies.

The women brewed vats of tea, which they served in bowls. Dr. Boerhaave, turning one round in his hand, said, "I believe this is made of the base of a musk-ox horn." As he bent and sniffed at the horn with his long, square-tipped nose, hair drifted from the tent and into everyone's tea, catching in their teeth as they drank. An older woman with heavily tattooed hands arrived, bearing a dish of boiled caribou. Erasmus made a strangled noise when she offered him a portion on a metal spoon.

"*Quiet,*" Zeke said.

He reached for the spoon and examined it: silver, shapely, as alien here as a palm tree. To Joe he said, "Tell Oonali that yesterday, I asked if he'd ever seen white men's ships. And he said no. Ask him if perhaps he's forgotten to tell me something?"

Oonali said nothing at first. Joe stood to one side, translating, while Zeke asked quick questions, his anger ill-concealed. Had they seen any white men? Had they seen two ships? Where had the spoon come from? Did they have more like it? Had they ever met a *kabloona* named Dr. Rae, who'd traveled east of here several years earlier, and who'd bought spoons and other white men's goods from some Esquimaux?

Joe struggled to keep up with the flow of Zeke's words and made, Erasmus thought, conciliating gestures toward Oonali as he translated. Then Oonali, who had been calmly eating, spoke.

"We have not seen such ships," he said, or so Joe translated his words. "But we have heard a story, from some Inuit we met hunting seal several winters ago. These men told us that, during the previous winter, they found a ship abandoned in the ice. They climbed on this ship but found no one there, only one dead man on the deck. They wished to see into the spaces below, but the passages to the lower part"——here Joe paused, looked at Zeke, and said, "Hatchways? Must be hatchways"——"were sealed over. These men told us that one side of the ship was wounded, and that they pulled wood away from there until they'd made a hole. Inside they found many useful tools and much iron, which they took so it wouldn't go to waste. They had many spoons, like this one. I traded two good hides for this."

"But you didn't see the ship yourself?" Zeke said.

"No ship," Oonali replied.

"You haven't seen any white men?"

"I have never met one, although I have heard about them. You are my first to talk with."

Zeke, excited now, drew his copy of the Rosses' map from his jacket. "We're here," he said, indicating the bay where they were anchored. "This is the Great Fish River, here"—he asked if Joe knew the Esquimaux name for the river, which he did—"and this is the western shore. Can you indicate where the ship was seen?"

Erasmus and his companions leaned around Zeke and Joe and Oonali, forming a circle. They all knew Parry's and Ross's tales of men who could outline long stretches of coast with remarkable accuracy. Esquimaux traced maps in the snow, carved them in wood, built them from little piles of pebbles. Drew them when offered pencil and paper. "I'll give you a knife," Zeke said. "If you can show us anything."

Oonali gazed at the paper. "Where the seals are good," Joe translated, as Oonali touched a finger to a bay and spoke.

Oonali touched an inlet, then the mouth of a river. "Where my friend was lost. Where the fish are caught in the rocks."

With his thumb Oonali pressed the edge of the map, which showed the east coast of King William Land butted up against the border. He moved his thumb off the paper and a few inches into the air, where the west coast might have been had the map been larger, and the west coast charted.

"This is where the ship is sunk."

"Sunk?" Zeke said.

Erasmus didn't know whether to watch Oonali or Joe, whose face was so surprised that he could hardly form words.

"Underwater," Joe translated. "Those Inuit, they did not at first take all the goods they found, but piled them on the deck to carry back later. Then they went hunting. The hunting was good that winter. When they returned the ice had begun to break up, and the ship was gone except for the tops of the three tall poles, which pierced the water. The things on the deck had disappeared. It is thought that taking the wood away from the wound in the side caused the water to pour in."

"Is there anything left?" Zeke said. "Anything for us to see?"

"There is nothing," Oonali said. "The men who told me this story, they took from the shores all the things that floated in. Nothing is left."

THAT NIGHT, WHEN they returned to the *Narwhal* with their bow and arrows, the musk-ox bowls Dr. Boerhaave had traded for, and their precious silver spoon, Zeke gathered the entire crew and told them what he'd learned. He meant the men to be impressed, Erasmus thought, to be seized with the knowledge that they were close to the site where at least one of Franklin's ships had been. But Sean Hamilton said, "This Oonali—he didn't actually *see* the ship? And the ship is gone? And all we have to show for this story is a spoon?"

"The spoon has a crest on it," Zeke said angrily. "We'll undoubtedly be able to show exactly which of the officers it belonged to."

Sean shrugged. "I don't see how that's more than what your Dr. Rae came home with. All this way, and you've got a story told by a lying Esquimau."

"When are we leaving?" Isaac Bond asked.

Erasmus reached over and rapped the spoon in exasperation.

"Aren't you *curious*? Aren't any of you one bit curious as to how this got here?"

"We're curious to know how we're going to get home," Barton DeSouza muttered. "And when."

Later Ned, alone in the galley, wrote to a friend in the mountains of northern New York. Erasmus came in for some hot water just as Ned went out to relieve himself, and he leaned over the sheet of paper on the table.

> *Commander Voorhees is having a difficult time. Hard luck seems to plague him. Today I thought we'd discovered something important, but now it seems that the story the Esquimaux told us means little after all. One of the two ships sank, perhaps. But where are the men? Our men are all against the commander, even Captain Tyler, and it makes me sad to hear them talking as if the commander is a fool. The more the others say he is young and inexperienced and gullible, the more I like him for his enthusiasm. I think he's only a few years older than me. But he's the one who knew enough to press this Oonali, and so got him to reveal the story of Franklin's ship. Perhaps this is all we can expect: it is ten years now since Franklin's ships left England.*

A good heart, Erasmus thought; Ned had come a long way from his first response to the story of Franklin, his loyalty to Zeke and their mission seeming to grow in inverse proportion to their luck. He was pleased to see Ned sticking close to Zeke over the next few days, while Zeke pored over his maps and fondled his new bow. The other men, during their hours off, wandered toward the Esquimaux camp in an ill-concealed search for feminine companionship.

Had it not been for this distraction, which Zeke seemed power-less to discourage, Erasmus wondered whether they could have pre-vented an open mutiny. The men wanted to leave at once: it was clear they couldn't reach King William Land at this time of year, and that even if they did they'd find no ship. But Zeke wasn't ready to leave. Again and again he told Erasmus he felt sure there must be other traces of the expedition, and although he had no clues he wouldn't move. They were trapped, too, by Fletcher Lamb's condition. On the night they returned from the Esquimaux camp he'd developed vio-lent spasms, and a stiffness of the jaw that grew worse hourly.

"It's lockjaw," Dr. Boerhaave told Zeke. "There's nothing I can do for him but try to keep him comfortable."

The other men shunned their sick companion and returned from their forays bright-eyed and flushed. They'd hidden spirits, Erasmus guessed, which they were now sharing with their new friends. Rob-ert Carey and Ivan Hruska, considerably inebriated, came to blows over the favors of one young woman. All Zeke did was to growl at Captain Tyler and order him to restrain his men.

Hourly Zeke, along with Dr. Boerhaave, visited Fletcher Lamb; when Fletcher died Zeke read the service over him and then crouched in the crow's nest and wouldn't come down. As if, Erasmus thought, he were watching over Fletcher's grave. Thomas Forbes constructed a coffin, but the ground was stony and after hours with a pickaxe and shovels still the grave was not as deep as they would have liked and there were foxes everywhere. Ned set palm-sized pieces of flat stone around it, as if that boundary would shelter Fletcher's bones.

NINE DAYS AFTER their first meeting, Barton DeSouza spotted a group of Esquimaux hunters returning to camp. Their dogs carried the meat, some with the front half of a caribou draped around them, ribs curving around the dogs' backs; some pulling heaps of meat lashed to pairs of poles. Later two hunters came to the ship and invited the *Narwhal*'s crew to a feast. The Esquimaux were sick of them, Erasmus knew. The seamen were hunting their caribou, distracting their children, disappearing with their women; he was disgusted with them himself. Although he and Dr. Boerhaave never spoke of it, he thought the doctor shared his feelings. The men's behavior made Erasmus restless and filled him with longings. When he retreated to the cabin, Zeke's strange, sulky paralysis drove him away again. Although the hunters didn't say it, Erasmus understood that they wished this to be a farewell feast. He hoped that Zeke would also see it that way.

Only Mr. Francis stayed behind to guard the brig. On the way to the feast the others chattered, carrying gifts of biscuits and tea and leaving a space around Zeke, who was silent even when Erasmus pointed out the lemmings slipping over the ground. Great kettles of food were stewing over fires as they arrived, but the atmosphere was strangely subdued with the hunters back in camp. Each hunter gathered his family about him, closely watching the *Narwhal*'s crew; the men's easy camaraderie with the women and children vanished. Joe strummed his zither. A few men tried to dance but their feet stuttered under those watchful eyes; the Esquimaux wouldn't dance at all and Joe soon fell silent.

Erasmus and his companions ate until they were full and then watched the Esquimaux continue eating. When they finished Joe, still trying to knit the two groups together, persuaded some of the hunters to demonstrate their skill with their bows. Their arrows flew into the distance, piercing with uncanny precision the sheets of paper Erasmus tore from Lavinia's journal and offered as targets, but the only people smiling were the little boys who seized the targets as soon as the shooting was done. Once more they ran away, shredding the paper as they ran; once more, Erasmus saw, they clustered on the stone cairn and set the shreds flying in gusts of wind, as if trying to imitate insects or small white birds. While he pondered the children's game, some of the women upended the cooking kettles and began scraping off the dense layers of soot. It was Ned who saw the first flash of copper.

"Look," he said, pulling the bunch of twigs from a woman's hands and scrubbing furiously. Metal, copper. Erasmus ran to the other kettles: copper, copper, copper. A film seemed to drop from his eyes, and he looked around and saw that the wooden tray on which some of the meat had lain could not have been made from any of the scrubby vegetation here; that in fact it resembled a part of a writing desk. Tent poles suddenly resembled oars, wooden spoons might have been shaped from gunwales, parts of spears and knives might have come from barrels.

"They've found a *boat*!" Zeke exulted. "These things come from a ship's boat." He seized Joe's arm and said, "Tell them I know."

"Know what?"

"Just tell them I know."

As Joe translated, Zeke seized a copper pot in one hand and a stirring stick that might have been made from an ash oar in the other. A hush fell over the camp. Oonali stepped forward.

"These things are from a *kabloona* boat," Zeke said. "Why didn't you tell us before that you had found one?"

Oonali shrugged as Joe put Zeke's questions to him. "You asked about ships," he said through Joe. Joe looked mortified, as if he'd been the one caught lying. "And about the land across from the coast. Not a small boat found on an island."

"What island?"

Oonali said something Joe couldn't translate. After Zeke took out another of his maps, Oonali pressed his thumb down on a large island at the mouth of Back's Great Fish River.

"Were there men?" Zeke said. "You told us we were the first white men you'd met."

"I did not meet them," Oonali said calmly. "They could not be met. They were dead."

By now all the Esquimaux, and all the brig's men, were pressed in a circle around Zeke and Oonali and Joe. Zeke offered axes, barrel staves, beads, and knives in return for any other items they might have picked up at the boat. In return for the story of how they'd found it.

Oonali said, "This happened some winters ago. On the island we found a wooden boat which was sheathed with this metal. Also the bodies of thirty or so men."

There had been guns, Joe translated, just one or two, and a metal box with some papers in it, some clothes, some things they'd not known the names of. They had taken many of these things, guessing they'd someday find a use for them.

"Show me," Zeke demanded. For a minute Erasmus thought all was lost. But Joe must have softened Zeke's words and framed them courteously, because Oonali, after considering for a moment, spoke to the other Esquimaux gathered around. Some ducked into the tents, returning with full hands.

A prayer book, a treatise on steam engines, a snowshoe, and two pairs of scissors. More silver spoons and some forks. Dr. Boerhaave, holding out his hands, received a mahogany barometer case, and Erasmus's hands filled with chisels and chain hooks and scraps of rope. Zeke stood open-mouthed, turning a broken handsaw end over end over end. "The boat?" he said. "Is the boat still where you found it?"

"We cut it up," Oonali said. "It was of no use to those men. We cut it up and took all the wood and useful things. Some things we have cached at our other camps."

"The bodies?" Zeke said.

"The sand has buried them. This was"—he paused to consult with two middle-aged men—"six winters ago. Or seven. We have visited this island since, and nothing is left of those men."

Erasmus wrote down everything, piecing the story together as fast as he could scribble the words. Thirty men, at least one boat, a winter that might be either 1848 or 1849; an island some two hundred miles from the point at which Franklin's ships had supposedly been beset. The men must have dragged the boat all that distance, perhaps on one of their sledges: and who were "they," and had they been the only ones left? And how had they thought to get that boat up the river's fierce rapids? In his rush Erasmus spotted his journal with caribou grease.

Someone sneezed, delicately; he looked up to see Oonali's wife. The three young women who'd served him tea during his first visit had turned out to be Oonali's daughters; this woman, their mother, had stood off to the side then, and he'd noticed her only when Joe pointed her out. She had a fine white scar running from the outside corner of her left eye into the hair at her temple, worn teeth, shy eyes. She was holding out something to him in her closed hand.

"For me?" he asked. But of course she couldn't understand his words. She had her back to everyone else and her gesture was furtive. He tore off the last of his jacket buttons and offered it on his open palm. With one hand she scooped the button up, holding the other hand over his palm and then spreading her fingers. A scrap of dried and hardened leather, spiked through with bits of metal, dropped into his hand.

He thanked her, put down the scrap, and kept writing. Then a few minutes later thought to pick it up again. Once more that film seemed to drop from his eyes: part of a boot sole, he saw, the front part, from the toes to the ball of the foot. Seven short, wide-headed screws had been driven through it, from the inside out—a line of two, at the tips of the toes, then a line of three and another line of two. Wood screws, the sort one might use to fasten a cleat or an oarlock to a boat. The heads had been countersunk, set flush with the inner layer; the tips of the screws protruded perhaps a quarter of an inch.

Staring at those broken, rusted tips, Erasmus imagined the rest of the sole, the worn heel, the broken-down upper. The broken-down man who, trying to walk across the ice, perhaps pulling a sledge or a boat behind him, might have studded his shoes for a better grip. Without thinking he slipped the scrap into his jacket pocket.

Across from him Zeke purchased every item brought for his inspection, naming each so Erasmus could note it in his journal. A riot of objects, an orgy of objects. Dr. Boerhaave bent over a mildewed black notebook. When he opened it, Erasmus saw it was only a shell, two covers with just a few pages remaining, all the rest torn out. "It could have been someone's journal," Dr. Boerhaave said. "Even Franklin's." But the pages still caught in the binding were blank, and Erasmus saw where the rest had gone: little boys, given this as a toy, had ripped the sheets out one by one. What could have been the words of one of Franklin's crew sent sailing on the breeze. He stared, then turned back to his own journal: tidy notes, long columns aligned. Everything listed except that bit of boot.

Finally, with everything piled and noted, Oonali said, "Perhaps you will return to your own place now. We have given you everything we have."

"I would like to buy some of your dogs," Zeke said. "All your dogs, if you'll part with them."

The land between here and the river was a soupy, pond-riddled, hazardous place, nearly impossible to cross at this time of year; Zeke, Erasmus saw, could only have one thing in mind. He meant, if he could obtain enough dogs, to stay here through the winter and then travel, if not to King William Land, then across the frozen strait to the island. For a moment Erasmus gave in to a vision: he and Zeke walking side by side into the Academy of Sciences, bearing these relics and full of stories. How much more glorious their entrance would be were they to say: *We saw men from Franklin's ships. We gave them proper burial.*

"It is impossible," Oonali said. "We need the dogs to carry our tents and other things. We leave tomorrow. Already we must begin packing."

As if to demonstrate, a woman began piling skins and clothes on a dog. The dog grimaced and drooped his tail, then turned to bark at a raven stealing some bits of fat.

"Let me have just a dozen," Zeke begged.

"Impossible," Oonali said.

FOR ANOTHER DAY Zeke wrestled with himself, writing and writing in his black book, talking and talking to Erasmus and Dr. Boerhaave, as he tried to figure out a way to explore more territory and find clearer signs of the lost expedition. The following morning he rose, stared at his coffee, and then said into the dim cabin, "He who does not see the hand of God in all this is blind."

Captain Tyler and Mr. Tagliabeau exchanged a glance, as did Dr. Boerhaave and Erasmus. Zeke turned and faced into his bunk, his arms spread above his head and his hands grasping the supports. As he spoke he swayed slightly, leaning into the bunk and then back out, against the air, while a white figure barked at him from a tub of ice in the corner: the little white fox Ned had trapped, which Zeke had appropriated as a pet to replace his lost Wissy. She ate from Zeke's plate; he had named her Sabine.

"I read the dogs' death as a bad omen," he said. "Or even an act of sabotage. Especially Wissy's. But it was not, it was an illness pure and simple. That we could not penetrate Peel Sound, and that Bellot Strait was closed to us, also seemed to signal the failure of our expedition. Fletcher Lamb's death, for which no one would have wished, delayed us when we might have departed. Yet in fact all these events have conspired to place us exactly here, at exactly this time, where we could meet precisely this group of Esquimaux. *We* are the favored ones. We've uncovered much more than did Dr. Rae. That we can't pursue this further is a sign that what we've found is sufficient. More than sufficient. Through patience and persistence we've twice seen past the Esquimaux deceitfulness and uncovered the true story. I was tempted to winter here—but those men are dead, and we know where they died. We'll leave as soon as we can ready the ship."

The men cheered when Zeke announced his decision. Erasmus, listening to them bustle about as they prepared the *Narwhal* for the last leg of her voyage, considered their accomplishments. While they hadn't seen either bodies or ships, their evidence was much more direct than Dr. Rae's. They'd dined with people who'd seen bodies and carved up one of Franklin's boats. They'd eaten soup with Franklin's silver spoons and lost only a single member of their own crew. He looked forward to arriving home in triumph, bearing his neatly written journal in its green silk dress. After dusting the grease spots with salt, he wrote:

> *I try to set my feelings aside; I try to record here simply what I saw, what I heard, what has happened. But I admit I've found these days exciting. These are very different Esquimaux from the civilized tribes of southern Greenland. And it was thrilling to delve below their superficial deceit and uncover the crucial story about*

the boat. I feel as though my small role—keeping Zeke steady and providing a sympathetic ear, while maintaining all the scientific observations—has contributed much to our success. Is it ridiculous to hope I may return home as a sort of hero: the steady, older naturalist who has been of inestimable aid to the commander, and made all the important observations? Lavinia will be so proud of Zeke. Of us.

Although there was no possibility of sending letters for some weeks, Dr. Boerhaave wrote to his English friend Thomas Cholmondelay:

Do you remember the story I told you, about Mr. Thoreau's pilgrimage to Fire Island and his attempt to gather up the relics of Margaret Fuller drowning? It sticks in my mind: how he found that shift with her initials embroidered on it; her husband's coat, from which he took a button; her infant's petticoat. The relics we've uncovered here—I append a list that will sadden your heart—put me in mind of that other shipwreck. There is something so terribly personal about these small objects.

We've had a death on our own ship as well: a pleasant young man named Fletcher Lamb, who succumbed to lockjaw after cutting himself with a razor. The smallest of accidents; it too meaningless in itself. Yet by that act our tiny crew is reduced by one. I kept him as comfortable as possible but could do nothing to avert the end. He died quietly, after having said his prayers and dictating a brief note of farewell to his mother and sisters. I've lost patients before, of course. But this death, so needless, hurt more than most. And it is disturbing that our commander reads into the delay caused by that death a form of divine intervention, which allowed us to make our discoveries. Are you well?

THEY SET SAIL on August 9. From the shrouds hung seven caribou, which, along with the clusters of birds suspended in the rigging, gave the *Narwhal* the appearance of a butcher shop under sail.
Sabine, chained to her tub of ice beneath the dead wildlife, watched
the bustle curiously.

"Don't you think I'm doing well with her?" Zeke asked Erasmus.
He slipped Sabine a morsel of bread, while Captain Tyler called out
the sequence of orders that would set them moving again. "She was
so shy when Ned brought her in, but I think she's becoming quite
civilized."

She was half grown or perhaps a bit more, four pounds of energy
with a coat resembling that of a fancy cat. As they began to move she
stood and howled to her relatives back on shore.

4

A Little Detour

(August–September 1855)

*I have no fancies about equality on board ship.
It is a thing out of the question, and certainly, in
the present state of mankind, not to be desired.
I never knew a sailor who found fault with the
orders and ranks of the service; and if I expected
to pass the rest of my life before the mast, I would
not wish to have the power of the captain diminished an iota. It is absolutely necessary that there
should be one head and one voice, to control
everything, and be responsible for everything.
There are emergencies which require the instant
exercise of extreme power. These emergencies do
not allow of consultation; and they who would
be the captain's constituted advisers might be the
very men over whom he would be called upon
to exert his authority. It has been found necessary to vest in every government, even the most
democratic, some extraordinary and, at first*

sight, alarming powers; trusting in public opin-
ion, and subsequent accountability to modify
the exercise of them. These are provided to meet
exigencies, which all hope may never occur, but
which yet by possibility may occur, and if they
should, and there were no power to meet them
instantly, there would be an end put to the gov-
ernment at once. So it is with the authority of
the shipmaster.

—RICHARD DANA, *Two Years*
Before the Mast (1840)

AT FIRST THE VOYAGE HOME WAS MUCH LIKE THE VOY-
age out, except for the intensity of the deep, enveloping light. The
light was like silver, like crystal, like oil—but not, really, like anything else; Erasmus could find no comparison, he gave up. The light
was like itself. Under it, in Lancaster Sound, he could imagine the
promise of Baffin's Bay: ships and mail and company and, a few
weeks beyond that, home. At first the weather was calm, and so were
the men.

Erasmus's only sleep came in little catnaps but he slept deeply
during those stretches and woke refreshed. In between he spent
hours with Dr. Boerhaave over their specimens. He made lists and
schedules, crossing off each item accomplished: these bird skins
dried and packed and labeled, these plants identified. All immensely

satisfying. One day he woke in the grip of an unfamiliar feeling—a compound of anticipation and physical well-being, all he'd accomplished in the previous days balanced with all he was eager to do that day. This was happiness, he thought with surprise. The sky hung above him like a gigantic glowing bowl.

On sunlit nights, when sleep seemed such a waste of time, Erasmus thumbed through his battered copy of Hooker's *Botany of the Antarctic Voyage of the Erebus and the Terror in the Years 1839–1843*, not only because those same ships had later carried Franklin, but also because it reminded him of what he might have done on his own first voyage, had Wilkes not blocked him. Now he believed he might put together an arctic volume that would stand as a companion to Hooker's. Next to him Dr. Boerhaave re-read Parry's journals, assessing the descriptions of the Esquimaux. Collating his own notes, he talked about writing an account of the Netsilik similar to Parry's famed Appendix.

"All the arctic peoples build a culture around the available food sources," he mused. "And those cultures may be very different. Yet the tribes share racial characteristics. Just as the plants and animals recur across the arctic zone so do the people, uniquely adapted to this environment. More and more it seems to me they must have been created here . . ."

"Why must they have been?" Erasmus said affectionately. He'd grown very fond of the way his friend talked: one cerebral, slightly stilted sentence linked to the next, whole paragraphs unfurling. He'd never asked, he realized, if Dr. Boerhaave still thought in Swedish, translating mentally before he talked; or if he now thought in English. And where did his French and German fit in, and when had he learned all those languages? His grandparents, he'd once mentioned, had been Dutch. "That doesn't follow."

"You're so old-fashioned," Dr. Boerhaave said. "All the leading naturalists, and all the most progressive philosophers, lean toward this idea of separate, successive creations—why do you resist it so? Why does it seem so improbable to you that man, like the other animals, might have been created multiply in separate zoological provinces?"

"I just don't believe it," Erasmus said. And held up his hands in surrender, and laughed. Whenever they discussed the geographical distribution of plants and animals, they always parted company at the final step of the hypothesis—that just as the arctic supported a white bear rather than black or grizzly bears, murres and dovekies rather than penguins, so too might the Esquimaux differ at a species level from the men in other places.

The idea seemed wrong to Erasmus—not just theologically unorthodox, but scientifically unsound. One practical definition of a species was the ability to interbreed; everyone knew matings of all the races of men produced fertile offspring. Canadian voyageurs and Coppermine Indians, Parry's crews and Esquimaux, plantation owners and their slaves: that no one wanted to discuss these conjunctions didn't make them less true. Erasmus thought of the botanist Asa Gray, whose work he admired. That idea of varieties moving toward species over time—if man was part of nature as a whole, subject to the same physical laws that governed other organisms . . .

"Separate," Dr. Boerhaave said, "does not mean inferior."

"Differentiation always implies ranking," Erasmus said. They smiled and left the subject, returning to the books before them.

Ned listened in on these conversations, occasionally asking questions of his own and practicing what the two older men taught him about the preparation of specimens. At first he worked on birds. In his lined copybook he wrote:

*Remember to measure everything before beginning to remove the
skin; record color of eyes and other soft parts; if possible make an
outline of the entire bird on a large sheet of paper before skinning,
otherwise sketch overall shape and stance. Break the wings as close
to the body as possible, then cut the skin down the center of the
breast to the vent. For the head, stretch the skin gradually until the
ears are reached; cut through the skin there close to the bone; then
cut carefully around the eye, making sure not to cut the eyelids.
Sever the head from the neck and pull out the brain with the hook;
remove eyes from sockets, cut out the tongue, and remove all flesh
from the skull. Poison the skin with powdered arsenic and alum or
arsenical soap.*

*If prepared carefully, Mr. Wells says, the skins will stay in perfect
shape until we return home and will be of much use to scientists.
Or they may be softened and mounted in a lifelike shape, so others
will have a chance to examine what we've seen. Ever since I pulled
Mr. Wells from the water at the base of the cliff he has treated me
very kindly; who could imagine I'd find another man willing to
help me like this? I have a gift for this work, he says. I might make
a living from it someday, if I wanted—in museums, he claims, are
assistants with no more formal education than me, who do the initial work on all the specimens. My father would have laughed and
thought this no better than undertaker's work. But that was there,
and this is another country.*

PART OF ERASMUS'S well-being came from the sense that he was
teaching Ned something useful. As Ned's hands moved among skins
and bones, Erasmus was reminded of his own boyish efforts—a
squirrel, he thought, had been his first preparation—and he watched

happily. On his other side Dr. Boerhaave, busy himself with an ivory gull, asked Ned, "How is it you read and write so well?"

"I was lucky," Ned said, comparing the spinal column in his palm to the sketch before him. "A man who took me in one winter taught me."

They were interrupted by the lookout calling, "Drift ice ahead!" As they leapt to their feet and stared, the ice turned into a herd of beluga whales, glimmering white in the water. After gaping at them, Ned told Erasmus and Dr. Boerhaave how he'd gotten his education.

He had left Ireland in '47, he said, at the height of the potato famine. All his family had died but his brother Denis and his older sister, Nora; the three of them had taken passage on one of the over-crowded emigrant ships bound for Quebec. But Nora had sickened on the ship, and at the quarantine station of Grosse Isle, downriver from Quebec city, Nora had been taken from them.

"We were starving," Ned said, gazing out at the water. "And Denis and I were sick ourselves, though we didn't know it yet. Nora was almost dead. These men carried her off the ship and said she had to go into the hospital on the island. Me and Denis were forced onto another, smaller ship, crammed full of Irish like us, and they sent us upriver to Montreal. We never saw Nora again."

In Montreal, he said, there were already so many sick with the fever that the residents had forced them along to Kingston. In Kingston, Denis had died.

"How old were you then?" Dr. Boerhaave asked.

"Twelve," Ned said. "I turned thirteen there."

He touched only briefly on the terrible years when, after being left for dead in a pauper's hospital, and then wandering the streets, homeless and thieving, he'd been taken in by some farmers who worked him hard. Soon after turning sixteen, he'd run away.

"All I wanted," he said, "was to be out of that cruel country. I thought that if I could just get to America, my whole life would be different."

He'd crossed the St. Lawrence into New York State and drifted from Cape Vincent to Chaumont to Watertown; then, hearing tales of logging work to be had in the Brown's Tract wilderness, he'd made the hazardous journey through the north woods. Deep in the forests near Saranac Lake he'd found work in a logging camp, though not as a logger. The men, immigrants like himself, had laughed at his slight physique but had been willing to hire him as cook's helper.

Midway through his second season, the cook had left and Ned had taken on the duties of feeding the entire camp. That year, while picking up groceries on Lower Saranac Lake, he'd met a pale Boston lawyer who planned to winter there in the hope of curing his consumption. The lawyer was building a cabin in the woods and hiring a staff. He'd engaged Ned as his cook.

All that winter, while the lawyer lay wrapped in blankets on a porch facing south, simultaneously basking in the sun and freezing in the subzero wind, he'd taught Ned his letters, so that Ned could read to him and eventually take dictation. During Ned's second winter a new cook had been hired, so that Ned might spend all his time with the lawyer and his books.

"It was a great thing he did for me," Ned said. "I'll always be grateful to him."

"Why did you leave?" Erasmus asked.

"He died," Ned said.

He was twenty, and in an hour's conversation he'd said, *they died, she died, he died, he died.* Rising to return to the galley, Ned explained in a few more sentences how he'd drifted south to Philadelphia, been unable to find any clerical work, and ended up cooking at the wharfside tavern where Mr. Tagliabeau had found him. He said nothing about the fight that had led to his dismissal.

"I couldn't seem to settle down," he said. "Everywhere I went, I missed my family." He paused for a moment, not sure how to say what he meant. What could where he traveled matter, when he had no hope of ever seeing Nora or Denis again? In a way, wandering like this was what gave him hope; he'd seen Denis die with his own eyes but Nora had simply disappeared, and if he kept moving it somehow seemed possible that she wasn't dead. That she might be wandering, like him.

"It's a strange thing," he said, "knowing you don't have a single living relative in all the world—how can you pick a place to live, when you're a stranger everywhere?"

Dr. Boerhaave smiled, as if he knew exactly what Ned meant. Both of them, Erasmus thought, had cut their ties to home in a way he still couldn't imagine.

"One thing I liked about the wharves was that all the men who came in were strangers too," Ned continued. "I was beginning to think about shipping out on a merchant ship and seeing the world, since I had no ties to anyplace. But then you all showed up, and look how well everything worked out. Commander Voorhees took me on, and here I am: in a place where hardly anyone has ever been. Where we're all strangers, except to each other."

THEY *HAD* BEEN STRANGERS, Erasmus would think later. Even to each other. But he forgot that for a while in the blinding light. Outside the sun shone and shone, and inside the relics obtained from the Netsilik, neatly boxed and stowed in the hold, shed a quiet radiance. Filled with purpose and caught up in his work, Erasmus was slow to register the mood of the men around him. They were fifteen people, isolated except for their brief time among the Netsilik, and they'd begun to tire of each other. Small habits loomed large: the way, for instance, that Zeke fed Sabine from his fork at the dinner table. Or Zeke's bored, superior gaze when Erasmus tried to tell him what he'd learned about Ned.

"Well, of course," Zeke said. Sabine sat on the chair beside him, following his hand alertly as it hovered over the plate. "Ned told me all of this ages ago." When had that happened? Erasmus wondered. When Zeke was brooding over Fletcher Lamb's death? Lately Zeke had seemed even more secretive than usual.

Several of the crew who'd quarreled at Boothia over women nursed those rivalries into fire again. On the voyage out, it had often been Joe who was best able to cheer and calm the men, entertaining them with his zither and his stories. But Joe had been glum since their departure from Boothia: so glum that, when a fistfight broke out between Sean Hamilton and Ivan Hruska, Joe left them to Mr. Francis's harsh discipline and came above, to hang listlessly over the rail where Erasmus was perched with his sketchpad.

"They'll get over it," Erasmus said. "They're restless, they're all thinking of home. Really we've been incredibly lucky so far. Everything we learned from those Esquimaux . . ."

The biscuit Joe tossed over the rail was caught in midair by a fulmar. "What makes you think those Esquimaux were telling us everything they knew?"

"Because—they *didn't* tell us, at first," Erasmus said, startled. The fulmar flapped away with its prize. "We had to dig out the truth for ourselves. We had to pry it out of them. If Ned hadn't seen those cooking kettles . . ."

Joe made a disgusted sound. "They told that story for their own reasons," he said. "To get the ship to go away, and the men to stop hunting their caribou and preying on their women. Couldn't you see that? They told us what we wanted to hear. And if Commander Voorhees hadn't been so blinded by his own anger and his desire to find something, he would have realized just how ambiguous the situation was."

"You're saying they *lied*?" Erasmus thought back to the look on Joe's face when he'd translated Oonali's revelations about the ship's boat. He'd assumed, then, that Joe was simply mortified by the earlier deceptions.

"Not lied," Joe said crossly. "There was surely truth in what they told us. But they knew what we were looking for, and what it would take to satisfy us, and so perhaps they bent the truth a little. Shaped the story to our desires."

"But you're the *interpreter*," Erasmus said. "It was your job to figure that out, and convey to us what was accurate, and what misleading."

"I shouldn't have to interpret gestures," Joe said. His hands, brown and broken-nailed, clamped on the rail. "If Commander Voorhees had looked more closely at Oonali, instead of at me—if he'd paid any attention to Oonali at all—he would have understood how to weigh the information."

Oonali, Erasmus recalled, had pushed two girl children behind him as he spoke at the feast, and shooed others away from the gathering of the men. Uneasily he said, "What did Oonali say, that you didn't tell us?"

"It's not what he said—it's the way he said it. It's the context in which he said it. I translated every word as accurately as I could. But I was also paying attention to other things. And you were not. Commander Voorhees was not. If you were in a negotiation with your people back home, you'd notice other things besides the words."

"Do you think there was no boat, then?" Erasmus asked. "But where did they get those kettles, the pieces of wood—everything?"

"Of course they found a boat. Dead sailors, too. What I'm not so sure of is that all the traces of them are actually gone. But they had every reason to discourage us from overwintering there, and from searching the island in the spring. Who knows what we might have found, if we hadn't been satisfied so easily with their tale?"

He paused and picked at the dry skin around his thumbnails. "Oonali's wife told me something awful," he admitted. "When we were standing apart from the others for a minute. She said at that boat, near the dead sailors—they found human parts that had been . . . interfered with. Bones with the marks of saws and knives. Skulls with holes smashed in them."

"Dr. Rae's report," Erasmus murmured, remembering the story he'd told Ned at the start of their voyage. "That's just what the Esquimaux he met told him."

"These stories are worse," Joe said. "Oonali's wife told me she found a sailor's boot, which someone had been using as a kind of bowl. There were pieces of boiled human flesh in it."

In his bunk, beneath his bookshelf, Erasmus had driven a tack and then wedged his secret scrap of leather between it and the shelf's lower side. The one thing he'd kept for himself; still no one knew he had it, not even Dr. Boerhaave. Later, perhaps when they were home, he might offer this as a last surprise to seal their friendship. Something separate from Zeke, and from the goals of the expedition, which only the two of them would share. Until now that scrap of leather had seemed like a symbol of courage, a weary foot moving across the ice no matter how tired. Yet perhaps Oonali's wife had meant it to signal something quite different. Perhaps it was the sole of the same boot she'd told Joe about . . . or perhaps these tales were horrible lies, and all Joe's worries unjustified.

"You should be telling Commander Voorhees this," Erasmus said. He decided not to show his treasure to Joe; it would only make Joe feel worse about what the Esquimaux might not have admitted. "Not me."

"You think I didn't try? I tried to tell him the night before we sailed. And he said, he said"—here Joe drew himself up and tucked in his chin—"'*I* have always read that the Esquimaux pride themselves on their excellent memories, and the faithfulness of their storytelling. I think we may have absolute confidence in what we've been told.'"

With that Joe headed up to the crow's nest, leaving Erasmus to ponder the eerie accuracy with which Joe had caught the inflections of Zeke's voice.

Later, napping briefly, Erasmus dreamed that Joe had turned into an Esquimau boy, indistinguishable from the children at the hunting camp. Then he dreamed that he was himself a tiny boy, listening to his father read. *Not far from the cave where the north wind rises live people who have a single eye centered in their foreheads. In Africa is a race who make in their bodies a poison deadly to snakes. On a mountain in India live men with dogs' heads, who bark instead of talking. Near the source of the Ganges are mouthless people, who subsist on the odors they breathe; beyond them live pygmies in houses of feathers and eggshells.*

He woke still within the enchanted circle of his father's words, and then blinked to see where he was. What had his father meant to do, reading those tales to his small sons? He and his brothers had soaked up those words, which had lit their own experiments. Cutting open a little green snake, they'd been equally ready to see eggs or infant snakes or three-headed monsters. *Try to see what you see,* his father had said. *Then integrate it with what you've already read and heard.* Still Erasmus felt a kind of pity for him. At thirteen his father had gone to work in the firm his own father founded; after that he'd read in snatches, always standing at a printing press or setting type or inking it, lugging bales of paper or bundles of pages, always on the move and starved for time. Once he'd taken over the firm he'd been busy in other ways. *I wanted things to be different for you boys,* he'd said. *For you not to have to work so hard. For you to be able to learn in peace, and travel wherever you wanted—especially after your mother died, I could never leave home for more than a few days.*

How could Erasmus not be grateful for all he'd been given? The next morning he made what amends he could to Joe, offering the heap of little disks he found in the stomach of a bearded seal. "Specimens of the operculum from the large whelk snail," he said.

Joe, who seemed to have recovered his good humor, examined them with interest and then butchered the carcass when Erasmus finished his dissection. Somewhere during those hours, both of them up to the elbows in blood, Erasmus said, "I'm sorry. You're right—I should have been paying more attention. But what can we do about it now?"

"Nothing," Joe said. "We must be thankful for what we did learn. And the Netsilik can be thankful that we're gone; and I can be thankful that we didn't do any more damage than we did."

NOTHING SHONE SO brightly for Erasmus after that. It rained for three days, windy squalls that made work difficult and left him too much time to think about what Joe had said. Then Zeke appeared on deck one afternoon and asked the crew to report to him in the cabin after their evening meal. As Captain Tyler started to ask a question, Zeke said, "I would like to see all the officers together, now."

They crowded around the cabin table in their usual formation: Zeke at one end, flanked by Erasmus and Dr. Boerhaave; Mr. Tagliabeau and Mr. Francis and Captain Tyler clumped together, as separate from Zeke as was possible in such a tiny space; Sabine annoyingly underfoot. Zeke placed a sheet of paper on the table.

"I should have taken care of this before," he said. The paper was densely written over, in his clear hand. "And I apologize for my tardiness. This is quite standard, something that most expedition leaders require their crews to sign, and I would appreciate it if you'd attend to it now."

"May I?" Dr. Boerhaave said. Zeke nodded and pushed the paper over. Dr. Boerhaave read for a minute, before handing the document to Erasmus.

The undersigned accept Zechariah Voorhees as sole commander of this expedition, and pledge to aid him to achieve the goals of the expedition in every way possible, as deemed best by said Commander Voorhees.

The contract, stilted and formal, went on to state that, should something happen to Zeke, the expedition would then be under the shared command of Captain Tyler and Erasmus, with the captain responsible for the safe return of the ship, and Erasmus responsible for fulfilling the expedition's goals. Erasmus had no quarrel with this: he was Zeke's right hand and this seemed a simple formality. But a more disturbing paragraph followed, stating that all members of the crew—not exempting Erasmus, nor Dr. Boerhaave—promised to turn their journals and logs over to Zeke at the conclusion of the expedition, and further promised to refrain from lecturing or writing about their observations for a period of one year after the journey's end.

Where had this come from? The blood hummed in Erasmus's temples, and when Sabine draped herself over his instep he nudged her aside more sharply than he meant to. Zeke had been distant since Fletcher Lamb's death but still Erasmus hadn't sensed how far they'd drifted apart. They were meant to be brothers; who would impose on a brother like this? When he knew he could control his voice he passed the contract to Mr. Tagliabeau and said to Zeke, "I'm sorry to disagree with you, but I think this is *outrageous*. You never said a word of this to me before. You're acting the way Wilkes did on the Exploring Expedition and I object to it, I object to it strongly . . ."

Zeke raised a hand to silence him. "It's a formality," he said. "But surely you can see the need to present our findings quickly, and in concert; not to contradict each other. Of course I'll expect all of you to help with the initial announcement of what we've learned, and I would fully acknowledge any material I draw from your notebooks."

Looking straight at Erasmus, and ignoring the whispers of the captain and the mates, Zeke said, "It's to *avoid* what happened with Wilkes's expedition that I do this. We must have no quarrels among ourselves, no results thrown into question by any appearance of disunity among us."

"Why should Mr. Wells share command with me, in your absence?" Captain Tyler said angrily. "He knows nothing about this ship."

"He shares my goals for the expedition," Zeke said. "I must be sure that if something happened to me, someone would take charge of delivering the relics and our scientific observations. As well as safely delivering the ship and its men."

Dr. Boerhaave, who'd said nothing yet, drew the paper from Captain Tyler's hand, took the pen Zeke had prepared, and signed. Then he rose. "Of course I will assist you in any way I can," he said. "As I have always done. But I'm offended that you feel a need for this. If you'll excuse me."

He nodded stiffly and went up on deck. Erasmus, left behind, stared at the paper that blocked his dream of lecturing by himself. But he'd be *with* Zeke, he thought. They'd be striding into the Academy of Sciences together—and already they were sharing the journal Lavinia had meant for Zeke. Their observations would be fused together, into a single narrative that Erasmus might write himself; Zeke disliked the act of composition and preferred to toss out broad ideas and let others shape them. This contract was the act of a young man, still nervous about his position. Surely Erasmus, so much older, could afford to give in here and work out the details later? Zeke would never prevent him writing a few articles purely about the natural history of the area, with no reference to Franklin or their Esquimaux companions.

"I won't sign this," Captain Tyler said. "In your absence, Mr. Tagliabeau would naturally be my second-in-command. Not Mr. Wells."

"I'm sorry you feel that way," Zeke said. "But if you don't sign, I'll be forced to relieve you of command."

Then everyone was shouting. In his awkward position, Erasmus felt he shouldn't speak—but all this quarreling had the effect of diverting his attention away from the paragraphs about the journals, and to the question of the succession of command. Perhaps Zeke counted on this. He wore down the captain, finally suggesting that the balance of the crew's payment for the expedition, due on their return, might be withheld if he refused to sign.

Captain Tyler signed, and then Mr. Francis and Mr. Tagliabeau; they flung themselves up the ladder and Erasmus could hear shouting from the deck. The captain—who was he talking to?—said, "I would never have taken this command if there'd been anything better around. This is no fit job for a whaling skipper, this bobbing around the arctic . . ."

"And you?" Zeke said to Erasmus once they'd left. Sabine hopped into his lap. "My trusted friend?"

Erasmus signed and shook Zeke's hand. When Zeke asked Erasmus to help him explain the contract to the men trickling into the cabin, Erasmus did that too. He inscribed the names of those who couldn't write and showed them where to make their mark. Both Nils Jensen and Isaac Bond said, "But Captain Tyler would still be in charge, if something happened?"

"Absolutely," Zeke said. "Nothing has changed."

Ned, ever amiable, read and signed the contract himself without a murmur. Joe, the last to arrive, said, "I'll want to make a report on the Netsilik to the Moravian missionaries in Greenland. Would that be permitted?"

"It wouldn't go outside the church?"

"No. But they might want to establish a mission in the area at some point, and my observations could be of use to them."

Zeke gave his permission, and Joe signed.

All throughout that evening, Sabine remained in Zeke's lap with her delicate paws on the table, peering at the contract as if she were about to sign it herself. Now and then Zeke fed her morsels and then pointed out the neat way in which she wiped her lips.

"Isn't she charming?" he said to Barton DeSouza, just as Erasmus was explaining the second paragraph of the contract. Barton looked disconcerted, the more so when Sabine turned, looked lovingly up into Zeke's face, and barked.

On deck, in the shelter of one of the boats, Dr. Boerhaave stared for a long time at his journal but closed it without writing anything. Then he took out his letter case and wrote furiously to his friend William in Edinburgh:

> *I've enjoyed this expedition very much but am coming to despise our commander. He lives in a world of his own making, only aware of his own thoughts and fantasies: a boy still, for all his bulk and bluster. On Boothia, he could not see the Netsilik except as agents of his own glory, and although I tried to gather information about their customs I was never granted enough time to do so, nor to gather and*

prepare plant and animal specimens, and he has no appreciation
for the fossils I gathered; and now this: all the notes I managed to
take despite him are to be his, so that he may construct a narrative
of the last days of Franklin and his men from the slight evidence he
has gathered—which is slight, do not mistake this, I append a list of
relics but in themselves they don't tell us more than we knew before
from Dr. Rae's explorations and what we really learned, or might
have learned, is something about this glorious place and its people,
but he will make no use of that—a whole year. Of course he hasn't
the least understanding that priority is granted to the naming and
description of new species not by their date of discovery but by the
date of published description.

Erasmus, the following morning, made a note about a fish in
his journal and then flipped through the pages, assessing his earlier
entries. Had he been too personal? He drew some scales and listed
the fish's stomach contents but longed to describe how he felt. He
began a long letter to Copernicus. It could not be sent; there was
no way to send it, and no one to receive it; Copernicus was still out
west somewhere, painting canyons and Indians. But Erasmus felt
the bond between them, across the length and breadth of the continent, somehow strengthened by Zeke's act.

ON AUGUST 20 they entered the waters of Baffin's Bay. They'd
planned to turn north and then east here, sailing around the upper
edge of the pack and retracing the great arc back to Greenland, but
Isaac Bond called down from the masthead and reported a ship.
Zeke, the captain, and the mates took their turns with the glass: a
large ship, they agreed, caught in the ice a few miles south of them,

apparently abandoned and adrift. Zeke ordered the *Narwhal* brought as close to the ship as possible. The ice loomed before them like land.

"I can't risk getting us caught in the pack," Captain Tyler said. "Not this late in the season. And not when we're so close to home."

"It's not your ship to risk," Zeke said coolly. He pushed the spyglass toward the captain and pointed out the black hull marked with a band of white. "British naval vessels are all painted like that," he said. "They're impossible to tell apart from a distance. That could be the second of Franklin's ships. The Esquimaux told us about *one* ship sinking. Only one."

Captain Tyler scanned the distant ship. "If it were . . . but there's so little chance of that. And you can see it's deserted—why should we risk ourselves?"

"Because I tell you to," Zeke said.

He turned his back and went below: as if a show of confidence that his orders would be followed would ensure that they were. Captain Tyler cracked his knuckles but worked the brig south through the ice, until they were finally blocked a few hundred feet from the other ship by a long, hummocked floe. The possibility that this *was* Franklin's ship made Erasmus tremble with excitement. To his surprise, Zeke named as the boarding party only himself, Erasmus, Dr. Boerhaave, and Ned.

"I need everyone else on hand to work the brig, in case we're nipped," Zeke said.

"Take Forbes, at least," Captain Tyler grumbled. "You may need a carpenter."

"We'll be fine," Zeke said.

They lowered themselves to the ice, picked their way gingerly across the cracks, and approached the ship. Zeke said, "If this were the ship, one of the ships, if we were fated after all to find this final sign, it would be such excellent confirmation of what we've already learned . . ."

The ship was fast in the ice. Zeke shouted as they approached, but no one answered. As they clambered aboard Erasmus's skin prickled, and he knew they all feared the same thing: that they'd find bodies inside, frozen or starved to death. The deck was in order, lines properly coiled and sails stowed, but empty of people.

Zeke pointed out the motto on the brass plate over the helm: *England expects every man to do his duty.* "Could it be the *Erebus*?" he said. "Or the *Terror*?"

As they descended into the cabin, Zeke was already talking about how they might free the ship and tow it home. Erasmus had to remind himself to breathe. If this were one of Franklin's ships, if, if, if . . . already he could imagine the newspaper headlines. They entered the dark and musty cabin. In a writing desk, Dr. Boerhaave found the logbook. He lifted it; he blew off the dust. Erasmus stared at the fine black hairs on the back of his friend's hands.

Dr. Boerhaave opened the book. "The *Resolute*," he announced.

And there they were, in a cold, dark ship that for a minute was only a ship. Then it was something else, though still not glorious. They'd all heard about this ship; it belonged to Edward Belcher's expedition, which had been frozen in during the winter of '53 and '54. Belcher, Erasmus knew, had abandoned his fleet that May, a thousand miles west of them. As he and Zeke were planning their own voyage, they'd heard the gossip about Belcher's return to England on a rescue ship. He'd been court-martialed for his poor judgment, and barely acquitted; there'd been little reason to think his vessels wouldn't be free come summer, and no one understood why he'd left them.

Zeke's face sagged as they recollected the squalid story. They stood in one of Belcher's ships, which had broken free and made the long journey eastward by itself. A discovery, but hardly an earth-shaking one.

"Should we try to tow her out?" Erasmus asked.

"Let someone else salvage her," Zeke said. "It's not our job to repair that man's mistakes." He took the logbook but left the *Resolute* to continue drifting southward with the pack.

Back across Lancaster Sound again, then along the coast of North Devon; Zeke sullen with the knowledge that their detour had come to nothing. From Jones Sound the water stretched east and north nearly free of ice, a sight that made everyone smile: all of them dreaming of home. Erasmus dreamed of his narrow bed in the Repository, his orderly specimen cases and shelves; of the cook bringing into his dining room a dish of roasted veal and glazed carrots. Dr. Boerhaave was looking forward to a trip to Boston; the men spoke of sweethearts and things they might buy with their wages; Captain Tyler said he missed his wife. Perhaps Zeke dreamed of Lavinia. Or perhaps he dreamed of other things.

IN PHILADELPHIA, WOMEN dreamed that the *Narwhal* was sailing toward them. Alexandra wrote:

> *Just another six or eight weeks, if all goes well. I thought I'd look forward to the end of this time, but in fact I'll miss being here: a retreat from the noise and crowding of my family's house. I've come to love my hours in the Repository and have grown very attached to Lavinia. We've completed the plates for the entomology book, but Linnaeus and Humboldt have no more hand-coloring work. They offered me a small stipend simply to continue as Lavinia's companion, but I've persuaded them to let me—and Lavinia too, I said; she needs to stay occupied—take engraving lessons from one*

*of their employees in lieu of a salary. I have a substantial nest egg
in my sewing box now. What I need is a skill I may take with me
when I leave. If this is the life I am to lead—here in this city, unat-
tached, dependent on my brother—I must do what I can to make
the best of it.*

*The brothers objected on the usual grounds but I cited the exam-
ple of Thomas Say's wife, Lucy. As their father helped arrange her
election as the first woman member of the Academy of Sciences,
this made them think. Lavinia made them look at Mrs. Hale's
book, which she brought back from town:* "Women's Record, or
Sketches of All Distinguished Women from 'The Beginning' till
A.D. 1850. Arranged in Four Eras. With Selections from Female
Writers of Every Age." *I mean to be an advanced woman, she told
her brothers. Like those women. Isn't that what you want for me?*

*We started last week. Mr. Archibault, one of the Wells's mas-
ter engravers, comes to us in the Repository, bearing burins and
needles and steel plates spoiled by the apprentices, which would
otherwise be scrapped. More broad-minded than the brothers, he
remarks that both Helen Dawson and the Maverick sisters did
excellent engravings; and so anything, he supposes, may be possible.
Straight lines, curved lines, incomplete lines, and dots—I have
much to learn, and little time. I gashed myself several times with
the burin.*

LATER, ERASMUS WOULD wonder if Zeke's disappointment over
the *Resolute* was responsible for what happened next. Or if Joe's earlier comments about Oonali had finally sunk in, until Zeke doubted
the worth of their relics. At the point where they all expected to turn
east, Zeke called the crew together on deck.

"We have four days yet of August," Zeke said. "And can look

forward to several weeks of good sailing in September. The weather's excellent and the season is far from over. Your hard work has already brought this expedition much success. And I know you'll be willing to delay our return just a few more weeks, so we might bring back not only our news of Franklin's expedition, but some significant geographical findings as well."

Erasmus, sketching the strata of a distant cliff, turned to stare at Zeke as Sean Hamilton blurted, *"What?"* Two seals popped their heads from the water and stared at the ship.

"We'll head into Smith Sound," Zeke continued, "testing the boundaries of the open water. A little detour. The bulk of the drifting ice is south of us; you can see for yourselves that there's no loose pack north of us. A swift, concerted probe through the Sound might bring us far before we have to turn back. We'll make as much northing as we can in ten days, chart as much new territory as we can, and then make a quick run for Godhavn. I promise we'll be there in less than four weeks."

"No!" Captain Tyler said. He grasped a shroud, squeezing until his swollen knuckles stood out like walnuts. "This is out of the question, you can't consider it."

Mr. Francis and Mr. Tagliabeau backed him up and others also raised their voices: *my mother is waiting; the season's too late; this isn't what you told us when we signed on*—Isaac Bond, Nils Jensen, Ivan Hruska. Zeke brought out his maps, talking about his theory of polynya formation and why there *should* be open water north of the constriction of Smith Sound.

"Please," Erasmus said in his ear. "What about Lavinia?"

But Zeke shook him off and did what Erasmus had dreaded from his first words. "You've pledged to support me," he said, waving the contract. "This brief exploration is part of our goals, as I have determined them, and you must support me in this. You must."

Sabine, perched on his shoulder like a white epaulet, regarded the crowd and barked.

THE ICEBERG'S FACE was sheer and as high as their mastheads, but Nils Jensen and Robert Carey managed to scale it. They were trying to anchor the *Narwhal* to the berg's lee side, where they might find some protection from the crushing ice. Nils drove the anchor in; Robert adjusted the lines. Just as they began their scramble back to the ship, the berg split in two with a noise like a cannon shot. Robert leapt for the water, and although he was nearly frozen to death Dr. Boerhaave was able to save him. But while his companions watched, unable to help him, Nils toppled into the chasm between the berg's two halves. Later this sight recurred in Erasmus's dreams and he'd wake with his throat closed, imagining what Nils must have felt when the larger half sighed and rolled in the water, grinding a submerged tongue into the smaller half and obliterating the chasm. They did not find even a scrap of Nils's clothing.

For Erasmus this scene came to stand for the twenty-three days during which they battled the ice beyond the twin capes guarding Smith Sound. As they sailed into the great basin, he'd talked himself into sharing some of Zeke's enthusiasm. But by September 3 thin ice was already forming around the *Narwhal* at night, bridging the floes that kept them pressed against Ellesmere and prevented them from crossing to the Greenland side of the sound. Joe gazed at the floes with a long face; any part of Greenland, even this far north where he'd never been, counted as home to him. The distant shores teased him terribly.

"I joined you to look for Franklin," he said to Erasmus, chipping at the ice on deck. "Not for this."

Meanwhile Ned cooked as if he'd never stop, rushing hot soup and coffee and biscuits to the frozen men. He made dried-apple pudding again and again, a food much beloved by Fletcher Lamb and Nils Jensen, who were gone. Although he'd not grieved openly for Fletcher when he died, now that Nils was also gone he set places at the table for the dead men, unable to stop until Erasmus gently reproached him.

Nils was killed on September 6. By September 8 drift ice surrounded them and foot-long icicles hung from the rigging; by September 10 they were confronted by solid pack; by the eleventh they knew that an open polar sea, if it existed at all, lay beyond this barrier of ice. Beyond their reach.

Zeke was stunned by Nils Jensen's death, and disappointed by their failure to sail farther north, but he told the crew they'd done well. "We've charted a long new stretch of coastline," he said, showing them the maps he'd drawn and the features he'd christened. Cape Laurel, Cape Violet, Cape Agatha—his sisters, his mother; but also, and more to the crew's pleasure, Fletcher Lamb Bay and Jensen Point. What pleased them most was Zeke's order that they turn and head for home.

But on September 14 they found their route to the south walled off by a dense mass of ice that had floated in since they'd entered the basin. A stiff wind jammed the ice against the brig and her against the coast; they sailed through hail and snow and freezing rain, which glazed the deck and the rigging. They probed the pack, searching for a passage south but blocked again and again. Plates of ice swept toward the shore, grinding over the gravel and tossing boulders aside before being crushed and heaved by other floes; the rumblings and sudden, explosive cracks made the men feel as if they'd been caught in a giant mouth, which was chewing on the landscape. Their area of movement decreased each hour, until Zeke, who'd stopped eating during the five days of their frenzied oscillation, finally conceded defeat and began to look for a suitable harbor.

Later Erasmus would wish he'd thought to remind Zeke of the advantages of a site that looked southward and eastward. But he was exhausted and so was Zeke, and so were all the men; hail was beating against their faces and they could hardly see what lay before them. From the gloom rose a towering triangular point, backed by smaller pyramids; they swept around it, forced by the wind, and to their great relief found a cove bitten into the point's back side. Sharp walls loomed over them, blocking their view of Greenland; across the Sound, but in the harbor's southeast corner was a small gravel beach and a bit of lumpy ground.

Still it was a poor choice, Erasmus thought, when the sky cleared the next morning. The cove opened to the northwest, the coldest prospect. As they warped the brig closer to the beach, three icebergs swept around the point and grounded on a reef, partially blocking the mouth of the cove and plugging them in like a ship in a bottle.

PART II

5

The Ice in Its Great Abundance

(October 1855–March 1856)

The intense beauty of the Arctic firmament can hardly be imagined. It looked close above our heads, with its stars magnified in glory and the very planets twinkling so much as to baffle the observations of our astronomer. I am afraid to speak of some of these night-scenes. I have trodden the deck and the floes, when the life of the earth seemed suspended, its movements, its sounds, its coloring, its companionships; and as I looked on the radiant hemisphere, circling above me as if rendering worship to the unseen Centre of light, I have ejaculated in humility of spirit, "Lord, what is man that thou art mindful of him?" And then I have thought of the kindly world we had left, with its revolving sunshine and shadow, and the other stars that gladden it in their changes, and the hearts that warmed to us there; till I lost myself in memories of those

who are not;—and they bore me back to the
stars again.
　　—ELISHA KENT KANE, *Arctic Explorations:*
　　The Second Grinnell Expedition in Search of
　　Sir John Franklin, 1853, '54, '55 (1856)

IN PHILADELPHIA IT WAS BEAUTIFULLY CLEAR AND
warm, the chrysanthemums rust and gold in the gardens and the
leaves of the sweet gum radiant on the grass. Alexandra, secure in
her spacious rooms, kept her diary faithfully. It was a form of discipline, she thought. A record of her education as well as a way of
honoring her parents. Her first diary, smooth black leather with gilt
thistles, had been a gift from them. *Today I am eight,* she had written. *I got a box of pencils, a Bible, this book to write in. A promise from
Emily not to touch my paints. I have a bad cold.* Seventeen volumes
now, one for each year since then; the only gap some months from
her fifteenth year, when her parents were killed and she could say
nothing. She wrote:

*I've finished my engraving of the Passaic smelt. Lavinia stopped
after three lessons, she hated cutting up her hands; but I have a gift
for this, I do. Even Mr. Archibault admits that my line is expres-
sive and clear and that I have a fine touch with light and shadow.
In a way I didn't expect it's much more than copying; more like
re-making, re-creating. When I'm working everything else drops
away and I enter the scene I'm engraving. As if I've entered a
larger life.*

I meant to start on a copy of the hand's nerves and tendons but the news set us in an uproar. First we heard that the abandoned British ship Resolute *was found floating in Baffin's Bay. A crew from an American whaler sailed her down to New London; we had hopes they might have met the* Narwhal *and have mail for us, but apparently not. Then Saturday the papers here carried the story of Dr. Kane's rescue. No one can talk about anything else—such enormous good luck, the way the rescue squadron, driven back from Smith Sound, met Esquimaux who'd spent time with Kane's party and been aboard the frozen-in ship.*

Learning that Kane and his men had abandoned their ship and gone south on foot, Lt. Hartstene made his way to Godhavn and discovered the party there, just as they were about to board a Danish brig. The front page of the paper was filled with Dr. Kane's report. Sledge trips, news of Esquimaux living farther north than anyone suspected; long stretches of coastline discovered on both the Greenland and the American sides of Smith Sound; he claims two of his men have viewed an open polar sea. Having endured extraordinary cold and starvation, and a long journey by sledge and small boat, he lost only three members of his Expedition and is now a great hero. Against this his father's behavior stands out even more despicably.

Emily, who visited yesterday with Jane, is as angry as I've ever seen her. Despite the efforts of the Ladies Anti-Slavery Society and others, Judge Kane committed Williamson to prison on Friday, for failing to produce the runaway slaves he's sheltered. One of the antislavery papers notes that 'such a man can surely be no relative of the noble-hearted explorer. His opinion makes every state a slave state. . . . He is the Columbus of the new world of slave-whips and shackles which he has just annexed.' The slaves are safe, Emily says—I'm not sure whether she has direct knowledge of this—but

the abolitionists who aided them may be in prison a long time. The
decision has caused a split in the city, and at every social gathering.
Lavinia sides with me and Emily on this, but when Emily asked
if she'd be willing to let her committee meet here she declined; her
brother and Zeke, she said, might be back any day, and the house
must be ready for them. Later I found her crying. She's not been
sleeping, though she tries to hide this.

I can't blame her for worrying. That Dr. Kane is home, while we
have as yet no word of Zeke and Erasmus; that Dr. Kane is lionized
for discovering the open sea Zeke hoped to find—we can only hope,
Lavinia says, that Zeke and Erasmus are safe and have found some
traces of Franklin. The truth, when one looks past the headlines, is
that while Dr. Kane did remarkable things, he was in the wrong
place; he didn't learn until reaching Upernavik of Rae's discoveries
a thousand miles south and west of where he'd been. Also he lost
his ship. But he is a hero nonetheless; and is not responsible for
his father's detestable decision; and will be in Philadelphia shortly.
Lavinia has asked her brothers to seek an appointment with him,
to find out if he's seen any evidence of the Narwhal. *But apparently*
he's seeing few people.

LATER ERASMUS AND the rest of the crew would learn that their
cove was only a corner of a bay previously named by Kane; their
home only the width of Smith Sound from Kane's winter quarters.
Later Erasmus would lay out calendar pages and his journal entries
and the newspaper stories of Kane's return, matching up days and
trying to understand how the *Narwhal* had failed to cross paths
with Kane's retreat party. They'd missed each other so narrowly
it seemed only fate could have kept them apart. But he'd remind
himself, then, that it had never been their charge to find Kane.

Even as they'd been loading the *Narwhal,* the Navy had outfit-
ted two rescue ships, which had left New York as the *Narwhal* left
Philadelphia. Everyone had understood that they'd head directly
toward Smith Sound, in search of Kane, while the *Narwhal* would
head for King William Land, in search of Franklin. A simple division of labor.

The *Narwhal* had arrived in Smith Sound so late in the season,
and so unexpectedly, that when Erasmus thought of Dr. Kane
at all, he felt sure he'd already been found. By October, though,
Erasmus couldn't spare even a thought for his fellow Philadelphian. Only once, when he was adding to his growing letter to
Copernicus, did he wonder if Dr. Kane had reached this far north.
He wrote:

> *Do you ever feel this in your travels out west? That all the unex-
> plored parts of the world are closing their doors; that so many of
> us, traveling so far, cannot avoid crossing each other's paths and
> repeating each other's discoveries? Perhaps you've passed the Absa-
> roka Mountains, into the Wind River Valley or Jackson's Hole, and
> wondered what it would have been like to be the first one there. I
> wish I could pretend to be another Meriwether Lewis, but those
> days are half a century behind us. Sometimes I have such a feeling
> of people crowding the world. Up here all is emptiness, we see no
> human beings; yet we can't know for sure that we're the first ones
> here. I have no idea where you are. You have no idea where I am.
> I would give anything to know what you're doing this very night.*

Then he returned to work, ashamed of having stolen even a
moment. Although there were men weeping in odd corners; although
those who couldn't write crept up to Ned and Dr. Boerhaave and
asked for help drafting last testaments; although Captain Tyler dis-

appeared periodically and was of little help; still Erasmus tried not to give in to despair. But the *Narwhal* wasn't yet ready for winter, and the ice thickened with each tide.

He did whatever Zeke asked, helping the men dismantle the upper masts and lashing the lower yards fore and aft amidships. Around that framework they laid planks, which housed in most of the upper deck, and a thick layer of insulating felt. Boats and spars and rigging and sails they stowed in a shed hurriedly built on shore, along with all their coal, the supplies from the hold, and most of the plant and animal specimens. Alongside the storehouse they built another hut in which Zeke set up the meteorological instruments.

Through a wavering cloud of frost smoke, Erasmus glimpsed the full moon gleaming. The thermometer read ten degrees, then zero, then ten below; cold hands, cold feet, shoulders hunched against the wind. All the men complained and swore they couldn't get used to it, then did. When the weather permitted, Joe went hunting in the brief slots between the parenthetical twilights. No dovekies, no murres, no ptarmigan; but before the other animals disappeared he shot two musk oxen, seven caribou, and many hares. Erasmus made lists of the meals these might provide, along with their initial store of provisions and the salted fish Zeke had purchased at Godhavn. He might have made another list—on one side Zeke's impulsive maneuvers, which had stranded them here; on the other Zeke's foresight with the supplies that fed and sheltered them. With the help of Joe and Dr. Boerhaave, he dug out the Esquimaux furs Zeke had purchased and fitted each man with a suit.

Later Dr. Boerhaave wrote to his friend William:

I couldn't even tell who it was at first; two furry figures huddled over a moaning third. But it was Isaac, who was careless and exploded his powder box; his hand is in danger. I extracted several shards of metal and sluiced out as much of the powder as I could. A poultice of yeast and charcoal may draw out the rest.

Everyone's cold. This place—in the morning, when the sun is low in the east, the peninsula shadows us. In the afternoon we're shadowed by the hills to our south, later by the three grounded icebergs; Commander Voorhees couldn't have chosen a colder place. Away from him the men refer to the icebergs sarcastically as "Zeke's Follies." Some folly. I meant to be back in Edinburgh by now, writing up papers and arguing happily with you and the others: walking, talking, drinking, thinking. Instead I have only Mr. Wells; but I've grown fond of him. If it were not for him and the work we do together, I think I would feel desperate.

THERE WAS NO POINT, Zeke said, in trying to maintain separate messes for men and officers. Their fuel was limited, they must conserve. Ned and Sean Hamilton moved the galley to a spot under the main hatch. Then Zeke rearranged the sleeping quarters, setting Thomas Forbes to remove the bulkhead between the men's forecastle and the officers' cabin.

"You'd never see this on a whaling ship," Captain Tyler grumbled. "How are you going to maintain discipline, if we're all mixed together?"

"I'm not doing this to be democratic," Zeke retorted. The previous night several of the men's bedclothes had frozen about their feet. "Just to be practical. We have only the one small stove besides the galley stove, and the best way to keep everyone warm is to allow the heated air to circulate."

As a concession to Captain Tyler, Zeke had Thomas build two shoulder-high partitions, each of which stretched from one side of the hull toward the midline, where the stove was set, and stopped a few feet short of it. From this common island the stove radiated warmth impartially fore and aft. Air flowed not only around the stove but also over the partitions, and although sound traveled freely between the men's and the officers' bunks, when the crew lay down they were hidden. When they pulled their stools close to the stove for warmth, the half-ring of officers aft and the half-ring of men forward could see each other, and talk if desired, yet were separated at least by the stove and its pipes. The division was more symbolic than real, yet it served, Zeke argued. By a judicious lowering of the voices and averting of the eyes, the officers might preserve an illusion of privacy. More importantly, they were warm.

Zeke took great pride in this, Erasmus saw, as he did in every aspect of their housekeeping arrangements. Otherwise Erasmus couldn't guess what Zeke was thinking. The mistakes that had lodged them here, the families anxiously waiting for them back home, the true nature of the relics they'd brought from Boothia—if any of these worried Zeke, he gave no sign. Mostly he seemed pleased with himself: that he'd had the good sense to bring the planks and felted cloth that sheltered them, the furs that warmed them, the extra fish to supplement their diet. That he'd had the sense to find Joe, who was so much help. Perhaps he was also pleased that Captain Tyler and the mates had no real function, now that the *Narwhal* was a cramped but stable household, and not a sailing ship.

"What do they know?" Zeke asked Erasmus one afternoon, as they paced the walk along the shore. Well within sight of the ship, for safety's sake, yet far enough away for privacy, Zeke had measured out a promenade and had the men mark it off with wooden wands. Another innovation he was pleased with.

"The whaler's whole being is oriented toward fishing successfully and then getting home before winter sets in," he said. "Captain

Tyler did well enough transporting us where we needed to go, but he knows nothing about the physical and emotional demands of surviving an arctic winter and keeping a crew healthy and cheerful. Have you noticed how sullen he is after dinner? I'm beginning to wonder if he's sick."

"He's foul-tempered enough," Erasmus said. "Should we ask Dr. Boerhaave to examine him?"

"I'll take care of it," Zeke said.

But he was busy with other things—bubbling with ideas, always cheerful, endlessly energetic. By himself he built a latrine of ice; then, while the men watched curiously, a low wall around it to cut the wind. Ned and Barton joined him when he began a walled lane from the ship to the promenade; Robert Carey, with Zeke's laughing encouragement, built a little watchtower overlooking the lane, which Zeke crowned with a roughly carved woman's head. How clever he was, Erasmus thought. Zeke never asked for help, or explained what he was doing. He simply busied himself within sight of the crew and made what he was doing look like fun, until those who lagged behind felt left out. Erasmus was reminded of Zeke's resourcefulness, one of the qualities Lavinia loved.

He was drawn in himself—the last two weeks of October, before the sun disappeared entirely, were filled with giddy play. Miniature ice cottages rose on the floes, and ice castles, palaces, gated walls. To the growing village Erasmus added a model of his father's house, building another, larger and finer, when the ice shifted and crumbled the walls. Dr. Boerhaave built a version of the castle in Edinburgh, and Zeke one of Independence Hall. Mr. Francis and Mr. Tagliabeau jointly sculpted a whale, overwhelming Dr. Boerhaave's moat. Foolish acts, grown men shaping ice like children raising sandcastles—yet the intent was far from casual. Erasmus noted the men's lifted spirits, the renewed sense of camaraderie, and was filled with admiration for Zeke's instincts. Perhaps, after all, Zeke knew what he was doing.

ALTHOUGH ERASMUS NO longer put anything in Lavinia's green journal except for purely scientific observations, in his bulging letter to Copernicus he wrote:

> *Let me sketch one day for you, and let it stand for the whole of our autumn. Half past seven and we rise to the ship's bell, tidying ourselves and our bunks. Some of us tend to the fires; Ned cooks and we breakfast at half past eight. Then the men turn to under the direction of the mates. Clearing the decks, filling and polishing the lamps, measuring out the day's allowance of coal and fussing over our precious stoves, banking snow along the hull, chunking ice from the nearest berg for water, hanging wet clothes from the rigging on washdays—all these duties are finished by lunch. After lunch the men pace the promenade briskly, as ordered by Zeke for their health. Sometimes they play games on the ice. When there was still a bit of light, Zeke and I and Dr. Boerhaave and Joe often went out with our rifles, hoping to shoot a bear or a seal to supplement our diminishing supply of fresh meat. The light was so dim we were seldom successful, but the hunt gave us an excuse to be away from the others for a while. Sometimes we stumbled on Esquimaux artifacts; while we've as yet seen no Esquimaux, we've found remains of ancient encampments: ruins of stone huts, a part of an old sledge, pieces of a stone lamp, harpoon tips. Surrounding these, the bones of walrus and bear.*
>
> *Later in the afternoon, while the men nap or whittle, play cards or repair their clothing, and while Zeke pores over his maps and books or tends to his instruments, Dr. Boerhaave and*

I catalog the specimens we collected earlier. We talk about what we've seen—how nature, in this place and season, is reduced to her bones. In the tropical places I visited with the Exploring Expedition all was lushness, and much obscured by overwhelming detail, but here each thing stands singly and strong. It is so, so beautiful here, despite the danger, despite the discomfort; I would never have chosen to winter here yet it's as if I was waiting my whole life to see this. I stand on the ice, I watch and watch until the dinner bell rings at six. Afterward, in hours I've come to love, we have our school.

Close the hatches, open the hatches, dry the bedding, melt ice. Cook, sleep, hunt, study, sleep. This is how my days are shaped. Joe, Ned, and I killed a bear two days ago, huge and dirty and yellow-white. Before we killed it, it almost killed us. The sun disappeared for good yesterday, October 30, but this doesn't mean, as I once imagined, that we're in continuous night. Instead the nights are black, like our nights at home, but during the days we have twilight—a few minutes less each day but even when the solstice arrives we should still have that glow at noon. The sky is like no sky I've ever seen before. Our masts and shrouds, entirely coated with ice, glimmer against that blue-gray cloth.

Zeke said, "We should use our evenings profitably. Let each of us teach what he knows."

Dr. Boerhaave began teaching the men who couldn't read their letters; Ned assisted him, wonderfully patient because he'd learned to read so recently himself. When Zeke complimented him, he said, "May I teach one of the men to cook? So we might take turns, so I'd have more time to help Erasmus and Dr. Boerhaave with their work?"

When Zeke agreed, Ned chose Barton DeSouza. During Barton's apprenticeship the crew swallowed beans as hard as pebbles, but Barton, whose beard was oddly chopped after part of it froze to his hood, took the jibes good-humoredly and soon grew competent.

Sean Hamilton gave a brief course in butchery; Dr. Boerhaave, using the same frozen carcasses, taught basic anatomy. Erasmus found it delightful to see Thomas Forbes, usually so quiet, arguing with Robert Carey over whether the bone on the table between them was a femur or a fibula. Twice a week Erasmus spread before the men samples of all he'd gathered.

"Fucus," he said, showing them fronds from Godhavn. Isaac Bond was surprisingly interested in the different seaweeds and where they grew.

"Auk," he said. "From Lancaster Sound." Barton DeSouza was fascinated by the structure of the feathers and the quills.

As the men, in turn, taught Erasmus the whalers' names for seals and salmon and cod, he understood that theirs was a different sort of knowledge, but no less valuable than his. He began to know them one by one, and not just as the group of men who did the unpleasant tasks. Sean Hamilton was very quick; Robert Carey was slower but persistent and steady. Ivan Hruska had a wonderful, cheering laugh; Barton DeSouza, who had trouble reading, drew quickly and accurately.

Joe told stories from the Bible, rendered simple and vivid by his long practice preaching to the Esquimaux; he mingled these with tales about the tribes among whom he'd worked. He also gave Zeke language lessons and helped him compile a simple dictionary. In his tattered black book—which still, Erasmus saw, housed the most remarkable hodgepodge of scribbles and extracts and sketches and plans—Zeke noted down words and their English equivalents: *idgloo* = a house; *nanoq* = a bear; *bennesoak* = a deer when it is without its antlers. *Okipok* = the season of fast ice.

Even Captain Tyler and the mates, who usually held themselves separate, were drawn into those pleasant evenings. Mr. Francis demonstrated a whole array of seamen's knots, while Captain Tyler taught some basic navigation. In the darkness Mr. Tagliabeau, who had a wonderful eye for the stars, led groups to the tops of the icebergs. In air so cold their breath formed clouds of snow crystals, he pointed out the whirling constellations.

The second time he did this Erasmus left his outer mitts off for too long while he sketched: November 29, at eight P.M. He froze all but the little finger on his left hand, and the next day woke to find giant blood blisters extending from the tips past the second joints. The blisters ruptured a few days later, rendering his cracked and bloody hands useless for more than a week. But he was lucky, Dr. Boerhaave said; the flesh never blackened or died. Zeke held Erasmus's hands up before the men, pointing out the oozing blood and enormous swelling.

"This is what you must guard against," Zeke said. "This is what happens when you're careless."

Zeke lectured on the open polar sea. Erasmus thought the men would resent this, since the search for it was what had trapped them here. Yet they seemed interested. During their whaling days they'd all seen the open patches of water persisting strangely amid the ice and swarming with fish and sea creatures. Both Ivan Hruska and Captain Tyler had, on earlier trips, seen narwhals crowded into a small polynya, with their horns pointed straight up in the air as their bodies were crammed together.

"The theory of an open polar sea stems from ancient times," Zeke told them. In the lamplight, with his beard shining and his cheekbones flushed, he looked like a young soldier. He made his own heat, he was often sweating. In the cabin he opened his shirt to the waist while others huddled in their jackets.

He held up a diagram of ocean currents. "Parry and others have shown that there are two sites of maximum cold on the globe, one for each hemisphere, both situated near the eightieth parallel. The isothermals projected around these points make it seem likely that, within an encircling barrier of ice, the sea remains perpetually open around the region of the pole." Sabine barked, a tiny exclamation point. By then Erasmus had grown so used to her presence that he hardly registered her bounding over the shelves while Zeke talked, or standing on the table and sniffing at the cracks around the bull's-eye, or sitting, tiny and bright-eyed and white, on Zeke's shoulders as he paced the room.

The men's spirits were good, he thought. Their days and nights were full, and their imaginations were fed by their studies, so that they seldom felt bored. Dr. Boerhaave brought out Agassiz's *Poissons fossiles* and toured the crew through the plates, translating key portions of the text for them as they gawked at the bony relics.

"Nature," he said, "is not random but is the product of thought, planning, and intelligence. The entire history of creation has been wisely ordained."

From extinct fishes he leapt to Thoreau; a great collector of turtles and trout, Dr. Boerhaave said. An avid reader of explorers' accounts, and a good friend of Agassiz's. Erasmus was the one who suggested he share with the men the contents of the books and essays he'd collected in Concord. On the night when Dr. Boerhaave lectured on Thoreau's essay on civil disobedience, Erasmus saw attention on every face.

"There is a higher law than civil law," Dr. Boerhaave said. "The law of conscience. When these laws are in conflict, Thoreau argues that it is our duty to obey the voice of God within rather than that of external authority." He held a tattered magazine in his hand: *Aesthetic Papers*. The first and only issue. Robert Carey raised his hand. "What is 'aesthetic'?" he said.

———

LATER, ERASMUS WOULD look back on those calm months and
wonder what had brought an end to them. Just hardship, he would
think. Enough hardship to disrupt the balance of any small commu-
nity. As the solstice approached the weather bit at them. Routinely it
was twenty-five degrees below zero, then thirty below, then colder,
with a wind that licked through clothes and walls.

Pacing with Dr. Boerhaave on Zeke's promenade, Erasmus would
watch his friend's beard, eyebrows, and lashes grow a crisp white frost,
while icicles hung from his moustache and lower lip. They talked to
keep their minds off the cold. Not of home, nor their friends and
families, nor women—what would have been the point? Better to
avoid any topic that would have drowned them in homesickness. They
explored each other's minds. In the light of the stars and the moon,
the landscape glimmered indistinctly and edges disappeared, until
they could imagine themselves at the moment of Creation. Could it
be, Dr. Boerhaave asked, that the earth and stars and the planets and
their moons had all condensed from swirling clouds of gas? And that
these condensations developed constantly toward man?

The intricate joints of the hand, Erasmus said. The amazing com-
plexities of the eye. From such everyday miracles one might infer a
Creator. The hand and eye are but manifestations, Dr. Boerhaave
replied. The Creator and the great design are the ultimate reality.

Their old difference rose again. A species, Erasmus said, was the
collection of all individuals resembling each other more than they
resemble others, and producing fertile offspring; presumably all
descending from a single individual. A species, said Dr. Boerhaave
as he whirled his arms in circles, was a thought in the mind of God.
Everything on earth was just as God had created it, during the biblical six days and again in subsequent, successive creations after catas-

trophes similar to the biblical flood. Each new set of living beings was progressively more complex.

"Look at Cuvier," he said.

"Look at Lyell," Erasmus retorted.

Talking grew difficult; their beards froze to their neckerchiefs and saliva sealed their lips. The wind tore tears from their eyes and froze their lids together.

On December 21, all they saw of the sun was a red glow at noon. The cabin walls began to drip moisture; the men's furs, dusted with snow and ice, drooped damply when they came inside and stiffened when they went out again. The weakest of the men—Robert Carey, who'd never completely recovered from the dunking that had killed Nils Jensen; Ivan Hruska, who'd always had the stunted look of an undernourished boy—grew reluctant to leave their bunks in the morning and claimed an assortment of aches and congestions. The night school fell apart.

They were hungry, Erasmus thought. Or not so much hungry as filled with violent lusts for all they couldn't have. The meat in the rigging was gone by then, and Joe could find nothing to shoot. Ned and Barton tried their hardest to make appetizing meals, but everything began to taste alike. Dr. Boerhaave took Erasmus aside and said, "You know, you're remarkably pale. Are you feeling all right?"

Erasmus stared at his friend's face, as white as a boiled potato, then looked around at the others. Each complexion was waxy and pale, except where the cold had bitten crusty sores. Four of the men complained of shortness of breath.

"With your permission," Dr. Boerhaave said to Zeke, "I'd like to make a brief medical inspection of the crew each Sunday."

"No one's sick," Zeke said, frowning. "We're doing well."

"No one's sick," Dr. Boerhaave agreed. "Yet. But as ship's surgeon I'd like to take this extra precaution, so nothing gets hidden until it's serious."

"I don't want to encourage malingering," Zeke said. "We can't coddle ourselves up here."

Dr. Boerhaave pressed his lips together. "I simply think it's wise to check them regularly." Zeke shook his head.

Although Erasmus agreed with Dr. Boerhaave's caution, he understood Zeke's reluctance as well; any acknowledgment of sickness made the men nervous. So did the darkness, and the daily task of scraping from bunks and bulkheads the frost that formed from their breath while they slept. It was disturbing, Erasmus thought, to watch the air that had lived inside their lungs turn into buckets of dirty ice. Tossing the shavings over the side, he felt as if he were discarding parts of himself.

SABINE THE FOX was cleaning herself in the tub of snow Zeke kept on deck for her delight. Even those who disliked having her in the cabin were charmed by her habit of burrowing her nose into the snow, tossing it over her back and hindquarters, and then rubbing herself with her paws. She was watching, unconcerned, as Sean and Ivan lugged a scuttle of ice to the melting funnel on the day before Christmas. Then Sean tripped, dropping his side of the scuttle, and Ivan slipped on the spilled ice and fell, thrashing his arms and his legs just as Barton emerged through the hatchway. Ivan's arm knocked Sabine from her tub and hurled her through the air: and in an instant she'd bounced off Barton's thighs and tumbled down the hatch.

She broke both hind legs. Zeke, who rushed from his bunk at the sound of her howls, was too busy comforting her to be of any practical help. Although Erasmus knew he should wring her neck right then, Zeke talked him and Dr. Boerhaave into splinting her bones and then dribbled water from a spoon down her mouth all day. Still he couldn't save her. He wrapped her in a length of gray flannel and buried her under a pile of stones near the promenade. He squatted next to the stones; he wouldn't come in. Erasmus had to go out after him.

"Zeke?" he said. "They've made dinner for us, Christmas Eve dinner. You can't let them down . . ."

Zeke brushed his outstretched hand aside. "Can't I simply have a minute alone?" He exhaled a cloud of frost, shaking his head as he rose. "All right," he said. "Let's go be *cheerful.*"

Joe had hidden seven ptarmigan, which he roasted with the help of Ned: half a bird to a man, a splendid change from salt pork. Isaac, Thomas, Robert, and Barton had secreted a portion of their flour and lard rations for the past several weeks, and with these supplies, and the dried cherries and raisins Sean contributed, they made a delicious duff. Erasmus brought out two of the plum puddings donated by a neighbor at home; Dr. Boerhaave prescribed from the medical stores two bottles of cognac, to protect them all from indigestion.

They ate and drank with good humor, despite Zeke sitting glum at the head of the table, and despite the silence falling after a memorial toast to Nils Jensen and Fletcher Lamb. Isaac pulled himself together and elbowed Barton. "A joke!" he cried. "Every man must tell a joke!"

Barton shook himself and told a coarse story about a one-legged man and a singer. Thomas responded with a joke about a carpenter and a cow. Around the table they went, all except Zeke; when silence fell again Mr. Francis and Mr. Tagliabeau led a round of whaler's songs. Then Ivan flourished his napkin and said to the officers, "Please take your seats in the theater."

Up on deck, under the housing, the men had arranged meat casks and boxes for seats and marked off a stage with a row of candles. In great secrecy they'd gotten up a little skit for the officers, prancing about in the freezing air with their fur jackets tied about their waists like skirts, and their shirts pulled open and tucked down to form flounces around their hairy bosoms. Bulky Sean played a young beauty; Ivan and Barton her jealous older sisters; serious Thomas her mother; and Robert and Isaac the two suitors competing for the beauty's hand as they fended off the sisters' advances. As the melodrama concluded with the duel of Robert and Isaac, frowning and slashing the air with their jack-knives, Sean stood on a candle box and shrieked so shrilly that Erasmus could hardly see for laughing.

Afterward Captain Tyler and the mates brought out the last surprise—three bottles of excellent port. Even as the men fell on it gratefully, and as Erasmus sipped his own delicious ration, he wondered where it had come from. Captain Tyler's bleary-eyed mornings, his snoring deep sleep—had he a private supply of spirits? Erasmus saw Zeke look down at the cup he'd just held to his lips and come to the same realization.

"Captain Tyler," he said coldly. "What is the meaning of this?"

"It's Christmas," the captain said, grinning and waving one of the bottles. "Relax yourself a bit. Celebrate. It is very fine port, is it not?"

"We are carrying no port."

Captain Tyler shrugged. "No ship's captain would travel without a small private stock," he said. "What I do with it is my own business. And what I choose to do with it tonight is share it with our fine crew."

"You are in on this?" Zeke said, turning to Mr. Francis and Mr. Tagliabeau. "I object to this. Very, very strongly."

"More music!" Mr. Francis said. Gathering the men on the makeshift stage, he started up a sailor's hornpipe. Joe played his zither, the men sang and danced, Captain Tyler joined them. Erasmus followed Zeke outside, where they gazed at one another and then at the moon. A complete halo hung around it, with the arc of another perched on top of the first like a crescent head-dress.

"More snow on the way," Zeke said gloomily.

Erasmus wished he could join the frolicking men. The invisible ice crystals filling the air and bending the moon's rays made Zeke's face look ghastly; Erasmus turned his eyes back to the sky.

"Homesick?" he asked. "Lavinia should be lighting the candles on the tree about now. Serving eggnog, and those little ginger cookies our mother used to make. Maybe the rest of the family is there and someone's playing the piano . . ."

"Torture yourself," Zeke said. "Go ahead."

"SHOW HIM YOUR GUMS," Dr. Boerhaave said, standing Sean and Barton in front of Zeke one January Sunday.

Obediently they opened their mouths. "See that?" Dr. Boerhaave said. Zeke leaned toward Sean. "How puffy and red the gums are in the back?"

"And I have a loose tooth," Barton said, reaching up with his right hand. "Here."

Zeke shook his head. "I know," he said. "We need fresh meat. Joe's been out looking for bear every day this week but he's seen nothing yet." Then he returned to his charts. He was making elaborate maps of the coastline, naming every wrinkle.

"My knees and shoulders are aching badly," Dr. Boerhaave said to Erasmus later. "How are yours?"

"Not bad." But he lifted his shirt to show Dr. Boerhaave the dark, bruiselike discoloration spreading down his left side.

"Ned has patches like that all over his arms," Dr. Boerhaave said. "Ivan's old harpoon scar is beginning to ooze. I fear we're in for real trouble." He and Erasmus went through the storehouse and suggested to Zeke that small portions of the few remaining raw potatoes and a little lime juice be added to the daily rations. They worried that everything was running short.

Erasmus counted items again and again, comparing what was left against his lists. All his work and planning, and still he'd miscalculated. Already the candles were almost finished, as was the lamp oil. Joe had made some Esquimaux lamps, which he fueled with the blubber he'd put down in the fall; these helped stretch the candles but were smoky and covered everything with soot. The coal was low enough that they had to ration it and could no longer keep the cabin so comfortably warm. Erasmus found plenty of beans and salt beef and pork, but Dr. Boerhaave said these were exactly the worst things for men beginning to suffer from the scurvy. They needed fresh food, and couldn't get it.

When Erasmus showed Zeke a detailed accounting of their stores, Zeke blamed the shortages on him. "All those days you were fretting in Philadelphia," he said. "How could we have ended up like this?"

Erasmus couldn't answer him. The obvious answer—that they hadn't meant to overwinter—he'd long since realized wasn't true; more and more he understood that Zeke had plotted since the beginning to search for an open polar sea. Only living members of Franklin's expedition could have kept him from this ambition. Zeke had insisted they stock the ship *as if* they might have to overwinter, *as if* they might need these supplies in an emergency, and Erasmus couldn't blame their present straits on ignorance. Somehow, despite all his lists, he'd made mistakes. He hadn't realized how ravenous the cold and the boredom and the physical labor would make them, or how little they could depend on hunting.

Dr. Boerhaave joined Erasmus in the storehouse one dark morning when he was counting the tinned soups for the third time. "This isn't your fault," he said.

Erasmus shook his head. "Then whose fault is it? If I'd planned better . . ."

"Blame Commander Voorhees," Dr. Boerhaave said. "It's *his* expedition, as he never fails to remind us." With his mittened hands he pushed aside a sack of flour and sat on a crate of salt beef.

Erasmus looked down at the array of tins. "I can't . . . don't put me in that position."

"I'm sorry," Dr. Boerhaave said. "I admire your loyalty—I just don't like to see you blaming yourself. He doesn't listen to anyone, he's so preoccupied with his own ambitions that he doesn't think things through. If he'd told us from the beginning we were going to winter up here . . . how could you know what to plan for, if he didn't tell you?"

Erasmus fiddled with the smoking wick in the lamp. "I have to do the best I can," he said. "I promised my sister." One end of the wick sank in the melted blubber, reducing the light to a flicker. "But why *didn't* he just tell me?" he burst out.

"Why indeed?" Dr. Boerhaave said. In the gloom something scuttled along the wall; perhaps a rat. "He sits in there with his papers and leaves you to sort out his mistakes."

Erasmus tried to think of something positive. "In the fall," he pointed out, "he was wonderful about organizing the men."

"And since Sabine's death," Dr. Boerhaave said, "he's been lost in his own world again."

IT WAS TRUE what Dr. Boerhaave had said; some days Zeke seemed to have abandoned his command. Yet even with this to worry about, Erasmus was sometimes peculiarly, privately happy. The animals had disappeared and the landscape was empty: not a plant, not a creature, not an insect or a particle of mold. The only living things he saw besides the men were the rats infesting the brig and the storehouse, further diminishing their supplies. But one day he stood with Dr. Boerhaave and saw sheets of light undulating like seaweeds in the sky. The ice where they stood was bluish gray, the immobilized icebergs a darker gray, the hills in the distance a friendly, velvety black. As he and Dr. Boerhaave discussed what they saw, the arctic's simultaneous sparseness and richness seemed to unfold. In his mind the long journey they'd made, and the plants and animals they'd collected, fell into a beautiful pattern. The dwarfed low willows and birches, hugging the ground to evade the blasting winds; the great masses of mosses and lichens and the sorrel growing like tiny rhubarbs; the small rodents skilled at burrowing—"It all forms a kind of rhythm," Erasmus said, and Dr. Boerhaave agreed. The fact that they didn't fit into it made it no less beautiful.

In Lavinia's journal—what could Zeke's contract mean now?—Erasmus began making extensive notes for a natural history book. Meanwhile Dr. Boerhaave wrote in his medical log:

> *These signs of scurvy so far—*
> *Captain Tyler: abdominal pains, swollen liver, gout in right foot.*
> *Mr. Francis: tubercles on three finger joins, accompanied by pain and stiffness. Mr. Tagliabeau: right premolar lost, other teeth loose, bleeding gums. Seaman Bond: purpurae on forearms. Seaman Carey: left knee grossly swollen; reports a sprain there as a child. Seaman Forbes: bleeding gums. Seaman Hruska: serous discharge from old lance wound. Ned Kynd: excoriated tongue, bruises on both arms.*
>
> *Mr. Wells has those bruises on his side; now I have a few myself. Our lime juice is almost exhausted. I've been prescribing vinegar,*

sauerkraut, and a dilute solution of hydrochloric acid: all I have
left by way of anti-scorbutics. Our commander, who has no symp-
toms at all, prescribes daily exercise on the promenade. And a
cheerful attitude.

He closed the log and picked up his journal. Still he loved to
touch it; a smooth tan spine, with elegant marbled paper on the
boards. He'd brought it with him all the way from Edinburgh.
Whatever he put here Zeke would read; he couldn't put anything
he meant: he copied into it six pages of Thoreau's essay "A Winter
Walk," just for the pleasure of hearing the words in his head, shaping
them with his pen. He put his head down on the cover, amid creamy
moons haloed with red and green swirls, and slept.

ROBERT CAREY WAS CRYING. Erasmus found him wedged
between two crates, his knees tucked under his chin as tears rolled
down his face. To Erasmus's gentle questions he said nothing. Hours
later, when he still wouldn't stop crying, Dr. Boerhaave gave him
some laudanum and carried him to bed. Then Ivan Hruska said no
one ever paid attention to him, that his fellow seamen ganged up
on him and teased him mercilessly. Everyone preferred Robert, Ivan
said, everyone coddled him; he rolled himself in his hammock and
refused food until Dr. Boerhaave threatened to put a tube down his
throat. Sean and Thomas got into a fistfight. Barton let the galley
fire go out. There were arguments, then long tense silences.

One night Erasmus, alone in the cabin, heard from the other
side of the stove an unfamiliar, nasty, muffled laughter. He stepped
through the gap in the partitions to investigate and came upon a
reprise of the Christmas skit, transposed into a coarser key. Isaac,
as the successful suitor, had opened his fly and was waving his thick

erect penis at Sean, who was rolling his eyes in maidenly shock. In the background Barton, as one of the jealous sisters, was swishing his hips. "Give *me* some of that," he was hissing, while Isaac gasped with laughter. "Let *me* . . ." He fell silent when Sean, who saw Erasmus first, elbowed him in the chest.

"Just having a little fun," Isaac said. He tucked himself back in his pants. "Can't hold that against us, can you?"

Erasmus didn't know what to say. Between the cold and the stress and the hunger his own penis felt like a tired leather tube, shrinking away from his hand each time he tried to urinate. What was all this urgent flesh? Before he had time to wonder if the playacting was play, or something more serious, Zeke stepped around the stove and joined him.

"What's going on?" he said. He blinked as if he'd just awakened. The men were silent, apparently abashed.

"Nothing," Erasmus said. "Just a little . . . a little quarrel." Clumsy lie.

"I won't have that," Zeke said. "We're all uncomfortable. But we must stick together, we must be cheerful." When he turned his back, Isaac grabbed his crotch mockingly.

ON JANUARY 24 the southern horizon glowed reddish orange, before fading away in a violet haze. This hint that the sun would return seemed to rouse Zeke at last, although not in a way Erasmus would have chosen.

At dinner Zeke said, "We'll have sun in another month and a half, but we won't be able to free the brig until July, at the earliest. I propose we occupy the spring months with sledge trips north. It's unfortunate about the dogs. But we can pull the sledges ourselves, and the ice belt along the shore will be in excellent shape in April and May. We can examine the coastline north of here, we can follow the trend of the Sound and look for the open polar sea."

Captain Tyler laughed wildly. "If you think we're going to pull sledges like draft horses, that we'll go one inch further north with you . . ."

"You will go where I say," Zeke said. And left the cabin, to walk the promenade in the dark.

Erasmus threw on all his clothes and followed him, too angry to feel the cold although the thermometer outside the observatory read fifty below. "Why did you do *that*?" he shouted, even before he'd reached Zeke. "You couldn't have made the men more anxious if you'd tried."

Zeke continued pacing, leaving a fog trail behind him.

"What is it you *want*?"

Zeke stopped and turned to face him. "What do you think?" As he spoke his face disappeared inside the cloud his breath created. "I want my *name* on something," he called. "Something *big*—is that so hard to understand? I want my name on the map. Your father would have understood."

"My father is dead!" Erasmus called back. "Why would you want to endanger yourself and the rest of us more than you already have?"

Zeke shook his head and his face disappeared again. "Don't turn against me," he said. "Everyone else is—don't you know how much you and your family mean to me?" When the cloud blew away his eyebrows jutted out, entirely white. "Your house was where I grew up," Zeke said more quietly. Now Erasmus stood by his side. "Where I learned everything important. You and your father . . ."

"If something happened to you," Erasmus said, "Lavinia would die. Don't you worry about her?"

"Of course," Zeke said. "About her, and you and your brothers, and what you think of me—I've always wanted to be part of your family, for all of you to be proud of me. If I led a successful sledge trip north, everyone would see what I can do."

"Lavinia loves you no matter what," Erasmus said. What was all this talk about his family? A man in love, a man engaged, might be a little more romantic. "Surely you understand that?"

Zeke's frosted eyebrows drew together. "The men need to get used to the idea," he said. "We're going north."

ERASMUS THOUGHT HE had several months to talk Zeke out of his useless plan; meanwhile he must do what he could to lift the men's spirits. When the sun approached during the second week of February, he and Joe and Dr. Boerhaave took a party out to meet it. They clambered up the hill behind the brig, up and over the two beyond. An arc of light split the horizon, violet and lavender merging into rich brown clouds. Then the shining disk broke free, perched on an icy range. They opened their jackets, the briefest moment, the pale rays touching their throats. Barton cried at the sight, and Isaac pointed at the giant shadows they cast on the snow. It cheered them, Erasmus thought. He was cheered himself and afterward saw mirages for hours, blue and green and pink balls of light. That night they all ate in some semblance of harmony.

When he woke at three A.M. and heard a faint noise, Erasmus thought at first that he was dreaming. The cabin was dark but for the gleam of one tiny blubber lamp. The fire was banked in the stove; Mr. Francis, who had the watch, had fallen asleep at the table. The curtain to his bunk was open but the others were closed and appeared undisturbed. Erasmus couldn't see beyond the stove, but he heard no sound from the men's quarters. The noise was above him, distinctly above him. He put on his boots and his furs and made his way up the ladder.

The noise ceased before he came out on deck. It was completely dark under the housing, much colder than in the cabin but not nearly so cold as it must be outside, where the wind was singing in the shrouds. He hadn't brought a lantern with him, and he would have slipped back down had he not heard another noise just then: a sort of snort or gasp.

"Who's that?" he said sharply.

Someone laughed.

"Speak up," Erasmus said. "Who's out here?"

More laughter, from more than one voice. Then, "Me. Isaac." And "Robert." And "Ivan."

A scuffle, some whispers, a giggle. "All *right*. Me, too—Thomas."

"You're sitting in the dark?" Erasmus said. "What are you doing?" He had a horrid memory of Isaac prancing around, half-clothed. "Who else is here?"

"Me" came a voice from the bow. "Barton."

And Robert—it was Robert who couldn't stop giggling—said, "Sean and Ned are here too."

"Ned?" Erasmus said. Sensible Ned. "Are you trying to kill yourselves?"

"Ssh," Ned said, from behind him. "Whisper."

He lit a candle stub, revealing the men in the feeble light. Bundled up in their fur suits and further wrapped in buffalo robes, they were huddled against the rough plank walls, far too sick and worn for any prancing. They'd been telling stories instead, Erasmus guessed, reliving memories from what seemed like another life. Some had had adventures on Boothia, which Erasmus had envied even through his disapproval: *I spent a night in a tent with a young widow; the breasts of mine were tattooed; mine was warm, warm, warm*—Thomas Forbes, Sean Hamilton, Ivan Hruska. Erasmus moved among them, coming to rest against the stovepipe housing.

"We're warming ourselves," Barton said. "And celebrating the return of the sun."

He held out a teacup with a broken handle, into which Erasmus peered. Water. He sipped, choked, sipped again: raw alcohol. Not Captain Tyler's port, nor Zeke's whiskey, nor Dr. Boerhaave's medicinal Madeira or cognac, which were in any case kept carefully locked away. He looked at the faces, scabby and marked by scurvy spots, bleary-eyed, relaxed. "Where did you get *this*?"

Robert laughed so hard he fell against Ivan. "It's what you put the fishes in!" he said. "The fishes and the little things you bring up from the seafloor."

"I took it," Sean admitted. "From the cabinet, last night." He held up an old oil bottle, half full of Erasmus's preserving alcohol.

"You drained it from my specimens?" Erasmus said. "Once you break the seals and drain off the alcohol the specimens are ruined, just *ruined* . . ."

"We wouldn't do that," Ned said. "Sean took one of the unused bottles of spirits."

"Lucky me," Erasmus said. He sipped again; the strong spirits burned the sores on his tongue.

"Lucky us, I'd say," Barton added. "Who wants to drink essence of dead fish?"

The men writhed with stifled laughter. "This is so bad for you," Erasmus said. "Never mind what Commander Voorhees would say if he caught you—alcohol only makes you *feel* warm, you'll all get frostbite." He took the candle from Ned and moved toward Ivan. "Let me see your hands and your face."

Ivan pushed his hood back and held out his hands. His left little finger and the flesh below it were waxy white, and another dead-white patch shone beside his nose. Erasmus groaned. "Look at this."

He passed the candle to Sean. "Each of you look at your neighbor and see if anyone else has frozen spots."

Only Isaac did, a patch at the base of one thumb. Erasmus told Ned to hold his hand over Isaac's, while he placed his own on Ivan's frozen flesh. Still they were all speaking quietly; and still everyone but him was sipping from the teacup and the bottle. "We must all go down now," Erasmus said. "I'll decide whether to tell Commander Voorhees about this in the morning."

"It's only a little celebration," Ned said in his ear. "We have small enough chance for it . . ."

And this was true, Erasmus knew. The men were smiling; their quarrels forgotten, their bad humor gone. Was it so bad, what they'd done? He'd been unable to sleep himself, bored and cabin-sick below, and up here where the air was fresher and no one was fighting it was amazingly pleasant. He lifted his hands; Ivan's frozen spots seemed to have thawed without damage.

"Couldn't we stay a bit longer?" Barton wheedled. "You're welcome to stay with us."

He knew he shouldn't; he knew he ought to order them below, or discipline them, or at least not condone what they were doing by his presence. But he felt as if he'd stepped outside time for a minute, as if all the pressures of the last few months had dropped away. He sat; he took the offered teacup. He listened without comment as the men mocked Zeke and his plans for sledge trips, and he told himself that by doing so he was letting them blow off steam. He felt warmer after the teacup passed his way. Ned sat beside him and spread a buffalo robe over both of them, so that his legs warmed and his face radiated against the cool air. Barton passed around some pemmican—where had he gotten this? It was hidden in the storehouse, deep in a cask, only for use on sledge trips—and Erasmus chewed dreamily.

The men spoke about other trips, whales and seals they'd taken, bad captains and good. Ned told about his travels in the Adirondack Mountains, and Barton about a trip to Portugal. It was cold, Erasmus knew it was cold, but he was warm and every time he meant to rise and lead them into the cabin someone was telling a story, which he didn't want to interrupt. The candle burned out and they sat in darkness, listening to each other. Each, despite the shape of his story, saying the same thing: *I am here. I am here, I am here.*

When the hatch door popped open, the sound was as shocking as the lamplight flooding out. Zeke, showing first his hair and then his face and torso and legs, a rifle cradled in his arms, rose among them as if from a grave.

"What's going on?" he said. "Visitors? Are there Esquimaux?" His yellow hair was matted with sleep; his jacket was open and his boots unlaced.

Erasmus stood, surprised at his own unsteadiness. "Everything's fine," he said soothingly. "None of the men could sleep, so they came up here where their talk wouldn't disturb the rest of us. I woke a while ago and came up to make sure they were all right."

Zeke held the lantern high, scanning Erasmus's face; then he bent and swung it before the sitting men. Barton's eyes were swollen, Sean's cheeks were red, Ivan still had the bottle in his hand. "You're *drinking*!" he said. "Without permission, in the middle of the night . . ." He spun toward Erasmus again. "Even you," he said. "Even you."

Erasmus was looking down at his boots when Zeke's rifle, slashing horizontally through the air, caught him square in the gut. He fell against the rail, unable to catch his breath.

"What is *wrong* with you?" Zeke shouted. "I try and try to take care of you, to keep us all safe and in shape to accomplish something in the spring, and while I'm sleeping you sneak off like thieves. Wait until Captain Tyler sees this, what our laxity has come to . . ." He hurled himself back down the ladder and returned a minute later, even angrier.

"Mr. Francis is asleep at his post," he said to Erasmus. "Or passed out; his breath stinks of wine. Captain Tyler is lying in his bunk in a drunken stupor and can't even raise his head—was this your idea? Or did Tyler and Francis set out to corrupt you all? I *knew* they were drinking . . ."

"I," Erasmus gasped, still unable to catch his breath. "I . . ."

"We had nothing to do with the captain," Barton interrupted. "That's the captain's own supply, he only shares now and then . . ."

"You're hateful," Zeke said. "All of you. You can't be trusted with anything, you have no pride, no discipline, no sense of *esprit de corps.*"

"It was the sun they were celebrating," Erasmus said. "They shouldn't have taken the alcohol but it was harmless, really, and I'd just about persuaded them to return to bed when you arrived."

"You," Zeke said.

He lowered himself a few steps down the ladder. "If I could I'd toss you all outside on the ice," he said. "But that would make me a murderer. You'll not see your beds for the remainder of the night, though. You like it so much up here, you stay here till breakfast." He slammed the hatch cover behind him, bolting it from the inside.

The men laughed drunkenly, amused at Zeke's display of temper and aware, Erasmus thought, of Zeke's temporary powerlessness. Up here all the traditional punishments were useless. They were already on short rations, and Zeke couldn't reduce them further without risking their lives; they couldn't be set on the shore in solitude, or confined on the brig any more than they were; they couldn't be mastheaded or set extra tasks outside: it was impossibly cold. They straddled such a fine line between life and death that they were, paradoxically, safe. Or so they seemed to think.

"We have four hours until breakfast," Erasmus said. "And it's well below freezing." He clutched his tender middle with one hand. "We have to keep moving."

He made everyone rise. They paced the deck in a languid oval, slowing as the liquor wore off and exhaustion overtook them. Barton dropped out of the line surreptitiously, propped himself against one of the lifeboats, and snoozed. Ivan kept walking but stopped swinging his arms; Sean lost a mitten. By the time the breakfast bell rang and Mr. Francis, sheepfaced and sullen, unbolted the hatch, they'd all been frostnipped: a heel, some fingers; lips, cheeks, a chin.

Later Zeke railed at them and then demanded that Erasmus turn over all his preserving alcohol, and Dr. Boerhaave all his medicinal brandy and Madeira. These he locked ostentatiously away. From Captain Tyler he demanded all his private supplies, but although the captain produced a half-case of port, no one but Zeke believed this was all he had.

"I'm *sorry*," Erasmus said to Zeke: on the promenade, in the cabin, outside the latrine. Was Zeke going to hold a grudge forever?

Zeke gazed at him stonily. "You betrayed my trust."

"I was trying to *help* you," Erasmus said.

Still Zeke shunned him, speaking to him only when absolutely necessary. At night, inside the cabin, the air was hazed with tension. Joe, who'd slept through the disastrous party, pitched a caribou-skin tent beneath the plank housing and began sleeping there. Dr. Boerhaave began reading a chapter of *David Copperfield* out loud each night—a way, he told Erasmus, of binding everyone together and lightening the mood. But only Ned, ashamed of his role and frightened by Zeke's frigid mood, joined Erasmus in apologizing outright.

Tired, hungry, scurvy-ridden, they moved through March in a pale imitation of their old routine. The sun, now hanging a few degrees above the horizon and gilding the mountains, cheered them despite the continued cold. They ate pickled cabbage, hardtack, salt pork and beef; all their fresh meat was gone. Zeke continued to draw up plans for sledge trips and Ned, somewhat shamefaced, helped him, thawing casks of pemmican and repacking it into small bags. He no longer helped Erasmus and Dr. Boerhaave with their work; Zeke kept him busy all the time, assisting with the meteorological records as well as the travel preparations.

One morning Zeke took Ned to determine the condition of the ice belt north of them. As soon as they left, the mood lightened on the brig. Joe trapped two foxes that afternoon, which Erasmus and Dr. Boerhaave were helping him skin and butcher. Everyone was looking forward to dinner when Zeke and Ned returned, carrying with them a human skull.

"We found an Esquimaux grave," Zeke said, resting the skull on the capstan like a prize. "Three mummified bodies wrapped in skins, and this—isn't it something?"

Erasmus, easing a fox hide from its tricky attachment over the heel, looked at Dr. Boerhaave, who was blotting the blood. Only months ago, Zeke had refused to touch the graves of Franklin's crew. Dr. Boerhaave, as if he heard what Erasmus was thinking, raised an eyebrow. Those had been the graves of Englishmen.

Joe stuck his knife into one of the fox haunches and examined the skull: brown, stained, old. "You broke open a grave?"

"It was already open," Zeke said. "Some bears had pushed away the rocks at the foot."

"And you moved the rest," Joe said.

Zeke rested his hand on the skull, looking away from the fox parts. Yet he would eat with the rest of them, Erasmus knew. No matter how sharply he remembered Sabine. He would have to eat.

"We did," Zeke said. "What was the harm in that? When we try out our sledges, I mean to bring one of those mummies back, for the museum at home."

"It's *wrong*," Joe said. "The spirits of these people can't rest if their graves are disturbed."

Joe stared at Zeke and Zeke stared back, until Joe left the deck.

Ned picked up Joe's knife and Joe's task, trying to shape pieces that would be appetizing and not resemble fox. Afterward he stood silently at the stove, although he would rather have helped Erasmus prepare the skins. *Sew up from the inside any bullet or knife holes,* Erasmus had taught him. He'd made notes. *Rub on the inside of the skin as much of the mixture of alum and arsenic as will stick there. Wrap a little oakum around the bones of each leg, to keep them away from the skin.*

But Erasmus was working away without him, not even asking if he wanted to help. After supper, though, Erasmus joined him on his nightly walk to fetch clean ice from the Follies. "I appreciate what you're trying to do," Erasmus said.

"Do you even *know*?" Ned asked.

"I know you're trying to keep Commander Voorhees company," Erasmus said. "Make him feel less isolated. He's still angry at me, he won't confide in me. I know you're trying to take up the slack."

"Something's wrong with him," Ned said. "He talked all day while we were out, he feels like everyone's against him. Someone has to listen to him."

They'd reached the first iceberg; together they began prying off chunks and heaving them into the washbasin. "My father got like this," Ned said. "Living on dreams, cut off from everyone. Flailing out at anyone around the minute he was criticized."

"It helps us all, what you do," Erasmus said. "Whatever you can do to calm him."

Ned made a face. Each time Ned did something like this, Erasmus realized, even a day's walk with Zeke, he set himself off both from the other men and from Captain Tyler and the mates. Soon he'd be stranded. As they dragged the ice back to the brig, Erasmus reminded himself that he and Dr. Boerhaave must be particularly careful to include Ned in their activities.

Inside the cabin Captain Tyler, who used to sit almost on top of the stove, positioned halfway between the men and the officers, glanced slyly at Erasmus and shifted his stool all the way to the men's side of the partitions. He'd been doing this for weeks: murmuring, murmuring—what was he saying?

"Can you hear him?" Erasmus whispered to Ned.

"I can't," Ned said. He packed the ice more tightly in the melting funnel. "He never does that when I'm in there."

Erasmus strained his ears, pretending unconcern when Mr. Francis and Mr. Tagliabeau slipped through the gap as well. Zeke was pacing the promenade, guarding the brig against nothing and no one with his rifle in his arms—unaware, Erasmus thought, that his command was slipping away. There would be no sledge trips, Erasmus heard Captain Tyler telling the men. Was that what he heard? We'll be out of here the instant the ice breaks up. Low laughter followed. Only when Dr. Boerhaave came in and said, "Are you feeling sick?" did Erasmus realize he was clutching his stomach.

Later, after everyone else had gone to bed, Erasmus and Dr. Boerhaave sat at the cabin table by the sputtering light of a salt-pork lamp. They couldn't talk about what was going on; anyone might be awake and listening.

"Try to do some work," Dr. Boerhaave said. "You'll feel better."

For a second he rested his hand on Erasmus's forearm. He was breathing slowly and deeply: in, out, in, out, looking into Erasmus's eyes. Erasmus felt his own breathing steady into a rhythm that matched his friend's. He took out his letter case and wrote to Copernicus about that skull, so delicate and troubling; halfway through, he found himself writing instead about Ned's attempts to calm Zeke. Dr. Boerhaave opened his volume of Thoreau's *A Week on the Concord and Merrimack Rivers*. Since Zeke's punishment of the drinking men, he'd begun using his journal solely to record passages from his reading. Now he copied:

> *"But continued traveling is far from productive. It begins with wearing away the soles of the shoes, and making the feet sore, and ere long it will wear a man clean up, after making his heart sore into the bargain. I have observed that the after life of those who have traveled much is very pathetic. True and sincere traveling is no pastime, but it is as serious as the grave, or any part of the human journey, and it requires a long probation to be broken into it."*

He turned the journal so Erasmus could read what he'd written. "Thoreau gave me this copy himself," he said. "He published it at his own expense."

Erasmus, puzzled, said, "And you copy his words out because . . . ?"

"Because they're worth learning." He cast his eyes in the direction of Zeke's bunk, and for the first time Erasmus understood that Dr. Boerhaave's journal had become an act of covert rebellion.

BARTON COLLAPSED FIRST, then Ivan, then Isaac; Sean and Thomas were very weak and after Mr. Francis fell down the ladder, tearing a chunk of flesh from his knee, the wound refused to heal and he too was confined to bed. Those who could keep to their feet nursed the others, preparing and serving meals and emptying slops and laundering bandages, drawn together again by their common crisis. They weren't starving, exactly: they still had food, although it was the wrong sort. Joe stalked a bear but lost it. There were walrus, he suspected, south of the brig, but as yet he'd seen none. He'd had no luck trapping since that anomalous pair of foxes.

Erasmus, moving among the sick as Dr. Boerhaave's chief assistant, was shocked at how quickly Mr. Francis deteriorated. The wound bled, suppurated, refused to close, deepened; in a week the bone was exposed. Captain Tyler sat with him for hours, and Erasmus was touched by this kindness until the afternoon when, bending over Mr. Francis shortly after the captain left him, he smelled brandy and realized his stupor was not just the result of infection.

Outside, far from Zeke, Erasmus seized Captain Tyler by the arms and shook him. "What are you doing?" he said. "Drink yourself to death, for all I care—but how can you give that poor man spirits? It's the worst thing for him, the very worst thing."

Captain Tyler pulled away with a growl. "Lay hands on me again," he said. "Touch me like that again and . . . Mr. Francis is a dead man. Why shouldn't he have some comfort in his last days? Dr. Boerhaave spares the laudanum—for you, for his *friends,* we're all going to die up here and he wants to make sure your last days are peaceful. The brandy eases my friend."

Two days later Mr. Francis died in his sleep. Thomas was too sick to work, but Ned and Robert managed to put together a rough coffin. Captain Tyler, Mr. Tagliabeau, Erasmus, and Zeke carried the body to the storehouse, and Zeke read the service for the burial of the dead, although they couldn't bury him. Later Erasmus, packing

up Mr. Francis's effects, looked briefly at his journal before handing
it over to Zeke.

March 2: Snow and fog. I have no energy.

March 3: More snow. Slept all day.

*March 4: Wind, very much wind. Could not sleep and felt tired
all day.*

March 5: Snow and wind. Much pain in my knee.

*March 6: Clear sky, very cold. The knee is worse and there is a
smell.*

March 7: Colder. Fainted when Dr. B. changed my dressings.

March 8: Felt very bad.

March 9: Felt very bad. If I could only see Ellen . . .

THE DAY AFTER that bleak ceremony, Erasmus was chopping ice
when five figures appeared near the tip of the point. By the time
he'd raced into the cabin, alerted everyone, and gathered those who
could move on the bow, the figures had reached the brig and were
peering gravely up at them. Zeke greeted the Esquimaux in their
own language, although he still needed Joe's help in interpreting
their responses.

Ootuniah was the name of one of the men; Awahtok another.
Erasmus couldn't catch the names of the three younger men, who
hung behind the first pair and seemed hardly more than boys. All
five were dressed in fur jackets and breeches, with high boots made
from the leg skins of white bears. The men's feet, Erasmus saw, were
sheltered by the bears' feet, with claws protruding like overgrown
human toenails. Walking, the men left bear prints on the snow.

"They'd like to come up," Joe said, after speaking with them for
a minute.

"It's too risky to let them all aboard at once," Zeke said. "Tell them one, the oldest one, may come. The others must remain outside for now."

Inside the deckhouse Ootuniah fingered Joe's tent approvingly. He opened the flap and stuck his head inside, then said something that made Joe laugh. Joe opened the hatch and led the way down the ladder, which Erasmus thought Ootuniah might find unfamiliar. But Ootuniah descended as calmly as if he'd been using ladders all his life. Inside, he opened the bunk curtains, picked up the books, fondled the stove. Erasmus saw him slip a wooden cooking spoon into his jacket.

Ootuniah squeezed between the stove and the partitions before anyone could stop him. But Dr. Boerhaave, who'd darted belowdecks as soon as he sensed what was going on, had managed to move the sick men onto stools and chests, so that they were sitting upright when Ootuniah saw them. Ootuniah smiled and said some words of greeting, which Joe translated. Then Joe added, for the men's benefit, "Don't be frightened, he's friendly."

Was he? Nothing seemed to surprise their visitor, Erasmus thought. Not the *Narwhal* itself, nor the number or condition of the crew. Dr. Boerhaave whispered to him, "What do you think of this? It's almost as if they've been keeping watch on us, and took Mr. Francis's death for a sign that we're weak enough to be approached safely."

Behind Ootuniah's back, Dr. Boerhaave signaled the men to sit up straight and smile. But when Ootuniah finally sat down at the table, the first thing he said, as Joe translated it, was, "Your people are sick. Do you have meat?"

Before him was a plate of salt pork and beans and bread, which Zeke had asked Ned to prepare. Ootuniah poked the food with his finger and then ignored it. "Only this food," Zeke said, and then translated his own words slowly. He looked up at Joe. "Did I say that right?"

Joe nodded. "Tell him," Zeke added, "or tell me how to tell him: 'We would like to trade with you for meat. We have needles and beads and cask staves. Do you have meat to spare?'"

Joe spoke to Ootuniah and listened to his response. "They have some walrus meat," he reported to Zeke. "Ootuniah says if you will allow the others aboard, he'll trade with us."

Zeke thought for a moment. "Not in here. But we'll receive them in the deckhouse."

Ootuniah shrugged when Joe spoke to him, then rose, went up on deck, and spoke to the group below. They ran across the ice floes, disappearing behind a line of hummocks to return with a heavily laden sledge drawn by eight dogs. They couldn't have been hiding there for long, Erasmus thought. But they might have spent days farther off, on the other side of the point—what an odd feeling, to think that the brig had been under observation!

The Esquimaux scrambled into the deckhouse, bearing great lumps of blubber and walrus meat. Erasmus and Dr. Boerhaave led the sick men up one by one, leaning them like bundles against the bulwarks. Ned and Sean put a handful of precious coal in the deck stove and brought up an iron cooking pot. In exchange for five cask staves the Esquimaux offered some chunks of meat, which Ned quickly boiled. They ate and ate, the crew slurping the hot broth and tearing at the parboiled flesh, the Esquimaux taking their own portions raw, alternating slices of meat and blubber. Zeke, after the first frenzy, said in a low voice to Joe, "See if they'd trade those dogs as well."

"They won't," Joe said after some discussion. Erasmus thought there'd been a lot said in Ootuniah's language to yield these few words in English. Yet Zeke, who claimed to understand many words now, didn't seem uncomfortable.

"It's been a hard winter, and many of their dogs have died," Joe continued. "They can't spare this team." He talked with Ootuniah more, and also with Awahtok. Wiping his mouth, he said to Zeke, "This is a hunting party; they come from across Smith Sound, from a small village called 'Anoatok,' I think. They must bring the sledge and the dogs and the walrus back to their families."

"How far away is their home?" Zeke asked. "Why haven't we seen them before?"

"It's some days' journey across the Sound," Joe said. "They believe no Inuit live on this side—they come here only to hunt."

Ootuniah spoke again, at some length, and Joe's face grew still. He asked something brief, then repeated it. Ootuniah said a word Erasmus thought he recognized, and when Joe turned back to Zeke, his eyes were round.

"They ask if we are friends with 'Docto Kayen.'"

"What?" Zeke said, leaping to his feet.

"That's what he said. He says last winter, and the winter before, they knew white men on the other side of the Sound. Dr. Kane, and his men. They lived in what he calls a 'wooden *idgloo*,' like this one. And had no luck hunting, and grew very sick. Ootuniah hunted for them, and traded with them. Last spring the party abandoned their ship and went south."

Zeke stared down at his feet for a long time. It would take weeks, Erasmus understood later, before Zeke would really absorb this information or what it meant. For now, he made only a calm proposal.

"I'd like to make a treaty with them," Zeke said. "If they'll continue to bring us food, and perhaps some dogs, we'll trade them iron and wood and other things they need. I need their help and the loan of sledges and dogs. In return I'll help them in every way I can. Like Kane did. Tell them I'm a friend of Kane's, and wish to be their friend as well."

There was more conversation, some of which Zeke seemed to understand but most of which Joe had to translate. "They thank you for this offer of friendship," Joe said. "They'll leave us half their walrus meat as a token of peace. And will discuss your proposal with their families. For now they say they must go home. They wish us well."

Zeke gave them all gifts of pocketknives. In return, Ootuniah gave Zeke an ivory-handled knife he'd concealed in his boot.

"He must have made the blade from one of Kane's cask hoops," Zeke said, turning the knife in his hand. "How do we know they haven't murdered Kane's entire party?"

Joe shook his head. "If they'd wanted to," he said, "they could have murdered all of us. Instead they've given us walrus, when I can't find any to save my life. Why would you think they're hostile?"

In the flurry of leave-taking, the iron cooking pot disappeared, and two spoons, a lantern, and a large piece of wood from the railing. The next day, when Erasmus went out to the storehouse, he found the door pried open. Only an axe and a barrel of blubber were missing—but Mr. Francis's coffin had been moved a few inches. As if, Erasmus thought, the Esquimaux crowding around it and peering down had bumped it gently and in unison with their bear-clawed toes.

6

Who Hears the Fishes When They Cry?

(April–August 1856)

Unfortunately, many things have been omitted which should have been recorded in our journal; for though we made it a rule to set down all our experiences therein, yet such a resolution is very hard to keep, for the important experience rarely allows us to remember such obligations, and so indifferent things get recorded, while that is frequently neglected. It is not easy to write in a journal what interests us at any time, because to write it is not what interests us.

—Henry David Thoreau, *A Week on the Concord and Merrimack Rivers* (1849)

ERASMUS HELD A CARIBOU SKIN IN HIS LAP, SCANNING it in the dim light until he found one of the telltale scars. He set his thumbnails on either side of the perforation. "Like this?" he asked. Across from him, on another cask, Dr. Boerhaave sat surrounded by the heaps of skins they'd obtained from the Netsilik. Their knees were almost touching; beyond the yellow circle cast by the oil lamp, the rest of the storehouse was dark.

Dr. Boerhaave framed a similar wound with his thumbs. "Richardson did this during Franklin's expedition to the Barren Grounds. Or so my friend William Greenstone claims. Let's try."

They dug in their nails, squeezing inward as if to express pus from a wound. Both were rewarded by the sudden appearance of a fat white grub, the shape and size of a little bean.

Dr. Boerhaave peered at his. "That's it," he said. "The third instar of the warble fly."

"Shall we?" Erasmus said.

"Richardson claimed they tasted like gooseberries."

They popped the grubs in their mouths. "It's rather good," Dr. Boerhaave said, after some tentative chewing. "Fresh-tasting, a little sweet."

Erasmus swallowed. "The Indians of the Coppermine River eat these?"

"Richardson claimed they treasure them. As we should. After all they are a form of fresh meat. And they saved Richardson and some of the other men from starvation. Really the man is an admirable naturalist."

Erasmus popped another from its hiding place and ate with more relish. One skin at a time, they searched for the wounds the larvae had bored before settling in for their sleepy winter's growth. As they worked they talked about other, pleasanter times, hunting larger game. Dr. Boerhaave recalled grouse on the Scottish moors and the seals of Spitzbergen. Erasmus said, "Spearing fish is very nice—I used to do it with my brothers, as a boy."

"Yes?" Dr. Boerhaave said. "How?"

Erasmus counted his little white treasures: eighteen, nineteen, twenty. "We went early in the spring, just after the ice melts and before the water weeds grow," he said. "When the fish are crowded together in the shallow warmer water. They're like us, then—still half-asleep from the winter, slow moving. We'd patch up the seams of our boat, and repair our spears and gather pitch-pine roots, then launch the boat at a small lake near our house."

He tucked his cold hands inside his fur jacket. "My brother Copernicus made an iron fire crate, which hung out over the water from the bow. On a still evening, very late, we'd light a fire in the crate and push off into the lake."

He was silent for a moment then, remembering the secret beauties of those nights. Where was Copernicus now?

"The fire lit the water," he continued. "A circle of light all around the boat, which let us see several feet down. Some of the fish hung with their bellies turned up to us. Others swam the way they do in summer. There were eels, turtles—the fish were so easy to spear that I felt like a criminal. When our fuel burned out we'd paddle home by the stars. A great fish roast for breakfast—what I wouldn't give for a grilled perch right now!"

Dr. Boerhaave, arranging the grubs on a tin plate, made a wry face. "Fish murderer," he said. "One of the things that made me want to meet Thoreau was an early essay he wrote about the joys of fish spearing; and then the way he grumbled later about the fate of fishes. Somewhere he talks about fish as if they have souls. About their virtues, and their hard destiny, and the possibilities of a secret fish civilization we don't appreciate. 'Who hears the fishes when they cry?' he wrote. He worries about the strangest things."

"All these interesting people you know," Erasmus said. "Thoreau, Agassiz, Emerson, some of them so famous—did you ever want to be famous yourself?"

Dr. Boerhaave ate another grub. "You mean the way Commander Voorhees does?"

"I . . ." Erasmus said guiltily. "I guess I do mean that."

Dr. Boerhaave shook his head. "I don't think about it. Somehow I always knew I wasn't cut out for that—I'm lucky, in a way. I never wanted anything more than the chance to do some useful work. It matters to me that I contribute my bit to our knowledge of the natural world. But not that people *recognize* me. I suppose I was cut out to be a kind of foot soldier—it always seemed like those of us in the background have the time and privacy to get the real work done. What about you?" He smiled fondly. "Do you hunger for glory?"

"I hunger for roast beef," Erasmus said, returning his friend's smile. "But glory—I don't know, I suppose I'm like you. I'd like my *work* to be admired, but I hate my *self* to be singled out. Shall we bring in our treats?"

They brought the plate belowdecks, where more than half the men were confined. Sean, picking at his gums, had brought out a chunk of what he thought was old food but which turned out to be his own flesh. Ivan and Robert had both lost teeth and could chew only with difficulty; Mr. Tagliabeau had been seized with biliary colic and Captain Tyler was recovering from a urinary obstruction, which had tortured him until he passed a large stone. Almost everyone suffered from hemorrhoids, which made them bad-tempered; and they were hungry as well as riddled with scurvy.

"We have something good for you," Dr. Boerhaave announced.

Joe, who was still on his feet, looked at the tin plate. "Oh, good," he said. "From the hides? I've heard about these, I should have thought of this myself." He took two and passed the plate to Sean and Ivan.

"What are they?" Sean asked.

"It's not important," Joe said. "Just eat them."

"Nothing goes in my mouth without I know what it is," Sean grumbled. When Dr. Boerhaave finally explained, most of the men refused to touch the grubs. Zeke ate heartily, Joe calmly and steadily; Ned, after some persuasion, also ate a few. Erasmus and Dr. Boerhaave ate the rest and then returned to the storehouse.

"It's a good idea," Dr. Boerhaave said. "But useless if we can't get them into the men who most need them. We could ask Ned to smuggle them into some soup, but cooking will destroy their value."

They gathered a few more skins and returned to work. "If the ice would just open up enough for the seals," Erasmus said.

"All the animals will be back before long," Dr. Boerhaave said. "We just have to hang on a few more weeks."

But on April 13 Zeke announced that he was done with waiting. "If the Esquimaux won't come to us," he said, "we'll go to them. We must have help hunting. We must have dogs."

On the table he spread Inglefield's flawed map of lower Smith Sound; then he abutted his own charts of the Ellesmere coast, up to the point where they were frozen in. "The crossing party will be composed of myself, Dr. Boerhaave, Joe, and Ned." While Erasmus and Dr. Boerhaave stared at each other, Zeke added, "It's thirty or forty miles across the Sound to Greenland, and the village the Esquimaux described can't be far. We'll take the middle-sized sledge, so we can bring back as much meat as possible. With luck we'll have dogs to pull it on the return trip."

"The composition of the traveling party," Erasmus said. "Surely . . ."

"I must have Joe," Zeke said. "For his skill with a rifle, as well as his knowledge of the language. I'd prefer not to leave you without the services of a surgeon, but we'll be in more danger and so Dr.

Boerhaave must come. You're needed here, as Captain Tyler and Mr. Tagliabeau are both sick."

But this was a punishment, Erasmus thought with dismay, as much as a practical decision. He was being punished for that night in the deckhouse with the drinking men. Separated, purposefully, from his friend. "Let *me* come," he said. "Instead of Ned." He touched Dr. Boerhaave's shoulder.

"You can't," Zeke said. "Why can't you understand that? I need you here, taking care of the men."

Dr. Boerhaave stepped forward. "If Erasmus has to stay," he argued, "why not leave Ned to help him care for the sick? We don't need a cook while we're out on the ice—wouldn't it make more sense to take one of the larger, sturdier men?"

"I need someone I can trust," Zeke said. "Someone who'll accept direction without questioning me."

My fault, Erasmus thought. If he'd managed to placate Zeke, Zeke wouldn't have turned to Ned.

Ned squared his shoulders. "I'll go," he said. "I'd be glad to go."

"I'm afraid to go," Dr. Boerhaave confessed to Erasmus later. "I don't want to, but it's my duty. What if something happens to Joe or Ned?"

They left the brig on April 16. Zeke made a speech to the men left behind; Ned pressed Erasmus's hands; Dr. Boerhaave embraced him and whispered in his ear, "Shall a man go and hang himself because he belongs to the race of pygmies, and not be the biggest pygmy that he can?" While Erasmus puzzled over that cryptic comment, the crossing party harnessed themselves to the sledge, heading for the place they'd only heard named once: Anoatok.

IN THEIR ABSENCE, Erasmus bent his energies toward improving the health of his companions. He was stronger than anyone else—perhaps from the grubs, which he ate every day for the rest of April, although no one else would touch them. Each time he ate he thought of Dr. Boerhaave. He let himself elaborate on the daydream he'd had for months: that somehow, when they finally reached Philadelphia, he might persuade his friend to settle there. Just across the creek from his home, a small stone house had been sitting vacant for several years. Dr. Boerhaave might live there, he thought—privately, yet just a short stroll from the Repository. Erasmus would give him a key. They might meet there daily; they might work on their specimens together. Sometimes they might dine together and sit by the fire afterward, reading companionably and drinking soft red wine. Nothing would separate them then.

He decorated that small stone house in his mind: the most comfortable armchairs, the neatest linen. Then suddenly there was wildlife around, and he dropped his daydreams and hunted with a passion and accuracy he'd never known before. He shot a burgomaster gull, three ptarmigan, and two caribou—the first since October. The men ate the venison gratefully and grew stronger. Ivan, the first to recover, helped Erasmus shoot a seal at a newly exposed breathing hole. One seal, then crowds of them climbing out to bask in the sun; Sean and Barton caught two more. Barton, who'd twice worked on a Newfoundland sealing ship, taught the others to eat the dark, oily flesh with slices of fresh blubber, disconcertingly sweet and delicious.

The succulent beef of the first musk ox Erasmus shot roused the last of the men. They cleaned the winter's accumulation of soot from the beams and walls, aired the squalid corners, laundered bedding and socks and shirts. Only Captain Tyler and Mr. Tagliabeau remained in their bunks. *When exhausted by sickness,* Erasmus remembered his father saying, *elephants will lie on their backs and throw grass toward the sky, as though beseeching the earth to answer their prayers. The elephant is honest, sensible, just, and respectful of the stars, the sun, and the moon—qualities rarely apparent even in man.* Just then Erasmus would have happily traded Captain Tyler and Mr. Tagliabeau for a pair of useful pachyderms. He tried alternately to bully and coddle them, but they would not be moved.

Since Zeke's departure they'd collapsed entirely, as if finally giving in to their grief over the loss of Mr. Francis. Or as if they no longer believed they wouldn't share his fate, despite the vibrant signs of spring. In his bunk, above his pillow, Captain Tyler had pinned a small sheet of paper. On it he'd drawn the outline of a gravestone and written:

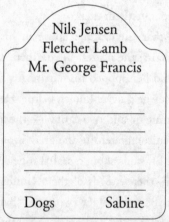

Nils Jensen
Fletcher Lamb
Mr. George Francis

Dogs   Sabine

He and Mr. Tagliabeau wouldn't hunt, or work on repairing the brig, or pace the promenade. They lay in their bunks, openly drinking and reading as if this might somehow save them. Mr. Tagliabeau burrowed into a copy of *Pendennis*; Captain Tyler into Dr. Boerhaave's *David Copperfield,* picking up where the doctor had left off reading aloud during the worst days of winter. When the men came by their bunks and said, "What should we do? What are your orders?" Captain Tyler and Mr. Tagliabeau shrugged and said, "Do what you want. What Mr. Wells says. It won't make any difference."

———

MAY 5, 10, 15. Still the sledge party didn't return. Erasmus worried about them—but only for their own sake; whatever meat they brought back from the Esquimaux would now be superfluous. The weather stopped chewing at them and twice the temperature rose above freezing. The light made it feel warmer; the light made up for everything. When Erasmus woke and first stepped outside, the dazzling whiteness pierced his eyes and made his head swim until he treasured the nights, when the sun sat lower in the sky and lent shades of red and yellow to the clouds. A soft mist hovered over the hills and the falling snow was heavy and wet, like spring snow back home. Home, where he might one day live in the company of his friend. *What would it mean,* he imagined asking Dr. Boerhaave, *to grow up hearing stories in which truth and falsehood are mingled like the minerals in granite?* To which Dr. Boerhaave might reply, *It could mean you were being taught to understand that anything you can imagine is possible.*

The brig was still frozen in solidly, but trickles of water seeped down the sides of the icebergs and the floes were bare of snow, sometimes wet on the surface. The broad strip of land-fast ice began to crack as the tides nibbled away at the base, and rocks tumbled down upon it from the cliffs above. Nothing like a lead opened in the solid sea ice of their cove, not even a crack appeared, but the signs of breaking up were everywhere.

Erasmus gathered the men on May 17. He was in charge now; he accepted it. Dismissing entirely Zeke's dreams of heading north, giddy with sun and the birds in the sky, he said, "I propose we break up the storehouse. The ice might begin to open any day now, and we should be prepared to stow the brig swiftly."

"Then we can go the minute a lead opens up," Isaac agreed.

They made heaps and towers on the ice and then slowly began moving the things they were least likely to need back into the hold. Erasmus, Sean, and Barton, with the guidance of Thomas, tore down half the deckhouse and closed off the remainder roughly. Erasmus began sleeping in that breezy shanty, and soon the men abandoned their stuffy quarters and joined him, leaving only Captain Tyler and Mr. Tagliabeau below.

Thomas said, "Should we rebuild the bulkhead? We're not so dependent on the stoves anymore, and Commander Voorhees will surely want the regular arrangements restored for our voyage back."

"Leave it for now," Erasmus said. "It's a day's work; we can wait and see what he wants to do when he returns."

As their spirits rose they knocked down the remains of their autumn ice village and rebuilt it more elaborately. A Greek temple rose white and elegant, next to a model of the Boston library and diagonally across from a miniature tavern which, Thomas swore, was just like the one nearest the wharf from which the *Narwhal* had sailed. Sean built a railway station and Barton, not to be out-done, built an imitation Japanese garden. Erasmus thought the men built even more gleefully and skillfully than they had in the presence of Zeke, perhaps because they knew each building raised was tem-porary. Not something they'd have to regard all winter, soiled and slumped and covered with snow, but a living, glistening thing that might dissolve in a few weeks. To their efforts he added a boathouse, with a little river carved before it and curving toward home.

A DISTANT SOUND woke Erasmus during the night of May 21. He threw on his clothes and ran outside, into the pearly, improb-able midnight light: two figures, dark against the ice, were creeping toward him. No matter how quickly he moved, how he halved the distance between himself and the figures and halved it again, still there were only two. Two. Ned, bent forward but still upright, resting a long moment before each step; and leaning against him, almost being carried by him, Zeke.

"Wait," Erasmus said to the blackened, bloody faces. "Only a minute more." Before he touched them, before even determining how far behind them Joe and Dr. Boerhaave might be, he flew back to the brig, rounded up Barton and Sean and Isaac, and tossed down the smallest sledge. Ned and Zeke, weighed down by the lumpy packages tied to their backs, had crumpled to the ice by the time the crew reached them. Zeke was unconscious and Ned hardly better, but Erasmus bent close to Ned's ear.

"How far back are they?" he asked urgently. "Can you tell us where to start looking? Are they with the sledge?"

Ned twisted his head into Erasmus's face.

"Can you talk?" Erasmus asked, pulling back. "You're almost home, we'll have you inside in five minutes—are they far?"

"Joe left us," Ned groaned. "He stayed in Greenland. Dr. Boerhaave . . ." He banged his cheekbone into Erasmus's mouth, hard enough to split Erasmus's lower lip. Joe in Greenland? How could that be? Once more Erasmus pulled his head away.

"Under," Ned whispered. "Under. We were, he was blind from the snow, we stopped. Zeke and I, we unharnessed ourselves, we left him in the traces while we were unloading the sledge to camp, we were, we were—it was safer to leave him tied in for a minute we thought, so he wouldn't wander, he couldn't see—we were unloading."

"Unloading," Erasmus repeated. He put a hand to his streaming lip. How could he be bleeding when time had stopped?

"It cracked," Ned whispered. "The floe, right under the sledge. There was ice and then there wasn't. The sledge went in and it pulled him. So fast. I couldn't even touch his hand before he was gone."

ZEKE REMAINED UNCONSCIOUS for eleven days and was weak for a fortnight after that; brain fever, Erasmus thought. Ned was in better shape physically, but too exhausted and brokenhearted to talk. In their sleeping sacks Erasmus found some clues from which he tried to piece together the story.

Before the sledge had vanished, Ned had unloaded those sacks, most of their supplies, and Dr. Boerhaave's small medicine chest and oilskin-wrapped journal; he'd carried home both despite his weakness. Erasmus went through the chest's contents, not mourning his dead friend—not yet, he couldn't admit that Dr. Boerhaave was truly gone—but searching for remedies for the survivors. Ointments, plasters, a few canisters of pills, oiled silk, lint, bandages, scalpels. Many small bottles and vials: tartar emetic, mercurous chloride, syrup of squill, tincture of opium. Not much use to Erasmus, but he heard Dr. Boerhaave's voice as he read those names aloud. When he retreated to his bunk after tending to the invalids, he browsed through Dr. Boerhaave's journal. Before leaving the *Narwhal* Dr. Boerhaave had written:

The last pages of my acquaintance's Walden *continue to comfort me. "Is it the source of the Nile, or the Niger, or the Mississippi, or a Northwest Passage around this continent, that we would find?" Thoreau writes. "Are these the problems which most concern mankind? Is Franklin the only man who is lost, that his wife should be so earnest to find him? Does Mr. Grinnell know where he himself is? Be rather the Mungo Park, the Lewis and Clarke and Frobisher, of your own streams and oceans; explore your own higher latitudes—with shiploads of preserved meats to support you, if they be necessary, and pile the empty cans sky-high for a sign. . . . What was the meaning of that South-Sea Exploring Expedition, with all its parade and expense, but an indirect recognition of the fact, that there are continents and seas*

in the moral world, to which every man is an isthmus or an inlet, yet
unexplored by him, but that it is easier to sail many thousand miles
through cold and storm and cannibals, in a government ship, with
five hundred men and boys to assist one, than it is to explore the pri-
vate sea, the Atlantic and Pacific Ocean of one's being alone."

Those words made Erasmus weep. A message for him, he thought: that Exploring Expedition was the one he'd been on as a youth, that search for Franklin had sent him here. If he and Dr. Boerhaave had truly heeded those words they might be safe in Philadelphia, comparing notes on crustaceans. Instead Dr. Boerhaave had crossed the Sound.

He'd written nothing during the crossing itself. His next entry read:

How difficult that was! Ridges of hummocks, barricades blocking
our way again and again; I've never suffered such bodily pains. Yet
we're safe, finally. Ned's snow blindness seems to have responded
to treatment. For the last two days of our crossing I washed out his
eyes with solution of boric acid, then put in morphine drops and
bandaged his eyes shut; we pulled him on the sledge. A terrible trip.

The birds have been remarkable: snow buntings, a passerine
that is probably the Lappland longspur, hoary redpolls, the Ameri-
can pipit (surely this is the extreme north of its range?), wheatears.
Red-throated loons, ivory gulls, a white gyrfalcon. The pipits fly
high then flutter down, repeating their song faster and faster as
they approach the ground. How these songbirds change the barren
landscape! Suddenly everything seems alive. The dovekies are the
most numerous; our hosts slaughter great flocks of them. We join
their feasts gratefully.

Campions, cochlearia, and lichens are beginning their growth
beneath the snow. In a sheltered pocket, where an ice crust had
formed, a purple saxifrage was flowering and a cinquefoil was

greening. On some dry stones, from which the snow had already
melted, I found two spiders.

And that was all. Not a word about the disappearance of Joe, the
nature of the Greenland Esquimaux, the response to Zeke's requests
for dogs and help. Not a word, of course, about his own trials on the
journey back.

He was blind, Erasmus thought, staring out into the harsh
morning light. Not just blind but in pain. On what day had that
happened? And why had he been walking blind, harnessed like a dog
to the sledge? Why wasn't he being pulled on the sledge, as Ned had
been pulled on the journey over?

DURING THE MONTH that Zeke was laid up, Erasmus tried to
prepare the brig for their departure. Ned still couldn't or wouldn't
talk. To the men, who clamored for explanations about the disappear-
ances of Joe and Dr. Boerhaave, Erasmus could say only what Ned
had whispered before his collapse: that Joe had left them, and that Dr.
Boerhaave had died in an accident on the ice. Erasmus grieved for Dr.
Boerhaave constantly, and was consumed with questions about his
end—but there was work to do, so much work to do, and Captain Tyler
and Mr. Tagliabeau continued to shirk their duties. Leaning into Captain Tyler's bunk and shouting at him that he must get up, they were so
short-handed, Erasmus saw that Dr. Boerhaave's name had been added
to the paper gravestone. After that he left the captain alone.

He gave orders, made lists, split the duties of nursing the sick
among the well, and assigned hunting teams. He waited impatiently
for Zeke's recovery, but it was Ned who recovered first and Ned,
leaning on his arm while they paced the promenade, who first told
Erasmus what had happened.

The ice in Smith Sound had been murderous, Ned said, like nothing they'd ever seen before: great tumbled blocks, amid which the sledge crashed like a toy. Sleeping had been almost impossible and they'd walked for twenty hours some days, half-blinded by the glare. Ned's eyes were the worst. For ten or eleven days they'd wandered, finally reaching the coast with still no idea of where they were. But Dr. Boerhaave found tracks, Ned said, the faint tracks of a sledge, and Joe steered by them to a small settlement.

How lucky they'd felt then! For there were Ootuniah and Awahtok and the three other Esquimaux who'd visited the *Narwhal*; also a few other men, four women, and a handful of children. They were feasting on walrus, and although they seemed startled by the arrival of their guests they shared their food freely and took them into their hut—a large dormitory, built of stone and lined outside with sods, very different from the tents of the Netsilik. Around a blubber fire their wet furs steamed.

For two weeks, these people had sheltered the four pale men. While Ned recovered his eyesight, Joe and Zeke and Dr. Boerhaave hunted with their hosts, capturing birds, seals, and two more walrus, which they afterward ate in the warm hut. Zeke had asked Ootuniah for dogs and men to help him journey north—he needed help, he said. And would pay for it generously. Or so Ned understood from what Joe told him.

Much of what Ned knew he'd gathered only by asking Joe. On their arrival Joe had begun to interpret, as always, but Zeke had ordered him to stop. He didn't need Joe's interpreting skills after all, he said; he'd studied hard and now he could understand the Esquimaux language himself.

"I'm not sure about this," Ned told Erasmus. "How much he understood—but he seemed to be doing well enough, and he really didn't want Joe to help him. He said he couldn't establish true friendships with these people if Joe always interposed himself between them and him. You're to be quiet, Zeke said. So Joe had time to interpret things for me. And time to talk with Ootuniah alone and listen to his stories. He told me some, they were like Esquimaux fairy tales."

The hunting trips, Ned thought, were where Joe and Ootuniah had grown friendly: he knew no more than that. On their last night in Anoatok, when Ootuniah finally, firmly, denied all Zeke's requests and said that they could spare no dogs or men, and that Zeke shouldn't travel north at this time of year, Joe slipped away. Ned and Zeke and Dr. Boerhaave woke the next morning to find that Ootuniah and his companions had loaded Zeke's sledge with a huge heap of walrus meat, but that Joe was gone.

Zeke had translated Ootuniah's explanations for Ned and Dr. Boerhaave, his face stricken as he did so. "This land is your friend's homeland," Zeke repeated. His face twisted, as though the words were sour on his tongue. "Although his own people live far south of here. He has borrowed a sledge and dogs from us and headed there. We wish him well in his journey, as we wish you well in yours. All this meat, it is for you and your men. Your friend has gone home."

Ned and Dr. Boerhaave hadn't been surprised; they'd both seen how tired Joe was of Zeke. Zeke's demands and requests and posturings, Zeke's plans and questions and maps; many times Ned had seen Joe and Ootuniah together, talking and laughing and sharing food. "It was Commander Voorhees's moodiness that drove Joe away," Ned said. "His carelessness—Joe was our most valuable crew member, and now he's gone. I could almost feel what Joe was feeling: he was in Greenland, even if so far north, and among Esquimaux, even if not a tribe he knew—and he had a chance to get away from us. Of course he took it. If I had a way to go home, I'd do the same."

Ned and Zeke and Dr. Boerhaave had been forced to travel back without Joe, loaded with precious walrus meat but with none of the things that Zeke had most desired. That trip was worse than the first, Ned said; the pack was shifting and the floes heaved beneath them. After a brief stretch of smooth, clear ice, they'd run into a maze of pressure ridges, ten-foot blocks heaped in snaking walls that forced them backward and then in circles. Zeke refused to lighten the sledge by discarding any of the meat. It was all they had to show for their trip, he said, and the *Narwhal*'s crew needed it.

"Although you didn't," Ned said bitterly. "How could we not have understood that if the Esquimaux were finding food, you would be too?"

On the fourth day, Dr. Boerhaave's eyes had given out completely. A vast confusion of rain and snow and glaring sun, wild winds and sudden sharp cold; their furs were soaked through and they had to keep moving to stay warm. Were Dr. Boerhaave to ride on the sledge, Zeke said, he would surely freeze to death. He must keep walking. Perhaps that was true. But it was also true that the sledge was already almost too heavy to pull. Dr. Boerhaave couldn't possibly lie atop that heap of meat and Zeke wouldn't discard his sole prize.

Zeke arranged the traces so that Dr. Boerhaave was harnessed next to the sledge, with Ned and Zeke himself a few feet before him, at the points of an equilateral triangle. Another set of ropes ran from Dr. Boerhaave's waist to Ned's and Zeke's, forming the triangle's sides, so that Dr. Boerhaave could then walk forward guided by the gentle pressure. And it had worked, Ned admitted. It was horrible the way Dr. Boerhaave stumbled over the ridges and mounds, the way his sightless face grimaced and colored—yet perhaps only the constant movement had kept him alive.

Or perhaps if Zeke had emptied the sled, packed Dr. Boerhaave on it wrapped in all their furs, he might be alive even now. Or if they hadn't untied the ropes connecting them to Dr. Boerhaave before unloading the sledge for their brief rest, or if they'd chosen any other place, any other time to stop . . .

"The waist ropes weren't long enough," Ned said, staring out at the white plain. Erasmus was sweating beneath his jacket, moisture trickling down his sides as if his arms were weeping. That Dr. Boerhaave had had to endure this . . . "We couldn't unload the sledge while we were still tied in," Ned continued. "Just a few minutes we weren't tied to him—how could the ice have opened just then?"

Erasmus remembered his first impression of his friend: Dr. Boerhaave's quick and shining mind, flashing like a silver salmon. Did a soul survive? His body moved among the fish but perhaps his soul had floated free. One fine idea in the mind of God, which might express itself in another form.

"It wasn't your fault," Erasmus said. And it wasn't; nor was it, exactly, Zeke's. Yet if Joe had been there it wouldn't have happened, Joe would have understood what to do: and who was to blame for Joe's desertion, if not Zeke? The sweat congealed on his chest. It could have been Zeke, sinking through that ice. It *should* have been Zeke. Behind that flare of rage was a bleaker thought. If he hadn't shared that one night with the men—if Zeke hadn't caught him drinking—he might have been there himself to save Dr. Boerhaave.

BY JUNE 15 Zeke was well enough to rise and resume command of the ship. He gathered all the men on deck, even Captain Tyler and Mr. Tagliabeau, and thanked them for their good work during his absence and subsequent illness. Erasmus stood next to him, his hands jammed in his pockets, trying to listen without shouting. Dr. Boerhaave was dead and here was Zeke. His sister's love, the leader of all these men, everyone needed him—*if I struck him,*

Erasmus thought, with the calm of real hysteria; *if he fell and hit his head . . .* but Zeke's death wouldn't help anyone except, very briefly, him. He dug his fingers through the cloth and into his thighs as Sean said, "But what really happened to Joe and Dr. Boerhaave?"

Zeke told a story that resembled what Ned had told Erasmus, but was somehow quite different. In his version, Joe was unhelpful on the crossing to Greenland, and once there poisoned Zeke's relationship with the Esquimaux. Because of Joe the Esquimaux, initially willing to supply Zeke with dogs, and perhaps even accompany him on some travels north, had turned against him. There was a woman involved, Zeke hinted; he suspected that Joe had formed a relationship with one of the Anoatok women, deserting so he might meet her later.

The tragic journey back, Zeke said, had also been Joe's fault. In his absence the sledge was too heavy for three men; they'd struggled heroically, wanting to bring fresh meat to the *Narwhal*'s crew, but they'd grown overtired and it was this that had beaten them. Had Joe been there, Dr. Boerhaave might still have fallen—that was fate, no one could help it—but a third pair of hands might have been enough to haul out him and the sledge.

"This is what happens," Zeke said frostily. "When a team breaks down, when commands are ignored. A weak link in the chain imperils us all."

In the silence Erasmus chewed his lips and watched Zeke gaze toward the plain surrounding the ship, dotted with ice buildings and heaps of supplies. A pyramid of barrels holding their beef and pork, quadrangles of flour and dried apples and beans, a little tower of bottled horseradish, twelve bottles to the case. "Who gave the orders to break up the storehouse?" Zeke asked.

"I did," Erasmus said, amazed that he could still speak. Two long-tailed ducks passed by, heading for their breeding grounds farther north. How Dr. Boerhaave would have enjoyed a glimpse of them. "I thought you'd want to be ready the moment the ice opened."

"Your diligence is admirable," Zeke said. "But I hope you haven't stowed the pemmican, or any of the other traveling supplies." Everyone stared at him. "The Esquimaux have promised to visit us in a few weeks," Zeke continued. "A few men, and a team of dogs for our sledge. They'll help us make a quick trip north, while we wait for the ice to break up."

"I never heard that," Ned blurted. "When did they promise that?"

"You don't understand their language," Zeke said. "You only heard what Joe told you. They'll be here shortly. Then a party of us will head north."

The men said nothing; they stood still and then disappeared below—as if, Erasmus thought, Zeke's announcement was so absurd they'd all agreed not to hear it. For a while he couldn't speak himself. Later that night, still wondering if he'd heard correctly, he was turning the pages of Dr. Boerhaave's journal when Zeke crept up on him. He tried to shield the pages with his hand before he spoke. "Why are you still talking about this trip?" he said. Why hadn't he asked this right away? "It's ridiculous, it's such a bad idea."

"So you've said," Zeke replied. "So you've been saying since January, you could hardly be less enthusiastic. Yet the success of our whole voyage turns on this."

"What *success*?" Erasmus closed the precious volume. "Nils and Fletcher and Mr. Francis already dead and now Dr. Boerhaave, Dr. Boerhaave, Dr. . . ." He dashed away what was spurting from his eyes.

"I'll take that," Zeke said, bending over the spotted book.

"No!" Erasmus said. "Please—it should be mine."

Zeke pushed his hands aside. "It's a part of the expedition's records now," he said. "Hence mine."

DURING THOSE LAST weeks of June, Alexandra wrote:

That my life would change like this; it's so extraordinary, my fate turning because of Mr. Archibault's crippled hands, me profiting by his problems—what am I to make of this?

He arrives each evening with his secret parcels and we work long into the night. We've taken over Erasmus's Repository, lighting it as best we can; a far cry from the sunlit space of the Wellses' engraving room. They work in teams there, several men to each plate; one engraves the landscape, another the animals, another the human figures. Here it's just the two of us, doing the best we can.

All this has come about because Dr. Kane drives himself so mercilessly—or is driven by his publisher, we can't be sure which. The facts I piece together are these. In the months since Dr. Kane's return he's generated almost nine hundred pages of text, much taken directly from his journals but some newly written; only the Preface and Appendix remain undone. Meanwhile Mr. Hamilton, who renders from Dr. Kane's pen-and-ink sketches the beautiful paintings on which the engravings are based, has been living in Dr. Kane's own rooms that they might work day and night.

*Mr. Childs, his publisher, began printing the early chapters even while Dr. Kane continued writing, and he's given specimen pages to the newspapers as a way of drumming up publicity. Mr. Childs chose the title—*Arctic Explorations: The Second Grinnell Expedition in Search of Sir John Franklin, 1853, '54, '55*—and plans to publish in September, but the engravings are far behind schedule. It's this frenzy that has been my great blessing. Mr. Archibault's team is the farthest behind; no one knows but me that something has happened to his wrists. When he bears down with his graver,* *pains shoot up from his wrists and his fingers lose their strength and grow numb; he's lost almost all control of them.*

He spends his days directing the other members of his team, who engrave views of the cliffs, the sky, the ship, and the human figures. He checks the plates at each stage, he points out mistakes and calls for corrections. He's supposed to be doing the animals—his particular gift—but claims he can't concentrate while supervising everyone else and must do his own work at night. Then he sneaks the plates and their corresponding paintings out of the building and here, to me. He has a wife, six children, a widowed mother living with him, and no other income beyond his salary.

Neither of us can quite believe this is happening. That he should be so dependent on a woman still in training; that I should be given the chance, so early, to work on the plates for an important book—it's difficult for both of us. We both know I'm not ready for this. And how exasperating it is that he can't correct my mistakes directly. He paces back and forth, cold compresses on his wrists, and can do no more than say, "Lightly, lightly." Or, "Carve deeper there, a little more pressure," or "Can't you see the way Hamilton's angled the jawbone?" I've never worked so hard. Some of what I do is good, I can see it. Sometimes I can match my line both to Hamilton's intent and to the work of the others who've already marked the plate. But sometimes my clumsiness shows. Partly I long for my work to be recognized. Partly I'm glad no one will ever know how I've served out my apprenticeship in public.

Caught in our strange union, Mr. Archibault and I try to be kind to one another. But twice he's arrived here pale with distress, and has let me know that Linnaeus, looking over a plate, has expressed dissatisfaction. Mr. Archibault's job rests on what I do, as does the firm's reputation. Yet it's no use to think of this, I can only do my best.

I still haven't met Dr. Kane, on whose behalf an army works day and night. This man who's changed my life and made a hell of Lavinia's. Why is he here? she asks. And not Zeke and Erasmus? She rages; then chides herself for being irrational. I find her asleep in odd corners, in the middle of the day, and when I wake her she weeps and twists her skirt in her hands. She knows my secret and doesn't hold my work against her, even tries to encourage me now and then but can do no work herself. Nothing I do seems to help her.

Still—still, still, still—we have no word of Zeke and Erasmus. Though whalers now make their way into upper Baffin's Bay, no one reports sighting the Narwhal.

"OUR ACQUAINTANCES HAVE DECEIVED US," Zeke said when he returned. He'd been gone for three days, exploring the far side of the point in search of the Esquimaux. His face was sunburnt and above it his hair, sweaty and rumpled, looked almost white.

Ned, who was standing next to Erasmus and sorting handfuls of scurvy grass, said, "You saw the Esquimaux?"

"I saw no one," Zeke said curtly. "The pack in the Sound is beginning to move, there are big leads everywhere and there's no possibility of travel across it. As the Esquimaux must have known when they sent us home. They never had any intention of helping us, they just meant to get rid of us. And so they have. We have no way of communicating with them now for the rest of the season."

"Why *would* they come here?" Ned said. "All they ever want to do is get away from us."

"Your opinion," Zeke retorted. "Which you may keep to yourself."

Ned turned and busied himself with the stove. Captain Tyler and Mr. Tagliabeau, still idle but well enough to sit in the sun wrapped in blankets, looked up at Zeke. "But this is good news," Captain Tyler said. "Isn't it? If the ice is breaking up in the Sound, surely we'll be freed soon . . ."

"I don't think so," Zeke replied. "I went south along the ice belt, looking for open water. The straits aren't open anywhere, they're only heaving and breaking. The ice on our side is completely solid between us and the North Water."

Mr. Tagliabeau groaned and put his head on his knees.

"We have at least six weeks before there's even the possibility of breaking out," Zeke said. "And there's no point wasting this precious time. So we don't have dogs. So the movement in the Sound blocks us from travel to the east. There's no reason we can't head north, exploring the coast. We'll break into two parties, one to guard the brig and ready it for our departure, and another to travel. Volunteers?"

No one said a word.

Zeke looked from face to face. Erasmus shifted his eyes when Zeke's gaze reached him.

"Some enthusiasm would be welcome," Zeke said. "I'll post a sheet of paper in the deckhouse tomorrow morning, and I expect six of you to sign up for the exploring party. Work it out among yourselves."

TUESDAY AND WEDNESDAY, the sheet remained blank. Ned took Erasmus aside, while Zeke rummaged through the supplies on the ice. "No one's going to sign up," he said. "Of course no one is. After what happened—I'll never go anywhere with him again. And neither will anyone else. I've talked to the men."

He looked Erasmus squarely in the eye, and Erasmus understood that, beyond the rebuilt bulkhead, Ned had been telling the crew his version of the trip to Anoatok, which must have won out over Zeke's.

On Thursday, Zeke sat down to dinner with an armful of charts. "Well?" he asked. "Who is joining me?"

"We must stay with the ship," Captain Tyler said. "Mr. Tagliabeau and I—it's our duty to guard the ship, and ready it for our departure."

The seven crewmen rose from the table as one. Ned stepped forward and spoke for them. "It's too risky," he said. Brave boy, Erasmus thought. "There's nothing to be gained. The ice may break up before you think, and we must be here when it does."

Zeke's face turned white, but he clenched his hand around his charts and said to Erasmus, "It's just you and me then, my old friend. But we'll move more swiftly without these malingerers. Shall we leave on Saturday?"

For a minute Erasmus struggled with himself. His duty toward Zeke and Lavinia, his duty toward Ned and the rest of these men—no matter what he decided, he'd fail someone. "It's a bad idea," he said. "I can't support you in this. I vote to stay."

Zeke rose, scattering papers. "This isn't a *vote*. Who said anything about *voting*?"

"I'm staying here," Erasmus said, hoping he sounded as firm as Ned had.

"You can't do this," Zeke said to him. He turned, faced the others, and repeated himself; then added, "You'll all regret this."

"We've followed you wherever you wanted," Captain Tyler said. "Look where it's brought us."

Mr. Tagliabeau said, "We might now consider this ship a wreck, since it has no power to move. Under maritime law, the commander of a ship has no further powers once a ship is wrecked."

Ned took a breath and steadied himself. "The *Narwhal* isn't a ship anymore," he said. "Maybe it's not a wreck like Mr. Tagliabeau says, but it's not a ship. It's our home, even if it feels like a prison."

Was this mutiny? Erasmus wondered. If Zeke started hurling orders at them, if he threatened them and still they refused . . .

"I'll give you all another chance to act like men," Zeke said, beginning to pace. "We'll meet here tomorrow at noon, and I'll ask each of you to state for the record your decision to support me in a journey north. Perhaps a party of six is excessive, given our reduced numbers. I need only three of you. Any three."

He left the cabin, clambered down onto the ice, and did not return. No one slept in the cabin that night. Erasmus tossed in the deckhouse, aware that below him, Captain Tyler and Mr. Tagliabeau had abandoned their bunks to join the men in the forecastle. He heard voices deep into the night, although only a few phrases floated clearly: *when a whaling ship's frozen in like this, the captain is bound to release the men; the boats should be at our disposal; if he won't do that we might confine him*—Barton DeSouza, Robert Carey, Isaac Bond. Erasmus longed for Dr. Boerhaave, who might have guided him.

At noon, they waited for fifteen minutes before they heard Zeke climb up on deck and then descend among them. From the shelf behind his bunk he took the small metal box in which he kept his charts and his journal and also, since their deaths, Mr. Francis's official log and Dr. Boerhaave's journal. He opened Mr. Francis's log. One by one, in a steady voice, he called out the crew members' names. One by one they said, "Stay." He entered each vote, turning last to Erasmus.

"I'm sorry," Erasmus said. "But I must also stay."

"Well, then," Zeke said. "So you reveal yourselves." He wrote a few more lines in the log and then locked it inside the box. "I'll be gone four weeks," he said, squaring his shoulders. "The ice won't open before August fifteenth, almost surely later. I'll be back before August fifth."

"You're going alone?" Ned said. "You're still going?"

"Of *course* I'm going," Zeke said. "Why would I return home without taking advantage of our excellent situation here? Dr. Kane may have preceded us to the Greenland side of Smith Sound, and may have befriended our fickle Esquimaux before us, but who's to say how far north he traveled? The open polar sea may be less than a hundred miles away, and I won't give up this chance to find it because of you."

He turned to Erasmus. "I'm very disappointed in you," he said. For a second, Erasmus was reminded of his own father. "But under the terms of the contract you signed, I leave you and Captain Tyler in shared command until I return."

He left the brig again, headed for the three guardian icebergs. Erasmus followed a few minutes later, cursing as he crossed the spongy white plain and looped around the turquoise puddles of meltwater spread so deceptively everywhere. Like windows into the open sea but shallow, just a few inches deep, all lies. He waded through them, soaking his boots, panting as Zeke's figure disappeared. His own feet disappeared in the water; how could the ice be so wet on the surface, so solid below, so obstinate in refusing to release them? At the first berg he stopped and rested against the slumping contours. Around the back of the third, largest berg, he found Zeke.

"Please," he said, still panting. "Don't go off alone."

"You're the one making me do it," Zeke said.

"I can't leave the men. Not after all that happened this winter."

Zeke made a sound of disgust. "They're not *your* responsibility— they're mine. And I know they'll be fine."

"But I'm responsible for *you*." Had he admitted this before? "Lavinia made me promise I'd look after you."

"As if I'm a child?" He stepped back from Erasmus, into a puddle; his feet disappeared and he seemed to be walking on water. "As if I need the protection of a woman, of you—why would I want to marry her, if she's like *you*?"

"Because you *love* her," Erasmus shouted. Then stood with his mouth still open. He leaned back against the largest of Zeke's Follies.

"I can't think about her up here. I can't think about anything except what I have to do." Zeke looked down at the blue pool obscuring his feet. "You could still change your mind," he said softly. "Come with me—I'd put everything that's happened behind us, we could still discover something wonderful. Be like brothers."

"It was Dr. Boerhaave who was like a brother to me," Erasmus said. "And now he's dead."

Again Zeke made that noise of disgust, clicking his tongue on the roof of his mouth: *tchik, tchik, tchik.* "Noted," he said. A string of eider ducks whirred by, their harsh cries shocking in the silence. "You've made your feelings perfectly clear all along. If your father could see what you've become . . ." He turned and walked off across the film of water.

Alone, without dogs or human companions, he couldn't pull a sledge. He left two days later on foot, with a spare pair of boots, a rifle, a good deal of ammunition, and provisions strapped in an unwieldy bedroll to his back.

SOMETIMES THEY WERE ASHAMED. Or Erasmus was, and Ned as well; perhaps some of the others: because their lives, through the rest of July and early August, were almost easy. Each day, while their ice structures dripped and consolidated into glassy mounds, they dismantled another heap of the *Narwhal*'s stores and repacked the items carefully in the hold. Pleasant work, under the warm sun. And with each trip to the hold and back, the men could examine the tiny, heartening gap, like a mouth beginning to open, where the dark hull met the ice.

Erasmus, checking new lists against the old, found more efficient arrangements for their remaining supplies. Now that the candles were gone, and most of the wood and much of the preserved food, he was able to convert part of the hold aft of the mainmast into storage for the specimens he and Dr. Boerhaave had collected. The crates of bird skins in one neat tower; fossils matched part to counterpart, neatly labeled and layered with hides; bottles crammed with floating invertebrates swathed in dried grasses and then wedged in boxes—only now, given some room and time, was he able to see how much he had. There was enough here to keep him occupied for the rest of his life, and he would have been happy if he weren't worried about Zeke, and if Dr. Boerhaave had been present. He packed his friend's books in a case he built next to the fossils, keeping out only a few for the shelf in his bunk.

On the gravel beach smoke hung in the air; the men had developed a passion for preparing caribou skins, and hides depended like flags from scaffolds of poles raised near little fires. Erasmus asked Ned, who seemed to be directing the efforts, what this was all about. Flushed and pink-cheeked, Ned was bent over a skin, scraping the fascia away with a piece of iron pipe. Next to him Barton was arranging a white skin some distance from a fire, while on deck Isaac and Ivan and Robert were sitting cross-legged amid a pile of skins already smoked and dried.

Ned said, "You don't mind, do you? I thought it was a good idea, a way to keep us all busy. The suits we've been wearing all winter are worn out and they smell bad—each of us decided to make a complete suit for himself, from the inside out. A sort of souvenir, for when we get home. The things you taught me helped me prepare the skins. Joe showed me the basic pattern of the garments last fall. Ivan worked as a tailor on a sealing ship when he was a boy, and he showed us all how to cut out the pieces."

"It's fine," Erasmus said. "I suppose. We don't need the skins for anything else."

"Have you seen the underwear?" Ned said. "It's wonderful." He showed Erasmus the shirt, drawers, and socks he'd almost completed. "These are from the skin of a calf a few months old," he said. "Very supple and delicate. You make them with the fur side in. Then these"—he held up a hooded coat, trousers, and mittens—"these we make from a yearling, with the fur side out."

Erasmus saw a wrinkle and several pleats where the hood of Ned's coat met the back. Something was wrong, too, with the way the sleeve met the armhole, and there were patches where the fur ran backward. It was touching, really. The eager clumsiness, the attempt to keep alive the fragments of Esquimaux lore Joe had passed along. "You're using sinew?"

Ned shook his head. "None of us can manage it. But we found some waxed button thread in the chest with the extra wool cloth . . . was it all right to take that?"

"It's fine," Erasmus said. "But maybe you could keep track of how many spools you use, and let me know."

"Of course," Ned agreed. Looking down at the garments, he said, "Ivan and I have been getting along faster than the others. So we're also making a suit for you, which we hope you'll like."

"That's very kind," Erasmus said. "But it isn't necessary. Everything that Dr. Boerhaave and I gathered, I have enough souvenirs for a lifetime."

Ned cleared his throat. "It comforts the men," he said. "If you know what I mean."

Puzzled, Erasmus said, "I don't."

"Because . . . we tell each other we're making these to bring home and show our relatives, but also some of the men worry about how late in the season it's getting, and how the ice still hasn't opened, and they dread getting stuck here again. We don't want to be caught so ill-prepared as we were last winter."

Erasmus felt his face stiffen. "It's just in *case*," Ned said hastily. "It's not that anyone questions your orders or thinks you're doing the wrong thing. But just in *case*, you know. The same way that Barton and I have been packing down some seal meat with blubber on the ice belt, where it's still cool."

"It's a good idea," Erasmus said. Was this something Zeke would have thought of, had Zeke been here? During the bright nighttime hours, when he should have been sleeping, he sometimes walked a mile or two north from the brig, trying to imagine what Zeke was doing. What he was seeing, what he might have discovered. How his provisions were lasting and whether he'd been able to feed himself solely by his luck with a rifle. He'd been proud of how well he was managing in Zeke's absence. He should have anticipated the men's worries, he knew; but he hadn't been able even to consider the idea that they might remain trapped here another year.

"We'll get out in August," Erasmus said. "We will. But if it relieves the men's anxiety to make these preparations, if it makes everyone more comfortable . . ." Abruptly he turned and walked away.

THE FOLLOWING WEEK, Erasmus walked the length and breadth of their ice-bound cove: puddles, hollows, soggy mounds, but not a single crack. Yet the North Water of Baffin's Bay must be expanding, he thought; and beyond the protection of the headland that sheltered their cove, the currents must be heaving the ice. What was wrong, what had always been wrong, was the site Zeke had chosen for their home. Erasmus studied the patterns of shadow cast by the hills around them. The brig bobbed in a tiny pool of water, where the refracted heat from her hull had parted the lips of ice for two feet all around.

"If we could get to the mouth of the cove," he said to the men that night, "past the icebergs, we'd be ready to move when the bay opens."

"But we can do that," Captain Tyler exclaimed. "We have tools." The sense of being afloat again seemed to cure both him and Mr. Tagliabeau, who claimed to know every trick of the ice saws and powder canisters Erasmus had purchased more than a year ago.

Suddenly the pair were fitting pieces of metal together, calculating charges, giving orders to the men. All their sullen lethargy vanished. On August 1 they began sawing parallel channels through the ice, extending forward from the bit of open water under the bowsprit. The exploding canisters heaved and cracked fifty square yards of ice; the men sawed the slabs into smaller chunks and hauled them from the water, until the *Narwhal* occupied a tiny, jagged pool, three ship-lengths long but only a few feet broader than her beam. Flat on his stomach and sopping wet, Erasmus watched in wonder as tiny wavelets lapped at the edges of the pool. Each wavelet wore away a few more particles of ice. If they couldn't carve a canal all the way out to the Sound, still every cut weakened the ice. A little more open water and a swell might arise, the tides might be felt.

They sawed and blasted, sawed and blasted; they crept up on Zeke's Follies and then were beside them, almost in line with the tip of the point. Captain Tyler anchored the *Narwhal* to the stable ice, so it wouldn't snake down the canal until they were fully loaded. Although Smith Sound was still far away, although they hadn't yet dug themselves out of their cove, never mind into the larger bay, the long black ribbon stretching before the brig was immensely cheering.

August 5 passed without signs of Zeke, but no one discussed this. Zeke knew the margin of safety; that he might be a week, even ten days late, and still reach the brig before it was freed. Surely he was only exploring as long as possible. They worked around the clock, in delirious daylight, expecting Zeke every moment. On August 10, Captain Tyler set up the cables and the capstans.

Taking turns at the capstan bars, sweating and heaving to the tune of Sean's whaling songs, the crew warped the *Narwhal* to the far end of the canal. After they anchored, Ned and Barton cooked a special feast, which they ate perched on crates along the thread of water. Their condition hadn't really changed, Erasmus thought, tearing at a succulent ptarmigan leg. The brig had been one place and now was another, but the white plain still stretched around them, marked only by the line they'd carved across it. Still, the view was subtly changed, and this made an amazing difference. The hills they'd gazed at for almost a year loomed down at a new angle. The ice belt bound to the base of the cliffs was half a mile off their stern, almost beautiful in the distance. The three icebergs were right beside them, shrunken and bordered by rings of water. And the rock cairn beside the storehouse, beneath which they'd interred the remains of Mr. Francis, was no longer visible.

STILL ZEKE DIDN'T RETURN. The temperature dropped and the sun sank toward the horizon; not night, not quite yet, but there were real twilights. On August 16 the temperature dipped below freezing and an inch of young ice formed on the canal. Perfectly smooth, Erasmus saw. Glassy and terrifying. Some slabs they'd sawed out but not yet removed were frozen into the delicate plain. The noon sun melted the ice, but on the seventeenth, when the sun set for the first time, a clear cold descended and the air grew still. The following morning Mr. Tagliabeau, long-faced, stood on the new ice and didn't fall in. That day they sawed more old ice, with less enthusiasm, and on the nineteenth found that all their efforts had been undone while they slept.

The men came to Erasmus after he'd already lain down to sleep. They stood in a half-circle around the pallet he'd made on deck: Ned, Barton, Isaac, Robert, Ivan, Thomas, and Sean. Captain Tyler and Mr. Tagliabeau, for reasons Erasmus soon understood, stayed belowdecks in their bunks. When Erasmus sat up, rubbing his eyes, Ned stepped forward from the circle.

"Commander Voorhees is lost," Ned said, after clearing his throat twice. "We all know it—we knew when he left this would happen. He's two weeks late and we have to admit that he's dead."

"He's not *dead*," Erasmus said. Although he'd been fearing just this for a week. "He's late. Anything could have happened to him, he could be near us right now."

"He's dead," Barton said, behind Ned's shoulder. "He's been trying to kill us all since the day we left home. And the ice isn't opening, and the young ice gets thicker every day . . ."

"And we're not going to be able to free the *Narwhal*," Isaac chimed in.

"We're stuck," said Ivan.

"Again," Sean said.

"There's so little fuel left," Thomas added. "Our supplies—you know, you have the lists. We can't make it through another winter."

A fog seemed to hover over Erasmus's head. He was tired, he hadn't been sleeping well. He could almost hear the new ice forming. He could almost hear the beat of wings as the birds gathered for their journeys south, almost hear hooves ringing as the ground hardened and the caribou fled. His eyes felt full of cinders. Hadn't he *wished* Zeke dead, if only for a moment?

"What is it you want?" he asked. "I don't know what's happened to Commander Voorhees any more than you do. I can't keep the ice from forming, and I can't do much about our supplies. We can assign more hunting parties if you'd like, keep half of us working at breaking up the ice and half stockpiling game; that's a good idea, perhaps we'll start that tomorrow . . ."

Ned stepped back, twisted around, and picked up something from the deck. The others mimicked his movements, and when they stood and faced Erasmus again, he saw that each held a stack of neatly folded fur clothing. "We have these," Ned said. "Each of us. And we want to leave."

For the rest of the night, and all through the following day, the men ground down Erasmus's objections. Captain Tyler and Mr. Tagliabeau kept working on the canal, punctuating the men's comments with explosions and the crack of shattering ice. The officers couldn't address the subject directly, Ned told Erasmus. It would be inappropriate given their positions; they couldn't give orders to abandon the brig. But apparently they were willing to join a retreat led by Erasmus.

The men had maps, Erasmus learned. Maps, plans, lists of their own, detailed strategies. How long had they been discussing this without him? Since the moment of Zeke's departure, perhaps; those fur suits, he now realized, had always been meant for this trip. The men had never believed that Zeke would return. And although they'd hoped that the *Narwhal* might be freed, they'd found it sensible to make an alternate plan. Among them they had a surprising wealth of knowledge.

Sean and Barton had worked out a possible route. They'd load the whaleboat onto the large sledge and drag it from their cove around the point and to the mouth of the bay; then along the ice belt to Cape Sabine, or perhaps a bit farther south. After that they'd head diagonally southeast across the Sound, dragging the boat over the solid floes and rowing across any cracks. Somewhere south of Cape Alexander, perhaps fifty or sixty miles from the *Narwhal,* they might hope to find open water or at least navigable pack ice; they'd launch the boat and work past Cape York to the inshore lead of Melville Bay. They might still hope to find whalers there; failing that, they might hope to sail to Upernavik.

"But we'd need weeks to pack everything and prepare the boat," Erasmus said. "And we'd never get far enough along before the pack closes for the season."

Then he learned that chopping out the channel, even as it refroze at night, hadn't been the only situation that resembled the work of Penelope. While he'd been—what? Sleeping, he supposed, or hunting, or scouting; apparently they'd used each moment—Ned had led the men in a secretive effort down in the hold. Remarkable nerve, Erasmus thought, for someone only recently turned twenty-one; he wasn't sure whether he felt more admiration or anger. Under Ned's direction, the men had broken neatly into his boxes, shifting contents until the labels no longer bore any relationship to what was inside. He'd heard them moving around in there; they'd told him they were hunting down the rats.

They'd calculated what they'd need for their journey: so much pemmican per man per day, so much biscuit and molasses and coffee; so much blubber for the stoves; so much powder and shot and so many percussion caps; so many sleeping sacks. All repacked and grouped together, ready to be fitted into the whaleboat. Isaac and Ivan had sewn sailcloth provision bags, made watertight with tar and pitch. And each man had already assembled a tiny sack of personal belongings.

"Thomas has taken care of the boat," Ned added.

He led Erasmus to the whaleboat resting innocently under its tarpaulin. Under that cover, Thomas had fixed a false keel to the flat bottom and built up the bulwarks with planks and canvas. Those wood shavings, Erasmus thought. Earlier, when he'd noticed them, Thomas had claimed to be making standard repairs in anticipation of Zeke's return. The large sledge, which they'd never used, had been fitted with a cradle to carry the boat. Isaac had made sturdy sets of traces, with which they might haul the loaded sledge. And Ned had made a diagram, showing where they'd fit in the cramped boat and how the provisions might be stowed; he'd thought of everything. All they needed, Ned said, was Erasmus to lead them.

"Captain Tyler and Mr. Tagliabeau cede command to you," Ned said. "If you'll only give the order, we could leave in two days."

Erasmus agonized for another thirty-six hours. If Dr. Boerhaave were here, they could have decided together what to do—but Dr. Boerhaave was gone. And it was impossible that he should leave this place that had taken his friend's bones; impossible that he should abandon the brig and Zeke. On the sodden ice he saw everywhere the Zeke he'd known as a boy: Zeke and Copernicus stringing together a reptile's skeleton; Zeke tagging along to the creek to listen to Mr. Wells read Pliny; Zeke rolling across the Repository shelves wondering what to borrow next. Wanting so badly to be taken seriously; moving beyond Erasmus's distracted gaze and then reappearing after a few years' work at his father's firm, transformed into a man they all *had* to take seriously. Erasmus could still hear his father saying, *You should give him more credit. He behaves oddly sometimes. But his mind is sharp.*

Was sharp. Is, was—how could he leave Zeke behind, even if he were only leaving Zeke's body? Yet it was equally impossible that he should condemn the crew to another winter here. They couldn't survive it, and the *Narwhal* couldn't be moved. The only possible compromise was to send Ned and the others off in the boat while he stayed with the brig, hoping for Zeke's eventual return. He might survive, with luck hunting and perhaps some help from the vanished Esquimaux.

"It would be mutiny," Ned argued. "Without you. The contract said the brig was to be under Captain Tyler's command, but you were to head the expedition. And the brig might as well be sunk. You're in charge now."

"You take the men," Erasmus said to Captain Tyler and Mr. Tagliabeau. "I'll stay here and wait for Commander Voorhees."

Captain Tyler stared at him with frank dislike. "I will not," he said. "The chain of command is clear. If you give the order to go south I'll aid you in any way possible. But I'll not take responsibility for this without you. If I made it home somehow, having abandoned the brig and you and Commander Voorhees, my reputation wouldn't be worth a penny."

"Nor mine," Mr. Tagliabeau said.

"Whatever happens, then," Erasmus said, "it will be on my head. Is that what you want?"

"It's not what *we* want," Mr. Tagliabeau said. "It's simply your duty. Your choice."

ERASMUS PACKED SOME instruments, his fur suit, and Lavinia's green silk journal. He took Dr. Boerhaave's medicine chest, both because it had belonged to his friend and because he was now the closest thing the men had to a doctor. From the relics they'd obtained on Boothia he made a painful selection: the small copper cooking pot, the prayer book and the treatise on steam engines, the silver spoons and forks and the mahogany barometer case Dr. Boerhaave had once held in his hands. The rest he had to leave behind, but he hoped that these, and the careful account in his journal, would be enough to confirm Dr. Rae's findings and their own contact with the Esquimaux who'd seen the last of Franklin's expedition. He packed the smaller items in the copper pot and sealed it with a piece of walrus hide.

From the hold he removed his specimens, too heavy to ferry home. Unwilling to let them sink when the *Narwhal* was eventually crushed by the ice, he returned them to the storehouse. He made a list of all he'd consigned there, and in a tin box he placed that, his own journal, one of Dr. Boerhaave's precious volumes of Thoreau, and Agassiz's work on the fossil fishes. He added the studded bit of boot sole, which had spent all this time lying flat and silent beneath his bookshelf: one little relic of his own. Then he broke into Zeke's private box and stole Dr. Boerhaave's journal, leaving Zeke's black volume behind. Zeke was dead, he must be dead. That frail boy with the vibrant eyes was gone and now he must look after Ned. Lavinia—he put Lavinia from his mind.

He added Dr. Boerhaave's journal to his own tin box and prepared to solder it closed. At the last minute, he took down the portrait of Franklin and stowed that as well. In Captain Tyler's bunk, he saw, everything had been removed except for the paper gravestone, on which the names of their lost companions had been inscribed. Zeke's name now occupied the bottom of the list.

He had the men clean the ship, and he left behind enough provisions to support Zeke in case a miracle brought him back. He wrote out a careful statement, explaining the situation that had driven them to leave and their proposed route; he noted the crates of specimens in the storehouse and the provisions left on board. *We leave this brig August 26, 1856.* In the season called *aosok,* he thought, remembering the word Joe had taught him. The short interval between complete thaw and reconsolidation of the ice. For their long, improbable journey they had, at most, until the end of September. Not nearly enough time.

While the men began the laborious process of hauling the boat across the level plain, toward the point that blocked them from the Sound and onto the ice belt attached to the cliffs, he checked over every inch of the *Narwhal*. Then he nailed his statement to the mast and walked onto the ice.

7

The Goblins Known as *Innersuit*

(August–October 1856)

Enterprises of great pith and moment command our admiration, sympathy, and emulation with the varied force which the quality of their motives and objects deserves. The agility and courage of a rope-dancer on his perilous balance do not affect us in the same way as the generous daring displayed by a fireman in the rescue of a child from a burning house. There is natural nobleness enough in anybody to feel the difference between a hard day's journey on an errand of benevolence, and the feat of walking a hundred successive hours for a wager. A novelist, an orator, or a player, may work upon the sympathetic emotions of virtue until our heart-strings answer like echoes to his touch; but we are not deceived nor cheated into an admiration unworthy of ourselves. We were not made in the Divine image to take seemings for things. Our instincts

stand by the real interests of the world and of the
universe, and we will not meanly surrender our
souls to any imposture. We say to every man who
challenges our admiration for his deeds, "Stop!
worship touches the life of the worshiper. If your
objects are nothings, expect nothing for them: if
your motives are selfish, pay yourself for them.
We will not make fools of ourselves: we will settle
the account justly to you and honorably to us."

—WILLIAM ELDER, *Biography of*
Elisha Kent Kane (1858)

LATER, DIFFERENT SCENES FROM THE BOAT JOURNEY
would float back to each of them. So much work, so much pain; so
little rest or food or hope. What happened when? What happened
in fact, and what was only imagined, or misremembered? Erasmus
made no diary entries, nor did Ned or the other men. Of the days
when they were out on the ice, heaving against the harnesses and
rowing through lanes of ice-choked water, or sleeping packed like
a litter of piglets inside the canvas-covered boat, nothing remained
but a blur of impressions.

From their cove down the ice belt to Cape Sabine, then across
the broken, heaving Sound to a point slightly north of Cape Hather-
ton: pack ice, water, old ice, hummocks, thin ice, pressure ridges.
Always pulling, except for the wearying, exasperating times when

their way was blocked by an open channel and they must unload everything, remove the boat from the sledge, ferry across, reload, and begin the whole process again. Their shoulders and hands were rubbed raw by the ropes, and Ivan would remember the acid burn of vomit on his lips; they all threw up, they were pulling too much weight. Near the leads the ice was covered with slush and often they sank above their knees. Sean would remember how his ankles ballooned, forcing him to slit his boots and finally cut them off entirely, so that he made the rest of the journey with his feet wrapped in caribou hides. Robert would remember his persistent, burning diarrhea, and the humiliation of soiling his pants when he strained against the weight of the sledge.

Erasmus would pause one day after skidding helplessly on the ice, and then he'd think of the bit of boot sole sealed in his box and wonder why they hadn't all thought to stud their boots similarly. In what seemed to him now like another life, his boots had shot him off the face of a cliff—and still he hadn't learned. But it was too late now, they had no screws; they fell and stumbled and were relieved only once, when the ice field was smooth and the wind blew from the northwest. That day they set the sails and glided for eight miles: a great blessing, never repeated, which Barton would dream about for years.

From a high point of land on the Greenland side of Smith Sound, Captain Tyler and Mr. Tagliabeau saw more ice south of them, but also, in the distance, an open channel between the land-fast ice and the pack ice slicing southward. Isaac, blinded by the snow, would not remember this sight, but the others would; and Thomas would remember his frantic rush, at night when he was already exhausted, to caulk the boat's seams and repair the holes. And how anxious he'd felt when Erasmus told him they all depended on his ability to keep the boat together with no proper supplies.

At the Littleton Islands the ice field thinned, abraded from beneath by the currents from a nearby river. Barton would remember inching forward the last few miles, sounding the ice with a boat hook at every step and eying the eddies gurgling just below his feet. And then breaking through, despite his precautions: one side of the sledge crashing under, the sickening lurch and the scramble to firmer ice. Ivan remembered that moment—always, always—because he'd been tied in closest to the sledge and, as his companions heaved, had lost his footing and been pulled into the water, to bob briefly under the edge of the ice. By the time Erasmus pulled him out by the hair, he'd broken two fingers and seen blood pour from a gash in Erasmus's forehead. In the ice-choked water Erasmus floundered, scrambling for the provision bags slithering out of the boat as the sea slithered over the sides. The copper pot containing the Franklin relics slipped out too, but the air beneath the walrus skin kept it floating low in the water and at first Erasmus thought he might retrieve it. Under the broken floe it sailed, the floe that had nearly claimed Ivan; and although Erasmus pressed his shoulder against the edge and swept with his arms and then a paddle, finally lowering his head beneath the ice, the pot disappeared. That night a hard wind blew from the northeast, nearly freezing the wet men to death.

Erasmus would remember this because it was here that he lost the evidence of their search for Franklin's remains, and also because, although he could never be sure, he suspected that here began the process of freezing and constriction and infection that would later cause him to lose his toes. He should have been resting, with his boots removed and his feet wrapped in dry furs. But instead, that night he and Captain Tyler, with whom he'd been arguing since they left the brig, stood screaming at each other in front of the men and nearly came to blows. Each blamed the other for the accident and the loss of the relics—as each had blamed the other for every wrong turn taken, bad camping site chosen, failure hunting—and Captain Tyler had slashed the air with a boathook and said, "I despise you." A moment that Mr. Tagliabeau, never more than a few feet from his captain but less and less certain that his loyalty was justified, would also always remember. He'd longed to turn his back and say, "I despise you both," but had said nothing; on this journey he learned that he was both a coward and a complainer.

Not long after that accident, though, they stood on a high mound and saw a lane of open water spreading before them. With much effort they made their way to a rocky beach, and then unloaded the boat for the last time and sank it for a day to swell the seams. Not long enough, Thomas would remember thinking. The surf was beating against the cliffs; was it his fault the boat still leaked when it was finally, properly launched? They were ten men in a whaleboat made for six, with too much baggage. Trembling inches above the water they rowed, and felt like they were swimming. Under reefed sails, in a fresh breeze, they rounded Cape Alexander.

Ned would remember the mock sun that appeared in the sky that evening; a perfect parhelion—Dr. Boerhaave had taught him that word—with a point of light on either side. But neither Ned nor anyone else would be haunted by the sight of Dr. Boerhaave's head, which in the months since his drowning had been severed from his body by a passing grampus and then swept south in the currents, coming to rest face up on the rubble below a cliff. Among the rounded rocks his head was invisible to his friends, and the singing noise made by the wind passing over his jaw bones was lost in the roar of the waves.

Sutherland Island, where they'd hoped to land, was barricaded by ice. They bobbed all night in irregular winds and a violent freezing rain, and Ned would remember this place for the weather and the onset of his fever, which caused this journey to be jumbled forever after in his mind with his two earlier crossings of Smith Sound. Eastward with Joe and Dr. Boerhaave and Zeke he'd gone; westward with only Zeke. He remembered that. Pushing like an animal against the harness, pulling the sledge sunk into the soft surface—those journeys, or this journey?

Once the worst of the fever hit and he lay helpless among his companions, he repeated to himself the stories Joe had told him as they pulled another sledge, in another month. The stories that, once they reached Anoatok, Joe had translated for him around the fire. They'd lain on a platform inside the hut, mashed in a crowd of Esquimaux and sharing walrus steaks. Meat was piled along the ice belt and walrus skulls glared eyeless from the snowbanks. A mighty spirit called *Tonarsuk,* Joe had said, spearing a morsel from the soup pot. In whom these Esquimaux believe. And many minor supernatural beings, chief among them the goblins known as *innersuit,* who live among the fjords and have no noses. The *innersuit* hide behind the rocks, waiting to capture a passing man so they may cut off his nose and force him to join their tribe. Should the victim escape their clutches, his nose may be returned to him by the intercession of a skillful wizard, or *angekok.* The nose may come back, Joe had said; he'd been translating Ootuniah's words for Ned and Dr. Boerhaave, as they steamed companionably in the hut. The nose may come flying through the sky, and settle down in its former place; but the man once captured by the *innersuit* will always be known by the scar across his face.

Ned's fever, or frostbite, or something putrid he ate, had caused his own nose to erupt in pustules that leaked yellow fluid and then crusted over and cracked and bled. He would remember dread-ing his whole nose might disappear. And then thinking it *should* disappear—along with his face, his entire body: Who was to blame for all this, if not him? He had lied to Erasmus; he'd made those fur suits and shifted supplies like a thief; he'd planned this trip and organized the men. On Boothia, he'd pointed out the copper kettles that had set everything else in motion; on his earlier crossing of the Sound, he'd failed to save Dr. Boerhaave. As they passed fjords and glaciers he heard singing—not Dr. Boerhaave, but someone else— and begged the man against whose knee he was pressed to guard him from the goblins. The *innersuit* cause much trouble, Ootuniah had said. They plague many a journey. Weeping with guilt and fear, his hands cupped over his nose, Ned remembered his grandmother's tales back in Ireland. Malicious spirits who made porridge burn, toast fall buttered side down, cows lose their calves. Perhaps it was the *innersuit* who'd haunted this journey and brought the fickle, difficult weather.

Perhaps, he told Erasmus one night—perhaps it was the *innersuit* who were to blame for their bad luck. They pushed through half-solid water, around icebergs and currents of drift ice. One night they anchored in a crack as a gale struck from the northwest, watching helplessly as a floe on the far side of the channel broke off, spun on an iceberg like a pivot, and closed upon their resting place. When it hit the corner of their small dock the floe shattered, their haven shattered, everything around them rose and crushed and tumbled. The boat was tossed like a walnut shell into a boiling slurry of crushed ice and water, and Robert would remember this more sharply than the other accidents, because it was here that he dislocated his shoulder. Captain Tyler held him down while Erasmus torqued his arm back into place, and Robert would remember being amazed, even through the blinding pain, that the pair had worked in concert.

On Hakluyt Island they found birds, but failed to shoot any. A seal they shot near an iceberg sank before they could retrieve it. They ran out of food, for a week eating only a few ounces of bread dust and pemmican each day with all of them feverish, all of them weak, and Ned muttered that perhaps the *innersuit* had stolen Joe from them, and tipped Dr. Boerhaave into the water. Erasmus would remember this comment and how sharply it pained him. Despite his worry for Ned, and for the others who didn't understand how weak they'd grown but were each day less capable, still the mention of Dr. Boerhaave could make his mind freeze up. He never thought about Zeke, the thought was impossible; he hardly thought about what was happening to his feet, although they were oozing and stinking and numb; he focused on getting them all through each day, pushing forward and cooking and eating and resting and pushing again, putting the miles behind them. But when Ned muttered about goblins and Dr. Boerhaave, Erasmus had to fight to keep his concentration.

Northumberland Island, Whale Sound, Cape Parry. The sea was covered with drifting pack ice, which poured from Whale Sound in a constant stream. At night thin ice formed in the open patches, and Erasmus would remember the panic this caused him. If they were caught here they would never survive; and Ned would be the first to go. Ned was delirious, and when Robert and Ivan shot a heap of dovekies, Ned sat upright, his nose a bloody, eroded mass, and babbled. Something about a great hunt: he and Joe and Dr. Boerhaave joining the Esquimaux on the cliffs where the dovekies were breeding. Sweeping the birds from the air with nets at the end of long narwhal tusks; thousands caught as easily as one might pick peas and the bodies boiling in huge soapstone pots, the children sucking on bird skins and tearing raw birds limb from limb, their faces buried in feathers and blood smeared over their cheeks. But Ned wouldn't eat these other birds, he couldn't bear to bring food near his nose. He said names, only some of which Erasmus knew—Awahtok, Metek, Ootuniah; Myouk, Egurk, Nualik, Nessark—and later, when those names and the people behind them would return to haunt Erasmus, he'd remember envying Ned all he'd seen on that trip, and wishing yet again that he'd been present: Dr. Boerhaave might still be alive.

Erasmus both heard and didn't hear Ned as he forced the boat farther south. Captain Tyler and Mr. Tagliabeau contradicted his every order, more and more confident as they passed Hoppner Point and Granville Bay and it began to seem that, if they could just beat the final freezing-in, they might actually reach the whaling grounds. They were racing, racing, the temperature dropping each day and the new ice forming, the pack consolidating, the narrow channel closing: yet despite the urgency Captain Tyler argued over every tack and turn. These were his waters, Erasmus would remember him saying; they were in his country now and Erasmus must cede command to him. Here he knew what was best for the expedition.

Erasmus had unlaced his boots that morning, unable to resist confirming by eye what he could already feel; eight of his toes were black and dead. In Dr. Boerhaave's medicine chest were amputating knives, still sharp and gleaming, but it was impossible that he should use them on himself. It was also now impossible that he should walk any distance if the ice closed around them, but no one knew that yet. Or maybe Captain Tyler did know; he seemed to sense Erasmus's growing weakness.

"You refused to lead the men earlier," Erasmus would remember saying to the captain. "When the men most needed you, you'd do nothing. Now that there's a chance we might reach safety you want command, you want the credit." The rifles and powder and shot were scattered throughout the boat, but he had all the percussion caps and felt secure. "I'll shoot you if you disobey me," he said.

All the men would remember that: how nearly they'd come to

having to choose sides, how only a waving gun had saved them. For the last few days, creeping around Cape Dudley Digges and then through a narrow lead at the base of the ice foot, no one spoke except to give or respond to orders. Every night the temperature dropped below freezing, although it was still warm at noon. Sometimes it snowed. They rowed through a dense sludge that dripped from the oars like porridge, and when at last they doubled Cape York they dreaded the emptiness. October 3, Melville Bay. Upernavik, on the far side of the breaking-up yard, was still so many miles away.

WHAT GREETED ERASMUS in Melville Bay was dense pack ice, broken only by small, irregular leads; he'd expected this. What he didn't expect were the dark specks on the horizon. A cluster of specks and threads of something that, wavering and wafting upward, made his heart leap. Smoke? By now he'd long been familiar with the way the blank ice shifted perspective and perception—how what looked like a bear, far away, might turn out to be a hare nearby; how a nearby gentle hill might resolve into a distant, mighty range. At first he couldn't believe that the smoke was smoke. The specks, which seemed far away and large, might be closer, might be Esquimaux hunting. But the upright lines among the smoke threads were really masts, and those were truly ships. Seventeen ships, the men told each other, counting as they smashed the thin ice blocking their way and spun in a frantic, looping course through the seams around the floes. The ships appeared to be frozen in; a mile from the cluster their boat was stopped as well. They'd already burned the sledge for fuel and were too weak to haul the boat onto the solid ice.

"I'll go," Captain Tyler said. "I'll walk to the first ship and bring back enough men to help."

"No," Erasmus said. "Too many of us are broken down, I need

you here with me. The wind could change in a minute, and if the floes separate we could drift very quickly." He longed to go himself, but knew he couldn't walk more than a few steps. "Whoever is strongest and can move fastest must go. Barton, I think."

Barton leapt to his feet. "I'll run," he said. "I'll run the whole way."

Four hours later he returned with a crew of startled Shetland Islanders from a Dundee whaler. It was snowing and dark and very cold, and the ice was grinding beneath their feet. Erasmus greeted the sailors briefly, saying only that their ship was lost and they needed help. When he saw the pity on the sailors' faces, he understood how ragged and worn they must look. "Can you help us back to your ship? Can you take us in?"

The sailors, so strong and healthy, made short work of the task. They hauled the boat up on the ice, attached the drag lines, unloaded everything but the men's personal belongings and then, after a quick examination of the *Narwhal's* crew, sat Ned, Erasmus, and Ivan on the thwarts. Twelve of them dragged the boat, as if it weighed nothing, across the ice, while the others supported the men who could still walk. Thomas cringed at the sound of the keel splintering and grinding away.

Their way was lit by the moon, and by several fires. As they drew closer, Erasmus saw that these weren't bonfires, or cooking fires, but the remains of two ships burning. Nipped by the ice, they'd been sliced all the way through and partially sunk. Only the decking above the waterline remained. "It's the custom," one of the Shetland men said when Erasmus questioned him. "Among us whalers. When a ship is stove in, suchlike, we burn her remains." By the firelight Erasmus saw masts scattered over the ice, broken whaleboats, and a whole ship lying broadside, her keel exposed forlornly.

"Twenty vessels caught here," said the Shetland man. Magna Abernathy, or so Erasmus understood; his accent was very thick.

"Three lost so far. Their crews have been taken in by the other ships, but we still have some room. Our captain started preparing for you as soon as your messenger arrived."

Then a bark loomed before them like a castle. The *Harmony*, of Dundee, Magna announced. Captained by Alec Sturrock. Between the time Magna bolted up the planks and returned with his captain, Erasmus took in the cranes and whaleboats and the scarred, oily hull. After that everything happened so fast. Erasmus and his companions were carried, pushed, washed, tidied, bandaged, clothed; shown to newly hung hammocks where their belongings were stowed and then whisked away again. In the cabin they were blinded by the light of clean-burning lamps and stunned by the smell of baking bread. Ned was taken away by the ship's surgeon, who was worried by his fever and the condition of his nose, but Erasmus was allowed to stay with the others; no one had yet seen his feet.

Inside the *Harmony*, pressed hard to port by the ice, everything was tilted but the table had been leveled. Chairs were drawn up for them, plates set before them and wine, small glasses of red glowing wine. Only after they'd chewed and swallowed in silence for several minutes did Captain Sturrock ask, "How was your ship lost? How long have you been out in that boat?"

Erasmus leaned forward, ready to speak, but Captain Tyler spoke first. "Amos Tyler, of New London," he said. "I've captained whaling ships for twenty years." A quick exchange of places and names followed; the two captains hadn't met before, but had sailed the same waters and knew many people in common. Immediately Erasmus felt the balance of power shift like the bubble in a spirit level.

"Which was your brig?" Captain Sturrock asked. "We didn't see you among the fleet earlier in the season."

Captain Tyler curled his lip. "Not this season, indeed," he

said. Holding his glass out for more wine, he told Captain Sturrock his version of what had happened. How not this season, but last, he'd accepted a position as Sailing Master for an expedition in search of Sir John Franklin; how everything went wrong and they got stuck in the ice, because the expedition's commander wouldn't follow his advice. The eager questions about the fate of the Franklin expedition he answered briefly, impatiently. Then he went on and on and on, through all their own trials and the dark hopeless winter and their eventual escape. Erasmus tried to interrupt him, but couldn't. He was dizzy, sweating; the room was horribly close after their weeks in the open air and it was so hot, there were so many smells. "The *Narwhal* will never be freed," Captain Tyler concluded.

"And your commander?" asked the other captain. He looked around the cabin.

"Dead," Captain Tyler said. "As are several others."

Turning to Erasmus, he said, "This is the *Narwhal*'s naturalist, Erasmus Wells, a friend of Commander Voorhees. Commander Voorhees delegated to him responsibility for the expedition's goals in his absence, and it was his decision to abandon the brig and organize our boat journey. I merely navigated us through the ice."

Not his decision, Erasmus thought. But Ned's. Even this he couldn't take credit for. He must let them know that Zeke wasn't surely dead, only possibly dead, that there might still be hope. When he stood to speak, the floor tilted under him and the lamps merged into one gold ball and then disappeared. He was on the floor, flat on his back. Someone had undone his boots. Captain Sturrock and his surgeon and two other men were looking down at him, talking among themselves. The surgeon touched his toes, as Dr. Boerhaave might have done. "They'll have to come off," he said.

AFTERWARD, RECOVERING IN the first mate's cabin, Erasmus heard the story of how the *Harmony* had been trapped. He and Ned lay side by side, too weak to talk but able to listen.

In July the *Harmony,* along with ships from Hull and Aberdeen and Kirkcaldy and Newcastle, New Bedford, Nantucket, and New-foundland, had crept through the heavy ice in Melville Bay. When the fleet had finally escaped into the North Water they'd crossed quickly to Pond's Bay and then had found their route to the south blocked by fields of drifting ice. An easterly wind had driven ice into the bay, sealing the fleet inside; they'd seen no whales at all. For weeks they'd waited, anxious and bored, only to find the route south still blocked when the wind finally shifted and released them.

They'd tried to return to Upernavik; reaching Cape York again they'd found Melville Bay still choked with icebergs and heavy pack ice. Back to the west they'd gone, to be stopped again; back once more to Melville Bay, where the ice was even denser; back and forth a third time, twenty ships unable to find a safe route south. Strong winds from the southeast had crowded the fleet together, then pressed them against the ice trapped in the curve south of Cape York.

With the jib-boom of one ship overlapping the taffrail of the next they'd towed the ships through the narrow cracks until the wind closed the ice around them. The *Alexander* of New London had been crushed, and the *Union* of Hull; the *Swan* had been heaved on her side, where Erasmus had seen her. Since September 15 the fleet had been stuck here. And now, said Mr. Haslas—the surgeon, who visited Erasmus and Ned several times daily, and chattered while he examined them—now they could only hope that the ice might part once more. A strong wind from the northwest might still separate the floes, and if they could beat their way free before the young ice sealed the open water they might yet reach Upernavik.

The crews visited back and forth, held great gatherings on the ice, made music and gambled and danced; meanwhile the officers entertained each other, holding long dinners in their cabins. Captain Tyler and Mr. Tagliabeau went from one ship to the next, feted everywhere for their courage and wisdom. Or so Erasmus heard when, occasionally, one of the men tore himself away from the festivities and dropped by to see him and Ned. It was Thomas, after a visit to a New Bedford ship, who brought news of Dr. Kane.

"He left his ship in the ice," Thomas said. "Just like the Esquimaux told us. He and his crew made a journey like ours, in three small boats but earlier in the season. They crossed all the way to Upernavik and then were carried by a Danish ship to Godhavn, where they met up with the rescue expedition. They reached New York last October, and the men who told me this said it was in all the newspapers. Dr. Kane is a great hero now. Even though he was looking in completely the wrong place for Franklin."

He gazed dreamily past Erasmus's ruined feet. "Maybe we'll be heroes too," he said. "When we get home, maybe everyone will be thrilled to see us."

Erasmus looked over at Ned, lying a few feet from him and listening intently. Mr. Haslas had debrided his nose and applied poultices. But the soft flare of his left nostril had corroded away, as if it had been burned; scar tissue, tight and misshapen, replaced the normal flesh. Instead of a neat round hole, his nose had a dark narrow slit on that side. His own deformity, Erasmus thought, could at least be hidden inside his boots—how had this happened to Ned, so young and handsome?

"Do you think?" Ned said. "Will it be like that? Or will everyone blame us for abandoning the *Narwhal,* and for failing to bring back any evidence of what happened to Franklin?"

Thomas turned to him, waving his scarred hands. "Dr. Kane left *his* ship," he said. "He had to, and so did we."

Ned turned his face away, and Erasmus knew what he was thinking: that Dr. Kane had left no one behind except the surely dead.

A FEW NIGHTS later a great snowstorm descended, and with it a gale that shifted slowly from southwest to west to northwest. Erasmus and Ned heard the rush of feet on the deck above, excited chatter all night long as the ship shifted beneath them and their tilted world slowly leveled. Early the next morning Captain Sturrock rushed into their cabin, his hair sticking up and his eyes dark with excitement.

"The wind has opened the floes," he said. "We're afloat, all the ships are afloat, and we're going to try to head south through the leads. If we could have just a few days of this, before the new ice cements everything—I've spoken to Captain Nicholson, of the *Sarah Billopp.* If we're successful he's agreed to take you to his home at Marblehead."

"Marblehead?" Erasmus said. Captain Tyler and Mr. Tagliabeau squeezed in through the door, both looking as if they'd been up all night. "We won't stay with you?"

"Of course not," Captain Sturrock said. "You wish to return to Philadelphia, don't you? And that's as close as anyone in the fleet can get you."

Erasmus turned to Captain Tyler. "Do you agree that we should join the Marblehead ship?"

"You should, certainly," Captain Tyler said. "And Ned, and whoever else wants to join you. Ivan for sure, his fingers haven't healed correctly. But Mr. Tagliabeau and Robert and Sean and I are staying on with the *Harmony.*"

"Why would you want to go to Scotland?" Erasmus said. "I don't think we should split up."

"The *Harmony* isn't heading home," Captain Sturrock said. "Not right away—our holds are empty, we have nothing to show for our voyage and no way to pay off the crew. We've decided to head for Newfoundland, in company with Captain Bowring. He tells me that if we overwinter there we can head out beyond the Strait of Belle Isle in March with the sealing fleet, and take on a load of furs before we go home."

"You don't want to go home?" Erasmus said to Captain Tyler. "After all this time?"

"Of course I *want* to," Captain Tyler said scornfully. "But what will I live on? Do you think I'll ever see the rest of the money Commander Voorhees owes me for the voyage? I'm not like you discovery men, I have to make a living. The trip will be a waste for me, if I don't make up for the lost wages somehow. If we do well sealing, my share will be enough to send me home with at least something."

By his side Mr. Tagliabeau nodded away. This whole trip, Erasmus thought, all the man had done was nod. Never an opinion of his own, never an idea.

"What are 'discovery men'?" Ned asked.

Captain Tyler and Mr. Tagliabeau snorted. Before either of them could speak, Captain Sturrock answered, looking at Erasmus as he spoke.

"It's what we call you arctic exploring types," he said. "All you men who go off on exploring expeditions, with funding and fanfare and special clothes, thinking you'll discover something. When every place you go some whaling ship has already been. We know more about the land and the currents and the winds than you ever will, and more about the habits of the whales and seals and walruses. I've met Russian discovery ships, and English, and French, and never known them to discover much of anything. What is it you *discovered* on your voyage?"

"New coastline," Erasmus said. "We charted a good deal of new coast, north of Smith Sound. And we found relics from Franklin's expedition, just as I told you—that they're lost is surely not our fault."

"That's what discovery men do," Captain Sturrock said. "Get lost. Lose things. Franklin is lost, and his ships and his men, and Dr. Kane's ship is lost, and yours and all your precious relics and specimens. If the captain of a whaling ship ever lost things at the rate you do, he wouldn't be long employed."

"If I had known," Captain Tyler said. "If I had ever known . . ."

"At least American discovery ships take note of whales and seals on their voyages, and report back when they arrive home," Captain Sturrock continued. "*Our* discovery men apparently think whales are beneath them; they never so much as mention them when they return to England and write their fancy books. They're jealous of us is what it is. On the west side of Baffin's Bay, all the points and bays were named by whalers, not by discovery men."

"That British discovery ship we saw?" Captain Tyler added. "The *Resolute,* the one that set Commander Voorhees to thinking he should go north in the first place—all we did was look at it, but I heard an American whaler brought it home. It was cleaned and given back to the British government."

"We could have done that," Mr. Tagliabeau said. "That could have been us."

SEAN AND ROBERT stayed on the *Harmony* with Captain Tyler and Mr. Tagliabeau. On the *Sarah Billopp,* small and cramped, Captain Nicholson made room for Erasmus, Ned, Ivan, Barton, Isaac, and Thomas. Six men only, Erasmus thought. Out of the fifteen who'd left Philadelphia. He couldn't imagine arriving home with such a small remnant of the expedition. He couldn't imagine what he'd say to the families of the men who'd been lost or even the families of those who'd survived but who, because the expedition had so failed to achieve its goals, were headed off for another half a year, slaughtering seals. Partly he couldn't imagine these things because he couldn't truly imagine he was headed home. Yet as if the goblins had fallen asleep, the weather stayed fine just long enough for them to escape. Slipping through the ice-choked water, the fleet made its way to Upernavik, then quickly to Godhavn. There the ships went their separate ways.

The *Sarah Billopp*'s surgeon assured Erasmus that his feet were healing and that he'd be able to walk again someday. And it was only afterward, with some of the ships heading around the tip of Greenland while the *Harmony* carried Captain Tyler and Mr. Tagliabeau and Sean and Robert away from him, that Erasmus really understood all he'd lost. Ships turned east, ships turned west, and the shell in which he'd enclosed himself so he could bring the men to safety split like a sprouting seed.

He lay in his bunk, weeping. His toes were nothing. The failed goals of the expedition were not exactly nothing, but they'd always been Zeke's goals, not his. He'd lost the glorious collection of specimens he and Dr. Boerhaave had made together: all the birds and insects and flowers and ferns, the skins and scales and fossils and bones—gone, gone, gone. And with them his hope of writing a natural history of the arctic. Yet those losses were misfortune, which anyone might learn to accept.

But the *Narwhal* had lost half her crew, and he'd lost Dr. Boerhaave, the only true friend he'd ever had. He'd lost him, he'd lost Zeke, he'd lost his sister's chance at happiness. Lavinia waiting so patiently at home—how could he face her? He thought of her life, stripped of Zeke. And of his own, stripped of everything he'd ever wanted. Next to his head was the skin of the ship, a wall of wood; and beyond that waves, water, wind, creatures flying and swimming and breathing, the world spinning and stars whirling around the fixed pole to the north. Years from now, so much later, he would remember wanting to punch through that wall and dive into the waiting water.

PART III

8

Toodlamik, Skin and Bones

(November 1856–March 1857)

. . . There is a manifest progress in the succession of beings on the surface of the earth. This progress consists in an increasing similarity to the living fauna, and among the vertebrates, especially, in their increasing resemblance to Man. But this connection is not the consequence of a direct lineage between the fauna of different ages. There is nothing like parental descent connecting them. The fishes of the Palaeozoic age are in no respect the ancestors of the reptiles of the Secondary age, nor does Man descend from the mammals which preceded him in the Tertiary age. The link by which they are connected is of a higher and immaterial nature; and their connection is to be sought in the view of the Creator himself, whose aim, in forming the earth, in allowing it to undergo the successive changes which Geology has pointed out, and in creating successively all

*the different types of animals which have passed
away, was to introduce Man upon the surface
of our globe. Man is the end towards which all
the animal creation has tended, from the first
appearance of the first Palaeozoic fishes. In the
beginning His plan was formed, and from it
He has never swerved in any particular. . . . To
study, in this view, the succession of animals in
time, and their distribution in space, is, there-
fore, to become acquainted with the ideas of
God himself. . . . It is only as it contemplates, at
the same time, matter and mind, that Natural
History rises to its true character and dignity,
and leads to its worthiest end, by indicating to
us, in Creation, the execution of a plan fully
matured in the beginning, and undeviatingly
pursued; the work of a God infinitely wise, reg-
ulating Nature according to immutable laws,
which He has himself imposed on her.*

—LOUIS AGASSIZ AND A. A. GOULD,
Principles of Zoology (1851)

THE   ENGRAVINGS   WERE   BEAUTIFUL,   ALEXANDRA
thought: even those on which she'd worked. Again she pursed her
lips and blew a gentle stream of air. Again the sheet of tissue folded

back, revealing the image below. Dr. Kane's *Arctic Explorations,* which Mr. Archibault had given to her; she could hardly believe she'd had a hand in its creation. Her gaze moved between the volumes and the advertisement Mr. Archibault had also brought:

DR. KANE'S GREAT WORK,

ARCTIC EXPLORATIONS,

Is now being read by more than five hundred thousand persons, old and young, learned and unlearned. It is just the book which should be owned and read by every American.

500 NEWSPAPERS

have each pronounced it the most remarkable
and marvelous work ever published.

THE FOREIGN JOURNALS

and the most distinguished *savans* of Europe are extravagant in its praise. It is more interesting than

ROBINSON CRUSOE;

being a faithful account of privations and hardships, the
narrative of which cannot be read without a shudder.

OUR MOST EMINENT MEN

have vied with each other in extolling its merits.
Read the opinions of a few of them.

W. H. PRESCOTT, the Historian, says—
"It is one of the most remarkable records I have ever met with,
of difficulties and sufferings, and of the power of a brave spirit

to overcome them. No man has probably done more than Dr. Kane to lift the dread veil of mystery which hangs over the Arctic regions. His sensibility to the sublime and the beautiful gives a picturesque effect to his descriptions of the wonderful scenery by which he was surrounded; and he tells the occurrences of his daily life, enveloped with the most frightful perils, with a good-humored simplicity and air of truth that win our confidence, and must have a fascination even for the youngest reader."

WM. C. BRYANT, the Poet, says—

"The merits of Dr. Kane's recent work are so universally acknowledged, that it seems superfluous to praise it. It is a record of one of the most daring—and, so far as the interests of science are concerned, one of the most successful—enterprises of modern times, and it is written in a most interesting manner,—a manner which gives the reader a high idea of the intellectual and moral qualities of the author."

Hon. GEO. BANCROFT, the Historian, says—

"His expedition—in view of the small number of his party, the size of his vessel, (which had not even one companion,) the extent to which he explored the Polar regions, the length of time he remained there, and the marvels of his escape—seems to me without a parallel.

"His constant self-possession during his long trials, his quickness of judgment, his unshrinking courage in danger, his fertility of resources in the hours of greatest difficulty, give him a very high place in the very first rank of Polar navigators as a leader, and commander, and man; and no one of them all has told the story of their adventures so charmingly as he has done. For execution, so far as the publishers are concerned, the volumes are among the handsomest that have issued from the American press."

WASHINGTON IRVING says—

You ask my opinion of his work. What can I say that has not been already said by more competent critics? I do not pretend to critical acumen; being too much influenced by my feelings: still I may give some opinion in this department of literature, having from childhood had a passion for voyages of discovery, and I know of none that ever more thoroughly interested and delighted me than this of Dr. Kane. While I read the work I had the author continually in my "mind's eye." I was present when he lectured in the Smithsonian Institution in 1853, on the Arctic Expedition, which he had already made; when we all wondered that one of a physique apparently so slight and fragile, having once gone through such perils and hardships, should have the daring spirit to encounter them again. I saw him after his return from that second Expedition, a broken down man, broken down in all but intellect, about to embark for Europe, in the vain hope of bracing up a shattered constitution.

It was this image of the author, continually before me, that made me read his narrative, so simply, truthfully, and ably written, with continued wonder and admiration. His Expedition, and his narrative of it, form one of the most extraordinary instances of the triumphs of mental energy and enthusiasm over a frail physical organization that I have ever known. His name, like that of Henry Grinnell, will remain an honor to his country.

Hon. EDWARD EVERETT says—

"It does the author equal credit as a man of science, and an energetic, skillful and courageous adventurer, and a true-hearted philanthropist. In conjunction with his former publication, it will secure him an abiding-place on the rolls of honest fame among the heroes of humanity. The style of typography and illustration is of superior excellence."

G. P. R. JAMES, the Novelist, says—

"I read the two volumes with deeper interest than I ever felt in any work in my life; and I concluded them with love and admiration for the man who wrote them. I only wish there were a dozen volumes more."

Gen. LEWIS CASS says—

"The expedition is a monument of human energy and endurance, originating in the most honorable and commendable motives, and conducted with rare courage, sagacity and perseverance. To the severity of truth it adds the romantic interest of perilous adventure and of the extremity of exposure and suffering. I never read a narrative which took firmer hold of my feelings, nor which excited to a higher degree my commiseration for the heroic men whose terrible calamities it records, nor my admiration for the fortitude with which these were met. It was a contest between man and nature—between the stern power of an Arctic winter and the human frame to resist it. And it is wonderful to see that in their worst extremity the objects of the expedition were never abandoned by the hardy explorers, but they seemed to triumph over the icy desolation whose broad expanse was marked by no animated being but themselves. All other life had fled before its power of destruction."

Hon. CHARLES SUMNER says—

"It is a book of rarest interest and instruction; written with simplicity, ease and directness; possessing all the attractions of romantic adventure elevated by scientific discovery, and, as we sit at our warm firesides, bringing under our eyes a distant portion of the globe, which, throughout all time until now, has slumbered unknown, locked in primeval ice."

Prof. LOUIS AGASSIZ says—

"It will give me the greatest pleasure to write a scientific review of Dr. Kane's last expedition, which I have read with the deepest interest, mingled with admiration for his energy and the warmest sympathy for his sufferings.

Caught up in the work itself, she hadn't imagined the results. She hadn't imagined everyone reading and discussing the book, leaving her to feel like such a liar. And she hadn't imagined its effect on Erasmus, because she'd believed him dead.

When the bulk of the whaling fleet returned in September, with no reports of the *Narwhal*, everything she'd learned about the arctic from her earlier reading had convinced her the expedition must be lost. Zeke's father had begun organizing a rescue expedition for the following summer, but although she'd reassured Lavinia constantly that the men were alive, she'd lost hope herself. Then a whaling ship had hobbled into Marblehead, miraculously bearing Erasmus and a fraction of his crew.

The newspapers had been writing about Dr. Kane's voyage to England and his glorious book; perhaps weary of praising so much, they'd leaped to blame Erasmus for abandoning Zeke and the brig. They wrote as if a mutiny had taken place, or at least acts of fatal misjudgment; they hummed with indignation and questioned the fates of Captain Tyler and the others who'd splintered off from Erasmus's command. For that boy with the ruined face, and Erasmus himself with his ruined feet, they seemed to have no pity. Erasmus had offered his journal and a piece of a boot he claimed had belonged to one of Franklin's men; the reporters had scorned him and all but called him an outright liar. Linnaeus and Humboldt, who'd brought Erasmus home, had tried to keep the worst of the press from him. But they hadn't been able to keep Lavinia from calling him a murderer. Nor could they keep him from learning that everyone, everywhere, compared him unfavorably to Dr. Kane.

Even now, staying on at his house far beyond the time she'd planned, even with Erasmus recuperating in the Repository and Lavinia confined to her bed upstairs, Alexandra couldn't make sense of this astonishing conflation of events. She tried to distract Erasmus with her copy of *Arctic Explorations,* but as he thumbed through the two blue volumes he groaned over the coincidences between his and Kane's voyage. He looked up from the pages one afternoon, as if noticing her for the first time, and said, "What are you doing here?"

She couldn't say that this was her job now. Linnaeus and Humboldt had begged her to stay, at least until Lavinia was able to leave her bed. But she couldn't repeat the way Humboldt had said, "There are things the servants can't do," or the way Linnaeus had added, "And you've been such a friend to the family. We'd be glad to pay you the wages of a housekeeper." Closets and cupboards and linen presses had loomed in her mind, and the faces of the cook, the maids, the groom. She'd thought of herself as repaying a family's kindness, not as a paid servant. "More than those wages," Humboldt had added, seeing her face. "We wouldn't want you to do any actual housework; if you need more help just let us know."

She couldn't repeat this uneasy conversation to Erasmus. Instead she said, "Your brothers have been kind enough to allow me to stay here, and to continue my education while providing some companionship for your sister. And for you, if that's agreeable."

The portrait of Franklin looked down from the wall; on a table lay a battered medicine chest; on the bed was a metal box. Erasmus hid the contents of the box from her, but she'd glimpsed a letter case, a handful of books, and the journal Lavinia had sent off with Zeke, now stained and worn. "I write a clear hand," she said. "Perhaps I could help you with some of the papers you brought back?"

IN A NEW BOOK, plain black covers with a red leather spine, Erasmus wrote:

I try to take comfort in what's around me, I try to be grateful to be back home, to see what's here to see. Outside my window the sky is a dark rich gray, shot through with occasional bolts of sun, the leaves alight then mysteriously dimmed, then alight again: golden leaves. Through them move a red cardinal, a black crow, a horde of crows swirling to roost in the big oak. As darkness falls they flock in from all over the city, birds crowding every branch and all of them speaking all at once, amazing noise: are you there? I am here. Are you there? I am here. Good night, good night, good night. Why can't I simply enjoy them?

After all the time I spent dreaming of home, now I dream nightly that I'm in my bunk on the Narwhal, *with the crew intact around me. Lavinia blames me, everyone blames me, for returning* *without Zeke. I blame myself. I knew, as much as anyone could, what dangers we might face; those years on the Exploring Expedition let me imagine the arctic without the blur of romance. But why didn't I see the great failure of Zeke's imagination? None of his reading taught him the crucial thing. He could imagine the hardships faced by the explorers preceding us; but not that anything bad might happen to <u>himself</u>. Always he thought of himself as charmed. A boy's belief.*

What I want is to talk with my companions, but they've scattered. Thomas, who dreamed we'd all be heroes, was so ashamed of what the newspapers wrote that he signed on with a merchant ship and has already left for California. Ivan and Isaac went home to their families. Barton found work on a farm. I'm all alone. Are you there? I am here; no one's there.

This week I finally started doing the things I should have done the minute I got back. I wrote to Lady Franklin, enclosing a list of the relics and a version of Oonali's account of the sunken ship. I wrote to the families of Captain Tyler, Mr. Tagliabeau, Robert, and Sean, enclosing the letters they entrusted to me when we parted and promising to inquire into the status of the unpaid portions of their wages. I wrote to Ned Kynd, who sent a letter from the Adirondack Mountains; I paid him from my own pocket, and offered whatever help he needs. He says his nose is healed, but is permanently deformed. I told him my stumps are almost healed, and that I'd give anything for his wounds to be mine.

The saddest task has been writing to Dr. Boerhaave's friends. In his writing case were several thick letters to William Greenstone in Edinburgh, and one to a Thomas Cholmondelay in London. I made a packet for each, enclosing the letters and my own account of Dr. Boerhaave's contributions to our expedition. How much he learned, how much he taught us all. How he died. Ned's version, not Zeke's; and even Ned's I softened. He died, I said, on a trip to gather data about the Smith Sound Esquimaux and the flora and fauna supporting them. How bitter it is to refer them for further details to Dr. Kane's book.

Kane visited almost every place we went; almost all the coastline Zeke laid down Kane shows on his map, with his own names; the very sea to the north of us—the sea whose coastline Zeke left us to explore—shows up as "Kane Basin." For descriptions of the Smith Sound Esquimaux I need only refer Dr. Boerhaave's friends to the appropriate pages in Kane's volumes; for illustrations of the people Dr. Boerhaave last saw I point to the engravings. And so forth and so on; unbearable. Even the Esquimaux names Ned muttered in his delirium are here. I wish I could compare experiences with Dr. Kane, but he's gone to England: his health ruined by his arctic experience and the exertions of writing so much so fast. To William Greenstone I offered one personal note; that our lives were saved by the little white grubs in the caribou skins, which indirectly he taught us to eat. I didn't tell him I have Dr. Boerhaave's journal. I can't stand to let it out of my hands.

WHEN ZEKE'S SISTERS visited in December, Alexandra led them to the Repository. Both were taller than Alexandra, blond and impeccably groomed, and as she drew up chairs she couldn't help comparing their rich, sleek, black dresses with her own tired poplin frock. Despite the money squirreled away in her sewing box she'd spent nothing on clothes and still had only this lilac, her brown silk, and the gray with a few fresh trimmings. Her clothes hadn't mattered when she'd spent her days wrapped in a long tan painter's smock. The chairs disappeared beneath the sisters' swishing skirts as Erasmus propped himself up.

"How is your health?" Violet asked. She gestured at the bed, where the box keeping the bedclothes off his feet made an awkward bulge.

"Better," Erasmus said. He'd seen no one from Zeke's family since his first days back in Philadelphia. "The doctor says I may be able to start walking after Christmas."

Laurel nodded. "Alexandra," she said. "It's good to see you again. You're enjoying your stay here?"

"I keep busy," Alexandra said. "I'm glad to be able to help Lavinia."

"She's still . . . ?" Violet said.

"Still," Alexandra said.

Then no one knew what to say. Zeke's parents, when they emerged from their first month of mourning, had commissioned the building of a ship for the study of marine biology, in honor of their lost hero; the keel of the *Zechariah Voorhees* had already been laid. Dignified grief, a family behaving well. Although they still avoided Erasmus they'd sent their daughters. Yet their example hadn't swayed Lavinia. Lavinia refused their invitations; she hid upstairs and wouldn't come down and seemed to be doing her best to emulate Lady Franklin. Incoherent letters poured from her pen—to the newspapers, the Smithsonian Institution, members of Congress. Someone must organize another expedition to search for Zeke's bones. Papers, papers; she gave them to Linnaeus, who promised to post them but hid them in his office safe instead.

Alexandra poured coffee and offered macaroons. In the silence Laurel finally said to Erasmus, "Our father sent some addresses for you—the families of the crewmen you asked about. And says to tell you he wrote to them himself, the first week you were back." A folded sheet of paper emerged from somewhere in the mass of black silk.

"Thank you," Erasmus said. "I appreciate that."

More silence. Alexandra felt Zeke in the room, as if he'd come through the window along with the sun and was standing there smiling and raising his tufty eyebrows. They all wanted to talk about him, and couldn't or wouldn't, she thought. His sisters were longing for something that would help them envision his last days; Erasmus was praying they wouldn't ask a single question; and she herself was caught in the stillness . . . she rose and walked to the window and back.

"I've been learning to engrave on copper and steel," she said, not knowing what else to talk about. "Did you know that? Lavinia and I began taking engraving lessons last summer from one of the Wellses' master engravers. I'm still taking them, it's very interesting."

Violet swiveled her head on her neck, like a large swan. "You were always artistic," she said. "Do you remember our lessons with Mr. Peale? One of your sisters came with you, I think."

"Emily," Alexandra said. "She hated painting, she hated those mornings."

"And Lavinia," Laurel added. "And the van Ostade girls, and the Winslows, and the three little Peale cousins. But you were always the best. When we did the flower paintings, yours were the only ones that looked like flowers growing. The still life with the dead rabbit, the one that made Martha van Ostade so sick; I still remember yours. You always had a flair. Do you like the engraving?"

"I do," said Alexandra. "Very much."

She had a sudden sharp memory of those Saturday classes in Mr. Peale's atelier. In a high-ceilinged room lit by oblong skylights the girls had gathered around their easels, frowning seriously at a stuffed bird or a heap of fruit and crooking their thumbs on their palettes. For those hours it hadn't mattered whose family was wealthy and whose was not. Later, as they turned eighteen and nineteen, Violet and Laurel would disappear into a world of dances and social events closed to Alexandra after her parents' accident. But in the atelier

Mr. Peale had encouraged them all equally, correcting shadows and skewed perspectives, teaching them to represent the real. Round objects onto flat paper: leaves, lizards, roses, pots. Sometimes they'd posed for each other, draped in bunting or wreathed with ivy, allegorically arranged and fully clothed. Never a naked human form—but how to learn the basic facts of anatomy? Secretly, at home, Alexandra had drawn her own limbs before a candlelit mirror.

Violet and Laurel were smiling now and had a little color in their faces, as if the chatter about their shared girlhood had loosened something in them. To Erasmus, who'd been staring at the sheet of paper, Violet said, "We don't blame you, you know. Some do, but not us."

"You must forgive our parents," Laurel added. "They don't blame you either, not exactly—but this has been so terrible for them, Father isn't ready to see you yet. But he knows we're here."

"That's . . . kind of him." Everyone was looking away from everyone else. Through the windows the leafless trees were black against the sky. "It's so cold," Erasmus said, pulling the quilt higher on his chest.

The stove was glowing, but the women looked at each other and nodded. "We should go," Violet said. "You'll give our regards to Lavinia? We'd be glad to see her, when she feels ready."

"I'll tell her that," Alexandra said.

When they were gone she stood a few feet from Erasmus's bed, puzzled by his reticence. "Why didn't you tell them something about what Zeke was like up there? How he was, something good he did . . ."

"Something good he did," Erasmus repeated.

She waited, but he added nothing. In his first days home, during his bouts of fever, he'd spouted wild tales about Zeke. She hadn't known what to make of these—what had happened between the two friends up there, amid the ice and darkness?

"I feel like all I'm doing is waiting," Erasmus said. "Waiting to heal, waiting to learn how to walk without toes, waiting to see what shape my life will take now."

Alexandra lit the other lamps and fiddled with the stove until the room was warm and bright. "What did you think your life would be like?"

Erasmus leaned toward the stove. "Like my father's life," he said. "Only more so. Like the lives of his friends, who did this as more than a hobby. This little building," he said, waving at the space around him. "If you could have seen what it was like when I was a boy—half zoo and half museum, my father let us do anything we wanted. For a while we had a big tree in the corner, with live birds roosting in it. Aquariums, and an ant colony, and turtles and sala-manders; and jars of preserved specimens everywhere, big slabs of fossil-bearing rock and mastodon bones and a plant press, books open on all the tables. A wonderful, fertile clutter."

Alexandra looked around the Repository, which still seemed clut-tered to her. So many books and specimens, so much equipment—the microscope, the dissecting table set before the window; shelves and saucers and little zinc labels; heaps of unbound books and pages ripped from pamphlets. But it was true there wasn't a single liv-ing creature.

"Almost every fine day," Erasmus said, "we'd gather at breakfast, the four of us boys and our father, and tell him our plans before he went off to work."

Where was Lavinia? Alexandra thought. While the boys were making plans?

"We'd pick some field or stream and go gather specimens. When we returned, three of us would work at mounting or dissecting what we'd gathered and the fourth would read aloud. Embryology, ich-thyology, paleontology; it was all so exciting. Sometimes we'd visit

Peale's museum and study the mammoth bones and the sea serpents. At night our father would join us and examine what we'd gathered and ask us what we'd learned. Then he'd look at our notebooks."

"You kept those even as little boys?" Perhaps Lavinia had kept one too. Or perhaps she'd simply watched her world shrink and shrink, while her brothers' worlds expanded.

"Always," Erasmus said. "It was part of our father's plan for educating us. We must read French and German and Latin, and learn how to draw accurately. We were to keep notebooks of all our observations, illustrated ourselves."

"I'd love to have seen those," Alexandra said, thinking of her own sketchbooks. In Browning's house she'd had only a cubicle off the parlor to herself, and almost no privacy. Always, though, she'd had a small locked trunk of her own. In it she'd kept—still kept, the trunk was under her bed—the sketchbooks in which she drew herself and her sisters, and whatever else came to hand.

"Look under E in the bookshelves," Erasmus said. "I believe you'll find them there. If you'd bring them to me . . ."

She pushed the rolling ladder into place. Between a book about ferns and a description of the invertebrates of the Orinoco River region she found five buckram-bound books with red spines and no titles.

"I started the first when I was ten," he said, when she returned with them. "The last ends the day before I left on the Exploring Expedition." He opened one. "See? This is what we did."

She peered at a drawing of a wasp's nest. The whole nest, from the outside; an interior view after a side had been cut away; larvae and full-grown wasps in various positions. The drawings, done in black ink with a light wash, were clumsy but vivid, labeled in a boyish, somewhat crooked hand.

"That's from when I was twelve," Erasmus said. "Copernicus's are much nicer, he was always the real artist in the family. Linnaeus's and Humboldt's are more orderly, and the drawings are probably better, but they're less detailed—keeping the notebooks was always a chore for them, they never liked it as much as I did. Even when I was a boy, I was sure I wanted to be a naturalist."

"They're charming," Alexandra said, with her hand poised to turn the page. "May I?"

Erasmus nodded, and she flipped through the volume: bones, fish, birds' organs, worms, spiders, pupae, lichens. Suddenly she had tears in her eyes. Lying there so worn and beaten, Erasmus had seemed old to her since his return although there was less than fifteen years between them; he was forty-two, she thought. His hair had thinned and faded; he'd lost weight and his face was drawn, with deep lines on his forehead. His attitude of defeat had aged him further. But in these pages she could see the hopeful boy he'd been.

"That Exploring Expedition," he said. "Everything that happened after we got home, it broke something in me. But this voyage was like another chance."

For a minute he spoke about Dr. Boerhaave—all they'd collected, their good conversations, all they'd shared—and Alexandra felt a pang of envy.

"I was going to write a book about the arctic," he concluded. "Perhaps a wonderful book."

"You could still do that."

Erasmus shrugged. "No one wants to hear about our expedition. The big failure, the big anticlimax. With Zeke dead and the brig abandoned, what is there to say? What is there to write about that Dr. Kane hasn't already covered?"

"But a natural history of the arctic," Alexandra said. "Not a travel book, not a book of memoir and adventure like Dr. Kane's, but something about the area's botany and zoology?"

"That's what I meant to do, really," Erasmus said. "But all my specimens are gone, and Dr. Kane printed those long compilations of plants and animals in his Appendix. All I have left are the lists I brought home, and some notes in my journal. And my friend's journal, I have that too."

He didn't offer to show her these, Alexandra noticed. She could look at his childhood notebooks but not at what was most important to him, not what he'd done recently.

A FEW DAYS later she entered the Repository to find the tin box open and Erasmus reading something with a mottled cover. Heaped on the bed beside him were Agassiz's books about fossil fish, and near those the worn journal that Lavinia had once pressed into Zeke's hands. Alexandra expected Erasmus to bury the books in the bedclothes, as he'd done before when she interrupted his secret researches. But he left everything open this time, drawing back his hands as she approached.

"You see what I do?" he said. "This is what I do with my time these days. I paw through my own journal"—here he touched the green volume—"Zeke wasn't using this, he let me have it." With his other hand he touched the speckled volume. "Then I read in here. This belonged to my friend. I was just looking at a passage he'd written about some fossil fish, and I was comparing his description with Agassiz's plates—these books were Dr. Boerhaave's too, I can hardly believe I managed to get them home. Do you know them?"

"Only by reputation," Alexandra murmured. "You didn't have a copy here."

"The plates are extraordinary," Erasmus said. "Copernicus can do things like this, but I never could." He flipped through the pages for a minute and consulted Dr. Boerhaave's journal. "My friend was acquainted with Agassiz," he told Alexandra. "They met when Agassiz was visiting the Scottish Highlands, looking at the fossil fishes in the Old Red Sandstone. He was recollecting that trip, and he mentioned a fish I was trying to find—here."

He pointed out a chromolithograph of an odd-looking creature, all spines and overlapping plates. Alexandra gazed at the subtle hues and textures. "That's gorgeous," she said. "Really remarkable. Work like this—it makes me see how important illustration can be, how it's truly one of a naturalist's tools."

"It is," Erasmus said. "With accurate drawings, one can compare specimens from all over the world without having to rummage in the cabinets of museums and individual collectors. It's as if I'm holding the fossil right here in my hands."

"I heard Agassiz lecture when he visited Philadelphia," Alexandra said. "Fascinating."

"I did too!" Erasmus said. "But you must have been only a child."

"Not quite—I was fifteen or sixteen."

They smiled at each other, and then Alexandra remembered the stories her sister Emily had told her. "What Agassiz is doing now," she said, "he's such an interesting thinker, and yet—have you read the essay he contributed to Nott and Glidden's *Types of Mankind*?"

"I haven't," Erasmus said. "It came out just as Zeke and I were getting ready to leave, and I never had time to look at it."

"You should," Alexandra said. "You've been among the Esquimaux yourself now, you'd be a better judge. He extends his argument about separate, successive creations of life in different geographical centers to man. The races of man correspond to the great zoological regions, he says, and perhaps they're *autochthonai,* like plants, originating where they're found. Eight primary human types, each originating in and inhabiting a specific zoological province—one of his types is Arctic man, your Esquimaux. He seems almost to be arguing that his types are separate species."

"I . . ." Erasmus said. He paused for half a minute. A white moth fluttered before him, released from a cocoon behind the books. "It's wonderful to have you around, for me to have someone to discuss books and ideas with. I appreciate all the time you spend with me. But . . ."

To Alexandra's horror, tears slid down the bony slopes of his nose.

"Forgive me," he whispered. "I'm so tired, still. I don't know what I think about anything, and Lavinia hates me and I miss Dr. Boerhaave so much—how can I know what I think about some foolishness Agassiz has written? All I can think is that he was my friend's friend, and that my friend is lost, everything is lost." He reached up, closed his hand around the moth, peered at it, and then released it.

Alexandra turned toward the window while he recovered himself. Across the garden Lavinia's window was visible, the blinds drawn although the sky was still light. Whenever she urged Lavinia to rise, Lavinia turned her head and said, "How can you understand? You were always so clever, you can do anything. But without Zeke, what am I? Zeke was the only one who really loved me."

"You should write your book," she said, turning back to Erasmus. "It's the best way to honor Dr. Boerhaave. And Zeke, and the whole expedition."

"How?" Erasmus said. "With what? All my specimens are gone."

"Thomas Say had all his notebooks stolen on his first western trip. His notes on the Indians, all his descriptions of animal species, everything. But he still managed to keep working." She picked up his journal. "May I?"

It was better than she could have hoped; on almost every page, among the descriptions and narrative passages, were sketches of birds and bones and cliffs, a tusk found in a creek.

"Say was still a young man when he died," Erasmus said, following the movements of her hands. "He died before he lost hope."

She reached for Dr. Boerhaave's journal: more sketches, in more detail. "Dr. Kane had nothing more than such notes and sketches when he got home," she said. "But from them all the paintings for his book were made and then engraved."

"I'm no artist," Erasmus said glumly. "Copernicus is the one who can paint."

"I'm not bad at drawing and painting." Alexandra looked down at her capable hands. "With your sketches, with you correcting everything, telling me the colors and what details you remember, I might be able to make something reasonable."

As if he could not stop the process, Erasmus's eyebrows knotted and his lips curled, blowing out a little derogatory puff of air. Alexandra dropped the journal and turned from him.

"I'm sorry," he said. "I didn't mean to imply, it's just—what do you really know about this?"

Alexandra seized Dr. Kane's *Arctic Explorations,* opening the second volume to one of her engravings. Before she could think about what she was doing, she stuck it under Erasmus's nose. "*I* did this, or most of it. And this." She turned to another plate. "And this, and the background to this, and this seal . . ." In her hurry she tore the tissue overlying one of the plates.

She described Mr. Archibault's injured wrists and their secret sessions. "No one knows," she said, smoothing the edges of the tissue back together. "No one can ever know, Mr. Archibault would lose his job and your brothers would be furious, you can't tell anyone. But I could help *you,* if you weren't so stubborn . . ." She could help herself as well, she thought. Together they might work on a project she could claim partly as her own.

"You worked on *his* book?" Erasmus exclaimed. "How could you betray our family like that?"

Bewildered, she pressed the volume to her chest. "Your own brothers directed the engraving for the plates."

"That was business!" Erasmus said. "They had no idea Zeke and I were in the same area as Dr. Kane. They thought I was dead, they didn't know I was coming back."

"And how would *I* have known that?"

"Would you just leave?" Erasmus said.

He turned his back and pulled his pillow over his head. After he heard the door close he fell asleep—he slept so much now, he couldn't help it—and he woke thick-headed, with the sun beginning to color the sky. He reached for his journal and wrote:

Dr. Kane's narrative of the First Grinnell Expedition was a boy's romp, an adventure story—but this new book is so good I can't bear to look at it. If he and I had become friends, if I'd gone on his expedition rather than Zeke's; but he didn't even consider me. Everyone has passed me. Maury's published his Physical Geography of the Sea, *supporting Kane's findings about the open polar basin. Ringgold's already written up some of his work from the North Pacific Expedition: another expedition that might have included me. He found small shelled animals on the bottom of the Coral Sea, two and a half miles down—a very important discovery, proving that there's no azoic zone. No place where the great weight of water prevents a plumb line from passing, creatures from living. My father used to tell me that, below a certain depth, nothing could sink and drowned bodies and wrecked ships floated far off the bottom in layers related to their weight. That's what I feel like myself. As if I'm*

*floating below the surface, above the bottom, suspended in fluid
as thick as mercury. Why hasn't Lady Franklin written me back?*

AFTER THAT QUARREL, Alexandra avoided him and spent more
time with Lavinia. They'd seen each other tired, crabby, partially
dressed; sullen, excited, impatient, broken: although Lavinia was difficult to be around these days, Alexandra thought of her as another
sister. The sight of Lavinia's uncoiled hair, matted around her shoulders, pained her. So did the scraps of paper drifting around Lavinia's
bed: letters pleading that people find Zeke's body, rescue Zeke's relics, discover new seas in the name of Zeke. None of which would
ever be sent. The sight of her brothers made her weep, the doctor
annoyed her, and nothing Alexandra said seemed to help. Sitting
useless by Lavinia's bed, Alexandra thought of calling on Browning.
Everyone in their neighborhood turned to him; despite a certain
humorlessness he had a rare talent for comforting the bereaved and
once had soothed a widow who'd locked herself in her attic after
losing her children in a skating accident. Berating herself for not
thinking of this before, she asked for his help.

For the next few weeks, Browning visited Lavinia frequently, gliding dark-suited up to her room with his Bible and a handful of other
books. Although Alexandra wasn't privy to their conversations she
could see how much they helped. Lavinia stopped writing letters and
began to come downstairs for a few hours each day; she dressed and
ate and took some interest in the workings of the household. What
had Browning said? With his guidance she'd begun to pray again,
Lavinia revealed. As she had as a girl; it comforted her. When Linnaeus and Humboldt proposed a family Christmas dinner, she agreed.

"I can't make the arrangements," she said. "But if Alexandra is
willing . . ."

"Of course," Alexandra said. "It would be my pleasure."

"Let's have both families, then," Lavinia said. "Ours, and yours—would your brother come, do you think? I would like that."

Alexandra chose the menu, consulted with the cook, directed the housecleaning and supervised the decorating of the tree. The house was beautiful and no one minded how much she spent. On Christmas day they gathered around the huge mahogany table, with all the leaves inserted and chairs borrowed from every room. Linnaeus and Lucy and their daughter; Humboldt and Ellen and their little son; Alexandra's sisters, Emily and Jane; Browning and Harriet and Nicholas, who was almost three. Harriet, expecting another child in January, sat in an armchair with a pillow behind her back. Lavinia sat at the foot of the table, presiding over all that Alexandra had arranged. Alexandra sat to her right, where she might remind Lavinia unobtrusively of some forgotten dish or ritual. Far away, at the head of the table, was Erasmus in his wheeled chair. A turkey at one end, a ham at the other; white porcelain dishes of vegetables steaming beneath their covers; relishes and sauces and gravies and condiments; a forest of stemware, a sea of silver.

The candles sparked a confusing network of reflections from the shining surfaces, and during Browning's long prayer Alexandra saw flames in wine and faces in spoons. "So much has been taken from us," Browning said. "Yet so much remains." Then something about thanking the Lord for the bounty before them and the family remaining to them, and a long loop through the Lord's mysterious ways. How hard it is, Browning said, to accept the accidents that befall us. The ferry exploding on the river, which had taken from him and his sisters their parents; the childbed fever that had taken Mrs. Wells from her children when they were still so young—we have these losses in common, he said. They bind our families. As does this accident in the unknown regions of the north. Zechariah is gone from us, but we are grateful for the return of Erasmus.

Throughout all this, Alexandra saw, Lavinia stared straight ahead. Straight at Erasmus, her right hand tucked in her lap while her left turned a silver spoon back to front, front to back, the reflections melting, re-forming, and melting again. When Browning said, "Amen," Lavinia said softly, "I forgive you." Everyone knew she was speaking to Erasmus. "I understand that you did your best."

"I did," said Erasmus. His end of the table was so far from hers. "I did everything I could."

There was a precarious moment of silence. Then Nicholas tipped over a dish of pickles, Humboldt's little William laughed delightedly, Harriet began to scold her son and was stopped by Browning's quiet hand on hers. Dinner passed, almost festive, everyone chattering while Lavinia and Erasmus regarded each other and Alexandra thought, *Have they made up, then?* Between them she'd felt pulled so thin that light might shine through her lungs. Perhaps Browning had repeated to Lavinia the words he'd spoken after their own parents' deaths—how, in a family with no parents, they must each stand as guardians and protectors of one another.

They ate and drank, plates came and went; Lavinia directed the servants convincingly. "I'm so glad you could do this," Alexandra said. "This is wonderful."

"You did most of the work," Lavinia replied. There were gray circles beneath her eyes, and she wasn't eating. But that she was here at all was a miracle.

Somewhere else, at other Christmas dinners, people were discussing Dr. Kane and his book, the continuing searches for Franklin, the arctic in general: anything to avoid the discussions of politics and slavery that fractured families and friends. But here the topic on which everyone else fell back was also forbidden, and they struggled, and talked about books. Jane and Lucy found common ground in *The Wide, Wide World*, agreeing that they both still coveted the mahogany desk given to the novel's heroine in its most famous scene.

"That little ivory knife," Jane said, "and the four colors of sealing wax, and the pounce box and the silver pencil!"

With a pang Alexandra thought of Jane's bare bedroom in Browning's house, and the gate-legged table that served as her desk. Harriet, who also had no desk of her own, brought up a few more cherished scenes. And Emily added, "Men make fun of it, I know you all do. You like tales of adventure, in which the hero truly explores that wide world. But the novel is about tyranny, really; the tyranny of family and circumstances, and how one survives when running away isn't an option. Which it never is for women like us."

Browning raised his eyebrows and turned the conversation toward more serious books. Coffee and the puddings and pies arrived, and by the time Alexandra could pay attention again Browning and Linnaeus were discussing the relative merits of *Uncle Tom's Cabin* and Mrs. Hentz's rebuttal of it in *The Planter's Northern Bride*. Then Emily was telling Linnaeus and Lucy about her work with runaway slaves who'd made their way to the city. Perhaps she'd drunk too much of the Wellses' lovely claret.

Linnaeus said, "That's all very admirable. But can you answer the argument Mrs. Stowe has St. Clare make to Miss Ophelia? Are we in the North willing to elevate and educate the floods of freed slaves that must arrive here on emancipation? I think we won't; we can't. They're so essentially *different* from us."

Humboldt leaned into the conversation. "Are they not," he said, "even a separate species from us? In the same way that Catlin thinks the Indian tribes he painted out west are indigenous, and extremely ancient—their languages resemble no other group, they must have been created there. And Agassiz and others have argued . . ."

"Agassiz's idea of centers of creation is simple sacrilege," Browning said sharply. "This position that species are created in their proper places and don't migrate far, this thing he calls 'polygenism': to argue that human races are different species, descended from different Adams who were created separately in different zoological regions—this is to argue that scripture is allegorical rather than literal. And I don't accept that. We all descend from Adam and Eve, a singular creation. Human races have degenerated differently from that original pair."

Erasmus, Alexandra saw, was flicking his thumbnail against his front teeth. Lavinia looked up when Emily began to contradict Browning.

"Never mind that," Emily said. "It's not the theology that's important—Agassiz's polygenism is harmful because of the ammunition it provides to the proponents of slavery. And anyway he's a horrid man. He didn't come here just to give those lectures; he wanted to see Dr. Morton's collection of skulls and gather more data for his theories. I was working among the Negro servants at the hotel he stayed at, trying to convince them to provide shelter for escaped slaves passing through, and I saw him there, in the hall. One of the maids was trying to give him a message from someone who'd come by looking for him. She spoke perfectly clearly but he stood there like a big ox, pretending he didn't understand her and asking her again and again to repeat the same phrases. The look on his face—he was frightened of her. Revolted by her. How can you trust the science of a man like that?"

Erasmus flicked his thumbnail again and then spoke for the first time since he'd finished carving the ham. "Is that true?" he said. "About Agassiz?"

"As far as I know," Emily said. "He makes no secret of his attitude toward other races. No more than did Dr. Morton."

Erasmus shook his head. "Morton did good work at the Academy," he said. "But that necropolis he kept in his office—for all the time I was acquainted with him, I managed to avoid seeing the cabinet. None of us ever saw it." Linnaeus and Humboldt agreed.

"Such an awful obsession," Erasmus continued. "Hundreds of Indian crania, hundreds more from the Egyptian tombs and men all over the world robbing graves to send skulls back to him—but I don't remember any connection to Agassiz, I just remember the lectures Agassiz gave. And all the dinners feting him." He was silent for a moment. "Can't we talk about pleasanter things?" He pushed his chair away from the table and rolled in the direction of the parlor.

ERASMUS DIDN'T SAY he hadn't met Agassiz because he wasn't invited to the dinners. In the aftermath of the Exploring Expedition his reputation as a naturalist had been so slight that, despite his father's connections, no one had thought to include him. Yet what did this matter now? Most of his attention was taken up by fittings for his new shoes with the little pads that replaced his lost toes and cushioned his stumps. Late one night, when he was sure he wouldn't be interrupted, he opened his tin box and then the fossil cabinet with the hidden compartment. His nostrils filled with the smell of leather as he lined the footwear along his bed: one tiny antique woman's boot, one new man's shoe, one piece of boot sole. The fragment he'd brought home from Boothia was distinctly larger than the corresponding portion of his new shoes; his shoes now matched his mother's.

He practiced moving on his dwarfed feet, aided by a pair of walking sticks. For a while this occupied him entirely. Later, as he grew more confident but still was trapped inside by the freak snowfalls and bitter cold, the Christmas conversation began to nag at him.

He read Agassiz's essay in *Types of Mankind* and studied the chart linking the world's zoological provinces and their human inhabitants. The arctic column showed a polar bear, a walrus, a Greenland seal, a reindeer, a right whale, an eider duck. Then the face and skull of what Agassiz termed a Hyperborean. The features, which looked like no person Erasmus had ever seen, might have been imagined from Pliny's description. The races of man, Agassiz had written, differed from each other more than monkeys considered separate species within the same genus.

Browsing through the long passages of biblical exegesis and the essays on geology and paleontology, Erasmus saw that the point was an attack on the unity of races, an attempt to prove their separate creation. A messy compendium, the drawings distorted—whether willfully or unconsciously—to make a point. The Esquimaux looked like misshapen gnomes and the Negroes like chimpanzees; how could anyone who'd traveled the world take this seriously? Yet he knew there were clergymen shouting that the book cast contempt on the word of God. He was no judge of theology, but he thought it was bad science to deny that humans were part of nature and all one species. He had the feet of a pygmy now, but he was still himself.

He longed, as always, for Dr. Boerhaave, with whom he might have had a proper discussion. What is life, where did it come from? Species may be placed in groups related to one another in structure—but where did that relationship originate? He and Dr. Boerhaave would have laughed as they argued. He was grateful for that memory—and grateful, too, that the horrid stretch during which he'd been able to hear his friend's voice but couldn't see his face had passed.

Bit by bit his friend had returned to him. As he lay sleepless he'd seen first Dr. Boerhaave's leafy brown hair, striped with white, perfectly straight and flopping in the wind. His long chunky nose with that charming square tip appeared next; then his narrow eyes, slightly too close together; his wide, thin-lipped, mobile mouth; and the long-fingered hands which, gesturing so fluidly, had seemed like outposts of his mind. *The world has a pattern,* he'd said. *Our minds are made to perceive that pattern laid down by the Lord.* With those words humming in his ears, Erasmus searched the shelves for his father's old copy of Morton's *Crania Americana.*

Tiny steps; he felt like a deer, balanced on pointed hooves. He propped the volume open on the table and copied out Morton's interpretation of the cranial capacity of three Esquimaux skulls:

> *"The Greenland esquimaux are crafty, sensual, ungrateful, obstinate and unfeeling, and much of their affection for their children may be traced to purely selfish motives. They devour the most disgusting aliments uncooked and uncleaned, and seem to have no ideas beyond providing for the present moment. . . . In gluttony, selfishness and ingratitude, they are perhaps unequalled by any other nation of people."*

Certainly those people had seemed alien, but this wasn't the way he remembered them. Nor was this the way—or not solely the way—that Dr. Kane portrayed them in his book. Which Alexandra had worked on; and it was her sister who'd brought up this side of Agassiz. How could that philosophical idealism, which Dr. Boerhaave shared with Agassiz and Thoreau, have these consequences? He wanted his friend's face shining clearly; he'd almost lost that precious memory.

All of this was confusing. On his desk lay something else confusing, his first response to the letters he'd sent to the families of the three dead crewmen. Fletcher Lamb's mother had sent a bitter letter, pencil on lined paper:

I had two sons. The oldest went off on a whaling ship and was drowned to death and I forbade Fletcher to go to sea. He ran away to you. And now this. What am I to do without him? What am I to live on, without a son to support me? I had hoped you'd include the balance of Fletcher's wages. I am in urgent need of funds.

He would pay her himself and sort out the details with Zeke's father later; he'd do the same for Nils Jensen's mother and Mr. Francis's wife. But the money wouldn't make things right. He'd mishandled everything.

Every corner of his life was confused. After the Christmas dinner Alexandra, out of the blue, had asked Linnaeus and Humboldt for some engraving work. She hadn't admitted her work on Dr. Kane's book; her glance at Erasmus had entreated him not to betray her. She'd said only that Mr. Archibault believed her efforts promising.

His brothers had stalled but agreed to consult Mr. Archibault; and Erasmus had understood, as they had not, that Mr. Archibault would support her. Almost a form of blackmail, Erasmus thought. Doubly so, as his brothers couldn't afford to cross her; if she left they'd have to make other arrangements for the care of him and Lavinia. Later that week they'd agreed to subcontract a small set of botanical engravings to Alexandra and had arranged a work space in her rooms, but Erasmus knew they blamed him. They were waiting for him to take charge of the household, so they could dismiss Alexandra.

Which would leave him, he thought, alone with Lavinia. How would they live together? She came downstairs each day and dined with him each night, but it was Alexandra who made conversation, finding the neutral topics that got them through meals. Only once had they approached the topic of Zeke. "If you knew how much I miss him," Lavinia had said. "How hard it is for me to imagine the rest of my life . . ."

"I know," he'd said. "I would have done anything not to have it be this way." Liar, he'd thought. What a liar.

And there they sat. Her mouth said she'd forgiven him, her body at the table signaled a truce, but her gaze eluded him. She seemed to have grown a set of translucent second eyelids, like a cat's nictitating membranes. Behind that film she raged with loss. Had she been able to choose, he thought, he would be dead and not Zeke. "I'm sorry," he'd said. Again, again. "So sorry." The servants swirled around, pretending not to notice the anguish behind their words: Agnes the housemaid, Mrs. Parkins the cook, Cardoza the groundskeeper, Benton the groom. Two years ago he'd hardly been able to tell them apart; now he knew all their names, as he knew their habits and moods and troubles. He had to know them; he depended on them, and on Alexandra. Together they helped him and Lavinia return to the world that had become so strange to both of them.

ALL OVER PHILADELPHIA, merchants and tavern keepers had picked up on the craze for Kane's book. Shops displayed white fur muffs and seal-trimmed jackets *a la Esquimaux*; hairdressers styled tresses in casual topknots emulating the Greenland belles. By the wharves one might order a dish called "Dr. Kane's Relief," which appeared crowned with a tiny wooden spear. A hot brandy drink was called "Ice and Darkness," an ale "Kane's Dew," a towering dessert with almond paste "Tennyson's Monument," after the striking engraving in Kane's book. No one mentioned Erasmus and his expedition, but there was still talk of Franklin.

In England Lady Franklin pressed for another expedition to leave next summer, heading for Boothia and King William Land and perhaps employing the *Resolute,* which had safely reached Portsmouth. *The most recent American expedition,* she'd said in a speech—meaning his own, Erasmus thought with a pang—*may have failed. But apparently they saw evidence of my husband's ships as clearly as did Dr. Rae. While we sorrow over their losses, we are grateful for their efforts. It is imperative that a <u>British</u> ship examine this site.*

She might have written him directly, Erasmus thought. Even the smallest word of thanks, acknowledging receipt of his list. Instead she'd ignored him and taken her facts from the newspapers, never asking him to confirm or deny them. The 'apparently' stung.

Then he learned from Linnaeus what everyone else in Philadelphia already knew—that Dr. Kane had left London in mid-November, sailing for Havana in the hope that a warmer climate might cure his persistent fever. On the passage from St. Thomas to Cuba he'd suffered an apoplexy and now lay in Havana partially paralyzed and missing much of his memory.

Erasmus hobbled down to the creek after he heard this, on his first solo trip outside. At his feet the rushing brown current swept twigs and litter past the tulip trees and deposited a shingle, like a little hat, on a tuft of dried grass.

"Your feet are much improved," Alexandra said. "It's time we got you out of here."

She threw open two of the Repository's windows; spring was in the air and the trees were unfurling small green leaves. The lists strewn over Erasmus's work table curled in the humid breeze.

"I'd like to visit the Academy of Sciences," she said. "It would help me with the engravings if I could consult some of the thallophytes there. And I can't very well go by myself—but if you were willing, we could pretend these were specimens *you* wanted to inspect. Would you come?" She had an idea that Erasmus might rouse himself if she could make him feel that he was helping her, rather than that she was helping him.

He frowned. "Do you really need to?"

"It would be an immense help," she said. "And it might be useful to you as well. You could compare the arctic specimens in the herbarium to your lists."

"I could," he said. "And it's such a lovely day. Would Lavinia join us, do you think?"

"Not today," Alexandra said. "I asked her at breakfast, but she wants to spend some time with the gardener."

"That's good," Erasmus said. "Isn't that good, that she's interested in the gardens again?"

"It is," Alexandra agreed.

The drive along the river was beautiful, the banks filmed by a haze of green and sheets of flowering blue squill spreading like water beneath the beeches. At the Academy they sat in the carriage for ten minutes while Erasmus examined the altered facade. "It's too peculiar," he said. "When I was away on the Exploring Expedition the Academy moved from the old Swedenborgian meeting house on Twelfth Street to here. I came back to find this big new building, everything moved and changed so I couldn't find anything—and now this."

"What's so different?" Alexandra asked.

"The extra *story*," Erasmus said. "It's twenty or thirty feet taller than it used to be, there's a whole extra story added on."

As she guided him inside, slowing her steps so she was at his elbow, she caught only fragments of his continual mutter. The lecture room fronting on Broad Street was now part of the library; the old meeting room was now full of shelves; all the specimens had been rearranged. There were people about, but no one Erasmus knew from the old days. The young man working in the library probably meant nothing unkind when, after Erasmus introduced himself, he said, "Of course I've heard of you. I imagine you'd like to see the collections from Dr. Kane's first trip north."

"It's . . ." Erasmus said. "I didn't have in mind those specifically, there's a set of thallophytes I'd like to see, and also all the arctic specimens. I don't know where anything is anymore."

"Let me show you," the young man said. He led them into a room lined with shallow drawers and smelling of earth and mold. "All the herbarium sheets are here. Most of the specimens came from Dr. Kane, as I'm sure you know."

"Indeed," Erasmus said faintly. At the far end of the room a stuffed dog was mounted on a pedestal, ears erect and tail curled springily over its back. Beside it stood a dog's articulated skeleton, posed the same way. "Where did you get *those?*" he asked. He drew Alexandra closer to the mount and the skeleton.

"That's Toodlamik," the young man said proudly. "Skin and bones. Dr. Kane's faithful companion on the sledge journeys, whom he managed to bring home. He sickened over the summer, while Dr. Kane was finishing his book, and when he died Dr. Kane brought him here to the taxidermist. We're so pleased to have him."

"Very lifelike," Alexandra murmured. She glanced at Erasmus, hoping this wouldn't upset him. None of this was what she'd intended; she'd meant only to ease him back into the scientific world. She'd imagined them bending over sheets of lycopodium and sphagnum, which would get him thinking about his own work. She was touched when Erasmus squared his walking sticks under him, lifted his chin, and said, "An excellent preparation. I had similar dogs myself. Now if we could look at the herbarium sheets, I'd like to compare some of the specimens with my own lists from the area."

"Of course," the young man said. "Anything you can confirm as having seen in a similar area, or perhaps if you note having seen something in a different place—your explorations didn't entirely overlap Dr. Kane's, did they?"

"They did not."

"We'd welcome your observations." He turned to leave but Erasmus moved in another direction.

Beyond the two versions of Toodlamik an open door led to another room. More bones, Alexandra saw, as she followed Erasmus. Bones and bones and bones. Erasmus moved toward the shelves. Human skulls, cheekbone to cheekbone, rows upon rows. And the skulls of bear and deer and squirrel and mouse; hundreds of bird skulls and fishes and snakes and two hippopotamus skulls.

"Dr. Morton's entire collection," the young man announced. "After his death, his friends raised funds to purchase the collection from his widow, and they presented it to us. There are over sixteen hundred crania, almost a thousand human and the rest from other species. You must have known Dr. Morton?"

"I did," Erasmus said. "But I wasn't aware you'd acquired these." He searched the shelves, peering at the labels. "Weren't there some Esquimaux skulls?"

"Those were only loaned to Dr. Morton, by a friend," the young man said. "The collection really isn't complete without them and it's too bad his friend took them back. If we could acquire even one or two specimens . . ." He paused. "You didn't happen to collect any? That you'd consider donating?"

Erasmus shook his head and the young man disappeared. Without a word Erasmus hobbled back to the herbarium, turned from Toodlamik, and went to work.

They spent the day making notes and comparing one sheet to another, all the sheets to what Erasmus remembered. Alexandra fetched and carried, making encouraging comments and diverting

Erasmus's attention from the strangers who appeared at the doorway, gazed curiously at them, and then disappeared. This was his place, she thought. He had as much right to be here as any naturalist in Philadelphia, and she was proud of the way he kept his attention on his task. If people were staring at him, and whispering in the hallways—they'd stare at her too, if they knew of the work she'd done on Dr. Kane's book. The quarrel between them seemed to have vanished, and as they worked in the shadows of Dr. Kane's dog she felt very close to him. At the end of the day, when although she hadn't glimpsed the thallophytes she thanked him for accompanying her, he said, "It is I who thank you."

FOR A FEW WEEKS, Erasmus's dreams were haunted by Toodlamik—bones and body, eyes and sockets, versions of the living and the dead. Then letters arrived, which chased the dogs away. Captain Tyler's family wrote, wanting to know what had happened to the balance of his salary. This Erasmus forwarded to Zeke's father. After that, Copernicus's letter limped in stained and travel-worn:

> *Humboldt's message finally reached me. Do you know how glad I am to have you back? I can't wait to tell you everything. At the Canyon de Chelly I saw the Anasazi ruins. Hopi villages, pueblo kivas; I've been all over California. In the Salinas Valley, not far from Soledad, I painted in a place that was scorched by the sun. About the time you were beating through the ice in your little boat, I was toiling along on a mule, in temperatures over 110 degrees. We'll have a lot to talk about, won't we? I can't wait to see you, am heading home immediately, hope you are recovering. Humboldt says there's been some trouble but whatever it is hold on, I'll be there soon. I am bringing you some seeds.*

The next day a letter came from Thomas Cholmondelay, Dr. Boerhaave's friend in London, expressing his appreciation for the packet Erasmus had sent. A portion was eerily out of date; he wrote about seeing Dr. Kane in London—*your fellow arctic traveler*—how much he'd been celebrated, how sad Lady Franklin and everyone else had been when Kane departed and how worried they all were about his health. On the heels of that, a letter arrived from William Greenstone in Edinburgh:

How can I thank you for forwarding Jan's last letters to me, despite your own difficulties? He was lucky to have you as his friend, and all of us who knew Jan are grateful to you and wish you a speedy recovery from your injuries. It was Jan's great wish to make another voyage north and I'm glad he saw so much before his terrible accident.

I think of him often—not just among our familiar Edinburgh places but whenever I hear any interesting news. Among our literary and scientific men, as I imagine among yours, there is much discussion of Mr. Wallace's "Sarawak Law" regarding the succession of species. Wallace remains in Borneo, but Lyell, Darwin, Hooker and others are in a flurry over Wallace's insights into animal distribution. There can no longer be much question, I think, of varieties representing separate, special acts of Creation—though I know Jan, influenced by Agassiz, leaned toward that view. I'd give a great deal to be able to argue with him over this. Meanwhile I thank you again for this gift of his words and also, belatedly, for your description of the Greenland meteorite.

He called him "Jan," Erasmus thought, looking from the letter to his friend's notebook. To each other they'd been Jan and William.

Whereas he—despite all they'd shared together, they'd parted as Dr. Boerhaave and Mr. Wells.

ON MARCH 14, Erasmus and Alexandra stood at the three tall windows of her family home: Emily with them on the left; Browning and Harriet and their new daughter, Miriam, in the center; Jane and little Nicholas on the right, gazing from the second floor down onto Walnut Street. There were neighbors below them, strangers above them, more strangers up on the roof—Browning had rented out these viewing spots for a fee—but everyone was silent and the street itself was empty. Erasmus could hear the drums, but the procession hadn't yet come into sight. A light rain, falling all morning, had soaked the crepe hanging from the balconies of every house; in windows people huddled against the wind while on the rooftops black umbrellas sprouted.

The street looked like an endless dark tunnel. And beyond it, Erasmus knew, the entire route was similarly shrouded. He was cold and his toes hurt, or the place where his toes would have been. Behind him, on a small cherry table, a stack of newspapers detailed the journey of Dr. Kane's body across America. In his imagination Erasmus saw all the routes preceding this final one, spreading like a jet-black labyrinth across the country.

From Havana, where Kane had died, to New Orleans by packet boat; the casket had lain in state in City Hall. For a week, while a steamboat conveyed the casket up the Mississippi and the Ohio to Louisville, people had stood on levees and wharves to watch Kane pass. In Louisville Kane's arrival had been announced by the tolling of bells and the firing of guns; more formal ceremonies, another procession; a lying-in at Mozart Hall. Halfway to Cincinnati the steamboat was met by another boat, crowded with memorial-committee members wearing mourner's badges. In Cincinnati the procession had wound from the wharf to the railway station; at Xenia people had swarmed the tracks, delaying the train's slow progress; all throughout that afternoon and night, crowds had waited silently at every stop. At Columbus Kane's body lay in the capitol building, silent focus of more long speeches. In the smaller cities of Ohio and West Virginia, where the casket remained on the train, people had gathered at railway stations while more bells tolled. In Baltimore there had been huge crowds and the grandest procession until today's.

On Monday the funeral car had arrived in Philadelphia, where it was met by a guard of honor: city police, an artillery company, and a dozen memorial committees from various civic groups, none of which had included Erasmus. The hearse had been accompanied by eight of Kane's companions, who'd spread the flag of the lost *Advance* over her commander's coffin and then, at Independence Hall, added Kane's ceremonial sword and a mound of flowers. Until this morning, people had streamed through the hall to pay their respects. Now, at last, the procession was coming into sight.

Policemen, more policemen, then the companies of the First Brigade and, flanking the hearse itself, the Philadelphia City Cavalry. The sight of the horsemen so excited young Nicholas that he wriggled halfway out the open sash and had to be pulled back and scolded by his aunt. The funeral car, Erasmus saw, was marked at the corners by golden spears bearing flags. Above the casket a black domed canopy kept off the rain; the silk ribbons that stretched to the spears drooped and the horses shone with moisture. Emily said, "There's that horrid father of his," but Browning murmured, "Not today."

The drums beat, the car moved slowly, waves of people marched. Erasmus crumpled the newspaper's guide to the procession in his hand. Almost every Philadelphian of distinction had been invited, from Kane's companions to the mayor and the aldermen, the members of the Philosophical Society, the medical faculty and students of the University of Pennsylvania, the Odd Fellows, the Fire Department and more, so many more.

"The Corn Exchange?" Browning said. "Why would they ask the members of the Corn Exchange?"

Erasmus had no answer. In all this great crowd, he thought, no place had been made for him. Nor for any of his companions: none of the living and nothing to honor the memory of the dead. At least the Toxophilites, he'd heard, honored Zeke at each monthly meeting.

Alexandra pressed his arm and he reached over and squeezed her hand gratefully. She was all he had to lean on; his brothers were comforting Lavinia, who'd refused to leave the house since Kane's body entered the city. Her presence at the procession, she'd said, would be an act of disloyalty to Zeke.

As if she knew what Erasmus was thinking, Alexandra said, "I'm sure it was only a wish to protect your health that kept the committee from asking you to join them. For you to walk so far, in this weather and with such a crowd . . ."

Erasmus looked down at his cunning shoes. "I manage very well with the walking sticks," he said. "As you know."

The funeral car was almost out of sight; below him were the members of the Hibernian Society and the St. Andrews and Scots Thistle Societies. They would pass for hours, he thought. At the church the procession would march past the casket, set up on a bier on the stone steps, and then all who could would crowd inside to hear the service. Words and words about Kane's goodness and glory and skills. As if Kane had not also lost a ship; as if his voyage had not also been marked by strife and rebellion. Someone, he noted from the program, would sing a Mozart anthem. One prominent minister would give an invocation and another the eulogy, which would be printed in the paper tomorrow but which Erasmus could already hear:

> *"We are assembled, my friends, to perform such comely though sad duties in honor of a man who, within the short lifetime of thirty-five years, under the combined impulses of humanity and science, has traversed nearly the whole of the planet in its most inaccessible places. . . . Death discloses the human estimate of character. That mournful pageant which for days past has been wending its way hither, across the solemn main, along our mighty rivers, through cities clad in habiliments of grief, with the learned, the noble, and the good mingling in its train, is but the honest tribute of hearts that could have no motive but respect and love."*

More prayers, more singing; a dirge and then a benediction. The arctic coastline Dr. Kane had explored and named, the ice he'd fought and the Esquimaux he'd discovered; the dark winters of his entrapment and the heroic journey by which he'd brought most of his men to safety—all of this was admirable and yet why should it have eclipsed Erasmus's own journey? He'd brought men home himself, he had done what he could, he had tried . . . he pulled his hand from Alexandra's.

"Lavinia was right to stay home," he said. "I can't bear to watch any more."

He withdrew from the window, moving cautiously to the davenport. In the damp lines of his palms he found the visions he'd been fending off since his return: Zeke dying, Zeke dead, all alone in that vast white space. Death coming violent or quiet or both—a bear, a slipped razor, a fall through the ice; tumbling iceberg or slow starvation; fury or resignation. He heard the ice cracking beneath Zeke's feet; he saw Zeke searching for a hand to grab, a line to grasp, where there was nothing but a field of fractured floes. Then Zeke looking up into the sky and sinking, his arms at his side. Above there was no one to rescue him, no one even to watch. Just a fulmar, perched on a walrus's skull and regarding the bubbles of his last breaths and the skin of ice beginning to seal the hole.

Against this great mourning for Kane stood Zeke's unwitnessed final days. *I should have been there,* Erasmus thought. *Somehow, I should have been with him.*

9

A Big Stone Slipped from His Grasp

(April–August 1857)

If a person asked my advice, before undertaking a long voyage, my answer would depend upon his possessing a decided taste for some branch of knowledge, which could by this means be advanced. No doubt it is a high satisfaction to behold various countries and the many races of mankind, but the pleasures gained at the time do not counterbalance the evils. It is necessary to look forward to a harvest, however distant that may be, when some fruit will be reaped, some good effected. Many of the losses which must be experienced are obvious; such as that of the society of every old friend, and of the sight of those places with which every dearest remembrance is so intimately connected. These losses, however, are at the time partly relieved by the exhaustless delight of anticipating the long wished-for day of return. . . .

*Of individual objects, perhaps nothing is
more certain to create astonishment than the
first sight in his native haunt of a barbarian—of
man in his lowest and most savage state. One's
mind hurries back over past centuries, and then
asks—could our progenitors have been men like
these?—men, whose very signs and expressions
are less intelligible to us than those of the domes-
ticated animals; men, who do not possess the
instinct of those animals, nor yet appear to boast
of human reason, or at least of arts consequent on
that reason. . . . In conclusion, it appears to me
that nothing can be more improving to a young
naturalist, than a journey in distant countries.
It both sharpens, and partly allays that want
and craving which, as Sir J. Herschel remarks,
a man experiences although every corporeal sense
be fully satisfied.*

—CHARLES DARWIN,
The Voyage of the Beagle (1839)

RUDDY AND BEARDED AND LONG-HAIRED, COPERNICUS
swept into the Repository and threw his arms around his brother,
squeezing so tightly he lifted Erasmus from his shoes.

"Oh, be careful!" Alexandra cried.

Copernicus shot her a startled glance, then followed her gaze to
his brother's feet. Quickly he lowered Erasmus into a chair.

"I'm sorry," he said. "But I'm so glad to see you!" He bent and grasped Erasmus's right ankle, then ran his hand along the foot: tarsals, metatarsals—but most of the phalanges gone. "Do they hurt?"

"No," Erasmus said, smiling in a way Alexandra had forgotten. "Say hello to Alexandra Copeland."

"Humboldt wrote me about you," Copernicus said. "What a help you've been with Lavinia, and what a good friend to our family. I'm delighted to meet you." As if, Alexandra thought, he'd forgotten all the times they'd met when she and Lavinia were girls. He clasped her hand and then spun around and said, "But where's Lavinia? I'm longing to see her."

"Let me go fetch her," Alexandra said, hoping Lavinia was up and dressed.

Later, as Copernicus unpacked the crates piled along the garden paths, she would see his paintings: Pikes Peak and the Grand Tetons and the Rocky Mountains; the Great Salt Lake, where the breeze had blown his floating body about as if he were a sailboat; alkali deserts and the Humboldt Mountains; the Yosemite Valley and El Capitan and the Indians he'd met in each place. Astonishing paintings, flooded with light and dazzling color. But for the moment she saw only the smile on Erasmus's face, and the possibility of Lavinia similarly transformed.

HAVING COPERNICUS HOME was a comfort, Lavinia confided to Alexandra. After all he was her favorite brother. She began to plan the household meals again: roast lamb with herbs and carrots, chicken bathed in cream. Nothing but Copernicus's favorites, she said. He'd been away so long. When her work was done, she and Alexandra sometimes joined the brothers as they sat exchanging stories of their adventures.

Each of Copernicus's paintings had a tale behind it, and a trail that could be followed through his sketchbook. A sort of visual diary, Alexandra saw, during those warm lazy afternoons. Fort Wallah Wallah on one page and a herd of buffalo on another; a group of men drying and pounding buffalo meat for pemmican. Delaware and Shawnee and Osage Indians; Kickapoos, Witchetaws, Wacos. Mormons. The black-tailed deer of the Rocky Mountains. Thousands of sketches and just a few words of description, the obverse of Erasmus's journal.

In turn Erasmus offered his own pages, Dr. Boerhaave's papers, and the long letter he'd written to Copernicus during the voyage. The papers cast shadows, Alexandra saw. Sometimes Erasmus would have to retire abruptly, leaving Copernicus alone. Sometimes, when she came down to breakfast, Erasmus would look as if he hadn't slept and later, in the Repository, he'd admit that all this talking brought him nightmares. Zeke haunted his dreams, he said. In the ice, nailed to the frozen ship, was a list of the dead in the shape of a headstone that he saw again and again. Still, the more the brothers talked, the more excited Erasmus grew. Copernicus showed Erasmus a sketch of the footwear that had protected him during a winter crossing of the Rockies: buffalo-skin boots over buckskin moccasins over thick squares of blanket over woolen socks. Erasmus showed Copernicus the tattered fur suit Ned had made for him and said, "I might write a book."

It would not be, as Dr. Kane's effort had been, an adventure tale built from transcribed journal entries, but neither would it be a simple description of the arctic. Rather, Erasmus said, the narrative would pull his readers along on a journey, as an imaginary ship moved from place to place and through the seasons. On the flagstone patio beyond the solarium, he described a sequence of verbal portraits, a natural history that caught each place at a particular time of the year. He wouldn't be in the story, Erasmus said. He'd be

erased, he'd be invisible. It would be as if readers gazed at a series
of detailed landscape paintings. As if they were making the journey
themselves, but without discomfort or discord.

"Why not include some color plates?" Copernicus said. "I could
do the paintings myself." From Erasmus's sketches and descriptions,
and his own knowledge of glaciers and light—what if he were to make
a series of paintings introducing the sections? Each could combine all
the important features of one region, all the representative animals
and plants—imaginary, and yet a portrait truer than simple fact.

Erasmus reached into his pocket and pulled out a withered
slab of leather wrapped in a handkerchief. He unfolded the cloth.
"Paintings like this?" he said. "That stand for a whole set of things?"

"What *is* that?"

Erasmus told him about his last day among the Boothian Esquimaux, and how the wife of the tribe's leader had slipped him this
relic. He didn't say where he'd hidden it; nor what Joe had told him
about the boot from which it might have come.

"Have you shown it to anyone?"

"Just some reporters," Erasmus said. "When I first got back, and
everyone was asking questions and I was trying to explain what happened and what we'd found. Even if all the other things were lost,
I said, this was one real bit of evidence that we'd uncovered from
Franklin's voyage. But no one believed me." He paused for a second. "That's not true; Alexandra and Linnaeus and Humboldt saw
it. They believed me, I think. I'm not sure, I was so sick. I don't
remember much from those first few weeks."

Copernicus balanced the relic on his palm. "But it's *real*," he
said. The tips of the rusty, broken screws raised the leather off his
skin, so that this thing which had once sheltered a foot now seemed
to balance on little feet of its own. "It's right here."

Two big blotches rose on Erasmus's cheeks. "It's my own fault," he said. "I didn't include it on my list of the items we found, because I wanted to keep it secret, for myself. I stole it, really. And now there's no one who witnessed me finding it, no written evidence of how I got it. One of the reporters accused me of manufacturing it. Another said I could have found it anywhere, and that it might be anything. A bit from a sailor's boot, picked up in Greenland. Or a remnant from Kane's expedition, found at Smith Sound."

"There's nothing that marks it surely as belonging to one of Franklin's men?"

"Just the context," Erasmus said. "Just where I found it, and who gave it to me."

Once more, as he had for months, he berated himself for having kept this secret from Dr. Boerhaave. He'd withheld this part of himself, failed to share every corner of his heart with the man who'd been his friend—why had he done that? What had he been waiting for?

The outline of the seven screws fit exactly within Copernicus's left palm. "It's too bad," he said. "This ought to have been the one thing that would make everyone understand all you found. But I understand what you mean: it's almost as if I can see the man this belonged to, and the entire expedition. And that *is* what I mean by these paintings: sometimes one scene can capture . . . everything. The *feel* of a place."

THE BROTHERS' PLANS delighted Alexandra, but also made her feel it was time to leave. Lavinia was more serene than she used to be, more thoughtful, more reserved; but perfectly capable of running the household and seemingly at ease with Erasmus now that Copernicus mediated between them. Meanwhile her own family could use her help, Browning said. They were grateful for the money she contributed each month, but how much longer could she count on that?

To this she had no answer; she was halfway done with her botanical plates and no more had been promised. Yet, as Browning pointed out, there were scores of ways she could help her family. A dense net of obligations, which she sometimes longed to shed . . . but no one was ever free of them. Lavinia was tied here with her brothers, perhaps forever. And she herself must be similarly tied to her siblings; she would never marry, she could feel it. Passing a mirror, she would glimpse herself in her gray frock, with her hair pulled tightly back, and think how invisible she must be to anyone who didn't know her.

"Your feet are healed," she said to Erasmus one day. "And you and Copernicus have so much work to do, you don't need me here anymore."

"But you can't go," he said, seizing her hand. "Not *now*."

"We do need you," Copernicus said.

"*I* need you," Erasmus added. "The paintings Copernicus plans to make—those are just the general portraits. Chapter headings, in a way. But we must have hundreds of detailed drawings of the plants and animals and their parts, just like the ones you're working on now. Won't you be our partner in this?"

"It's not as if I'm *replacing* you," Copernicus added. Although she'd assumed that he was.

"The way we've been working these past weeks," Erasmus said. "I thought we'd just continue. We work so well together."

Erasmus in one corner, writing steadily except when he leapt up to offer suggestions; she with pen and ink in another corner, drawing sedges and seaweeds and gulls; Copernicus already painting in blue and green and gold and white, icebergs calving from a glacier above Melville Bay—they *did* work well together, but she'd assumed this was just for a few weeks until Copernicus took over her work and her responsibility for Erasmus. But perhaps things didn't have to go that way. Neither of the brothers had said a word about money, though.

"Let me think about it," she said. "Let me talk to my family."

IN LATE MAY, Copernicus took Erasmus to visit two fellow painters who shared an attic studio. Under the skylights they drank red wine and chatted gaily—a pleasure, Erasmus thought. He went out so seldom; he'd missed the company of other men. Afterward he tapped along Sansom Street with his walking sticks, delighted with the day and with his own increasing stamina. He smelled lilacs, the sharp green odor of sumacs, freshly scrubbed paving stones. He was moving across the stones—not as swiftly as Copernicus, who kept darting ahead, and then looping back to him—but still he was moving. The sweet air poured into his lungs. Those painters had liked him. Found him interesting. They'd asked him questions about his book.

At Broad Street they caught the empty omnibus. Past them sailed storefronts, window displays, pigeons rising and falling as if all attached to the same rippling sheet. Copernicus pointed out the shadow rippling beneath the flock; Erasmus asked about the shadows water cast on ice. At their stop they were talking happily when the driver interrupted them.

"Would you be Erasmus Wells?" he asked, staring at Erasmus's feet. Erasmus nodded, still thinking about what Copernicus had explained. Water cast a shadow *up* . . . "My name's Godfrey," the driver said. At first the name meant nothing.

"William Godfrey," he added. "*Kane's* Godfrey."

William Godfrey, the deserter and traitor Kane had written about so bitterly in *Arctic Explorations*! Erasmus caught his brother's eye. "This is my last run of the day," Godfrey said. "I'd like to talk with you, if you could give me a few minutes . . ."

They agreed to meet in half an hour, at a nearby tavern. What harm could it do? On a bench by the tavern's front window, Erasmus looked out at a catalpa tree covered with foamy white blossoms and wondered what this stranger might have to say to him. "It's a good idea," Copernicus said, and Erasmus agreed. "You can compare notes."

Soon Godfrey slid in next to them. "Buy me a drink," he said. "A couple of drinks. You can afford it." A whiff of horse dung rose from his shoes.

While Copernicus fetched a round, Erasmus started to ask Godfrey about the sights they'd shared. "The Esquimaux," he said. "The ones that helped you . . ."

Godfrey leaned in too close to him, seizing the glass of beer Copernicus offered. "What was Commander Voorhees like?" he asked abruptly. Before Erasmus could answer, Godfrey said, "As bad as Kane? Was he that bad? You know, what *I* went through up there . . ."

Dr. Kane lied, he said. His book was a lie, much of what had really happened glossed over; he himself no mutineer but rather a hero who'd saved Kane's life several times. "*I* pulled him from the water when the sledge fell in," Godfrey said. His voice shot up and people turned to look at them. "*I* shot the bear he missed, the one that charged him . . ."

A carriage passed by the window, two beautiful chestnut horses and behind them, half-hidden, a woman in a blue silk dress much like one Erasmus remembered on his mother. Still Godfrey was talking: lowbrowed, pockmarked, seeming more unpleasant by the minute.

"And what did I get?" Godfrey continued, gulping at his beer. He held out his glass for a refill. "Nothing. Worse than nothing. Kane ruined my reputation, no one will hire me: look at me, driving men like you through the streets."

"I'm sorry," Erasmus offered, but Godfrey trampled over his words. Why he'd opposed Kane's orders, why part of the crew had set off on their own . . . the beer was sour and that, or Godfrey's complaints, made Erasmus queasy. That droning voice dissolved the pleasures of the day and cast him back to the dark winter, the paper headstone pinned to Captain Tyler's bunk and the names of the dead, the list that always grew longer. Erasmus was about to make an excuse and leave when Godfrey said, "You know, if anyone does, what it is to be falsely accused. And how the arctic can drive men mad."

He bent toward Erasmus and squinted. "Tell me the truth—did you kill him?"

Was that what people thought? Not just that he had abandoned Zeke, but that he'd murdered him? Erasmus rose but Copernicus pushed him down.

"How dare you!" Copernicus said. "My brother *saved* that expedition, he's the one who got everyone safely home. Zeke made his own decisions, what happened to him was his choice and you have no right . . ."

Godfrey drained his second glass and set it down. "Well, excuse me," he said to Erasmus. "Excuse me for making assumptions. But, you know—Kane's account of our voyage is so different from what actually happened . . . all I know about you is what I've read in the papers. How would *I* know what you really did?"

"I did everything I could," Erasmus said. "Believe that or not, as you choose." He rose again, sure that everyone in the tavern was looking at them. "We have to go."

Godfrey grasped his arm. "Don't," he said. "I know you despise me, everyone does—but you and I have things in common."

More carriages rolled by, a stream of handsome, well-dressed people talking and laughing, making plans, doing whatever it is people do. What did they do? They passed, leaving Erasmus cut off once more from the simple stream of dailiness. He and Godfrey had nothing in common, he thought. Nothing at all.

"I deserve a hearing too," Godfrey continued. "A fair and impartial hearing before the American public—I'm writing a book, *my* version. Will you help me? I need money. Surely you among all men can sympathize . . ."

If he would stop talking; if this awful man would just stop talking . . . Erasmus dug in his pockets, dropped a few bills on the table, and fled with Copernicus. His dismay stayed with him long after they'd reached home, and that evening he wrote in his journal:

What a horrid man! Yet something in Godfrey's account makes me wonder if our two voyages were so different. Perhaps I've been making a mistake in comparing what I did with what others claimed in print to have done. Godfrey said Kane's anger was boundless when the eight crew members seceded and set off on their boat journey; and that four months later, Kane was vindictive when the frozen men straggled back to the ship. According to Godfrey there was no saintly welcome; Kane was an iron-willed tyrant who grudgingly saved his crewmen only when their wills were broken. Godfrey boils with resentment and self-interest; yet some of what he says may be true.

If Kane was less of a hero than we all believe, am I less of a failure? The world knows Kane's version of that expedition, not Godfrey's; as it knew Wilkes's version of the Exploring Expedition and no one else's—and as it might have known Zeke's version of our own journey, had he not been lost.

Copernicus says we ought to try to talk with him again, this time without beer; he may have observed things on his side of Smith Sound I never saw, which might contribute to our portrait of the area. But I can't bear to see him again, I can't bear to think of anyone drawing a parallel between us. How can I write one word about the arctic when a person such as Godfrey is also writing a book, one that says me, me, me, me, me?

COPERNICUS'S FIRST PAINTING GREW, it was radiant. When his dealer visited the Repository to collect a group of the western paintings, Copernicus showed him the unfinished picture of Melville Bay and the dealer's breath whistled in his throat. "It's one of a set," Copernicus said. "For a book my brother's writing."

"When you finish them," the dealer said, "after the color plates have been made, if you'd let me sell them as a group . . ."

"We'll discuss it later," Copernicus said. "After the work is done."

He talked about the book as if it already existed, and so Erasmus wrote on. He took courage not only from his brother but from the presence of Alexandra, who turned out one handsome drawing after another. At night he fell asleep thinking about her face, her hands, the ink on her hands, the way her arms merged pale and strong into the sleeves of her smock. At the back of her neck, beneath the coil of smooth, straight, oak-brown hair, small strands escaped and whispered over the bumps of her vertebrae. He hadn't found her plain for a long time now.

On the *Narwhal* sex had been something he seldom thought about, after the first summer; perpetually too cold, too worn, too hungry, so worried he'd barely remembered the feel of skin on skin, which had seemed like something from another life. And before that, when he was still healthy and energetic, the cabin was always full of men coming and going, the light had been endless, there was no privacy. A few times, landing on the shoreline to hunt or left briefly alone on Boothia, he'd touched himself in the shelter of some rocks—but he'd thought of a red-haired woman in Washington then, a woman on Front Street, the flowery faces of Lavinia's friends. Now he lay in his lonely bed imagining Alexandra.

Thinking all the heat flowed from him, Erasmus was unaware of Alexandra's humming confusion. It was the presence of both brothers, she thought, that made her feel so strange. Copernicus's strong, broad body, his easy good humor and the way he rested his hand on her shoulder; Erasmus's focused attention, the way he followed her hands and looked into her eyes and spoke as if they were equals: which was it she wanted? Both, perhaps. Although she was aware even then that the affection she felt beaming from Copernicus was part of his general affection for the world. Perhaps it was only the delirious early summer weather that made her toss and turn in her sheets and stare at herself naked in the mirror. One lit candle, the gleam off her flank slipping into the glass and out as she imagined how she might look to another set of eyes. At night someone appeared in her dreams who was neither Erasmus nor Copernicus but both of them. During the day when she wasn't working she sat with Lavinia and talked about transplanting the irises.

All this made her blush when finally, reluctantly, she spoke to Erasmus about her financial situation. He looked so startled, even ashamed—did he never need to think about money? "I have an income," he said quickly. "More than I need. It was foolish of me not to realize that Linnaeus and Humboldt had stopped paying you. The three of us are full partners on this project, and it's only fair you should receive a salary for your efforts."

IN THE GARDEN the four of them sat, eating strawberry-rhubarb pie and listening to Erasmus read. The bleeding hearts were still in bloom, the weather had been cool; the lawn stretched soft and green between the wicker chairs and the drive. Along the drive the peonies planted so long ago rose in great clumps covered with flowers. Erasmus turned the pages on his lap. Lavinia nodded her head thoughtfully when Erasmus read a passage about the fevered coming of summer to Disko Island. It was a gift, she said. She could almost see the cliffs and ice floes sailing toward her. Even if Erasmus wasn't writing directly about Zeke, he was letting her see the last things Zeke might have seen, and she was grateful for that. Erasmus read on. A carriage appeared at the end of the drive and a man got out. After that everything happened as if in a dream.

Money changed hands and boxes were dropped onto the grass. Then another, smaller figure stepped down from the carriage, bundled in unfamiliar clothes. The figure lifted out a child; the pair sat, when the man pointed, on one of the boxes. The man began to walk up the drive, between the rows of peonies. Pink globes, creamy globes, the man touching the globes as he passed; Erasmus rose from his chair without his sticks and toppled to the ground. Then Lavinia was running toward the man, stumbling over the hem of her dress, and Copernicus and Alexandra were bending over Erasmus.

Alexandra would never be able to sort out the next few minutes. How Zeke and Lavinia got from their embrace halfway down the drive to the solarium; how Copernicus got Erasmus to his feet and into the shelter of the Repository; how she herself made her way to the mound of boxes and the two figures sitting there, so out of place—all this jumbled in her mind. One minute she was standing over the strangers—one was a woman, an Esquimau woman, and the smaller figure a little boy—and saying, as she would to anyone, "Won't you come inside?" The next she was leading them into the house and giving orders to the bewildered servants.

Zeke was a ghost, but Zeke was here; he had his arms around Lavinia, who couldn't stop weeping, but he was also calmly greeting Alexandra and asking if his companions could stay here. Lavinia touched his arm, his neck, his face. "Yes," she said. "Anything you want."

"This is Annie," Zeke said. "And Tom. They come from Greenland." He pressed Lavinia's hand to his cheek. "They have other names, Esquimaux names, but these are the ones they use with me." He kissed Lavinia's fingers. "They speak English, I taught them how. Annie saved my life."

For a while, as Alexandra glided automatically up the stairs, that was all she knew. She turned halfway up and found no one behind her. The visitors stood at the bottom, clinging to the bannister and testing the first step as if checking the thickness of ice. Annie wore breeches, a hooded shirt, soft boots even in this heat—all made from some sort of hide, deer or seal, something Alexandra couldn't name. Tom was dressed in a similar suit and the hides smelled, or perhaps the smell came from the people. She lifted her skirts above her ankles so Annie and Tom could see her feet; she took the steps slowly and let them see how each step was safe.

In the spare room across the hall from Copernicus's room she said to Annie, "You will stay here, with your . . ."

"It is my son," Annie said. "Called Tom." She seemed to understand Alexandra perfectly.

Alexandra went to her own room, where she gathered undergarments and her gray dress. When she returned Annie and Tom

were at the window, pressing their palms to the glass as if trying
to reach the outside air. Alexandra opened the sash and Annie
pressed her palm against the air where the glass had been, and
then smiled. She shook her head at the gray dress Alexandra held
to her shoulders.

"You'll be more comfortable," Alexandra said. "In this heat."
Tom stuck his upper body through the window and Annie joined
him. "Annie!" Alexandra said. She touched the woman's jacket and
Annie pulled away and frowned. Alexandra left the dress on the bed.

Downstairs, she tried not to stare at Zeke. There were sharp lines
carved around his eyes and his hands were battered and scarred;
part of his left ear was gone. His clothes were patched and torn and
stained. Slowly she recognized the remnants of the elegant gray uniform once worn by all the *Narwhal*'s crew.

"I put them in the second guest room," she said, hypnotized by
the way Zeke's hand moved over Lavinia's back and shoulders. What
was he doing here, how was he alive? Where had Erasmus gone? "I
brought Annie one of my dresses, but she won't put it on."

"I'll take care of it," Zeke said. He rose. "Stay here. I'll be
right back."

Alexandra took his place on the sofa, sitting still while Lavinia
leaned against her shoulder and wept. Later, when Zeke went out
to the Repository, Lavinia pulled Alexandra upstairs. They found
Annie seated on the floor with Tom in her lap, her head resting
on the windowsill and her body draped in Alexandra's dress. Best
not to think what Zeke had said or done to get her into it. The
bodice was loose, the sleeves too long. The white collar set off
her shining dark skin. When they entered she swiveled her head
and looked at them without interest. "Tseke?" she said. "Where
is Tseke?"

I DIDN'T KILL HIM, Erasmus thought. That moment in the garden, when he'd tumbled to the ground: what was the name for the feeling that had toppled him? Guilt, shock, horror all mingled with joy, with relief—*I didn't kill him*.

He stood near the herbarium case, supported by his sticks and finding it difficult to breathe. Copernicus sat by the window and Zeke orbited the Repository, gazing at what was new among all that had once been familiar. "I thought you were dead," Erasmus said.

"Well, I'm not," Zeke said. "As you see."

He looked much older, Erasmus saw. Stronger, more contained. And frighteningly calm. Why didn't Zeke embrace him, or strike him, or demand an explanation or offer one of his own? Not a word; he turned to Copernicus and said, "When did you get back?"

"Two months ago," Copernicus said. "I headed home as soon as I heard about Erasmus."

"I waited as long as I could," Erasmus said. How could he explain himself? "All the men were sure you were dead and they were frightened about spending another winter there. They made a plan without me—they said I had to lead them south, because you'd left me in charge. I had to take them, I thought you were dead."

"I'm sure you did," Zeke said. "I'm sure you did everything you could. I had news of you in Godhavn. I heard you got at least some of our men home safely."

"All of them," Erasmus said, more sharply now. "All that *chose*— the four that split off, I couldn't stop them from going."

"As you say," Zeke said. "Anyway I forgive you. Whatever you

did, I'm sure it was the best you could do. It turned out to be a blessing. To be *alone*, the way that I was alone—I know things about
myself now. Things you'll never understand."

"Tell me," Erasmus said.

"Why should I?"

Zeke's face was clenched. After a long silence, Erasmus thinking
every second, *Hit me. Get it over with*, Zeke said, "Why would I tell
you anything, ever again?"

Copernicus cleared his throat. "But where were you? How did
you survive?"

"That," Zeke said, "is a long story."

Apparently he wasn't going to tell it now. He wandered around
the Repository, peering at a drawing of a fossil Alexandra had left
pinned to her easel, ignoring Copernicus's draped painting, looking
down at the books open on the long table. He touched Dr. Boerhaave's journal, then the green silk volume Lavinia had once given
him. "I wondered what had happened to these," he said. "When I
got back to the *Narwhal*, and found my box broken into and Dr.
Boerhaave's journal gone, I was very . . . curious."

"I thought you were dead," Erasmus said. "I wanted to preserve
what I could." He couldn't bear the questions on his brother's face.
"Who are these people you've brought with you?"

"Who are you to criticize what I do?" Zeke asked. "You abandoned me."

"I'm not *criticizing*," Erasmus said. "Only asking."

"Would you have had me spend the winter with no comfort? In
a place where it's an insult to refuse what's offered? Annie's family
took me in." Zeke turned to the pile of manuscript pages. "You're
writing something? A little memoir?"

"Not a memoir," Erasmus said. What did that mean: *Annie's
family took me in?* "Something different."

"You agreed not to write anything for a year after the voyage," Zeke said. "And to turn the journals over to me."

"It's already *been* a year," Erasmus said. Then was appalled at the tone of his voice; and still couldn't stop himself. "You were gone. And anyway, anyway—this isn't a book about our journey, there's nothing in it about you or me or the Franklin relics, or what happened to any of us. It's about the *place*—a natural history of the place through the seasons."

"Write if it pleases you," Zeke said. "It's hard to believe anyone will want to read such a thing, though. Not when they see what I have to say, the story I have to tell."

From his pocket he took the black notebook Erasmus had seen so often during their journey. "It's all in here," he said, tapping the worn cover. With each tap, Erasmus felt a part of himself dissolve and re-form as a version of William Godfrey. "My journey north and all I discovered, what happened to me after I got back to the ship and found you gone, my life among the Esquimaux—everything."

Tap, tap, tap. "I'm going to marry Lavinia," he added. "The minute I can arrange it. I'm tired of being alone. What happened to your feet?"

"I lost my toes," Erasmus said. At least Lavinia would be happy; at least there was that. "Frostbite. What happened to your ear?"

"Polar bear."

Erasmus couldn't take his eyes off the black book. Zeke hadn't taken it north; he'd left it behind; *I have to travel light,* he'd said. When Erasmus broke into Zeke's locked box to retrieve Dr. Boerhaave's journal, he'd seen Zeke's black notebook waiting there.

THE EXTRACTS APPEARED in the Philadelphia paper two weeks later, appended to a reporter's brief introduction and beneath a curious set of headlines:

EXPLORER RETRACES MUCH OF KANE'S ROUTE
ABANDONED BY HIS MEN
RESCUED BY WIZARD'S PROPHECY
DETAILED ACCOUNT OF LIFE AMONG KANE'S ESQUIMAUX
ESQUIMAUX SPECIMENS HERE IN PHILADELPHIA

Zechariah Voorhees, given up for lost since the arrival here in November of the battered survivors of his expedition, has returned to us safe and well in the company of two of Dr. Kane's Esquimaux. I spoke with Commander Voorhees at his parents' home, where he greeted me cheerfully. Asked the question on everyone's lips, he responded, "My men did the right thing. When I set off on my journey north, I set a date by which I would return. Three weeks after that date elapsed, the officers to whom I had delegated responsibility determined that the safety of the group demanded they attempt a retreat. That's exactly what I would have wanted them to do. They had no way of knowing I was alive."

He was alive though, remarkably. And has much to report. To his companions' revelations about the discoveries on Boothia, among the Esquimaux possessing relics of Franklin's ships, he has nothing to add—the account provided earlier by Mr. Erasmus Wells is true and accurate, he says. As is the account of the expedition's winter in the ice. But since his men's escape to safety he has passed an astonishing year among the Smith Sound Esquimaux discovered by our own much-missed Dr. Kane.

These kind people delivered him to Upernavik in May, where he learned of Dr. Kane's tragic demise and was given a copy of *Arctic Explorations* by a Danish trader. Having read this aboard the ship that brought him home, he notes that Dr. Kane's descriptions of the western side of Kane's Basin are accurate in outline, but that his own explorations have added more detail to these areas. A corrected version of Dr. Kane's map follows on Page 3. Commander Voorhees is already at work on a narrative of his stay with the Esquimaux in the most northerly settlement of Greenland. In the meantime, as a kindness to our readers, he's generously provided a few extracts from his daily journal.

*   *   *   *   *   *   *   *   *   *   *   *   *

AUGUST 30, 1856. The men are gone; I can't believe I missed them. The *Narwhal* lies frozen in a useless canal. Heartbreaking to see how hard they worked but I must be glad they failed; here is my winter home. Everything aboard is scrupulously clean, provisions were set aside against my possible return, Mr. Wells left a note explaining what happened. I'm grateful but—four days! I missed them by so little, yet those days mean another winter here in the ice. I begin work today. I'll spend part of my time boxing off a small section of the cabin, insulating it with moss and peat so it can be efficiently heated, and stripping siding for fuel. The rest of the time I must hunt as I've never hunted, trying to cache enough food for the winter. It's an excellent time for walrus, if I can manage to take them by myself. The seals are fat, so are the musk oxen, and hares abound. I made a mistake last year, spending this month in a frantic struggle to escape rather than stockpiling supplies: a mistake I can't afford again.

I'm here for the winter, there's no denying it. The thing to do is face it. Make the best of it. Enjoy it even, learn from it. This is my chance to live, as nearly as possible, the way the Esquimaux live. To prove that a man willing to learn the ways of the north may live in relative comfort here. I have books, food, shelter; maps to make, a journal to keep. I may be a regular Robinson Crusoe.

OCTOBER 10, 1856. I rebuilt the partition, farther aft this time. I lined the bunk with fresh skins, I built a new entrance, I built what deckhouse I could with the wood they left me. I tore off the sheathing down to the waterline on the port side and chopped and stacked it. I put meat down in barrels and filled casks with blubber and oil. I cleaned the guns and moved all the ammunition into one dry place and counted every round; I'm growing short. I made new boots and a new jacket. I fixed the stove. Everything is perfectly snug. My tiny apartment belowdecks is easily heated and all is arranged in the most convenient and efficient way. With only myself to look after, no disagreements or moody men or those who pretend to be sick to avoid hard work, everything's been easy. The body of the sun is gone, but the sky shines red and yellow and blue and the ice glows green and violet. And the hunting has been so fine it's as if the animals give themselves freely to me. I'm ready for the winter, ready for everything.

OCTOBER 21, 1856. One minute nothing, the next a sledge track; it was like seeing a footprint in the sand. They appeared as I was cooking my supper—three of them, camped on the deck as I write this: Nessark, Marumah, and Nessark's wife. Nessark was among the hunters we met on our visit to Anoatok but the other two are new to me. All three spent time with Dr. Kane two years ago and the woman, who is lively and intelligent, learned some English from him and his men. She calls herself Annie, and between her English and what Joe taught me we talk fairly easily. They've come to take me to their winter settlement, she says. They don't want me in danger. I don't know how they knew I was here.

I told them I was safe, I was fine, I appreciated their offer but I could care for myself. They withdrew for a long discussion, then returned and let Annie speak for all. She says they—I—have no choice. They've been sent here by their *angekok*—the word they use for their tribal wizard. This angekok had a vision, she explained. Some children among them sickened recently and two died. The angekok determined that this was because of me.

She asks if I remember Ootuniah, who visited us last year and befriended Joe during our stay in Anoatok. I do remember him very sharply. I felt he didn't have our best interests at heart despite his gifts and this was proved when he loaned Joe the sledge and dogs I needed for myself. Now it appears that Joe told Ootuniah about the meteorite I found, the one he told me not to touch. When the angekok heard it had been destroyed, he decided I'd disturbed the iron stone's spirit. Their children sicken, he says, because that spirit is angry I'm still in this country.

What was I to say? It was a stone, I told Annie. A big stone, which slipped from my grasp. I meant no harm. She says no one blames me, it's understood that this was an accident and I'm not to be punished. Still, reparations must be made. The message the angekok sends is this: that I may pacify the spirit of the stone by making to them a free gift of all the iron that may be easily removed from the ship and transported on their sledges across the Sound. And by returning to their village with them, and allowing them to care for me. If I die here, the angekok says, I'll pollute the land somehow. Thus I must allow them to guard me.

Take the iron, I told them. Take anything you want, all the fittings, I can't use them anymore. But apparently this isn't enough. The two men seem prepared to carry me off bodily if I refuse. And so I am to go. Perhaps it's not a bad thing. They mean me no harm, I think; and I'll have warmth and company and food for the winter; and who else has lived among the Esquimaux like this? I may see things no one's seen before, live in this part of the world as no white man has. Annie does her best to make her tribe's offer attractive—we welcome you, she says.

Meanwhile Nessark and Marumah are loading their sledges with hoops and hardware they tear from the brig. On top of the iron the men pile meat from my caches; I want to go to their village as a strong hunter, not a beggar. Also I'm bringing two of the smaller sails as a gift. Everything else must stay here but my personal belongings. I pray the Franklin relics Erasmus took with him have reached home safely. That the men have reached home. We leave in a few hours.

DECEMBER 23, 1856. Anoatok is much changed since my first visit. During this season the Esquimaux usually move to Etah, where Dr. Kane visited them, but since my arrival the hunting has been unusually good and several extended families have stayed on after repairing and expanding the huts. Fresh sealskins cover the walls, a bear skin warms the floor, the blubber lamps burn steadily. The angekok, Annie says, has determined that my presence is drawing the animals. By their rescue of me, and their continued care—I sleep with Nessark, Annie, their little boy, Annie's parents, and her two young brothers—the spirit of the iron stone has been pacified.

The traps yield foxes, and despite the darkness we've harpooned many seals. We take bears as well—although I'd assumed they all disappeared at this time of year, it isn't so. On Monday the moon was full, we were hunting seal. Suddenly an iceberg near us began to tip and shift position—and a huge bear clambered out of the snow alongside it, disturbed in his rest. Our dogs pursued him and mine was the first shot. By tradition I'm credited with the kill and the skin is mine, but it was Nessark whose spear finished him—and lucky for me, the bear was upon me. I'm now missing most of the fleshy portion of my left ear. The wound is healing and the pain isn't bad. Nessark stopped the bleeding with snow and showed me how to slice the bear's skin from the body and fold it into a shape like a sled, then how to carve out legs, ribs, backbone, and shoulder blades and set each chunk to freeze on the ice. We pulled the meat home on the frozen skin.

JANUARY 28, 1857. A most remarkable event yesterday. The Esquimaux call it *saugssat* or so it sounds to my ear. A high tide two days ago, combined with a strong wind, opened a large lead in the cove. Into it poured hundreds of narwhals in search of breathing space and food. When the end of the lead froze over again the animals were trapped. It was horrible to see them thrashing around in the ever smaller hole, pushing each other underwater as they struggled for air, pulled tighter and tighter until their tusks projected above the surface like a forest of clashing spears. Yet wonderful, too, that it should happen so near to us.

Annie's little boy spotted them first and ran home nearly speechless with excitement—he's very clever, I've taught him much English and call him Tom. We all gathered our weapons and followed him, everyone rushing before a crack opened and freed the desperate creatures. But luck was with us not them. We stood around the edges of the pool, needing only to thrust the harpoons into the nearest animals and haul them up. Even in this we were aided, as the thrashing survivors heaved the carcasses upward.

Twenty-seven narwhals! Such a celebration we had. Tom is a hero and so, somehow, am I. Not for anything I do but because this season has been so generous. There hasn't been a saugssat here for seven years, nor such successful winter hunting. My presence—or more accurately my survival among them—is thought to have caused this good fortune. So I am pampered, fussed over, Annie makes me pants from my polar bear skin and an undershirt from the skins of murres while her mother feeds me dovekies cached since the summer in a seal-skin bag. The birds, permeated with blubber, are a great delicacy. Nessark has also been most generous and begrudges me no hospitality. They're generous not only with material things but with their time and knowledge; men and women alike spend hours with me, answering my questions.

MARCH 14, 1857. I leave with both reluctance and excitement. The food caches are empty, it's time to move to new hunting grounds, we have sun for nearly twelve hours daily and the dogs are strong. It's the best time of year to make a long sledge journey and the whole encampment has decided to accompany me to Upernavik. They would move now anyway, Annie tells me. But not so far, never so far—they do this, as everything else, on the advice of the angekok. He never speaks to me directly but only through Annie. The winter has been so good, he says, and everyone so healthy, because all the elements of his vision dream were satisfied. Yet he believes the spirits will still turn against them unless they convey me safely to Upernavik—which they've only heard about, where no one of them has ever been—and hence out of their country. Annie tells me this as if ashamed. I suppose they all assume I'd want to stay here forever. And how can I tell them nothing could be luckier for me than this—that they should bend their energies, their time and skills and dogs and sledges, to bringing me just where I want to go, and likely couldn't reach myself.

I've had time, these last months, to consider all the mistakes I made my first year here. One was certainly my failure to cultivate these people more fully when they first visited us. Because Dr. Kane's ship was frozen in on this side of the Sound, he was in more immediate contact with them. Always they aided him; and might have aided us had I pressed them more last winter. Perhaps we might have escaped with their help last spring. Instead we saw them only twice; our great loss. Now it seems clear that something one of my crew said or did—I won't speculate as to whom—gave these people the impression we were evil and to be avoided. Only after I was alone did they approach again, giving me the chance to adapt myself to their habits. The white man can only survive comfortably here by living as the Esquimaux do. Almost all the things we brought with us are useless. Esquimaux clothes, hunting techniques, eating habits are what make life possible.

I imagine that Dr. Kane also discovered this—but he never lived among them, as I've done for six months now.

APRIL 30, 1857. Upernavik, at last! The Danish traders welcomed me and gave me news of Dr. Kane—how tragic, this unexpected death after escaping the arctic! Also they tell me my men arrived here safely and are thought to be home. The walrus are streaming north and my Esquimaux must follow them; they're uncomfortable here, they've had no previous contact with the natives of this settlement and their customs are very different. I've given each a parting gift: a knife or a packet of needles, the last of my flannel shirts cut into pocket squares for the children.

Two remain behind as the sledges head north again. Annie and her son, Tom, have agreed to accompany me home, despite the hardship of leaving their family behind. They're excellent representatives of their race, intelligent and agreeable; fine ambassadors to the civilized world. With their help I can convey to others the interest and wonders of their culture. And together we may teach other travelers how best to prepare for future journeys of discovery in the arctic.

HUNCHED OVER HIS work table, Erasmus read those columns with his stomach lurching and heaving. *Trump this*, he could almost hear Zeke saying. *You collected bones and twigs, and then lost them; you and your _friend_. I've brought back people. Not skulls, not brains in a jar: living, breathing people.*

He read through the columns again. Which parts of Zeke's account were true, and which were not? He'd glimpsed Zeke's notebook a few times, when Zeke was pointing out things to

Lavinia; the pages were clean, no more tattered than when Erasmus had last seen the notebook in the box. No grease stains, watermarks, drops of blood or food or filth. Perhaps he'd written it all in the spring, during his journey to Upernavik. Perhaps he'd written it all on the ship that carried him home. Or perhaps only the entries regarding his journey on foot were faked, and the others were true.

He longed to ask Annie and Tom about their time with Zeke. A few times, when Zeke was off giving interviews or had gone home to sleep, Erasmus had approached the Esquimaux. Each time Lavinia had hovered. "You mustn't tire them," she'd said. Not leaving him alone with them for a single minute; equally unwilling to spend a minute alone with him herself.

From the Repository he watched strangers moving in his house. His eyes were sore, his head ached, something hurt at the base of his ribs; he drank brandy, hoping for comfort and warmth, but it only made him dizzy. He hid for the next few days, unable to eat or sleep. He could not remember ever feeling so sick, he was sure he had a fever. A figure appeared on the flagstones, crossed the garden, opened the Repository door: Zeke. He came ostensibly to ask if Erasmus felt all right but then said, in a calm dry voice, that Erasmus was upsetting his sister. "It makes her unhappy to have you around," he said. "Especially when you behave like this."

Erasmus touched a glass of water to his parched lips. "I can't talk," he said. "I'm sick."

When Zeke left, he slipped from his chair and lay under the table. It was true that Lavinia shrank from his gaze; he'd come upon her and Zeke embracing in the solarium, holding hands in the garden, pressed against each other's shoulders. Always she looked happy until, catching sight of him, her lips would tighten and the color rise in her cheeks. Zeke, he thought, must have told her stories. Stories so ugly that she no longer trusted her own brother and could not enjoy her new happiness in his presence.

He wrapped his head in pillowcases wrung out in cold water— where had he gotten this fever? Finally, when he felt better, he dressed in clean clothes and joined the others for dinner. Candles, flowers, Alexandra quiet at one end of the table and Lavinia glowing at the other; Copernicus and Zeke between them. He sat, after a murmured apology, and confronted a platter of sauteed calf liver: the food he hated most in the world, as Lavinia had always known. Not once had she ever served it to him. The slabs gleamed at him, sending out an evil smell. Why wouldn't Zeke stay at his parents' house, where he belonged? His Esquimaux were still upstairs; he rested his arm on Lavinia's chair; his papers were scattered everywhere. He ate the liver greedily, once more asking after Erasmus's health.

Erasmus pushed away from the table, trembling and queasy. When he stood, the surface of the table dipped and swam, shimmered and danced, the glasses waltzing with the spoons. Chasing the meteorite that had been the instrument of Zeke's salvation, he'd dropped through a hole in the ice just the size of this table. In the moment before he lost consciousness he'd opened his eyes and seen murres racing and darting around him, swift as fish, amazingly graceful. They were clumsy in the air but flew like angels through the water, and suddenly he'd seen why they were built as they were: the water was their natural home, as with walruses or whales. Now he saw that he'd misjudged Zeke in the same way. This house was the home Zeke had always craved; he'd slipped into it the minute Erasmus lost his place.

"Lavinia," Erasmus said. She glanced up at him, her eyes glazed with that translucent film. He cleared his throat and steadied his walking sticks beneath him. All he'd ever wanted for her was that she have the chance to live with the person she loved, as he had not. And if he couldn't bear the way she became around Zeke . . . "Would you excuse me?" he said.

THE FOLLOWING WEEK he made arrangements to move out of the Repository until Lavinia and Zeke were married and settled into a home of their own. "I *know* it's my house," he told Copernicus, who tried to talk him out of his decision. "I know it's a bad idea, but I'm angry all the time and I can't stand to be around Zeke like this, and I'm sick and I don't want to fight with Lavinia . . ."

"One meal," Copernicus said gently. "She ordered it because Zeke likes liver. So do I, for that matter."

Erasmus held out the folds of cloth hanging from his belt. "It's weeks," he said. "I didn't want to worry you. But I can't keep anything down."

Alexandra was equally bewildered. "*I* have to move," she said. "Of course I do, Lavinia doesn't need me anymore. But *you* don't have to."

"I can't think," he said. "I can't work, I can't sleep, I can't eat." She frowned but helped him pack a few things. Erasmus moved slowly, deliberately, hoping that Lavinia might walk in and interrupt him. Might rest her hand on his and say, "Where are you going? Why don't you stay?"

She hid in her room, saying nothing. He hesitated near her door, wanting to knock, afraid to knock. Then, almost as an afterthought, he stopped at the room farther down the hall to take his leave of Zeke's Esquimaux. He'd seen little of them; Zeke prepared their meals, which they ate here. Zeke took them for walks each day, and at night, when he returned to his parents' house, he locked them in their room and asked Copernicus—*Copernicus*, Erasmus thought, *not me*—to check on them.

Their room looked like the inside of a summer tent; skins were hung on the walls and spread on the floor. Annie was crouched in front of the window with Tom in her lap, a plate of boiled chicken, barely touched, on the floor beside her. "Where is Tseke?" she asked. "When does he return?"

"With his parents," Erasmus said. Though he knew that was just for the afternoon. "He'll be back soon." He had no idea if Annie understood Zeke's relationship to Lavinia, or the oddness of his own position.

"I'm going away for a while," he said. What difference could this make to her? "I wanted to say good-bye to you and your son." Just as he was thinking he could never know anything about her, a dusty tan moth emerged from the fur near her knee.

"Good-bye," she echoed. She caught the moth with an absent-minded gesture. As he watched she opened a crack in her fist, peered at the fluttering creature, and then released it. Exactly as he would have done. Why shouldn't they talk?

"Why did you come here?" he asked. "Did Zeke force you?"

"It was necessary," she explained. Her eyes followed the moth's path: window, ceiling, window, closet, window, window, window. "He says, 'I am a kind of angekok—did I not bring you the iron, the bears, the narwhals? Did not all the children stay well while I am with you? But I need you to come home with me and meet my people, so they will understand where I have been.'"

Her voice, repeating this, mimicked the pitch and rhythm of Zeke's in an uncanny way. The moth bounced against a row of books: *pfft, pfft, pfft.* Then soared up to the ceiling and into the window again. "He must bring me home to meet his people or my tribe will suffer. He said your ship had a spirit also, and was angry at being left behind in the ice. I must come here to where the ship is born, so the spirit does not punish my people. He says it is the same as with the spirit of the *saviksue* he disturbed."

Her English was remarkable, Erasmus thought. Zeke had taught her so much. "Did you believe that?" he asked.

As she shrugged, Tom slipped off her lap and hid beneath the caribou skin that had earlier sheltered the moth. She might have answered the question Erasmus didn't ask: *Why did you all want Zeke to leave?* They'd kept Zeke alive because the angekok ordered it, and their efforts had been rewarded. But he couldn't stay with them once winter lifted; he had no sense of his place and could only bring them ill luck. Her tribe was one great person, each of them a limb, an organ, a bone. Onto the hand her family formed, Zeke had come like an extra finger. They'd welcomed him, but he'd had no understanding of the way they were joined together. He saw himself as a singular being, a delusion they'd found laughable and terrifying all at once. When he strutted around, it was as if one of the fingers of that hand had torn itself loose, risen up, and tottered over the snow.

She might have tried to explain all this, but instead she shrugged again, eloquent shoulders in Alexandra's ill-fitting dress. "I understood he wouldn't leave without me; he said he *couldn't*. This is why my family let me go."

ERASMUS RETREATED TO Linnaeus's house. He might have rented pleasant rooms, might even have bought a house—but this was temporary, he thought. He needed to catch his breath and longed for some familial comfort while he did so. Still, he wondered if he'd made the right choice. His books and clothes barely fit into the small guest room allotted to him; the only maid frowned when she came for his chamberpot in the morning and disturbed the papers he left on the tiny desk. He missed Alexandra, who'd returned to Browning's house the same day he'd left home. He missed Copernicus; he missed especially the long days during which the three of them had worked together. Yet somehow everyone seemed to think he had brought this on himself.

He sat in the small, hot room, watching the flies hurl themselves at the window. Day after day slipping by, and now this, the worst of all. Zeke and Lavinia were being married this afternoon, at his own house. A small ceremony, only Zeke's parents, his sisters and their families; Erasmus's brothers and their families. Everyone but him. Lavinia had sent a note:

> *Why are you acting like this? It's your house still, and I won't keep*
> *you from it. I would like you to be with me on my wedding day.*
> *But not if you come in a spirit of bitterness. If Zeke can forgive you,*
> *if I can forgive you—why can't you accept our new lives together?*

To Linnaeus he'd said, "What choice do I have?" Linnaeus, looking uneasily at the heap of books piled near Erasmus's bed, had said, "You must do what you think best."

Erasmus had sent a silver tea set and instructed Linnaeus to tell everyone his fever had returned. Now, as if his untruth had brought it on, he had a terrible headache. The maid brought him a pot of coffee, too strong, and forgot the sugar bowl. When she returned with the bowl but no spoon, he said, "Kate—why are you doing this?"

"Doing what?"

Her broad face, covered with freckles, reminded Erasmus of Ned Kynd; a hint of Ireland was still in her voice although she'd been here since she was a girl. Hard-working, intelligent, usually good-humored; only sullen when she was alone with him. He said, "You know."

"Didn't I bring exactly what you asked for?" But she knew what she'd done, she'd done it on purpose. "Is there anything else?"

"Just go," he said.

After scooping sugar into his cup with a twist of paper he settled down to write a letter to Ned. Such a confusion, he couldn't imagine where to begin. He started with this room—the desk, the bed, the flies—and wrote out from there. About all that had happened since Zeke's return home, the two Esquimaux camped in his house while he was sequestered here; about the wedding he couldn't attend. About the newspaper article, which, although it hadn't criticized him directly, had turned the whole city against him. He folded up the three long pages of newsprint he was including, and then confessed his theft of Dr. Boerhaave's journal and the related glimpse of Zeke's black book. Six pages, eight pages. His hand grew tired.

After a pause he wrote to Ned about the party the United Toxophilites had thrown for Zeke. Part welcome-home party, part bachelor party; all the Toxies in full regalia.

You may remember those suits. From the day Mr. Tagliabeau signed you on; all those men in green coats and white pants, with their bows and arrows. They're an archery club. I used to belong.

He told Ned about the speech Zeke had given, regretting that the Esquimaux bow and arrows he'd obtained for the club on Boothia had been lost through no fault of his own. And the drinking, the wild toasts, the dancing women and the arrows presented to Zeke with jokes about his aim on his wedding night. He wrote about the work he and Alexandra and Copernicus had done on his book before they were stalled. Then he found himself longing to write about the lonely nights here in this room.

The walls were tissue thin, and on Sunday nights—always, but only, Sunday nights—he could hear Linnaeus and Lucy making love. Those squeals, those little groans. He couldn't imagine Lucy with her hair down, her mouth unpursed, the things she must do to make his brother make those sounds—they wanted another child, he knew. Perhaps that was the reason for their clocklike regularity. As for the way their noises made him think of Zeke and Lavinia, finally together . . . He kept himself from writing about any of this, describing instead his strange meeting with William Godfrey. Eighteen pages, twenty-one. At the end he wrote:

This is how everyone sees me now; as if I'm just like him.

IN BROWNING'S KITCHEN, the night after the wedding, Alexandra brooded as she cooked. *Dismissed*, she thought, as she lifted biscuits from the oven. She and Lavinia had never been equals, not really. What they'd done was wait together, and wait and wait and wait; and although this had bound them as survivors of a disaster were bound, so that they'd always have a connection, still she'd been Lavinia's paid companion, never exactly a chosen friend. As Lavinia had made quite clear. The instant Zeke came back, Lavinia had turned from her. "You've been so good for me," she'd said, when Alexandra proposed returning to Browning's house. "But of course you'll want to get back to your own work, now that you've managed to *establish* yourself."

Their time together was over; she'd learned a great deal and must be grateful for that. And she was determined not to lose her relationship with Erasmus. Working together, she'd felt them building what she'd always imagined a friendship might be. They'd shared thoughts, work, reading, interests; they confided in each other but also respected each other's privacy. She missed him every day.

On the tray before her she arranged the food she'd prepared for the Percy sisters: boiled chicken in jelly, the hot biscuits, butter, plum jam, lemonade. Browning had taken on the care of the two elderly women who lived across the street, and somehow they'd become Alexandra's responsibility as well. They weren't crazy, not exactly, but they were ancient and isolated and for the last six months had been convinced that people were trying to poison them. They'd take food only from Browning's hands, and eat it only in his presence. Morning and evening he brought food that had once been cooked by Harriet but which now Alexandra prepared. Then he sat patiently with them while they ate.

The texture of his life, Alexandra thought. Which was becoming the texture of hers. A crowd of people needing help, among which he spread himself and his wife and his sisters willingly but too thinly. Already she was tired of the way Browning assumed he could direct her.

Yet no matter how many hours she spent preparing meals, or helping out with the children or the family projects, there had to be some fragments of time left to her. If she slept less, perhaps. If she rose very early, even before Browning rose to prepare his classes; if she could steal an hour or two for her own work before her family began their demands: then she could feel as if she still had a life of her own. She could do what was asked of her with good grace, if she could have this time alone. The thing was not to give in completely.

As she cleaned up the kitchen and prepared to make yet another meal, she decided to retrieve the tools and materials she'd left behind at the Repository. She'd seen Erasmus only twice since her hurried departure; he was very low and didn't seem to be working at all. But despite their altered circumstances they could work secretly, she thought. Quietly, in stolen hours and stolen rooms. Still they might do something worthwhile. She stirred Browning's favorite soup, and then went to tell him she'd be away from home all the following day, and that he must do without her.

———

COPERNICUS WAS PAINTING in the garden. With Zeke and Lavinia gone on a brief wedding trip, he was taking advantage of his freedom; his loose muslin shirt was open over his chest and his forearms were smeared with paint. Blue streaked his hair and daubed his sweating face.

"Alexandra," he said. "What a nice surprise." He darkened a shadow, then stepped back to see the effect. Pinned to a second easel beside him were sketches he'd copied from the notebooks of Erasmus and Dr. Boerhaave. "What brings you here?"

She fanned herself; even the flagstones were sticky in this heat. "I left some drawing materials in the Repository," she said. "But I can't imagine we'll be working in there again. I thought I'd take them home, and see if I can do something there."

"You won't work here again," he agreed. "Nor will I." He wiped his hands on a rag and gestured toward his painting: icebergs, huge and luminous. In the foreground he'd recently added a stump of broken mast and a ringed seal. "As soon as this one's done, I'm moving."

"Where will you go?"

"I have friends at a boardinghouse on Sansom Street—I'm going to take a room there and share the studio on the top floor. I can't work here, it's too odd being around Zeke and Lavinia."

He led her toward the Repository. "You won't believe this," he said. "Don't be shocked."

Yet she was, when she passed through the high double doors. Inside it was so dim that for a minute, blinded after the glare outside, she could see nothing. Two huge black dogs bounded up to her, bumping their heads against her thighs and licking at her hands— "Zeke's," Copernicus said. "He brought them over the day of the wedding." She wiped her hands on her skirt. Why was it so dark in here? There were skins blocking most of the windows. On the floor Annie and Tom lay in a mass of linen that resembled a pile of sails. Why were there people lying on the floor?

"Hello," Alexandra said hesitantly. "I'm sorry, I didn't mean to intrude. I didn't know you were staying in here."

Annie had lost weight, and her hair was dirty. "Tseke gave us this as our home," she said. The dogs loped over and flopped down beside her. "Where is Tseke?"

"He'll be back in a few days," Copernicus said. "I promise." He bent over one of the basins on the floor, dipped a rag in the water, and wiped Annie's face. "Does that help?" he said. "Is that better?"

"I feel burning," Annie said mournfully. "So hot."

Tom coughed and spat. Stains and wet spots and the dogs' round-toed tracks marked the smooth polished wood; drifts of hair rolled under the furniture.

"Are they sick?" Alexandra whispered to Copernicus. "What's happened?" Her supplies had been pushed against one set of shelves; Erasmus's books were scattered and nothing remained of Copernicus's working area but a stack of crates. By the library table, someone had cast loose herbarium sheets that curled forlornly in the stink sent off by a full chamberpot.

"Zeke moved them as soon as you and Erasmus left," Copernicus said, close to her ear. "I suppose he thought they'd be better off here than in the house. But they keep shifting from spot to spot, trying to get comfortable. Nothing seems to help but the cold water. They both have fever—I'm not sure whether it's a reaction to this weather, or something more serious."

"They're to stay here?" she asked. "Permanently?"

Copernicus shrugged. "If I had anyplace to take them to, if I had anything at all to say about this—but I don't, they're in Zeke's care."

In air so foul she could hardly breathe she gathered her things together; her brushes, which she'd arranged carefully, had been jammed upright in a jar and the tips were spoiled. There were dirty fingerprints on the folder containing her drawings, but the drawings themselves seemed intact. Copernicus found a small box for her pens.

They worked without speaking, amid Tom's cough and Annie's rough breathing and the heavy panting of the dogs. Once they stepped outside again, Copernicus said, "I don't know what Zeke is thinking. I really don't. This is no place for them, they're miserable here. And the Repository is being ruined. If Erasmus saw this . . . as soon as Zeke returns, I'm leaving."

"Where did they go?"

"Washington," Copernicus said. "Zeke is meeting a group of people at the Smithsonian Institution. They're making a little party for him there, celebrating his discoveries, and he thought Lavinia would enjoy that. They only went for four days, because of Annie and Tom. Meanwhile *I'm* supposed to be the perfect person to take care of Zeke's Esquimaux. As if I'd know what to do with them, just because I've had some experience with the Indians out west. But Annie and Tom have different habits and different temperaments from any tribe I ever met—I don't know what to feed them. I don't know how to help them, or how to make them comfortable."

"I'm sorry," she said. "Is there anything I can do to help?"

"Not unless you know how to nurse them," he said. "Not unless you know something they'd like to eat. They don't like the meat I bring them. Annie wants some green plant she says will make her feel better."

"Some herbs?" Alexandra suggested.

Copernicus spread his hands. "If there's something you know. I'll try anything."

"There's some tansy and mint in the perennial border." She led him there and asked for his handkerchief. Side by side they gathered leaves in the burning sun.

"I'll miss this place," Copernicus said. "I never imagined, when I came back home, that I wouldn't have a home anymore."

The bruised leaves released a scent that began to cleanse the fumes of the Repository from Alexandra's head. "Is this—is this permanent?" she asked. "You and Erasmus would really let Lavinia take over the house for good?"

"It's just for a year or so," Copernicus said. "I think. Zeke's father has promised to build them a new house, on a plot of land he owns near Fairmount Park. But they have to draw up plans, and then build it—who knows how long that will take. Meanwhile what can we do but humor Lavinia? She's been through so much."

"You and Erasmus have been through a lot as well," Alexandra pointed out.

They knelt side by side in the border. She could smell paint, and the mint they were crushing, and the faint scents of his body and his breath. What would it be like to have him seize her, as Zeke had seized Lavinia on his return? Just as she was thinking this, he reached for a sprig and his forearm drew across her wrist like an arrow across a bow. She froze, thinking how easily she might move her hand a few inches, place her fingers in his palm. Anything might happen after that. He liked her, she knew. Even found her attractive. But he liked everyone; he made no secret of the Indian and Mexican women he'd kept company with out west, nor of the women he met in the theaters here. What she wanted, when she let herself imagine wanting anyone, was someone who might be wholly hers.

"I'm going to try to get Erasmus working on the book again," she said, rising and brushing her skirt. "And myself as well. Can I count on you? If he knew you were still painting, and supported what he was doing . . ."

"I do support him," Copernicus said, sounding surprised.

"I know. But . . ." She turned her eyes from his sun-browned throat and squinted at the garden. He was strong and good-hearted, yet perhaps not really reliable. "You've been gone for almost five years and maybe you'll want to travel again. And there's nothing wrong with helping your sister's husband while he's away. But once he returns—Erasmus needs your help more."

"I *will* help," Copernicus said. "I said I would, and I will. As soon as they return I'll let Zeke take care of his Esquimaux and I'll work on the paintings full-time."

Alexandra folded the handkerchief over the pile of fragrant leaves. "Steep these for ten minutes in a quart of boiling water," she said. "Have Annie and Tom drink the tea while it's hot, it will bring out a cleansing sweat."

She stepped into the Repository again, laying her hand on Annie's hot forehead and then on Tom's. "Zeke will be back soon," she said. She gazed at the chaos around her and moved quickly back into the light.

Ned Kynd received Erasmus's letter late one July night, as he was cleaning up after a long stint cooking for a dozen boisterous hunters. Rabbit stew and porcupine pie and sauteed trout; wild mushrooms and venison filet. He had a reliable stove, good supplies, a grateful employer. The patrons called out loud compliments, and if one grew overenthusiastic and came back to the kitchen and then recoiled at Ned's face, he could claim he'd had a hunting accident and be believed. In these North Woods his was just another legend. "A she-bear tore off that half of my nose," he'd say. "Then left me for dead. I was lucky."

And he *was* lucky, he thought, washing his hands with strong brown soap. Lucky to have landed here. Behind the hotel the mountains rose in solid ranks, cliffs and ledges jutting like bones through the fur of trees and stars shining, sharp and violent, as bright as those in the arctic. In Philadelphia there'd been nothing for him, only more bad jobs in taverns near the wharves. Only the lowest sort would consider him, because of his face. Some asked if he had leprosy, and if he told them what had really happened they stared at him blankly. On an impulse he'd made his way back to the Adirondack Mountains, to a village mentioned by a man he'd known at the lumber camp: Keene Flats, on the eastern side of the highest peaks. A place, his friend had said, where a few hotels catered to city men eager for a wilderness experience.

The noise from the dining hall diminished; the hunters shambled off to their beds. After hanging up his apron and changing his shoes, Ned began the long walk along the Ausable River, to the cabin he'd rented near John's Brook.

Inside he lit the stove and a pair of candles, then opened the envelope from Philadelphia. He wrote back to Erasmus that same night:

Your letter reached me with little trouble though I've moved since you last wrote—this is a small place, and everyone knows everyone else. Your news disturbed me. I've gotten settled here, it's a kind of new life. I hoped you might have one as well.

For Commander Voorhees to show up like this—I didn't wish him dead, I'm glad he's alive but don't see why you must suffer for it. You only did what we asked you to, you led us all to safety and should be honored. Those newspaper pages sounded more as if Commander Voorhees is making up an adventure tale than reporting what he saw. Why should he get to say what he wants, and be believed? I know what he did with that meteorite, despite Joe's advice, yet it seems he was rewarded for his errors. I remember Nessark from my stay at Anoatok, and he didn't strike me as someone who'd willingly let a family member go. Do you suppose Commander Voorhees deceived them in some way? It's the Esquimaux who make him a hero—without them he'd have nothing more than you do, just his story. It's the Esquimaux who set him off from you and me, from Dr. Kane—and I think he knows this, I think he had to bring them back. All this makes me suspicious.

I feel that if you're patient your reputation will be restored in time, as will your family's affections. Perhaps it would be helpful if you left that place for a while. Up here, no one talks about us or any other expedition, they're busy taming this wild place and no one requires explanations.

My job as cook is not exciting, but it's good enough. On my days off, I still practice what you taught me; some of the hunters wish to bring home the skins of the animals they've shot, and I do what I can to prepare them. My big triumph lately has been with deer—finally I've mastered removing that leaf-shaped piece of cartilage from the ear while keeping the skin intact. For my own amusement I've prepared some small skeletons: a bat, a fox, a salamander. You're a better man than Commander Voorhees. I'm not surprised he's taken those two Esquimaux from their homes, I always thought he'd do something like this. I wish he'd lost more than his ear. Should you need me you can reach me care of the hotel, at least for the remainder of the season.

"I'M GLAD HE'S ALL RIGHT," Alexandra said to Erasmus, when they met in early August by the Schuylkill River. She folded the pages of Ned's letter neatly. "I was worried about him when you first came back—his poor face. But he's right that you're a better man than Zeke. And I agree with both of you about that diary, I had the same reaction when I read the sections in the newspaper. Everything

I saw of Zeke before I left—he just seems *false* to me somehow. Even the way he is with Lavinia. I don't understand him. I never trusted him, not from the beginning."

Erasmus looked out at the ducks paddling in the eddies behind the rocks. When the Esquimaux at Disko Bay had tipped and rolled their delicate kayaks, the crew of the *Narwhal* had tossed them scraps of food, as strollers here might feed these creatures.

"He's already got a name for his book," Alexandra added. "*The Voyage of the* Narwhal—aping the famous works of exploration, I suppose. Copernicus told me he's written a hundred pages."

Erasmus shook his head. As if sensing that he'd not done a stroke of work since Lavinia's wedding, she'd asked him to bring some new pages and promised she'd bring some drawings. He had nothing to exchange for the detail of a whale's mouth she now spread on the bench between them.

"That's good," he said. "It's really quite close. If you could shade the baleen plates a bit more . . ."

Her face fell. "I knew I wouldn't get it right without you," she said. "And it's the only one I've been able to work on, it's so hard to get time at home."

"At least you've done something. I can't work at all."

"There must be someplace," she said. "Someplace we can go."

"We might be able to use the Repository as a studio," he said. "If we didn't bother Lavinia, if I didn't have to see Zeke . . ." Beneath the hem of her dress, one of Alexandra's shoes inscribed an arc in the dirt. "You don't think that's a good idea?"

"Have you talked to Copernicus?"

"What do you mean?" She looked so unhappy that, despite his own misery, he felt sorry for her.

"Probably he didn't want to upset you," she said. "But you should know."

She told him, then, how Zeke had converted the Repository into a kind of camp for Annie and Tom. He tried to envision it, but failed—bales of skins and puddles of water and dogs lurching against the tables. The precious books and specimens disturbed, and Annie and Tom both ill. Zeke had known and cherished that place as a boy.

"I'm sorry," Alexandra said.

"My father must be rolling in his grave. But it can't be helped, can it?"

"You could go back," she pointed out. "It *is* your house."

"There's something . . ." he said. "I can't explain it, but I know as surely as I've ever known anything that Lavinia can't be happy with Zeke in my presence. She thinks I'm judging her, she doesn't understand it's *him*, that I don't trust *him*."

"Then we have to live like this for a while," Alexandra said. "I suppose. They're building a house of their own, they'll be gone in time."

"In time for what?" He thought of Annie and her little boy. "Are they really sick?"

"They didn't look well," she said. "But I don't know what's wrong with them."

"Zeke," he said. "Zeke . . . Copernicus offered to let us work at his new studio, but really there isn't room without crowding his friends. He said that when Zeke got back from Washington, he was all puffed up from meeting politicians and members of the Smithsonian Institution, and that everyone was pressing him to exhibit Annie and Tom. A sort of lecture tour around the lyceum halls of the Northeast. One night a ventriloquist or a phrenologist, the next some itinerant professor giving lessons in physiology or showing wax models of Egyptian ruins. The next Zeke in his polar-bear pants, exhibiting Annie like another Hottentot Venus. It's such a dreadful idea, but Copernicus says he's going to do it. He's going to hold the first exhibition right here in Philadelphia. But if they're already sick . . ."

"Do you think that will stop him?"

"Nothing stops him," Erasmus said. "Nothing ever does. If he gives a lecture here, will you go with me? I have to see what he does."

"If you want," Alexandra said. "Of course I'll come. And I was thinking, in the meantime—what about asking Linnaeus and Humboldt for some space at the engraving firm? All we'd need are two desks near each other. There must be a corner they could spare."

She was looking at the river, not at him, but he could see the longing on her face. "I can't live like this," she said. "Not after having a chance to do real work. I can't stand this."

"I'll ask them," he promised. "If it doesn't work out, I'll rent us a workroom someplace else."

He let his fingers creep over her knuckles. Her hands were smooth and white, the fingernails clipped short; although her palms were small her fingers were unusually long and her nails, he saw, were deeply arched.

Later he'd think of this as the first moment he saw himself back in the arctic. Not a dark dream, like those he'd had during his first days home, but a bright waking vision: the muddy Schuylkill turned into a glacial stream; the ducks turned into murres and dovekies; the limp, moist foliage dwarfed into a crisp tangle of willows. Beside him Alexandra, who'd had only his stories from which to build her vision, dreamed in less detail. But she imagined a ship passing through dense ice, both of them scouting a route from the bow as the floes glided past.

Specimens of the Native Tribes

(September 1857)

Miserable, yet happy wretches, without one thought for the future, fighting against care when it comes unbidden, and enjoying to the full their scanty measures of present good! As a beast, the Esquimaux is a most sensible beast, worth a thousand Calibans, and certainly ahead of his cousin the Polar bear, from whom he borrows his pantaloons.

—ELISHA KENT KANE, *Arctic Explorations: The Second Grinnell Expedition in Search of Sir John Franklin, 1853, '54, '55* (1856)

HERE IN THE THEATER'S GALLERY, NEAR THE PROSTI-
tutes scattered like iridescent fish through the shoals of dark-clothed
men, Alexandra felt drab in her brown silk dress. Two seats down
from her, a woman in a chartreuse gown with lemon-trimmed
flounces was striking a deal with a pleasant-looking man. They
would meet on the landing, Alexandra heard them agree. Directly
after the lecture. The man's voice dropped and the woman shook her
head, shivering the egret feathers woven into her hair. "Twenty dol-
lars," she said. The man nodded and disappeared, leaving Alexandra
to marvel at the transaction.

"There must be a thousand people," Erasmus said, scanning the
crowd. "Maybe more."

"It's frightening," she said. "How good Zeke is at pro-
moting himself."

All around the city, on lampposts and tavern doors, in merchants' windows and omnibuses, posters advertised the exhibition.
A clumsy woodcut showed Zeke holding a harpoon and Annie a
string of fish, Tom peeping out from behind her flared boots. In the
background were mountains cut by a fjord, and above those a banner headline: MY LIFE AMONG THE ESQUIMAUX. A caption
touted the remarkable discoveries made by Zechariah Voorhees:

TWO FINE SPECIMENS OF THE NATIVE TRIBES!
MORE EXOTIC THAN THE SIOUX AND FOX INDIANS
EXHIBITED BY GEORGE CATLIN IN LONDON AND PARIS!
SEE THE ESQUIMAUX DEMONSTRATE THEIR CUSTOMS!

Zeke had run a smaller version in the newspaper and mailed invitations to hundreds of his family's friends and business associates—
organizing this first exhibition, Alexandra thought, like a military

campaign. Ahead of him lay Baltimore, Washington, Richmond, New York, Providence, Albany, Boston.

Erasmus said, "Can you see Lavinia?" and Alexandra, scouting the boxes on the second tier, finally spotted her dead center, flanked by Linnaeus and Humboldt and Zeke's parents and sisters. She was touching her hair then her cheek then her brooch then her nose, turning her head from side to side as if the mood of the entire audience were expressing itself through her. Everyone, Alexandra thought, made nervous by this month's chain of disasters. Across the ocean, off the coast of Ireland, the telegraph cable being laid with such fanfare had broken. Two trains had crashed south of Philadelphia, killing several passengers; last week a steamship on its way to New York from Cuba had sunk. Each of these seemed to heighten the financial panic set off by a bank failure in Ohio. Banks were closing everywhere; the stock exchange was in an uproar. The papers were full of news about bankrupt merchants and brokers. Alexandra's own family, who had no money to lose, hadn't been touched so far, and the engraving firm seemed stable. But Erasmus, whose income came primarily from his father's investments, had suffered some losses. And Zeke's father's firm was in trouble, which suddenly made Zeke's future—and Lavinia's as well—uncertain. Suddenly it mattered what Zeke charged for the exhibition tickets, and how many tickets were sold. The theater was full of people desperate for distraction.

In the glow of the gaslights Zeke strode out in full Esquimaux regalia, adjusted the position of two large crates, and took his place at the podium. The roar of applause was startling, as was the ease with which he spoke. If he had notes, Alexandra couldn't see them. Swiftly, eloquently, he sketched for the audience an outline of the voyage of the *Narwhal,* making of the confused first months a spare, dramatic narrative.

Their first sights of Melville Bay and Lancaster Sound, their encounters with the Netsilik and their retrieval of the Franklin relics; the discovery of the *Resolute* and their stormy passage up Ellesmere until they were frozen in; their long winter and the visit of Ootuniah and his companions; the first trip to Anoatok. No mention, Alexandra noticed, of Dr. Boerhaave's death, nor of the other men who'd died: nor of Erasmus. It was "I" all the time, "I" and "me" and "mine"; occasionally "we" or "my men." No names, only him. Beside her, Erasmus fidgeted.

Twenty minutes, she guessed. Twenty minutes for the part of the voyage involving the crew; then another fifteen for Zeke's solo trip north on foot and his return to the empty ship. "Now," Zeke was saying, "now began the most interesting part of my experience in the arctic. I was all alone, and winter was coming. I had to prepare myself."

From the crates he began to pull things. His hunting rifle, sealskins, a tin of ship's biscuit, a jar of dried peas. His black notebook, the sight of which made Erasmus groan. Into his talk he wove some stray lines from that, and then read aloud the section about the arrival of Annie and Nessark and Marumah. "The *angekok* is the tribe's general counselor and advisor," he explained. "As well as its wizard. His chief job is to determine the reason for any misfortune visiting the tribe—and the *angekok* of Annie's tribe determined that the cause of their children's sickness was me. So was my life changed by a superstition. From the day these people arrived I entered into a new life."

He described the journey to Anoatok and his first days there. Then he said, "But you must meet some of the people among whom I stayed." He stepped back from the podium and whistled.

There was rattling backstage, and the crack of a whip. Two dogs appeared—not his huge black hunting dogs but beagles, ludicrous in their harnesses, gamely trotting side by side. Apparently Zeke would not subject his own pets to this. Behind them they pulled a small sledge on wheels, with Tom crouched on the crossbars and Annie grasping the uprights and waving a little whip. Both Annie and Tom wore fur jackets with the hoods pulled up and shadowing their faces. When the sledge reached the front of the podium, Zeke gave a sharp command that stopped the beagles. They sat, drooling eagerly as Zeke held out bits of biscuit, and then lay down in their traces with their chins on their paws. Their eyes followed Zeke as he moved around the stage, but Annie and Tom stared straight out at the audience, shielding their eyes against the glare.

"These are two of the people who rescued me," Zeke said. "The names they use among us are Annie and Tom."

While they stood still he recited some facts. Annie and Tom belonged to the group of people John Ross had discovered in 1818 and called Arctic Highlanders—there were just a few hundred of them, he said, scattered from Cape York to Etah. Fewer each year; their lives were hard and their children sickened; he feared they were dying out. They moved nomadically throughout the seasons, among clusters of huts a day's journey apart and near good hunting sites. All food was shared among them, as if they were one large family. Because no driftwood reached their isolated shores, they had no bows and arrows, nor kayaks, and in this they differed from the Esquimaux of Boothia and southern Greenland. They'd developed their own ways, substituting bone for wood—bone harpoon shafts and sledge parts and tent poles. "A true sledge," Zeke said, "would have bone crosspieces lashed to the runners with thongs, and ivory strips fastened to the runners." He went on to explain how they subsisted largely on animals from the sea.

"The term 'Esquimaux' is French and means 'raw meat eaters,'" Zeke said. "But there's nothing disgusting in this, the body in that violent climate craves blood and the juices of uncooked food." From the nearest crate he took a paper bundle, which he unwrapped to reveal a Delaware shad. A few strokes of a knife yielded three small squares of flesh. Two he held out to Annie and Tom, keeping the third for himself. The beagles whined. Zeke popped the flesh in his mouth and chewed, while Annie and Tom did the same on either side of him. The audience gasped, and Alexandra could see this pleased Zeke enormously.

"With the help of my two friends," he said, "I would like to demonstrate for you some of the elements of daily life among these remarkable people."

Now Alexandra saw the bulk of what the crates contained. Certainly he hadn't carried all these objects home with him; he must have made some here, with Annie's help and whatever supplies he could find. There was a long-handled net, which Tom seized and carried to the top of one crate. He made darting and swooping motions as Zeke described capturing dovekies. "These arrive by the million," Zeke said. "When the hunter's net is full, he kills each bird by pressing its chest with his fingers, until the heart stops."

A soapstone lamp—where had this come from?—with a wick made from moss; Zeke filled it with whale oil and had Annie light it with a sliver of wood he first lit with a match, telling the audience they must imagine lumps of blubber slowly melting. In the huts, he said, with these lamps giving off heat and light, with food cooking and wet clothes drying and children frolicking, it had been warm no matter what the outside temperature. He brought out more hides and had Annie demonstrate how the women of her tribe scraped off the inner layers to make the hides pliable. "This crescent-shaped knife is an *ulo*," he said, and Annie sat on her knees with her feet tucked beneath her thighs and the skin spread before her, rubbing it with the blade. Beside Alexandra, Erasmus pressed both hands to his ribs.

"Are you all right?" she said. She couldn't take her eyes from the stage.

"That's exactly the way I soften a dried skin before I mount it," Erasmus said. "I have a drawshave I use like her *ulo*."

Zeke said, "The women chew every inch after it's dried, to make it soft," and Annie put a bit of the hide in her mouth and ground her teeth. "I can't show you the threads, which are made from sinews," he said. "But the needles are kept in these charming cases." Annie held up an ivory cylinder, through which passed a bit of hide bristling with needles.

Zeke took Tom's hand and seized a pair of harpoons; then he and Tom lay down and pretended to be inching up on a seal's blowhole, waiting for the seal to surface. As they mimicked the strike Zeke spoke loudly, a flow of vivid words that had the crowd leaning forward. They were seeing what Zeke wanted them to see, Alexandra thought. Not what was really there: not a rickety makeshift sledge, two floppy-eared beagles, a tired woman and a nervous boy moved like mannequins by the force of Zeke's voice. Not them, or a man needing to make a living, but the arctic in all its mystery: unknown landscapes and animals and another race of people.

Her face was wet; was she weeping? As Zeke's antics continued Alexandra found herself thinking of her parents and the last day she'd seen them. Pulling away from the ferry dock, waving good-bye, sure they'd be reunited in a week. Then the noise, the terrible shocking noise. Great plumes of steam and smoke and cinders spinning down to the water—and her parents, everyone, gone. Simply gone.

She turned to Erasmus, who had his face in his hands. Gently she touched him and said, "You have to look."

He raised his head for a second but then returned his gaze to his shoes. "I won't," he said passionately. "I hate this. All my life the thing I've hated most is being *looked at*. I can't bear it when people stare at me. I know just how she feels, all of us peering down at her. It's disgusting. It's worse than disgusting. People stared at me like this when I returned from the Exploring Expedition, and again when I came back without Zeke. Now we're doing the same thing to her."

Had she known this about him? She looked away from him, back at the stage; she felt a shameful pleasure, herself, in regarding Annie and Tom. She longed to draw them.

Annie had pushed her hood back from her sweating face, while Tom had stretched out on the sledge and was pulling at one of the beagle's ears. From his crate Zeke took a wooden figure clothed in a miniature jacket and pants. "The children play with dolls," Zeke said. "Just as ours do." Tom released the beagle's ear, seizing the doll and pressing it to his chest. Then Zeke was winding string around Annie's fingers, saying, "Among this tribe, a favorite game with the women and children is called *ajarorpok,* which is much like our child's game of cat's cradle, only more complicated."

He said something to Annie and stepped away. Annie's hands darted like birds and paused, holding up a shapely web. "This repre-sents a caribou," Zeke said.

Alexandra tried to see a creature in the loops and whorls, not knowing that, for Annie, it was as if the stage had suddenly filled with beautiful animals. Not knowing that for Annie this evening moved as if the *angekok* who'd brought Zeke to them had bewitched her, putting her into a trance in which she both was and was not on this stage. The *angekok* had shared with her the secret fire that let him see in the dark, to the heart of things. For her Zeke's bird net wasn't a broomstick and knotted cotton but a narwhal's tusk and plaited sinews; on her fingers she felt the fat she'd scraped from the seal. She was home, and she was also here, doing what she'd been told in a dream to do.

She was to watch these people, ranged in tiers above her, and commit them to memory, so that she could bring a vision of them to her people back home. Their pointed faces and bird-colored garments; the way they gathered in great crowds but didn't touch each other or share their food. Their tools, their cooking implements, their huts that couldn't be moved when the weather changed. In a dream she'd heard her mother's voice, singing the song that had risen from her tribe's first sight of the white men.

Her mother had been a small girl on the summer day when floating islands with white wings had appeared by the narrow edge of ice off Cape York. From the islands hung little boats, which were lowered to the water; these spat out sickly men in blue garments, who couldn't make themselves understood but who offered bits of something that looked like ice, which held the image of human faces; round dry tasteless things to eat; parts of their garments, which weren't made of skins.

"At first," her mother had said, "we thought the spirits of the air had come to us." On the floating island her mother had seen a fat, pink, hairless animal, a man with eyes concealed behind ovals of unmelting ice, bulky objects on which to sit, something like a frozen arm, with which to hit something like a needle. The two men who'd stepped first on the ice had worn hats shaped like cooking pots. Through them, her people had learned they weren't alone in the world.

Much later, when Annie was grown, she'd had her mother's experience to guide her when the other strangers arrived. Kane and his men had taught Annie to understand their ungainly speech, and Annie had learned that the world was larger than she'd understood, though much of it was unfortunate, even cursed. Elsewhere, these visitors said, were lands with no seals, no walrus, no bears; no sheets of colored light singing across the sky. She couldn't understand how these people survived. They'd been like children, dependent on her tribe for clothes, food, sledges, dogs; surrounded by things which were of no use to them and bereft of women. Like children they gave their names to the landscape, pretending to discover places her people had known for generations.

From them she'd gained words for the visions of her mother's childhood: a country called England and another called America; men called officers; ships, sails, mirrors, biscuits, cloth, pig, eye-glasses, chair. Wood, which came from a giant version of the tiny shrubs they knew. Hammer and nails. Later she'd added the words Zeke had taught her while he lived with them; then the names for the vast array of unfamiliar things she'd encountered here. In the dream her mother had given her this task: to look closely at all around her, and to remember everything. To do this while guarding her son.

Her hands darted and formed another shape, which Zeke claimed represented ponds amid hills but in which she saw her home. She felt the warm liver of the freshly killed seal, she tasted sweet blood in her mouth. In the gaslights she saw the moon and the sun, brother and sister who'd quarreled and now chased each other across the sky. At first her mother had thought the strangers must come from these sources of light. Her hands flew in the air.

"Can you see what she's doing?" Alexandra whispered to Erasmus. "I can't see what she's making."

"I have to go," Erasmus said. "We have to go. Can we go?"

HE HADN'T EXPECTED the exhibition to pain him so much. Back at Linnaeus's house, Lucy said, "Well, of course I wish he'd mentioned *you*. But still it was interesting, wasn't it? You should have stayed until the end, he had Annie and Tom sing some Esquimaux songs. The way she ate the raw fish . . ." Lucy shuddered, yet she was smiling.

"She's sick," Erasmus said. "She's miserable. Zeke has no right to show her off like that, like a trained bear . . ."

"It was the stage lights that were making her perspire," Linnaeus said. "And I think he does Annie's people a service, as well as himself. The more people see what Esquimaux life is like, the more they'll respect their ways. How can that be anything but good for her and her tribe?"

Erasmus retreated to his stuffy room, where he tossed and turned and dreamed about the copper kettle packed with relics, which had slipped beneath the ice. In his dream the prayer book and the treatise on steam engines, the silver cutlery and the mahogany barometer case had all sprouted eyes and were staring at him; the kettle was staring; the walrus skin sealing the top was staring. Annie, across that crowded space, was staring directly into his eyes, as Lavinia had stared when she was a girl of ten and he'd left, bereft and barely aware of her, to join his first expedition.

Only Annie had met his eyes in that theater, he thought as he woke. Only Annie—as only Annie knew if Zeke's stories were true. He'd gone to the exhibition hoping her behavior might give him a clue; hoping, perhaps, that she'd interrupt the flow of Zeke's words and say, "But it wasn't like *that*." Instead she'd performed in silence, gazing across the hall at him.

For a week he tried to resist what he knew he should do. He visited Copernicus, who had settled into his new place and begun another painting, this one of Lancaster Sound in mid-July. Into the vista he was crowding everything Erasmus had described to him, the whales and belugas and seals and walrus churning through the water, the fulmars and guillemots whirring and diving, the murres and kittiwakes guarding their eggs from the foxes. Everywhere life, vibrant and massed, and the streaming, improbable light.

"I should go to Baltimore," Erasmus said.

"What can you do for them?" Copernicus said. "No matter how much you disapprove, you can't stop Zeke—everyone loved his talk, he's having a huge success. And he needs the money now."

He added a blue shadow to the flank of a beluga. Erasmus found the painting beautiful, but he kept seeing Annie in that landscape and soon he left.

He tried to work. He tried not to think, over the weekend, about Zeke and Annie and Tom in Baltimore; when the newspaper reported another huge crowd he tried not to see Annie's face. He went to the engraving firm on Monday and met Alexandra at the pair of desks placed back to back, which Linnaeus and Humboldt had grudgingly granted them. Six square feet for her and six for him, in the dead space in the center of the storage room. The light was terrible. From the pages of Dr. Boerhaave's journal, and the sketchier notes of his own, he was trying to build a description of some peculiar fossils they'd found before winter had confined them to the ship. A jawbone that seemed almost crocodilian; leaf casts resembling gingkos. Alexandra was drawing one of these.

"How could such a fossil be in that place?" she asked. "Where now there are no trees?"

"I don't know," Erasmus said, looking from his dead friend's sketches to his new friend's drawing. "It must have been *warm* there once. At Tierra del Fuego, years ago, I saw the fossil remains of a whale on top of a mountain."

"You could argue," Alexandra said, "that it was left behind by the Noachian Deluge. That these leaves ended up in the arctic the same way."

"You could," he said. "If you didn't believe any of the geological evidence Lyell's assembled. All of which suggests that the earth and these fossils are millions of years old."

In England, he knew, even as Lyell and Darwin and Hooker discussed the mutability of species and the nature of geological change, a respected clergyman had put forth a theory that the surface of the earth had never changed, and that life forms never altered or developed. He said, "A man in London argues seriously that when the act of creation took place, the earth sprang into being complete with all its fossils and other suggestions of an earlier life. It's a test, this man says. Another version of the tree in paradise. God hid the fossils in the rocks to tempt us into questioning the truths revealed in the Bible. Supposedly the fossils aren't even the relics left by the Flood but just—I don't know, just *decorations*."

"Do you believe that?" Alexandra said. She picked up one of the leaf casts and regarded the symmetrical veins.

"I don't know what I believe anymore," he replied. "About anything. In Germany, there's a man who says the fossil-bearing rocks fell to earth as meteorites. And so the fossils represent beings from other worlds." He looked down at the loops and whorls of Dr. Boerhaave's writing, and then closed the journal and stood.

"I can't stay here," he said. His father had coaxed him into joining Wilkes's expedition; Zeke and Lavinia had lured him north; Ned had dragged him away from the *Narwhal*; Alexandra had steered him toward his book. But this one small decision might be his. "I have to talk with Annie. If Zeke's forcing her somehow to perform like this— I'm going to go to Washington. Maybe she'll tell me what Zeke really did up there. Maybe I can make him cancel the rest of the tour."

HIS TIMING WAS BAD—as always, he thought. Off by a year, a month, a day; in this case by just a few hours. He hadn't allowed for his new feet, which slowed every stage of his journey. He couldn't have predicted that the biggest bank in Philadelphia would close its doors and that depositors anxious to get to other banks would be crowding every form of transportation. And he'd forgotten what Washington was like in September, so hot and humid that the Potomac seemed to have risen into the atmosphere. There were pigs in the streets. Mud, and people shouting; everywhere the litter of construction and the long faces of men whose financial dreams were ruined. He followed a trail that led from a newspaper advertisement to a handbill to a poster to the new Smithsonian building. When the carriage let him off he confronted a mass of stone, wings and a cloister, battlements and a host of towers. He made his way to the main entrance and found himself in the Great Hall.

The beautiful display cases being built in the galleries behind the rows of columns caught his eye, as did the mounds of crates near the finished cases, but he moved past them toward the stairs at the hall's far end. People streamed at him, busily talking; hundreds of people who passed the tall windows and were lit by beams of muddy, late afternoon light, shadowed by the columns, and then set gleaming again. A river moved against him, parting with murmurs of apology. He was carried forward by a fantasy that he'd stand beside Zeke and, after pulling Annie and Tom to safety, tell his version of the story. Just once, in these august surroundings, he'd justify himself and Dr. Boerhaave and Ned, all of them, everyone.

The staircase looked like a waterfall. He fought his way up the inside railing, knowing all the time where this river of people must have its source but praying he was wrong. At the rear of the apparatus room, a few people trickled past him; he slipped past the hydro-electric machine and the pneumatic instruments, the Fresnel lens and the big battery. He drew a deep breath and passed through the wide door into the lecture room. The room was empty. The oval skylight above the speaker's platform shone down on an empty podium. The curved rows of seats spreading out in the shape of an open fan were empty; the horseshoe-shaped gallery above was empty as well. A poster attached to a pillar announced Zeke's lecture: 4:30 to 6:30 P.M., in this room, on this day. It was just past six now, yet somehow he'd missed it.

Where was Zeke? Where were Annie and Tom? The room was as big as a theater and held perhaps fifteen hundred seats; he could imagine Zeke's voice resonating from the smooth plaster walls as Annie and Tom went through their paces under the skylight's false sun. He sat for a minute and caught his breath, before making his way back downstairs again. Now the Great Hall was empty as well. Bewildered, unsure where to go next, he moved slowly. At the end of the hall nearest the stairs, the galleries were empty. Farther on, neat stacks of wood and panes of glass, sawhorses and boxes of workmen's tools sat between each pair of columns. Then he passed rows of half-built cases, rising in three tiers from floor to ceiling but without their glass doors or hardware; beyond them were a few rows of finished cases. A Negro carpenter adjusting a door on one of these looked up at him.

"May I help you?" he asked. "If you're having trouble walking . . ."

Erasmus looked down at his feet. "I'll be all right," he said. "It just takes me a little longer."

"Take all the time you want," the carpenter said, tapping the brass hinge. "So many people at that lecture, you were smart to wait until the room emptied out."

"I missed the lecture," Erasmus said, and moved on. Zeke and Annie and Tom could be anywhere, he thought. At any hotel, at anyone's home. He stared blankly at a mountain of crates, considering what to do next. Then realized what he was looking at.

Back home he'd read in the newspaper that Congress had appropriated money to build these cases, which were meant to house specimens from the expeditions of the last two decades. The centerpiece, he'd read, was to be the collection from his old Exploring Expedition. Stuffed in the Patent Office for fifteen years, mislabeled and poorly displayed, the specimens were to find a home here. He'd been thinking about other things when he read that; it had hardly registered, although once this would have been the most important news in the world. Now it didn't seem to matter where the things on which he'd wasted his youth ended up.

On the crates were labels, apparently meant to go on the doors of the cases once they were filled. He bent over one and read it wonderingly.

Case 71.

*Collections made by the U.S. Exploring Expedition
in the Feejee Islands . . . Cannibal Cooking Pots.*

*The Feejees are Cannibals. The flesh of women is preferred to that
of men, and that part of the arm above the elbow and the thigh
are regarded as the choicest parts. So highly do they esteem this
food, that the greatest praise they can bestow on a delicacy is to say
that it is as tender as a dead man.*

*Vessel for mixing oil . . . Fishing Nets of twine, from the bark
of the Hibiscus . . . Flute of Bamboo, and other musical instruments . . . Paddles . . . Mask and Wig worn in dances . . . War
Conch, blown as the sign of hostilities . . . Fishing Spears . . . War
Clubs . . . Feejee Wigs . . . Native Cloth, worn as a turban on the
head . . . Feejee Spears . . . Feejee drum made of the hollow trunk
of a tree.*

He leapt back as if he'd been burned. He both could and couldn't remember those objects, and the young version of himself who'd helped gather them. Two members of the Expedition had been killed by those Feejee Islanders. He hadn't taken part in the retaliatory raid, but he'd known what was happening. From the ship he'd seen the smoke from the burning villages and heard the rifle fire. Wilkes had argued that man-eating men deserved any punishment he might inflict, and although Erasmus had hated Wilkes's harsh ways with the native peoples, in this case part of him agreed. But that had been before Dr. Rae returned from the arctic with the first news of Franklin's fate, and those hints of mutilated corpses and human parts found in the British cooking kettles. Before Joe told him about the British boot.

He moved uneasily among the other crates. There were signs describing corals and crystals, cuttlefish and prawns: *Notice the Sea Mushroom*, one directed. How could he notice anything, with the objects locked inside their crates? He tried to imagine the ranks of display cases finished and gleaming: each case numbered, each shelf labeled, each item on each shelf tagged. How many miles of shelving, if he put every shelf from every tier of every case end to end? On those shelves would be thousands—tens of thousands—of specimens. Snakes and fossils and shards of wood, canoes and skulls and feathers and slippers all jumbled together. Stuffed dogs, stuffed fish. Exotic birds, gannets and toucans: *The Booby is so stupid that he will sit still and be knocked on the head.*

When all the specimens were arranged, this would be the largest collection in the country. Everything the biggest, the only, the best. Already there was a meteorite here, squatting dumbly behind two crates: *The largest specimen in the country, obtained at Saltillo. When found it was being used as an anvil. It is thought to be of lunar origin.* Behind it, the sign on another crate: *Human Skulls from the Feejee Islands, New Zealand, California, Mexico, North American Indians &c. One of the skulls is of Vendovi, the Feejee Chief and Murderer.*

Erasmus imagined Zeke striding past these crates with Annie and Tom and a crowd of followers, ignoring everything that didn't touch directly on him. He hadn't been so different himself when he was Zeke's age. Vendovi, whom he'd only glimpsed briefly, had killed one of the expedition's seamen and then been taken hostage by Wilkes in return. He and Erasmus had been on different ships, and Erasmus had hardly thought about him; hardly noticed when Vendovi was carried ashore at New York, to die the next day in the hospital. How had that person turned into a skull, and how had the skull landed here?

None of these skulls, none of those days, had entered into the version of the Exploring Expedition he'd recounted to Dr. Boerhaave when they'd first met. Perhaps he'd been ashamed even then. All the skulls but Vendovi's had come, he was almost sure, from burial grounds; other men on other ships had gathered them. Not he. Was it worse to capture a Feejee chief and let him die in a strange land than to tear an Esquimau woman from her home and exhibit her to curious strangers? Vendovi's death pained him now, but then he'd hardly noticed it. He'd gawked at the Feejee Islanders as if they were apes. As Zeke gawked at the Esquimaux, but with less enthusiasm and a colder eye. One more sign caught his eye:

Case 52.
The identical dress worn by Dr. E. K. Kane, the celebrated
American Arctic Explorer, and brought by him to this Museum.
We quote the following from the account of his travels:
"The clothing or personal outfit demands the nicest study of experience. Rightly clad, he is a lump of deformity, waddling over the ice, unpicturesque, uncouth, and seemingly helpless. The fox-skin jumper, or kapetah, *is a closed shirt, fitting very loosely to the person, but adapted to the head and neck by an almost air-tight*

hood, the nessak. *Underneath the* kapetah *is a similar garment, but destitute of the hood, which is a shirt. It is made of bird skins, chewed in the mouth by the women until they are perfectly soft, and it is worn with this unequalled down next the body. More than 500 auks have been known to contribute to a garment of this description. The lower extremities are guarded by a pair of bear-skin breeches, the* nannooke. *The foot gear consists of a bird-skin sock, with a padding of grass over the sole. Outside of this is a bear-skin leg. In this dress, a man will sleep upon his sledge with the atmosphere at 93 degrees below our freezing point. The only additional articles of dress are, a fox's tail held between the teeth to protect the nose in a wind, and mitts of seal skin well wadded with sledge straw."*

What was this doing here? The one thing Zeke might have noticed, even envied; Erasmus could see now why Zeke had come here on his honeymoon trip. Why he'd found it so crucial to curry favor with the Smithsonian's officials and scientists and to give his lecture not in one of Washington's theaters but in the glorious lecture room above.

This was Zeke's chance, his time to shine. In July another expedition had left England in search of Franklin and his men: Captain McClintock, aboard the *Fox,* headed with Lady Franklin's support for Boothia and King William Land. He meant to complete the search that Zeke had started but bungled—and if he succeeded, all Zeke's feats would be eclipsed except for his retrieval of Annie and Tom. They were his Sioux Indians, his two-headed infant in a jar. Zeke, Erasmus understood, had a tiny slot of time in which to make his name, a window between Kane and McClintock.

Erasmus poked at the crate, but it was solidly built and he could see nothing inside. He tapped it lightly with one of his sticks; then he hit it more strongly. By the time a hand clamped down on his shoulder he was braced on one stick and whacking with the other, as if he might shatter the thick pine boards and find his own life trapped inside.

"You must stop that," the carpenter said. "Right now. What's wrong with you? Are you ill?"

His skin was black, much darker than Annie's. Erasmus could think of no excuse. Weakly he said, "I had a fever earlier this year. I think it's come back."

"It rises off the river," the carpenter said. "It's running all over the city. The arctic woman and her son were so sick they had to stop the exhibition before it was done." He led Erasmus to a low box and said, "Sit down for a minute. Calm yourself."

"You saw them?" Erasmus said.

"Not the exhibition," the carpenter said. "But I saw the explorer come in with them, and I saw them leave. Four of the scientists who work here were carrying her. Another had her little boy."

"Do you know," Erasmus said, "did you happen to hear—where did they go?"

"To one of the towers, I think," the carpenter said. "Where the young men stay. The assistant scientists—they're just boys, some of them. When they aren't out in the field the director lets them stay in the empty rooms up in the towers. All day they sort and label their bones and then at night they drink too much and slide down the bannisters and run footraces here in the hall. They make a mess of things. I've told the director he can't expect me to work like this but he refuses to discipline them, even though last week they broke one of my doors . . ."

"Could you take me there?" Erasmus asked.

"I don't speak to those men." The carpenter fingered one of Erasmus's sticks, as if checking the quality of the work. "And I won't go near their rooms. But I'll tell you how to get there."

ERASMUS RESTED AT every landing, pinching his nose against the odor of sewer gas that seeped through the walls and permeated the staircase. He was in the largest of the main building's towers, a narrow rectangular oven that soaked up the sun's heat. On each landing paneled doors confronted him. These led, he supposed, to hot boxy rooms, and in those rooms were—what? Fervent young botanists and paleontologists, heaps of dusty equipment, spare books; concerns he couldn't imagine. He wished the carpenter had been more explicit. He heard laughter above him, and climbed another flight.

The three men he glimpsed through a half-open door were arguing too passionately to see him. Fossil dogs, fossil wolves; for a second Dr. Boerhaave's voice seemed to float across the surface of their discussion. *Large groups of plants and animals share a common morphology, a unity of plan. These plans exist as ideas in the mind of God, who expresses them differently from age to age. Individual species may disappear, but the blueprints persist, with variations; variant forms of the Form.* A wiry man in his early twenties leaned forward and said, "Cuvier doesn't even contest the existence of man during the epoch of the giant mammals."

"The question," said the red-haired man next to him, "is whether the associated human bones should be assigned equal antiquity with the dog bones found among them, and the hippopotami and extinct bears . . ."

Erasmus leaned inside the door. "Excuse me," he said. "I'm sorry to interrupt, but perhaps you could help me."

"A visitor!" the third young man said. In his hands he held something that looked like part of a human pelvis. "Come join us."

"I'm looking for Zechariah Voorhees," Erasmus said. On the windowsill a tumbler of whiskey caught the light, casting golden rays over bones and books and the huge-canined skulls of Asian swine. The room had the feel of a clubhouse, chaotic and busy, and for a moment he was reminded of the Toxophilites who'd sent the *Narwhal* off with such a splash.

"You're a friend?" asked the red-haired man.

"A colleague," he said; thinking, *Brother-in-law?* "I missed the lecture, but I heard the Esquimaux were taken sick. I was hoping to help."

"He was here a minute ago," said the man with the pelvis in his hand. "But I think he went to fetch the doctor."

"Where are *they*?" Erasmus asked. "The Esquimaux." If these were the men who'd helped carry Annie and Tom, they seemed mightily unconcerned about them now.

"Follow me," said the man. He looked curiously at Erasmus's feet, but asked nothing as he led the way to the next room over.

Erasmus knocked, pushing the door open when no one answered. Inside the stuffy room, Annie lay on one narrow cot and Tom on another. A desk and chair and a litter of dirty clothes filled the rest of the space. On the desk was a precarious tower of flat stone slabs, and in the chair a pale young man, already balding, who looked up when Erasmus entered.

"I didn't hear you knock," the pale man said. "You'll have to excuse me, I'm nearly deaf."

"May I come in?" Erasmus said, enunciating clearly. "These are my friends."

"Whose friend?" the man said, cupping his hand to his ear.

"Annie's friend," Erasmus shouted. He made his way past the

desk, pushing socks and linen aside with his sticks. Annie's eyes were closed, but she stirred when Erasmus touched her shoulder. "Tseke?" she said.

"Erasmus. Do you remember me?"

Her skin was very hot. A coarse sheet was pulled up to her chin; when Erasmus turned back the corner he saw that she was naked beneath it, filmed with sweat. Hastily he covered her and checked on Tom. Unclothed as well, he lay on his side, staring at his own hands.

"Where is Tseke?" Annie whispered.

"He's coming," Erasmus said. He turned to the pale man. "Who undressed them? Whose room is this?"

"It's my room," the man answered. "I'm Fielding, I work here. The explorer who lectured this afternoon is an acquaintance of mine. His Esquimaux collapsed during the lecture—the heat, we think—and he asked if they could rest here until the doctor arrives. She undressed her son and herself, after Zeke left. I stepped outside. Of course. You know them?"

"I'm Zeke's brother-in-law."

"You know Zeke!" Fielding said.

"Yes!" Erasmus shouted again, exasperated despite himself. He couldn't imagine why Zeke had left Annie and Tom in the care of a man who couldn't hear their requests. "Where *is* he?"

"Next door," Fielding said. "With the others."

Through the wall Erasmus could hear the young men's voices. "He's not," he said. Then he gave up trying to explain and concentrated on Annie and Tom. He found a jug of water near the door and dampened his handkerchief, dabbing at Annie's face and Tom's face and hands. Fielding hovered, polite but useless. "Do you suppose they're really sick?" he asked. "The fellows next door told me they were just overheated."

"You have eyes—look at them."

Fielding shrugged and stepped back to his desk. "I don't have much experience with women and children," he said. "I'm in here all the time . . . the other scientists never want me to drink with them and we disagree about almost everything." He lifted a thin slab of stone, pointing to something that looked like a crinoid. "What *I* think about this," he said.

"Please," Erasmus said. "Not now." He heard feet pounding up the stairs, and then Zeke was in the room.

"Where have you been?" Erasmus asked, just as Zeke said, "What are *you* doing here?" After glaring at each other for a silent moment, they both bent over Annie.

Annie was someplace hot and dark, streaked with red, filled with noise and the smell of blood. She was a seal who'd come up for a breath of air and met a bear; the bear had been waiting and she was caught by surprise; there was a blow and then burning. She tried to heave herself back in the cool water but she was being dragged across the ice. She was being bitten. She was being eaten. She moaned and turned and opened her eyes and her son was staring at her. The worst thing about what was happening to her body was the way it kept her from protecting him. But her journey must mean something, her reasons for coming with Zeke must be true.

The piece of peculiar ice her mother had seen had turned out to be a thing called *mirror*; more were on the ship, and in the building full of dead insects and birds. She and her son had inched up to those mirrors, stared into them, touched each other's reflections. In the room below, before she'd stumbled and fallen and been unable to rise, she'd seen herself reflected in the watching people's eyes. She'd been sent here like a shard of splintered mirror, she thought, to capture an image of the world beyond her home.

"Annie," Zeke said. "Can you hear me?"

"Is the doctor coming?" Erasmus asked.

Annie heard their voices but not their words. The strangers' language left her and she longed for someone to say her real name and speak to her in real words, but these large figures murmured incomprehensibly. One was Zeke, a walking finger who pointed at her and then turned into the barrel of a rifle. The rifle had brought her tribe meat and fed the children. But the rifle was a finger and the finger was Zeke, who had not understood his connection to the other fingers, the hand, the wrist, the body that was her tribe. The body that had once been her. When she coughed a bullet seemed to enter her lungs.

Her son asked in their shared language if they could go home now. One of the bears took the other by the shoulder and both stepped out of view, leaving only a white figure, a little white fox, behind. The fox put his paws on a piece of stone. A fox might follow a bear, waiting for scraps from the kill. She closed her eyes again. At home, she thought, her body would be wrapped in skins and carried away from the huts, then laid on the ground with a rock for her pillow. Around her someone would place her soapstone cooking pots, each one broken into pieces, and her needles and thread and her *ulo,* all she'd need for her life beyond. Over her body a vault of rocks would be built. Over her jawbones the wind might play a song.

"He's here," Zeke said. "Right behind me." He turned and beckoned to the doctor; Fielding tiptoed away.

Brisk and gray-haired and competent, the doctor felt Annie's pulses, rolled down her lower eyelids, and slid his arm beneath her covering sheet. "Enlarged liver," he said. His hand crept beneath the cloth. "Enlarged spleen." He moved over to Tom and repeated his investigations, asking Zeke how long these people had been away from their home, where they'd been staying, when their symptoms had first appeared. He made a note when Zeke described the site of the Repository.

"Near a river *and* a creek?" He felt the sides of Annie's neck. "Most likely it's a miasmatic bilious fever," he said. "Normally you'd see a yellowing of the skin, but of course on them . . . you can see, though, the way the whites of their eyes have yellowed."

"Can I move them?" Zeke asked.

"Carefully," the doctor said. "And not far." He rummaged in his bag, pulling out boxes and vials. "Preparation of Peruvian bark," he said. "Decoction of boneset as an emetic, a calomel purgative to relieve congestion of the liver, a diaphoretic in an effervescing draught—we'll try to break the fever with these. Then they need to rest in a clean, dark, well-aired room."

"I talked to a friend here in Washington," Zeke said. "He's willing to let us stay with him for a few days."

"Not one of those young men," Erasmus protested. "They're hardly more than children."

Zeke shook his head. "Someone else," he said. "A physical anthropologist who's in charge of a whole section—he has a big house a few blocks from here, servants, spare rooms. His children are grown and his wife is very . . . tolerant. He's had Indians from the Andes staying with him before."

"That sounds suitable," the doctor said. "I can call on you twice daily there. I want to bleed them now; this almost always helps." He looked down at Annie and Tom. "Race does modify the action of remedies, though."

Erasmus leaned against the desk, watching as Zeke held the basins and lancets and helped the doctor spoon a dark brown liquid into Annie and Tom. He had a real affection for them, Erasmus saw.

Afterward Annie and Tom looked more comfortable. "Go out for a bit," the doctor said. "I want to listen to their bowels."

In the narrow hall, with the stairwell yawning below them, the two men regarded each other. "I can't believe you brought them here in this condition," Erasmus said. "You have to cancel the rest of the tour."

"I already have," Zeke said. His hair was glowing like a helmet. "Did you come here just to tell me that? I know they're sick, I'll take care of them. I'm not a *monster*."

Erasmus had planned to say something about the conditions in the Repository, which Alexandra had described to him; about his impressions of the Philadelphia exhibition; about Lavinia, left alone so Zeke could trot around accumulating fame. Then he thought of the way Annie's first words, whenever he saw her, were always "Where is Tseke?"

"Let me stay with you and Annie and Tom," he said. "I want to help them."

"There's nothing you can do to help," Zeke said. "I'll be with them, though." He peered over the railing, apparently fascinated by the zigzagging flights of stairs. "You can visit them all you want, when they're better. But you can see for yourself how sick they are. You're not a doctor—what can you do?"

He reached over and flicked one of Erasmus's sticks with his thumb. "You belong at home," he said. "You always did."

The stick rose, until the tip was pointed at Zeke's right knee; Erasmus couldn't help this, his arm did it, it had no connection to him. "*I* belong at home?" If the stick swung, at just the right angle, Zeke would topple, topple. "I'm not the one . . ."

"Stop worrying," Zeke said. He leaned over and pressed on Erasmus's forearm, pushing the stick back to the ground. "At least until they regain their health, I'm done with this tour."

Behind them the door opened. "I'm finished," the doctor said. "If you'd like, you can come back in."

"I want to talk to Annie," Erasmus said to Zeke. "I want her to tell me what *she* wants. Let me see her alone for a minute." Without waiting for an answer he backed into the room.

"Annie?" he said. "What can I do for you? Tell me how I can help."

"Tseke?" Annie said yet again.

"*Erasmus,*" he said.

She opened her eyes. The whites were filmed with yellow—as was the rest of her, he thought, peering more closely at her face. It wasn't true what the doctor had said; the sickness glazed her normal color and gave her a slight greenish tinge, as if she'd been dusted with lichen spores.

"Oh," Annie said. "You."

Over the windows the curtains lifted, reaching toward the bed. She turned her head into the breeze and closed her eyes. "Go home," she said faintly.

For a minute more he gazed at her. She said nothing else. Perhaps she had gone to sleep. Tom too had his eyes closed; the curtains lifted and fell, lifted and fell, refusing to give Erasmus an answer. He gave up and returned to the hall.

"It's you she wants," he told Zeke bitterly. *You Lavinia wants,* he thought. "She keeps asking for you."

"I'll take care of them," Zeke said. "I promise."

He ran a thumb over his bushy eyebrows. Erasmus stood before him, hot and miserable. Not a breath of breeze moved through this windowless hall.

"I need her," Zeke said. "I've learned a lot from her, she's been helping me with my book." He bit off a fragment of thumbnail and dropped the shard down the stairwell. "It's going to be good," he said. "Personal, a sort of adventure tale—my encounters with the Esquimaux, my last vision of the *Narwhal*. It's going to be like Dr. Kane's book, only more interesting, more dramatic."

Erasmus's stomach knotted and rose. Why were they talking about this now, with Annie and Tom lying sick next door? They had never talked about anything, not Dr. Boerhaave's death or Ned's nose or all that might have been prevented if only Zeke hadn't been determined to head north. And now, now . . . *my encounters, my vision.* The lecture in Philadelphia had been shaped exactly this way. Erasmus said, "Why would you write an account that pretends all the rest of us weren't there?"

"You're all in it," Zeke said. "But no more than you deserve to be. Minor, minor characters."

"I haven't written about *you*," Erasmus said. "I didn't think that would be fair."

"What's fair?" Zeke said. "Was it *fair* that you abandoned me? Is it *fair* that I have nothing left, except the story I tell? You can't know what it was like for me up there. Coming back to the ship, finding you'd all walked out on me: it was very—*clarifying.* I learned who I could depend on. No one. No one but myself. You . . ."

The contempt in his eyes was shocking. "You're *nothing.* Not in the book. Not to me."

In his hands Erasmus felt the walking sticks dancing, as if the floor had metamorphosed into the open sea. "I may be nothing," he said. "But at least I don't destroy whatever I touch. What you're doing to Annie and Tom . . ."

Zeke stretched his arms over his head, opening and closing his fingers. "Go home," he said. "No one needs you here. I'll take care of Annie and Tom."

ANNIE WAS IN A ROOM. Her son was in another; Zeke came and went between them. At home the *angekok* sought his visions in a hollow hidden in thick ice grounded on the shore; she pulled the white curtains of the canopied bed around her and imagined ice. The doctor came; the man who owned this house came. The servants, as fearful and disdainful as those in the house to which

Zeke had first brought her, sponged her body and brought her food, which she didn't touch. The doctor forced pills and liquid between her teeth, some kind of poison. No one would listen to her. Not the doctor, not Zeke; not even Erasmus, who'd asked what she needed but then turned his back and disappeared when she'd said, *I want to go home.* Wasn't that what she'd said? Her body would never go home now and she must do what she could for her son. A white cloth over the bed, white cases over the pillows; she had little time; she worked. The great power, the *angekok* had once told her, comes only after struggle and concentration. By the strength of her thought alone, she must strip her body of flesh and blood and be able to see herself as a skeleton. Each bone, each tiny bone, clear before her eyes. Then the sacred language would descend, allowing her to name the parts of her body that would endure. When she named the last bone she'd be free; her spirit could travel and she could watch over her son. She burrowed under the white cloth and squeezed shut her eyes, beginning the terrible process of shedding her flesh. Let me be bone, she thought. Like the long narwhal spines at home, the walrus skulls, the delicate ribs of the seals. White bone.

THE LESS ALEXANDRA worked on the thing she most loved, the more her family appreciated her. The easiest days were those on which she didn't try to work at all. When she stopped looking so fiercely for a moment she might call her own, when she stopped rushing through her household tasks and simply gave into them, the days had a reasonable rhythm. And it was lovely, in a way, when her family thanked her—yet at night she weighed those thanks against the nagging sense that she'd wasted another set of precious hours.

Her family won during the days of Erasmus's absence. But as soon as she saw him again, she regretted every lost minute.

At the engraving firm, he told her Annie and Tom were sick. Which was terrible, but at least their condition had forced Zeke to stop the exhibitions. Zeke was looking after them and would soon bring them home, where he'd settle down to work on a book that was almost done, and in which Erasmus had no place.

"In his book," Erasmus said, "I am—he said I am a *minor character.*" He peered over Alexandra's shoulder. "That's excellent," he said. "*Our* book will be beautiful. You've caught the gills and the scales exactly."

They spent long hours at their desks, working in a kind of splendid trance. Erasmus wrote ten, twelve, twenty pages a day; Alexandra's drawings accumulated and when they visited Copernicus they found the second painting done, and two more started. Around them the firm was humming, as if their frenzy were contagious. Humboldt concluded negotiations for the plates for a new encyclopedia, which seemed more than usually lucky as businesses elsewhere closed. Pleased with themselves, they all gathered one afternoon in the main office to celebrate over a drink.

The brothers, Alexandra saw, had settled into a new relationship. Perhaps it was their enforced proximity, or the way Erasmus worked so hard, with such clear purpose, and never complained about the small corners allotted to him. Or perhaps Linnaeus and Humboldt, cast for years as the steady, uninteresting middle brothers, were secretly pleased to be doing favors for the eldest. Linnaeus, in particular, seemed to relish his new role. He gave Erasmus frequent advice, visited Lavinia three times each week, no longer criticized Alexandra's work.

He was with Lavinia now; they lingered over their sherry while they waited for him. There would be an awkward moment, Alexandra knew, when Linnaeus would report that Lavinia was fine, but that she still didn't want to see Erasmus. It would be awkward, but it would pass. At six-thirty Linnaeus entered the office. Waving away the glass Humboldt held out to him, he flopped down in an armchair, very pale.

"What is it?" Erasmus said. "Is she—unwell, again?"

"Zeke is back," Linnaeus said. "He walked in right after I got there." Then he drew a long breath.

"Annie is dead," he said. He rested his hand on Erasmus's arm; Alexandra had never seen them touch before. "She died two days after you left."

"She's dead?" Erasmus said. "How can she be dead?"

Linnaeus closed his eyes and then took the glass Humboldt offered again. "I know," he said. "It's horrible. He brought Tom with him; he's recovering but still very frail."

Alexandra thought of Annie and Tom as she'd last seen them in the Repository. Shouldn't she have known—shouldn't they all have known—where this was heading? "But Lavinia and Zeke will take care of him," she said. "Won't they? They'll find a home for him, at least until he's better and can be returned to his family."

"Lavinia's very upset," Linnaeus said. "She asked Zeke who was more important to him, her or those Esquimaux. If you'd heard her voice—it was terrible. And then, and then . . ."

"What's *wrong* with her?" Erasmus burst out. "He's just a little boy, and now he's lost his mother. You'd think she'd remember what that was like."

"That's not the worst of it," Linnaeus said. "She had one of the maids settle Tom in the Repository; he's to sleep there with only those two dogs for company. Zeke didn't even try to stop her, he said he'd do whatever she wanted."

"Zeke can't," Erasmus said. "Can he?"

Linnaeus curled his lip. "I suppose he can do anything he wants. He claims he was nursing Tom in Washington; I'd like to see him nurse anyone but himself. Then he admitted he'd stayed a few extra days, to take care of Annie's remains."

"He had her buried down there?" Erasmus asked.

Linnaeus gulped at his drink. "There was no burial," he said. "No body, even. There are men at the Smithsonian who—who do this sort of thing. I don't know how, I don't want to know how. I think the man Zeke was staying with had the idea, he knows about bones and skulls. Zeke gave him his permission and he, they, *someone* prepared and mounted her skeleton for the museum. Zeke stayed to oversee it."

Erasmus groaned, and Alexandra thought about Toodlamik's bones and skin. Then about Annie as she'd first seen her, leaning against the windowpane until the sash was raised and she reached, so gratefully, for the air.

"He did it for Lavinia," Linnaeus continued. "Or so he claims. The skeleton's to go in a glass case in the hall across from Dr. Kane's exhibit, with a plaque about Zeke's expedition. You know how he is, he thinks this will make him famous. Everyone will want to buy his book and then he and Lavinia won't have to depend on his father's generosity, they won't have to worry about anything again."

"Is that what he's thinking?" Humboldt asked.

"I don't know. But Lavinia said she didn't care what happened to Annie's remains, she knew all about Zeke and Annie and she'd never been fooled, she wasn't *stupid*."

Humboldt raised an eyebrow and Copernicus said, "Surely we're not surprised by that? He spent six months in her company, after better than a year without any female companionship. Didn't we assume . . . ?"

"I don't know what *you* assumed," Linnaeus said. Alexandra could not help glancing at Erasmus; what had she assumed about him? "I assumed that he'd honored his commitment to Lavinia, and that Annie was just what he said. A member of the tribe that saved his life. If she was ever more than that, why would he be so unfeeling as to exhibit her bones?"

"Nothing," Erasmus said, "has ever gotten in the way of Zeke's ambitions."

She was gone, he thought. They'd hardly had the chance to know each other. For a minute Linnaeus's words drifted past him. When he could bear to listen again, Linnaeus was still discussing Zeke's plans: returning Tom to Washington, arranging to have him cared for by someone associated with the Smithsonian. Someone who might be willing to take Tom in and educate him.

Copernicus turned to Erasmus. "You have to do something."

"I know," Erasmus said. He reached for Linnaeus's hand. "It's not your fault."

"We're all at fault," Copernicus said. "You should have fought back when Zeke returned, and not let him persuade everyone that you acted wrongly on the voyage. We shouldn't have doubted you. And you and I should have refused to leave our home."

"I know," Erasmus repeated. They'd doubted him? "I know." He stared out the window, toward the river and his lost home on the opposite bank.

FROM THAT HOUSE, in the gathering twilight, Lavinia was gazing back. Somewhere, perhaps along the creek, Zeke was pacing through the haze that had carried the fever to Annie. And somewhere else, she imagined, her brothers were together. When had they ever put her first? Copernicus had traveled across the continent and

Erasmus had sailed to both ends of the earth; neither had ever asked if she minded being left behind, alone and waiting for them. What had Erasmus given her? Her mother's walking shoe; a few odd books and lessons; a promise, which he'd broken. *Erasmus let me down,* Zeke had told her. *When I most needed him.* Because of Erasmus, he'd had to go north alone; because of Erasmus he'd ended up staying with Annie's family, bringing Annie home.

Outside the window the shadow of Annie rose before her, as it did every night at this time: piercing dark eyes, the smooth skin of her arms and throat, the quiet voice Zeke seemed to have found so alluring. Annie had been helpless here, completely dependent on Zeke—and what man could resist that? Her very existence had set Lavinia in the wrong. But she'd been patient, so patient, willing Zeke to turn away from Annie by the sheer force of her own desire. She had won him back, only to see the hurt and disappointment in his eyes as she turned away from the dead woman's son. Was it so awful, after their long separation, to want a scrap of normal life?

She'd stopped praying when Erasmus first returned without Zeke, started again with the help of Browning, stopped again when Zeke came home and her pleas were answered. Now she folded her hands across her waist and prayed she might be carrying a son.

The Nightmare Skeleton

(October 1857–August 1858)

These are the qualities which are required to make a first-class collector: He must have a fair general knowledge of zoology, especially the vertebrates. He must be a good shot, a successful hunter, and capable of great physical endurance. Then he must be a neat and skillful operator with the knife, and conscientious in the details of his work, down to the smallest particulars, for without this quality his specimens will always be faulty and disappointing. In addition to all these requirements he must be a man of tireless energy, incapable of going to bed so long as there are birds to be skinned, and who, whenever a doubt arises in his mind in regard to the necessity of more work on a specimen, will always give the specimen the benefit of the doubt.

—W. J. HOLLAND, *Taxidermy and Zoological Collecting* (1892)

HE WOKE TO THEIR SOUNDS IN THE DARK: WHISPERS,
rustlings, something dropped. In the moonlight the portraits above
him shimmered, faces caught behind panes of glass like dead men
peering through the ice, and at first he thought the sounds came
from them. But there were footsteps moving his way. The two black
dogs beside him rose and bristled; he sat upright on the mattress of
caribou skins, terrified but determined to be brave. They had come
to kill him, he thought. Zeke and his wife, who talked about him as
if he weren't present or couldn't understand them. They wished him
dead, as his mother was dead, and had chosen this night. They were
leaning over him, while the traitorous dogs said nothing.

"It's all right," the woman said. "Can you be very quiet?" He
could hear the dogs snuffling at her hands.

The man said, "We need to take you from here, so you won't be
hurt. Will you come with us?"

Tom said nothing. He recognized the woman as the one who
wasn't Lavinia; the one whose garment his mother had worn the
first day here. The man was one of the brothers but he could never
tell them apart. Then the man reached out and Tom knew him as
Copernicus, from the bright painty tang of his hand.

"Tom?" Copernicus said.

He wasn't Tom; his real name was his secret and he'd never speak
it among these people. Two days ago he'd decided to stop speaking
altogether. But he rose to his feet when Copernicus asked; he walked
from this building so full of death; he sat where they placed him
and felt the ground slip as if he were on a sledge. Two other brothers appeared, but one stayed only briefly. In and out of other doors,
other rooms, some still and others moving; he slept when he could,
ate now and then, said nothing. The walls rattled, the floors shook,
trees moved past him and then more buildings. His clothes were

taken and other clothes put on him. Erasmus was here, he knew Erasmus. Sometimes he dozed against his shoulder.

The landscape changed and changed again, but it was never the one he wanted. The people so close to him talked in low worried voices, but also sat still for long stretches. Where was Zeke? Somewhere else: farther and farther away, he hoped. His people had a name for Zeke, a chain of soft syllables that meant *The One Who Is Trouble.* To his face, they'd said the syllables meant *The Great Explorer,* and Zeke had smiled and nodded his head and done his best to repeat them.

He had plans for Zeke. Tucked into his jacket were bones he'd stolen from the place where Zeke had caged him: a bird's curved ribs, a serpent's spine, a mouse's foot. He needed more. When he had enough he would make a *tupilaq,* a nightmare skeleton built from bones of all kinds of creatures, wrapped in a skin. By the edge of some water he would set it down and say the secret words; then the *tupilaq* would come alive and swim across any form of water, no matter how far. Blank-eyed it would swim up to Zeke, disguised as a familiar animal; sleek fur, smooth ears. Perhaps it would travel as a deer before allowing itself to be killed. After Zeke slit down the belly and parted the flesh he'd find all the wrong bones, connected in all the wrong ways. Then he'd die.

That vision kept Tom quiet as he traveled. This wasn't like the journeys he'd taken with his people, moving happily behind the dogs to another hunting ground. This was like the later journey, the days in the box moving over the water. They moved over land now, but he was still confined. When he could, when Erasmus would let him, he hung out the windows and filled his lungs. There were trees, and then mountains. Then very large mountains and air so cool and fresh it almost made him think of home.

When it rained he held his hands out to catch the water. Resting on the top of the sky, he believed, was the land where the dead lived—a place of light and warmth and abundant game, feasting and song and dance. His mother was there. She'd abandoned her body so that she might watch over him; those men who came later, to take what was left, had only made visible the process she'd begun. Light from the land where she'd gone shone through holes in the sky, appearing as stars. Water fell through those holes from the rivers; that water was rain. Each drop that touched his skin was a message from his mother.

The movement stopped. The door was opened from the outside. When he stepped down and saw a man missing part of his nose, his scream was the first sound he'd made in days and it rang in his own ears. He pitched forward and crouched on the ground with his arms over his head, and would not be moved.

EVEN WHEN THEY reached the cabin on the Ausable River, no one could convince Tom to open his eyes. His arms wound tightly around his knees, his eyes screwed shut, his mouth sealed, he sat without moving where Copernicus placed him, on the small, red-blanketed bed.

"Has he been like this the whole trip?" Ned asked.

"Not quite this bad," Erasmus said. He touched Ned's shoulder. "I'm so glad to see you." Then he turned to Tom again. "He hasn't said a word since he was taken from the Repository."

Ned made coffee for the tired travelers and quietly, with the boy in the background radiating a distress that no one could soothe, they caught each other up on the events of the past few weeks. Erasmus told Ned how Linnaeus had driven the carriage to their old home, although he'd do no more than that; how Copernicus and

Alexandra had tiptoed into the Repository and swept the boy away. Each of them had told a separate lie, he said. Copernicus had told his companions he was heading west. Alexandra, during a terrible quarrel with her siblings, had said she was taking a position teaching drawing at a female academy in Cincinnati. Erasmus, knowing the way Zeke thought and imagining how he'd set about searching for them, had purchased passage for two on a ship bound for Liverpool; it would take some time before anyone discovered that they hadn't arrived.

"I think we've covered our tracks," he told Ned. Although his feet had prevented him from taking an active role, the plans had worked smoothly so far, and they were his. "But none of this could have happened without you—how can I thank you for all your help?"

"It's not a problem," Ned replied. "I told you I'd help any way I could, and I meant it."

He bustled around the small kitchen, avoiding the knees of his guests. "I've found a house for you, about a mile from here," he said. "It's pleasant, and quite isolated, but it won't be ready until tomorrow. We'll have to stay here tonight." He watched his guests look around his tiny home. "I'm sorry," he said. "But it'll be all right. I've borrowed some extra bedding from the hotel."

"Of course it will be fine," Alexandra said. Her dark hair and strong features reminded him of his sister, Nora, as did the way she leaned toward the boy every few minutes and stroked his back. "You were good to take us in like this. And it's wonderful to see you well, after you were so sick in Philadelphia. I understand you have a fine job now?"

"It's good enough," Ned said. How could he tell her that he was in danger of losing it? The time he'd had to take off, while he searched for a house to lodge his guests; the flurry of letters arriving at the hotel, which had made the owner suspicious; the letters he'd had to write back and the supplies he'd had to purchase: all this to help a boy he'd never met. The tone of Erasmus's letters had been so distressed, though, and the tale he'd told so upsetting, that Ned could not deny him anything. *I failed his mother*, Erasmus had written. *I can't fail Tom.*

Ned walked toward the grubby, silent boy, the source of all this trouble. Searching for some words Joe had taught him before their trip to Anoatok, he introduced himself haltingly in the boy's language. To his surprise, Tom opened his eyes—and then his mouth, as if he might scream again at the sight of Ned's nose.

Ned had no more Esquimaux phrases, but Erasmus had written that Tom could speak and understand English. He thought about his own arrival at Grosse Isle, when he was just a boy himself: when he and his brother had been torn from their fevered sister and packed like cattle on a crowded barge, then shipped upriver and cast on the kindness of strangers. Who hadn't been kind, and hadn't spoken any language he could understand. The rippling, incomprehensible flow of French, which he'd never heard before; the English so different from the English he knew; and never a word of Gaelic, never a taste of home. Never a story he could recognize, nor a person willing to take responsibility for him. He looked into Tom's dark eyes, reading there *help. Can you help me?*

"We were on the ice, in a great storm, in terrible weather," Ned said. He tapped his eroded nostril. "In the darkness the *innersuit* appeared from behind the rocks and swept me away to their hiding place. They took my nose and forced me to stay with them, but I prayed for strength and at last was able to escape them. When I was returned to my people, this man"—here he pointed to Erasmus— "this man, who was our *angekok,* did magic and my nose was returned to me. But a piece was missing, a scar by which the *innersuit* let it be known that I was once captured by them."

Tom unwrapped his arms, straightened his legs, and reached forward to touch Ned's nose. "It is painful?" he asked; the first words he'd spoken since leaving Philadelphia.

"Not anymore," Ned said. "Will you eat something?" From the cupboard he pulled a tray of roasted ducks he'd prepared at the hotel.

"The *innersuit* tried to take my mother," Tom said. "But she conquered them." He bent over the tray.

"What now?" Ned asked Erasmus.

Erasmus lowered himself onto a chair. "I don't know," he said. "We've gotten this far, and that's something. Thanks to you we have a place to stay. The rest—I don't know yet."

While they talked Tom finished the first duck and started on a second, pushing aside the baked bones; the heat made them brittle and ugly, useless to him. But around the walls, just as in the place from which he'd come, there were also skeletons: bat, fox, serpent. Later, after everyone had gone to sleep, he would steal a bone from one of the bat's wings.

THE HOUSE NED had found for them was drafty but large, set amid a stand of hemlocks at the base of a mountain, not far from the trail that led to North Elba through the meadows. Six days a week, drawn by Tom's lonely eyes, Ned took a long detour on the way to the hotel and breakfasted with the little band of runaways. As he got to know Tom better, he brought a clasp knife, a hatchet, rabbits' feet. On his days off, he took Tom for rambles in the forest. Erasmus asked several times if he'd like to join their household, but he preferred to keep his own place. After his time on the *Narwhal* he'd sworn he would never again share living quarters with people not his family.

"Would you think about it?" Erasmus said. "Anytime you wanted, we'd make room for you." Ned brought strings of fish for breakfast, but continued to say no.

While the weeks slipped by, Erasmus tried to understand what he should do next. He walked and thought, thought and walked—a pleasure that had grown unfamiliar. At least they were safe here. With the snowshoes Ned had made for him he could cast his sticks aside; the broad netted platforms restored his lost toes and as long as it snowed he was free. A few miles from the house, he might have been in another country. The forest was dark and unbroken; he saw wolves, deer, panthers, loons: *okipok,* fast ice. Snow glazed the fields and sealed off the mountain peaks. All around him, in every tree and stone, he felt Annie and Dr. Boerhaave. Once he stood in the meadows, after a snowfall, and in the moonlight saw the dark abrupt peaks casting shadows onto a plain that resembled a frozen sea. The shadows took the shape of his dead friend's face, and then of Annie's.

Sometimes he met a trapper, and once he stumbled on a hermit's cottage, but away from the river valleys all was emptiness. He could see why Ned had been drawn back here; the settlers kept to themselves and asked few questions. Remembering Ned's evasions, he invented an ice-fishing accident to explain his feet, and also new identities for his little group. Even Copernicus wasn't well enough known to be recognized here in the wilderness, so he didn't bother to change their names. But to the people he met when he fetched supplies, he lied cheerfully. He claimed they were from Baltimore; that he was a journalist and his brother a painter, who'd both spent years out west. The boy with them was an Indian, whom they'd adopted. And Alexandra was his wife. He paused over that: his wife? Copernicus's wife? Then chose what seemed most believable.

Through the astounding cold of winter, he and Copernicus and Alexandra worked as they had at the Repository, writing and painting and drawing. Copernicus built a small easel for Tom, and gave him brushes and paint; Alexandra gave him paper and pencils. They taught him how to read and write.

"Show me how to make my parents' names," he demanded, and Alexandra wrote NESSARK in large block letters and, not knowing his mother's true name, ANNIE. Tom gripped a pencil in his fist and covered sheets of paper: NESSARK ANNIE NESSARK ANNIE NESSARK ANNIE ANNIE ANNIE. Around the names he drew hundreds of stubby birds. He ignored the brushes Copernicus gave him but he liked the paint, and after the first messy experiment Copernicus stocked up on turpentine and gave Tom a smock that covered his clothes. Tom painted with his thumbs, feathering the color with delicate strokes. The same scene again and again: an icy white plain, a jagged cliff, some low dark lumps that might have been huts, smaller dark dots. Two-legged dots and four-legged dots: people, dogs. Erasmus said, "This must be his version of Anoatok." Alexandra, watching Tom's efforts, said nothing but one night drew a carefully simplified dog and left it on Tom's bed.

He slept in the last of the square chambers lining the lofty main room in which they cooked and ate and worked: one, two, three, four boxes. Four single beds; four people sleeping alone. When Tom went into his room for long stretches and closed the door the others tried to grant him the same privacy they gave each other. They had to do this, Alexandra thought. Otherwise they couldn't have lived in this odd, interesting, almost communal way, as if their new home were a miniature New Harmony. Although the local people believed them a family, they weren't: they were four people sharing a house and chores and work on a book, the three adults also sharing responsibility for the child. Why was this so different from living with her brother and sisters and nephew and niece? Yet it was; every moment she felt as if she were inventing her life. Tom copied her dog drawing again and again, adding harnesses and linking these with a tangle of traces; later, with her help, he drew a sledge. He needed her, she thought. In a way her family didn't. But he made no demands.

She wrapped two shawls around the man's overcoat she'd purchased in the village and went out by herself for long walks across the meadows or along the deer paths winding through the woods, exulting in the astonishing cold and the dry snow whipping her cheeks. On the pair of snowshoes Ned had given her, she tromped the trail along Slide Brook to the South Meadows Brook. No one asked her where she was going or when she was coming back. She chopped wood for the stoves and took her turn cooking and wrestling with the laundry, but because Erasmus and Copernicus shared these tasks they felt like pleasures. At home, she thought, she'd felt like a servant doing similar work: because that had been Browning's household. Browning's home, somehow, in which she and Emily and Jane and even Harriet were guests. Here no one *expected* anything. There were rules, lists, things that had to be done—but they all had to do them.

Each morning she woke with a jolt, electrified by all she wanted to do and purely amazed at herself. Where had she gotten the nerve to confront her family and tell such enormous lies? Sneaking up the dark walk to the Repository, Copernicus beside her, she'd pushed open the door as noiselessly and confidently as if she'd been a criminal all her life. Kidnapping: that was the word for what they'd done, at least in some people's eyes. She'd known just what to say to Tom, just how to bundle him up and slip him into the carriage—as, here in these forbidding woods, she knew how to find her way along the streams without getting lost, how to gather wood, how to stoke the stove. She knew how much sleep she needed, which proved to be very little; how, even, to navigate her way through her feelings toward the two brothers. She kept to her own bed, although she sensed she would have been welcome in either of the two rooms flanking hers.

For a while, which she knew wouldn't last forever, she enjoyed the delicate, teasing tension that kept the three of them afloat like a raft.

None of them knew where they were going next. They would finish the book, they agreed. Or as much of it as they could. After that—after that was a blank page Alexandra couldn't imagine. When Erasmus had first approached her with his plan, she'd volunteered to help rescue Tom, and then to help care for him while she completed the drawings for the book. She hadn't been able to think any further than that. Now the drawings were halfway done.

A letter arrived, which Erasmus read aloud as they sat eating venison stew. *Zeke has spoken with the police,* Linnaeus wrote. As if Zeke hadn't kidnapped Tom from his home to begin with. *And named you and Copernicus as suspects, but not Alexandra. When I agreed to help I didn't expect to be left in such an uncomfortable position. Don't you think you should explain yourself to Zeke?*

Erasmus made a face, and Alexandra looked into her bowl. If this was a kidnapping, what were the words for the other things they'd done? The mess they'd left behind in Philadelphia, their angry families, Erasmus's tangled investments, which were all that supported the four of them yet were still confused—these things were difficult, yet the book was growing swiftly. Around them were mounds of manuscript that Erasmus read to her and Copernicus at night; mounds of drawings she pinned to the walls for the brothers' inspection and comments; two more of Copernicus's giant paintings. Each bird and seal and cliff that Erasmus and Dr. Boerhaave had captured in their notebooks, each whale and swarm of plankton, found a home in them.

"That's it," Erasmus said as each corner of Copernicus's paintings emerged. "That's what it looked like."

All of them, Alexandra thought, could envision the book clearly now: the design, the type, the way the drawings and paintings would fall among the words. Beside them Tom watched and listened, making his own words and pictures. He drew his mother, he drew his father, he drew walrus hunts and polar bears. He waited for Ned's visits. The snow piled up until everything around him was white and almost looked like home.

Sometimes Ned took him deep in the woods, where the traps were set. They caught beaver, muskrat, rabbits; when they found a fox caught in one, growling and gnawing its frozen paw, Ned let Tom kill it. Tom stood on the fox, as he'd seen his father do, pinning its head and feet and then pressing his hands down on its chest so hard that its heart stopped and it died. Alexandra drew the way he skinned it with Ned's knife and staked the pelt out to bleach and dry. Erasmus and Ned cleaned the bones, reassembled them, and taught Tom their names. From a second fox, they allowed him to keep the leg bones and the skull.

"It's wonderful what he's learning," Ned said to Erasmus. "But how much longer can we keep him here like this?"

That morning Tom had woken to the sound of water dripping: not his mother, seeping through the sky, but icicles shrinking on the eaves. Something happened inside his eyes, as if the fog that had wrapped him since leaving his home had lifted. He gazed at Ned; at Erasmus and Alexandra bent over their tables; at Copernicus busy with a huge painting of the shoreline across the water from Anoatok. He said, "I want to go home."

Erasmus wrote two more lines and set his page aside. He looked up at Tom. His father, he remembered, had once looked at him with exasperation and said, "Can't you get over *anything*? Why do you have to lock yourself up here, just because things haven't gone the way you wanted?" All this time he'd been waiting for his next move to be revealed to him; here was the point of all his lies and lists. "I'm taking you home," he said. As if this was what he'd always meant to do. "As soon as the season is right."

LINNAEUS WROTE AGAIN:

Last week they went to Washington, to attend the ceremony at the Smithsonian; the collections of the Exploring Expedition have all been arranged in the Great Hall, and with them Annie's skeleton in a central display case. Zeke was given some sort of award but I don't know the details. Humboldt and I and our families are fine and we hope you are too, but I wish I didn't have to lie to everyone.

Zeke knows you didn't arrive in Liverpool, but no more than that—I don't think he <u>wants</u> to know more. After he contacted the police, he figured out that it cast a bad light on him and Lavinia if you were suspected of wrongdoing. Now he or someone else has started a rumor that Tom, ungrateful boy, has signed on as a cabin boy on a merchant ship. But really no one is interested in Tom's fate anymore. Everyone is talking, instead, about Zeke's book.

The bookshops sport great stacks of The Voyage of the Narwhal. *At a dinner at the Laurens' last week a woman bent toward me and, with great seriousness, began describing the differences between the Arctic Highlanders and the Netsilik, just as if she knew what she was talking about. I have to tell you it's a most interesting work—vivid, well-written, full of adventures. Are you surprised to hear you play a very minor role in it? As do your shipmates. Captain Tyler, Mr. Tagliabeau, Robert Carey and Sean Hamilton visited the city briefly, to settle some question of wages with Zeke's father. They aren't happy with the way Zeke por-*

trayed them but said it's no more than what they expected. When I told them you'd sailed for England they asked me to thank you for forwarding the letters to their families and to tell you they bear you no grudge—they profited from their sealing voyage and leave soon on another whaling ship. Also they said you'd want to know that the Greenlander called Joe is in Denmark, preparing reports for the missionary society and writing something about the Ano- atok Esquimaux and their folktales. Is everyone writing a book?

Lavinia hardly speaks to me or Humboldt and I think is very unhappy. Zeke's father is having financial troubles and had to give up his plans to build them a house; and although Zeke should make plenty from his book there are apparently some debts we didn't know about. If I hear from you, she says, if I have a way to contact you—how awkward this is!—would I ask if you would consider letting her continue living in your house for the next year or two, or until you return: when are you returning? "Remind him of what he gave me when I was ten," she says, which I hope means more to you than it does to me. She knows we don't like Zeke but reminds me that she loves him. What does she mean by love, I wonder?

Erasmus made arrangements. There would be no spe- cial ship this time, no provisions to arrange, no men to interview. After several inquiries he settled on a reliable whaling firm in New London, and a captain whose ship was due to leave mid-May and who didn't mind conveying paying passengers to Godhavn. The rest of the journey he must make on his own, but he'd settle the details in Greenland. Annie was gone; he couldn't bring her family her bones and couldn't imagine how he'd explain this failure. But he could return Tom to them. One last chance; he understood his luck. He wrote to Linnaeus, giving Lavinia permission to stay in the house indefinitely. His father's house; their father's house. On the ice, before everything had changed, he'd once built a model of it—and that was how it now existed in his mind. A small thing, blank-windowed and closed and cold. Let her stay there with Zeke.

He sat down with Copernicus. From the beginning Copernicus had refused to commit himself beyond the next week or month: one painting at a time, he'd said. He'd finish as many as he could. Still Erasmus had hoped he could convince Copernicus to come north. "If you could see it for yourself," he said. "The ice, the light, Tom's people in their own place . . ."

"It's not what I want," Copernicus said, startling him.

In the room's farthest corner, so absorbed in drawing bowhead whale that the men might have assumed she wasn't listening, Alexandra made a dark stroke she hadn't intended and then bit her lip. Of course Copernicus would go, it was his nature always to be going somewhere. His luck to be offered all the chances. Almost she rose, so the brothers could talk privately. Ned came into the room with a muskrat skin and paused as he heard the discussion; when Copernicus gestured for him to stay, Alexandra kept her place as well.

"I know it's hard to understand," Copernicus said. "But I can't take in one more thing. The West is still in my eyes, and the visions of the arctic you gave me, and now these mountains—this is an amazing place. As wild as the West, in certain ways, and changing so quickly—I could paint for the rest of my life and never get it all down. I'll finish what I can before you go, but I have to capture what's *here* as well."

"Are you sure?" Erasmus said. When they were boys, he remembered, a delegation of Indian chiefs had paraded through Philadelphia on their way to Washington. Even then, Copernicus had flown to his notebook and captured their spirits on paper. "Tom and I could use your help."

"I know," Copernicus said. "And I'd love to see those places for myself someday. But I'm here now, and my eyes are full. I have to get this place down while I can. Ned's going to help me."

Who would help her? Alexandra wondered. Never Copernicus, or not more than he already had. He might believe he was staying here in these mountains, but soon he'd be wandering again, alone again. She turned her gaze from him and back to her work. Erasmus turned as well, not toward her—she felt as invisible, among their swirl of plans, as Lavinia had once felt among her brothers—but toward Ned.

"I was wondering if you might like to come with *us*," Erasmus said to his old companion. "With me." His left foot throbbed and he reached down to rub it.

"I'm going to be Copernicus's guide," Ned said. "I can take him down the rivers and through the lakes, and we'll make camps in the woods. I know the area well. He'll paint. I'll hunt and cook. It will be good for both of us."

He didn't say that Copernicus had offered him a higher wage than he received at the hotel; nor that he had a plan of his own. He'd saved some money and meant to save more. As they traveled the mountains, he hoped to find a site suitable for a small hotel of his own. A resort, not just for hunters but for their families, where there might be healthful outdoor recreations and indoor comforts. Where a fleet of guide boats might glide like gondolas up to sturdy docks, and take those who were adventurous, but not so strong or skilled, down the braided streams. On the side, he thought, he might establish a small taxidermy firm.

"I've always tried to help you," he said to Erasmus.

"You've been a huge help," Erasmus agreed. He tried to smile, he tried to show his gratitude. On the *Narwhal*, he remembered, Zeke had asked for company on his last trip north and been refused. Had that felt like this? To Ned he said, "After all you've done—you must do what *you* want."

Through the winter Ned had been plagued by a dream, which he kept to himself. In it he and Zeke and Dr. Boerhaave were lost again among the maze of pressure ridges. Dwarfed by the treacherous heaps of ice they spun in circles, chopping passageways only to discover their own tracks on the far side. Cold and hungry and weak, then weaker, they climbed and fell, burrowed and heaved, and never got anywhere. The dream was endless and without resolution; its only saving grace the fact that in it, the moment never arrived when Dr. Boerhaave slipped beneath the ice. Now he looked into his surviving friend's eyes.

"I can never repay you," he said. "For all you've taught me. But when we got back from the North, I swore I'd never set foot on a ship again." He stretched the muskrat pelt in his hands, turning the fur side toward Erasmus. "Tom asked me for this," he said. "Is that all right?"

"Of course," Erasmus said absently. As Ned ducked into Tom's room, Copernicus said, "I feel a bit like him."

"Like Ned?"

"I've traveled too much already."

Alexandra crosshatched a shadow. Imagine being able to say that, she thought. *Too much*; when all she'd ever felt was *Not enough*. He was wrong about himself, he'd always be in motion. No woman would ever hold him more than briefly. In the village, she knew, the shopkeeper's daughter slipped from her family's home late at night to meet Copernicus in the woods. Because he never brought her to this house, they all pretended it wasn't happening.

"I need to stay put," Copernicus continued. "I need to *work*. It's wonderful that you're going, though. And not just because of what you're doing for Tom. It will help the book."

"Will it?" Erasmus asked. He'd almost grown resigned to the idea that he couldn't finish it before he left. Alexandra's drawings were nearly complete, strong and accurate; the paintings were like windows onto the world he'd once glimpsed and he'd be happy with whatever number Copernicus finished. But the text itself was missing something. As he thought this Alexandra, so quiet while they talked, rose and slipped out the back door and into the sheltering trees.

"People live there, along with the plants and animals," Copernicus said. "If you could bring their way of life into the narrative . . ."

Erasmus wrote the firm in New London, letting the captain know he'd need only two berths; while he waited for his sailing date he packed and made lists and mused over Copernicus's advice. *Carl Linnaeus,* their father had said, *proposed a separate species of man, possessed of a tail and inhabiting the antarctic regions.* Erasmus had seen for himself that no one, tailless or otherwise, lived near the South Pole. *Beyond the north wind live the Hyperboreans.* Those he'd seen, but hadn't seen clearly. He felt, still, that he'd been right to leave himself out of the story; he was a minor character after all. Not just in Zeke's story, but in the stories of Ned and Annie and Tom, even Copernicus and Alexandra—he was only the wave that rocked the boat. Yet he'd omitted from his book not just himself, but the Esquimaux.

Observing people wasn't his business; even on the Exploring Expedition, the work of the linguists and anthropologists had made him uneasy. Instead he'd cultivated a kind of reserve. He had not, like Zeke, invaded an Esquimaux tribe; he hadn't, as had his dear Dr. Boerhaave, tried to record their way of life before it vanished. Thinking himself virtuous, he'd averted his eyes and studied the plants and animals instead.

But perhaps he'd simply been afraid? As if, by not passing judgment on the people he saw, he'd hoped to avoid having anyone pass judgment on him. The best thing might be never to visit such places—but he *had* visited, the damage was done; and he had to visit again. When he returned Tom to his family, he might watch everyone. Women, patiently scraping and chewing skins. Men with feet encased in bears' paws, bent over a seal's breathing hole; children swooping nets through clouds of dovekies. He might talk to them. Would they talk to him?

ON APRIL 26, late at night, Alexandra walked into his room. Twenty-two buttons down the front of her gray dress; she unfastened the first six, as simply as if she were shedding her dress for her painter's smock. Erasmus undid the rest. The first sight of her bare shoulders struck him like his first sight of the ice—how could he have forgotten that? He ran his thumb along her collarbones. Never would he forget this. He was leaving soon; she might be staying here or going somewhere new; she hadn't revealed her plans. Perhaps, as she'd told her family, she might be a teacher. Against her thighs, under her hands, with her tongue touching the base of his neck, Erasmus felt his life pulsing and streaming. Up north, when he was lonely, he could unfold this night against the sky. He wound Alexandra's hair around his palm and pulled it like a curtain over his eyes. Alexandra thought with surprise: *Oh, it was this.* This pleasure that bound Lavinia to Zeke, no matter what.

Later that night Erasmus gave Alexandra the little slab of screw-studded leather, which he'd carried all the way from Boothia and failed to share with his first friend. He opened his hand, he released it. She rested the sole on her bare stomach, with the metal points touching her weightlessly. How delicious, the contrast between the cool metal and his warm hand.

"It's for you," he said. "Something to remember me by."

She walked the points up her skin. She'd meant to enter this room weeks ago, as she'd also meant to make, separately, another request. Two different things, one not necessarily linked to the other. But she'd waited too long and now everything was happening at once. If she waited longer, though, she'd lose it all. "Take me with you," she said. "Instead of Copernicus."

Erasmus was silent. Once she'd pried him out of his desolation by pretending to need his company at the Academy of Sciences. Not for months had he understood what she'd done. "I'm so glad you're here," he said finally. "This—us together like this—I've wanted this for a long time. But you don't have to feel *bound* by it. I promise I'll be back. And if you happen to still be free then . . ."

She sat up impatiently and pressed the scrap of leather back into his hand. "I *want* to go," she said. "Don't you understand? It's what I've always wanted. When you were gone I read Parry's journals out loud to Lavinia, all the time wishing I could be where you were. And since you returned and we started work on this book . . . I want to *see*. I want to travel, I want to see everything."

A strand of her hair wound down her neck, across her left breast, unfurling over her ribs. Lovely, lovely. He gazed at her, then down at the graying hair on his own chest. *"Look at me,"* she said. "I didn't come here to try to trick you into taking me, or shame you, or anything else. I wanted this, to touch you like this—but that's something different from wanting to go north."

She bent her knee, placing his hand above it on the inside of her thigh. "Any terms," she said. "You choose the terms. If you don't want us to be . . . to be together like this, we don't have to. I'll go as your assistant, your friend. Anything."

———

IN THE ROOM they shared for those last few weeks, Alexandra moved one hand along the curve of Erasmus's ribs. Next door, she heard Tom rustling in his bed. All the time they'd wasted—they might have made their way to each other months ago, but only when Tom had cracked a channel in Erasmus's heart could she sail in. Of course she would take care of Tom, she owed him everything. They would marry, they'd agreed, before the ship sailed.

"What are you thinking about?" she asked.

"How slow I am," he said.

Outside their door Copernicus painted. An extra painting, not one they'd planned—but the story Erasmus had told him months ago, about the underwater world he'd glimpsed when he fell through the ice, had suddenly seized him. He was anxious to finish, so he could begin painting the mountains around him. But for the moment he focused purely on the layer of ice, white on top then darkening to green and gray, lit by rays of sun pouring through a giant crack.

"How slow to make crucial decisions," Erasmus said. "To sense what's going on around me. I think how long it took me to understand Zeke, how I almost missed being friends with Dr. Boerhaave, how Ned had to force me to lead the men from the *Narwhal*."

The bottom of the ice was covered by a rich field of algae, on which infant fish and small crustaceans grazed. Three belugas, glowing and pale, occupied the lower left corner; a walrus, hanging vertically with its flippers swaying, was just about to surface. There were schools of capelin and swarms of jellyfish; murres he'd caught flying through the water. Copernicus pushed the stepladder to the right, so he could work on the narwhal whose tapered horn skimmed the walrus's flippers.

"How I was too late to save Annie," Erasmus said.

"Zeke moves quickly," Alexandra said. "Do you want to be like him?" She touched his chest.

"I almost missed *you*," Erasmus said. The gentle rasp of Copernicus's ladder against the floor was the sound that sent both them and Tom to sleep.

Tom dreamed a darker version of the scene Copernicus painted. The same ice, humped and shattered, but twilight rather than streaming sun; cold October rather than brilliant July. He dreamed a scene that preceded Zeke, at first as if he were dreaming simple history. His mother's brother left the camp with his sledge and six dogs, hoping to hunt seal on the thickening sea ice although the weather was bad. He left and didn't return. In Tom's dream, as in real life, a fog arose, and a terrible wind, which trapped them in their huts. When they were able to search for the lost hunter, they followed the tracks of the sledge until they vanished. In the moonlight a round area of new ice, surrounded by broken blocks, marked where the hunter had fallen through. The men chopped through it, widened the hole, and prepared the lines and harpoons and the sturdy bone hooks.

In his dream, Tom was no longer a small boy watching, but one of the men. In his arms he felt the pull of the line, and the gentle shudder of the hook as it bumped against something and then caught. In his back he felt the weight as he joined with the others, pulling up first the sledge and then, one by one, the dogs still tangled in their traces. On the traces he saw the marks of their teeth, where they'd tried to free themselves. Laid head to head on the ice, the dogs froze solid instantly. His hands grew numb as he coiled the line and sent the hook back into the water.

In his dream he could see everything, all he'd only been able to imagine when it happened; beneath the ice he saw the hook touch a booted leg. As if it were alive, the hook bounced three times along the leg and then caught the ankle. Gently, gently. He was the hook; he was the line; he was the strong body above, pulling delicately. He was the woman wailing as the boot broke the surface of the water, and he was the man watching as the body was born, feet first, from the sea. Feet, legs, hands, chest, head. The mouth was open in a terrible grimace, the fingernails broken where they'd clawed the edges of the hole. The body, laid out on the ice, glazed and stiffened and turned pure white. Tom bent over the face and saw not his uncle, but Zeke.

The sight jolted him awake; around him were only walls. At the foot of his bed lay the cache of bones and the muskrat pelt that would someday be his *tupilaq*. He turned so his head was near them. The place he had fled, and would never return to again, was called Philadelphia; and in that place, unaware of his fate, Zeke was sleeping. The sunny, golden length of him sprawled across the sheets, one arm almost touching the floor, one foot sticking off the mattress, bobbing as he dreamed of Annie.

Not Annie as she'd been in this house; not Annie as she'd been in Washington; not, not of her skeleton gleaming through a glass display case. But Annie as she'd been in Anoatok, utterly strange and utterly herself. She was smiling at him beneath a bird-filled sky. The life he'd lived with her and her family was the life Erasmus's father had taught him to seek; his dream shifted and he was part of that family, the true son, the son Mr. Wells had always wanted. The four sons of his body were only boys, listening wide-eyed to tales of bees brought back to life when covered by a fresh-killed ox's stomach. None of them had understood, as Zeke had, that those tales were natural history and not science. Surely that was what Mr. Wells had meant to teach him?

A FEW MORE TIMES, in the drafty house, the four companions slept and woke. Then they were gone. Into the woods went Copernicus, easel and paintbox strapped to his back and Ned at his side: just for the summer, he said, just for the brief months of buttery, tree-filtered light. Erasmus and Tom and Alexandra set off for the coast. Later that summer, they'd learn that McClintock's *Fox* had been caught in the ice of Melville Bay during their own winter in the mountains. Swept twelve hundred miles south in the moving pack, the *Fox* had started north again as soon as the ice released it—headed, Erasmus knew, for exactly the place he and Zeke had explored. He guessed McClintock's crew would meet the same or similar Esquimaux and find their way to King William Land as he and Zeke had not. Driving a sledge bearing a red silk banner embroidered by Lady Franklin herself, they'd find relics and bodies and evidence, returning to the glory that might have been his.

But by the time all this happened, he wouldn't care. He'd be in Greenland, after an easy trip during which no disasters happened and no one died. A Scottish whaling ship ferried the three of them from Godhavn to Upernavik; after that came a Danish fishing boat, and then a skin-covered *umiak*. They had little luggage, and weren't much trouble. Past cliffs and glaciers and low gravel beaches strangers guided them: *where the geese nest; where the goblins hide; where the ice cave grows beneath the ledge.*

Erasmus took no notes: he would do that later. Beside him, though, Alexandra drew in a larger version of the black-bound notebooks she'd been filling since she was a girl. The sights she saw resembled those she'd first glimpsed in Erasmus's green journal and then reconstructed with his guidance: and were also completely different. She lay on gray rocks, eyes level with a tuft of tiny, bladder-shaped blossoms. In Philadelphia she'd drawn these twenty times but only now saw what Erasmus hadn't captured: each flower was really a calyx, inflated and striped and deceptive; the true petals were hidden inside. The stems, the texture of the rock, the ice, the sky, the streaming clouds—they looked one way to Erasmus, another way to her. Also—*also,* she thought, *it was <u>everything</u>*—they were themselves.

Erasmus watched her draw. Nothing she rendered was new to him, yet each stroke of her pencil—he had bought her special pencils, Dr. Boerhaave's pencils—was like a chisel held to a cleavage plane: tap, tap, and the rock split into two sharp pieces, the world cracked and spoke to him. Annie spoke to him each time it rained, Dr. Boerhaave when the wind blew; Tom was silent much of the time but Erasmus could hear the language of his body as he strengthened and straightened and breathed the air and ate the food he'd missed.

They found Tom's people late in August. Against the hills beyond Anoatok were two-legged dots, four-legged dots, which Tom was the first to spot. He ran up the rocky shore, Alexandra and Erasmus following more slowly but still steadily: Erasmus had grown used to his feet and regained his balance, casting aside his walking sticks for a single ball-headed cane. As he approached the dots turned into figures, and faces appeared. Among that small crowd moving toward him were Tom's father—which one was he?—and men who'd hunted and talked with Dr. Boerhaave. A tall man in a worn fur jacket stumbled forward, stretched out a hand, pressed Tom to his chest and then lifted him into the air.

Sometime later, the people moved toward Erasmus and Alexandra, and Tom made introductions: Ootuniah, Awahtok, and the three other young men whom Erasmus remembered visiting the *Narwhal*; Nessark, Tom's father, who had known both Dr. Boerhaave and Zeke; the *angekok*, who wore around his neck a thong strung with long teeth. A few more men and then, behind them, shy women and children. Alexandra took four steps and stood among them, bending so the children could touch her hair. One of the women touched the back of her hand and she turned it, offering her palm; the woman rested three fingers there. Erasmus felt that touch in his own hand but he kept his gaze on the men before him, repeating each name, burning each face into his mind. When it was time, speaking slowly, waiting after each phrase for Tom to repeat the words in a language he was just beginning to grasp, Erasmus explained to them what he knew of Annie's death.

As he spoke Nessark clasped his son's shoulders, nodding but saying nothing, looking down when Tom continued to speak for some time after Erasmus had stopped. Two geese flew by, and a swarm of murres. The *angekok* stepped forward to speak for Nessark and the rest of the tribe but for a moment said nothing at all; only the birds' thrumming wings broke the silence. Erasmus lowered his eyes and waited. He would be judged now, he thought. Alexandra's presence by his side had altered every other aspect of this final journey, but she couldn't spare him this. He might not be forgiven. He looked up again and caught the *angekok*'s stern gaze. When he spoke, Erasmus could hear in the words only the sound of running water and an echo of the wing beats.

The *angekok* paused so Tom could translate. They did not blame Erasmus for the loss of their sister's body, Tom said. *Their sister,* Erasmus thought, looking from the boy to his judge and back. *Tom's mother.* He would never be Tom again, that had never been his name; to which of those syllables did he answer? He himself, the *angekok* said, had determined that the tribe should guide Zeke out of their country; and he had permitted their sister and her son to leave them. His fault. His left hand folded around the teeth swaying on his chest. On her voyage of discovery, he said, she had been betrayed;

when the poison took hold she had left her bones, so that she might save her son. The *angekok* pointed toward Erasmus's feet—so small, he said. Who had taken the rest? He gave Alexandra an *ulo* and Erasmus an amulet of little bone knives, with which to cut through bad weather.

Still later the *angekok*, after speaking with the boy, led him down the shore and across the worn floes leaning against each other like drunken soldiers. At the water's edge the boy handed over his collection. A skin laid flat against the ice, a bone laid here and another there; the *angekok* folded the pelt around the ill-sorted shards, chanting as he tied the bundle with a thong.

A few years later, as Zeke floated in the Rappahannock River, his face and chest above the blood-ribboned water, his shoulders bumping the hundreds of men who struggled, like him, to cross to the other side, something like a muskrat would brush his hands and Copernicus—drawn by the chaos, drawn by the wounds, always in movement but that day painting furiously on that bank—would see those dark shapes intertwine and wonder what they were. A war would have started by then, obscuring the arctic in people's minds as if it were no more than legend: *here are the hinges on which the world turns and the limits of the circuits of the stars.*

But for the moment Erasmus and Alexandra stood on the shore, peering down at the water as the boy who had led them here knelt and slipped the bundle in.

Author's Note and Acknowledgments

MOST OF THE BACKGROUND CHARACTERS IN THIS novel—including Titian Peale, Charles Wilkes, John Rae, John Richardson, Elisha Kent Kane, Sir John Franklin and his crew, Louis Agassiz, Samuel Morton and the other naturalists and philosophers mentioned, as well as Ootuniah, Awahtok, Nessark, and the other Smith Sound Inuit who befriended Dr. Kane—are historical persons. The foreground characters—including Zechariah Voorhees, Erasmus Wells, Alexandra Copeland and their families, as well as Dr. Boerhaave, Ned Kynd, the crews of the *Narwhal* and the other ships mentioned, and Annie and Tom—are invented.

I'm indebted to the journals and memoirs of many nineteenth-century arctic explorers, particularly those of George Back, John Barrow, Edward Belcher, Alexander Fisher, John Franklin, William Godfrey, Charles Francis Hall, Isaac Hayes, Elisha Kent Kane, William Kennedy, George Lyon, Francis McClintock, Robert McClure, Sherard Osborn, William Edward Parry, Julius von Payer, John Rae, John Richardson, James Clark Ross, John Ross, Edward Sabine, Frederick Schwatka, William Scoresby, and Thomas Simpson.

Also helpful were many more recent books about the arctic in the nineteenth and twentieth centuries, especially Pierre Berton's *The Arctic Grail,* George Corner's *Dr. Kane of the Arctic Seas,* Richard

Cyriax's *Sir John Franklin's Last Arctic Expedition*, Ernest Dodge's *The Polar Rosses*, Peter Freuchen's *The Arctic Year* and *Book of the Eskimos*, Sam Hall's *The Fourth World*, Chauncey Loomis's *Weird and Tragic Shores*, Barry Lopez's *Arctic Dreams*, Jeannette Mirsky's *To the Arctic*, Vilhjalmur Stefansson's *Arctic Manual*, and Doug Wilkinson's *Land of the Long Day*.

Anthropological and ethnological works by Asen Balikci, Franz Boas, Jean Malaurie, Samuel Morton, Richard Nelson, Gontran de Poncins, and Knud Rasmussen; William Elder's *Biography of Elisha Kent Kane*; Matthew Maury's *The Physical Geography of the Sea*; William Rhees's *An Account of The Smithsonian Institution, Its Founder, Building, Operations, Etc.*; W. J. Holland's *Taxidermy and Zoological Collecting*; and George Glidden and J. C. Nott's *Types of Mankind* provided other useful background. Stephen Jay Gould's *The Mismeasure of Man* steered me toward the work of Nott and Glidden; William Goetzmann's *New Lands, New Men: America and the Second Great Age of Discovery* provided initial information about the Exploring Expedition. The lines Erasmus Wells remembers his father reading to him are paraphrased from Pliny the Elder's *Natural History*.

I'm indebted to the MacDowell Colony, where I wrote the first lines of this novel; and to the Guggenheim Foundation, for a fellowship that enabled me to complete it. My thanks as well to Dave Reid, Charlie Innuaraq, Mathias Qaunaq, Limach Kadloo, and Joelie Aulaqiak of Pond Inlet, for showing me the beauties of the floe edge. Douglas M. Orr Jr. introduced me to the ballad "Lady Franklin's Lament"; Mark Sawin, of the University of Texas at Austin, shared with me both the bibliography of his research into the life of Elisha Kent Kane and his excellent master's thesis, "Raising Kane: The Making of a Hero, the Marketing of a Celebrity" (1997).

Wendy Weil and Carol Houck Smith offered constant support and the best kind of criticism; their help was invaluable. Peter Landesman's thorough, perceptive comments guided me through the final draft. Without Margot Livesey, who was with me throughout the entire voyage, there would have been, as always, no book at all: my deepest thanks.

THE FAMILIES

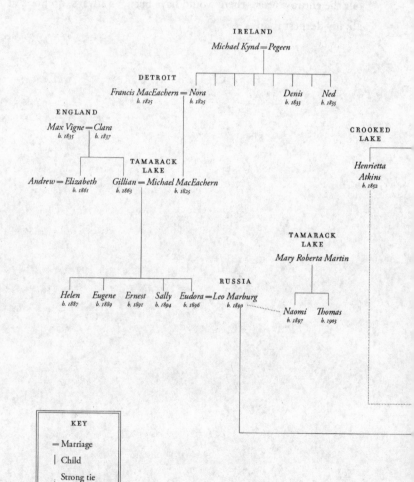

IRELAND

Michael Kynd = Pegeen

DETROIT

Francis MacEachern = Nora
b. 1825   *b. 1825*

Denis   Ned
b. 1833 *b. 1835*

ENGLAND

Max Vigne = Clara
b. 1835   *b. 1837*

TAMARACK
LAKE

CROOKED
LAKE

Henrietta
Atkins
b. 1852

Andrew = Elizabeth   Gillian = Michael MacEachern
b. 1861   *b. 1863*   *b. 1825*

TAMARACK
LAKE

Mary Roberta Martin

RUSSIA

Helen   Eugene   Ernest   Sally   Eudora = Leo Marburg
b. 1887 *b. 1889* *b. 1891* *b. 1894* *b. 1896*   *b. 1890*

Naomi   Thomas
b. 1897 *b. 1903*

KEY

— Marriage

| Child

Strong tie
beyond blood
or marriage

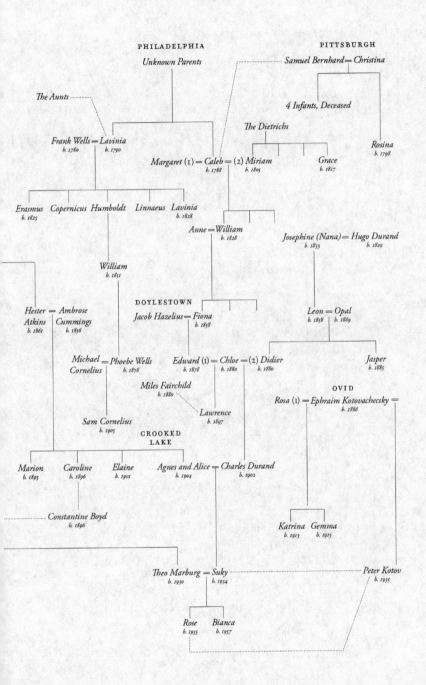

PHILADELPHIA
Unknown Parents

PITTSBURGH
Samuel Bernhard ══ Christina

The Aunts

4 Infants, Deceased

The Dietrichs

Frank Wells ══ Lavinia
b. 1780   b. 1790

Grace
b. 1817

Rosina
b. 1798

Margaret (1) ══ Caleb ══ (2) Miriam
              b. 1788   b. 1805

Erasmus   Copernicus   Humboldt   Linnaeus   Lavinia
b. 1825   b. 1828

Anne ══ William
        b. 1828

Josephine (Nana) ══ Hugo Durand
b. 1833   b. 1829

William
b. 1851

DOYLESTOWN
Jacob Hazelius ══ Fiona
                 b. 1858

Leon ══ Opal
b. 1858   b. 1869

Hester ══ Ambrose
Atkins   Cummings
b. 1861   b. 1856

Michael ══ Phoebe Wells
Cornelius   b. 1878

Edward (1) ══ Chloe ══ (2) Didier
b. 1878   b. 1880   b. 1880

Jasper
b. 1885

Miles Fairchild
b. 1880

OVID
Rosa (1) ══ Ephraim Kotovachecsky ══
            b. 1886

Sam Cornelius
b. 1905

Lawrence
b. 1897

CROOKED
LAKE

Marion   Caroline   Elaine   Agnes and Alice ══ Charles Durand
b. 1893   b. 1896   b. 1901   b. 1904   b. 1902

Constantine Boyd
b. 1896

Katrina   Gemma
b. 1913   b. 1915

Theo Marburg ══ Suky
b. 1930   b. 1934

Peter Kotov
b. 1935

Rose   Bianca
b. 1955   b. 1957

THE VOYAGE OF
THE NARWHAL

Andrea Barrett

THE VOYAGE OF THE NARWHAL

Andrea Barrett

THE AUTHOR ON HER WORK

"Writing *The Voyage of the Narwhal* took me on an unexpected journey. While writing my previous book, *Ship Fever*, and researching the stories of Irish emigrants on their way to Canada, I read a few pages about a ship that was sunk by drifting ice floes off Newfoundland. That image—the jagged ice, the hole in the ship, the people sinking helplessly—flung me back to the territory of a childhood obsession with polar explorers. What was it that had drawn me so deeply into those stories? The ice, the snow, the winter-long nights and the days that last for months: why had those tales gripped me so? On Cape Cod, where I grew up, I hid under bridges and up in trees and in hollows at the base of sand dunes, reading about Peary and Nansen and Shackleton, shutting out everything else in my world; longing so fiercely to be those explorers and not grasping for years that they were men, and I wasn't; that the forces and desires driving them could never be mine, and were not all noble; and that what separated me from them was not just gender but time and space and politics and the changing nature of the world. Yet something real joined me to them as well: an escape from the pettiness of the self, and a longing to embrace the whole world. Somewhere in my teens that obsession went underground. Then it resurfaced two decades later, altered but stronger than ever.

"Ned Kynd, a minor character in *Ship Fever*, continued to haunt me long after I'd finished writing about him and his family: what might have happened to him, I wondered, after he was separated from his sister at Grosse Isle and shipped upriver? At first I envisioned a companion novella, something short and largely about Ned. But almost as soon as I started work I realized that I'd entered an imaginary world very much shaped by my own Arctic obsessions, and that this was going to be a full-length novel.

"I embarked on this novel almost by accident; so, too, does the American naturalist who became its protagonist set off almost accidentally for the north. It's hard for us to imagine, now, how exciting those Arctic expeditions were; they caused a fever resembling the early days of the space program. The commanders of these expeditions were the astronauts of their time, celebrated with banner headlines and huge parades. When one of the most famous—Elisha Kent Kane, who appears in the background of this novel—died, all of America mourned him at a funeral exceeded only, a few years later, by Lincoln's.

"My naturalist isn't one of those actual Arctic explorers, though; he's an invented character, and all his companions and their expedition are also invented. You might wonder why I'd want to invent yet another expedition, when the late 1840s and 1850s were so rich with actual expeditions. One reason is that no single expedition encompassed all I wanted to say about the nature of exploring in that time and place. Another, perhaps more important reason is that only by *inventing* an expedition, and following where that led me, could I share in the process of discovery those real explorers experienced. It was a strange, secret pleasure to take material so far removed from my own quiet life, and to remake the traditional matter of a quest narrative in my own way."

DISCUSSION QUESTIONS

1. By today's standards, the crew of the *Narwhal* sailed north with almost nothing: no radio, cellular phone, or electronic equipment; no reliable navigational devices; inadequate food and clothes; maps with big blanks of uncharted space. Compare this kind of nineteenth-century exploration with "adventure travel" today. How do these experiences differ, both for the adventurers and for those waiting for them at home? Do you think travel in the mid–nineteenth century took a different kind of courage?

2. Many of the characters here might be described as obsessed, although the nature of their obsessions differs. What is driving each of the central characters? Is the search for glory and recognition different from the search for knowledge? How would you relate these characters' goals and aspirations to those of people who set off now on such

purposefully dangerous adventures as crossing Antarctica, skiing over the North Pole, or climbing Mount Everest?

3. All fiction is in some way about the encounter of the self and the other. Our ideas of "otherness," though, vary with culture and time. Mid-nineteenth-century American and European explorers, for example, sometimes described their encounters with people from other cultures in pejorative terms, as if those people were not fully human. And few written records from the period tell the other side of the story—how the Inuit, for example, perceived the strangers stumbling into their land. Who does Erasmus perceive as the other? Is he in some way a foreigner not just to the Inuit, but to his own culture? What about Alexandra and Zeke—or about Annie's and Tom's relationship to their own culture, and the other culture they briefly experience?

4. Compare the responses of Zeke and Erasmus to the Arctic landscape and the Inuit culture. Can you describe the ways in which each makes use of what he's seen and learned?

5. What is the function of the quotations from Pliny the Elder's *Natural History*, which Erasmus remembers his father reading: are these linked to the discussions, late in the novel, about race and the human species?

6. How do you view the relationship of Erasmus and Dr. Boerhaave? Toward each other they are tender, respectful, supportive, even loving; the best of friends. In another century, in other circumstances, do you think their feelings toward each other might have expressed themselves in a different way?

7. Initially, the central women characters—Alexandra, Lavinia, Annie—seem to be in the background of the novel. Does this reflect a sense of what was permitted to women then? How do their roles alter as the novel unfolds? Compare their relationships with each other to those among the central male characters.

8. Describe the journey that Alexandra makes during the course of the novel. How does it parallel the more visible, exterior journey made by Erasmus and the crew of the *Narwhal*? Does she find a

form of freedom within the constraints imposed on her by her class and gender?

9. Annie makes a journey as well—in its own way as profound and daring as that of the novel's male voyagers, and with deeper consequences. Do you think she's aware of herself as a kind of explorer? What does she see as her task when she agrees to leave her home with Zeke?

10. Why is it so important to Lavinia that Erasmus guard Zeke from harm on his journey north—and why does she feel so betrayed when he fails? What do her responses say about the role of marriage for women in her place and time?

11. Letters, journals, and diaries play a crucial role in this novel—as they did in the lives of many educated nineteenth-century people. What do they contribute to the novel? Do they reveal aspects of Erasmus, Zeke, Alexandra, Dr. Boerhaave, and Ned we wouldn't otherwise know?

12. In Erasmus's first journal entry, describing the scene at the dock earlier that day, he writes: "But when I describe it in words one thing follows another and everything's shaped by my single pair of eyes, my single voice. I wish I could show it through a fan of eyes. Widening out from my single perspective to several viewpoints, then many, so the whole picture might appear and not just my version of it." How does the structure of the novel as a whole mirror that initial statement? Did it seem important to you that the novel incorporate many viewpoints? How would the novel have been different if it had mirrored the published journals of the real nineteenth-century explorers and been written solely in Erasmus's voice—or, for that matter, in Zeke's?

13. The epigraphs heading each of the chapters are from nineteenth-century texts, which the characters might have been reading. Take a closer look at these: do we read them differently now than the characters would have read them then? Now take another look at the opening epigraph, which is from a text written exactly a century after the events in the novel and is about an antithetical landscape. Why do you think the author chose this? What is she asking you to think about?

Meghan Kenny	*The Driest Season*
Nicole Krauss	*The History of Love*
Don Lee	*The Collective*
Amy Liptrot	*The Outrun: A Memoir*
Donna M. Lucey	*Sargent's Women*
Bernard MacLaverty	*Midwinter Break*
Maaza Mengiste	*Beneath the Lion's Gaze*
Claire Messud	*The Burning Girl*
	When the World Was Steady
Liz Moore	*Heft*
	The Unseen World
Neel Mukherjee	*The Lives of Others*
	A State of Freedom
Janice P. Nimura	*Daughters of the Samurai*
Rachel Pearson	*No Apparent Distress*
Richard Powers	*Orfeo*
Kirstin Valdez Quade	*Night at the Fiestas*
Jean Rhys	*Wide Sargasso Sea*
Mary Roach	*Packing for Mars*
Somini Sengupta	*The End of Karma*
Akhil Sharma	*Family Life*
	A Life of Adventure and Delight
Joan Silber	*Fools*
Johanna Skibsrud	*Quartet for the End of Time*
Mark Slouka	*Brewster*
Kate Southwood	*Evensong*
Manil Suri	*The City of Devi*
	The Age of Shiva
Madeleine Thien	*Do Not Say We Have Nothing*
	Dogs at the Perimeter
Vu Tran	*Dragonfish*
Rose Tremain	*The American Lover*
	The Gustav Sonata
Brady Udall	*The Lonely Polygamist*
Brad Watson	*Miss Jane*
Constance Fenimore Woolson	*Miss Grief and Other Stories*

Don't miss other titles by National Book Award–winning author

ANDREA BARRETT

ANDREA-BARRETT.COM

Ship Fever

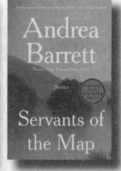

Servants of the Map

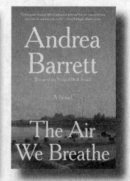

The Air We Breathe

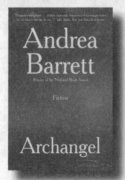

Archangel

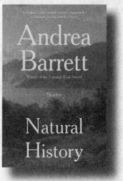

Natural History